The Exterminators

The Exterminators

An Assassin Bug Thriller

Bill Fitzhugh

Poisoned Pen Press

Poisoned Pen Press
6962 E. First Ave., Ste. 103
Scottsdale, AZ 85251
www.poisonedpenpress.com
info@poisonedpenpress.com

Printed in the United States of America

To all the fans of "Pest Control"—
thanks for waiting so long.

This one is dedicated to Paul Anik and
David Thompson, both taken too soon.

And for Kendall without whom
there would be no bug books.

Preface

The underlying idea for *The Exterminators* came about in May of 1991 during a brainstorming session with a former screen-writing partner. That idea became *Pest Control.* We wrote a screenplay but it went nowhere. Four years later I wrote the story as a comic novel. After rejections from 124 agents, *Pest Control* finally secured representation. Over the next fifteen years, *Pest Control* was published all over the world, the film rights were sold to Warner Brothers, a German company produced it as a radio play, and it was staged as a musical (of all things) in Los Angeles where it won the Ovation Award for best costume (a six foot tall cockroach with expanding wings). During all this time my agent frequently urged me to write a sequel to *Pest Control* but I didn't have a satisfactory story. When I finally came up with a story I liked, my agent retired.

Chapter One

La Paz, Bolivia: 1998

In his thirty years as an assassin Klaus had traveled the world, seeing many strange and terrible things. But, as far as he could remember, this was the first time he had stared into the black, bulging eyes of a dried llama fetus.

He was in the back seat of a hired car in the old quarter of La Paz known as Mercado de las Brujas, the Witches' Market, where traffic snaked slowly through the crowded, narrow lanes.

As the car crept along Calle Sagarnaga, the driver noticed Klaus studying the native women in their bowler hats and vivid dresses as they hawked the heads of boa constrictors, goat testicles, and toad talismans.

"They are witches," the driver said. "They sell these things for the rituals."

Klaus said nothing.

The driver looked in the mirror hoping to catch Klaus' eyes. "The peasants still make offerings to Pachamama. They burn these things as offerings in exchange for luck, health, prosperity." He put his arm on the seat back and turned to face Klaus, more serious than he had been. "Few outsiders have seen these rituals." Here he lowered his voice and continued, "But if you are interested, I could arrange for you to see. For a price."

Klaus said nothing. This was obviously a con of some sort, a clip joint operation. The driver steering wealthy, thrill-seeking foreigners into the hands of associates who would take them into the mountains with the promise of perverse entertainment then trade them a shallow grave for whatever was in their wallet.

Klaus' silence gave the driver another idea. He said, "Or perhaps you are the type of man who prefers a more sophisticated type of diversion."

Klaus fixed a grim stare into the mirror and said, "Or perhaps I am the type of man who prefers that you shut up and drive."

And that was that. The driver took a left out of the market and zig-zagged south and east until he was dodging stray dogs and children scavenging for the same food in the shadows of the snow capped Illimani.

Chapter Two

It was dark by the time the car stopped outside a vast, gated estate set into the mountainside. Klaus took his attaché case and told the driver to wait. While armed guards searched the car, others led Klaus into the compound, patting him down and inspecting the case before letting him continue.

Klaus followed the footlights illuminating the stone path through the lush subtropical landscape. The green canopy throbbed with singing samba and red-skirted tree frogs, their long, trilling croaks competing with the stridulating organs of ten thousand insects.

Klaus thought of his new friend and the room filled with assassin bugs in the basement of his house—well, his former house. His former bugs. What a waste they had to be destroyed. But, at the same time, what a brilliant idea. The first part of their great gamble.

And now it was time for the second part.

Klaus paused to examine an orchid, vivid purple with a yellow stripe like a tongue sticking out of a child's mouth after a lemon candy. Continuing up the path, Klaus noticed something out of the corner of his eye, flying at him. A gray blur, an irregular flight pattern. His first thought was bats. There was no time to react. The thing was on him, grabbing. Klaus looked down at his shirt. A giant Brazillian cockroach (*Blaberus giganteus*), nearly four inches of mottled translucence, the odd oval head covering, and the twitching antennae frisking him impolitely.

Klaus choked back a girlish scream before it could escape his throat. He dropped his attaché case and did an embarrassing dance on the pathway while trying to brush the twitchy cockroach off his shirt. But the sharply spined tarsii held fast to the fabric. Finally, with great trepidation, Klaus grabbed the thing and tossed it back into the flora, wiping his hands feverishly on his pants. He shivered and took a moment to compose himself before continuing up the path.

Only when he emerged from the jungled landscaping could Klaus see where he was going. He had to tilt his head back to take in the enormity of the place. Too big to call a house, wrong architecture to call a mansion or a palace, more like a fortress. Klaus guessed it was forty thousand square feet built into the side of a mountain. It was the estate of Miguel DeJesus Riviera, the man who put a ten-million-dollar contract on the head of an assassin known to him as the Exterminator.

As a result, a dozen of the world's best killers swarmed into New York, where the Exterminator was living at the time. But none of them succeeded at their task. Indeed, none of them left the city alive, let alone did they make the trip to Bolivia to collect the reward.

Klaus was the only one to get that stamp on his passport.

Chapter Three

Klaus was taken to a room. It was a vast space with a decorative stratagem whose theme was, at best, evasive. A garish Caucasus Mountain kilim was draped on a wall near a Peruvian corner cabinet of questionable design. Off to the side, Miguel's two young sons were sprawled across an overstuffed French lambskin sofa staring slack-jawed at a fifty-inch high-def wall-mounted plasma screen as it played *A Bug's Life.*

At the far end of the room, Miguel sat behind an antique Victorian desk. As Klaus approached, Miguel sized him up. Mediterranean features and a tailored suit that didn't hide how fit the man was. Gray at the temples and thin crows feet put him around sixty, but not a man to be toyed with. Miguel leaned back in his chair. "Ahh, the infamous Klaus," he said. "Your reputation precedes you."

Klaus smiled, but not politely. "I trust that will speed matters," he said in an accent that hinted at Europe. He handed over a slip of paper, a ten digit number printed on it. He sat opposite Miguel, in an African chieftain's chair made from zebra skin and elephant tusk.

Miguel looked at the paper then smoothed it onto the desk top and said, "I give up. Lottery picks?"

"One of my accounts."

"Ah." Miguel looked at the slip of paper again. "And this is a gift? For me?"

"I have a better idea. A transfer. Ten million, U.S." Klaus pulled a cell phone from his attaché case. "When the amount clears, my banker will call and I will be on my way."

Miguel feigned surprise. "Why would I give you ten million dollars?"

"For killing the Exterminator."

"*You* killed him?"

"Has anyone else claimed the hit?"

"Anyone else?" Miguel gestured toward the hallway. "I'm surprised you didn't trip over some of the assholes on your way in. They've been traipsing through here like it was an Easter Egg hunt." He shook his head. "Anyone else. That's rich."

"But did they claim it?"

"Claimed it? Yes. Proved it? No."

Klaus pulled a file from the attaché and tossed it onto the desk. Miguel opened the file and saw several newspaper clippings about a house in Queens, New York that blew up with several people inside. Police were quoted as saying it appeared to be the residents, one Bob Dillon, his wife Mary, their daughter, Katy, and a fourth man, later identified as CIA agent Mike Wolfe. Also killed in the explosion was a man who lived across the street, identified by his wife as one Dick Pratt. "I have seen the papers," Miguel said, pushing the file back toward Klaus. "I heard he was dead. Of course I also heard you died with him."

"You saw this in one of the newspapers?"

He shook his head. "I have other sources."

Klaus reached into his case again. He held out his closed hand, turned it over and dropped two items onto the desk.

"Let me guess, their wedding rings?"

Klaus gave a nod.

"Oh, please." Miguel slapped the desk, making the rings jump. "*Vete a otro perro con ese hueso!*"

Klaus hesitated, unable to translate Miguel's Spanish ejaculation. "Sorry?"

"It's an idiom," he said. "Means go see another dog with that bone." He waved dismissively at the jewelry. "For all I know, you picked these up in town."

Klaus nodded then said, "The French also have an idiom. *Voir jaune.* It means you are seeing things yellow, with a jaundiced eye."

"Perhaps." Miguel looked past Klaus and pointed at the television. "Oh, this is great," he said. "The scene where the grasshoppers show up looking for the food. The big one is Kevin Spacey. Did you see him as Bobby Darin?" Miguel began snapping his fingers and singing "Mack the Knife" until he noticed Klaus staring unpleasantly at him. "Oh, sorry. You were saying?"

Klaus reached into his satchel and pulled out another file, a series of photographs. He dealt them onto the desk top, one at a time. "This is his house just before…during…and after the explosion. Notice the time code. The only person who could know exactly when to take these photos would be the man who set the bomb's timer, no?"

"Sure," Miguel said. He pointed at the first one. "But this could be any house, anywhere. I can't give you ten million of my dollars just for taking these pictures, even if they are quite spectacular." He pointed at the second one. "Especially this one. Though I think you should have cropped this part but, hey, have you considered entering these in any contests?"

"No."

"Pity," Miguel said. "Perhaps you could win the ten million that way." He smiled and pushed the photos back toward Klaus. "In any event, this is inadequate."

"Yes, well, I would have brought the man's head," Klaus said. "But they are rather difficult to get through customs."

"So, you have no further proof?"

"Proof." Klaus scoffed as he rooted through his attaché case. "Do you recall the original intelligence photograph of The Exterminator, the one originating with the CIA?"

"Recall?" Miguel opened a drawer, pulled out a grainy fax of a dangerous looking man wearing a red and black baseball cap with "Exterminator" emblazoned across the front. He stared at it for a moment. "He has the eyes of a killer," Miguel said, thumping the fax with a finger. "Like yours, remorseless."

"Yes, keep that in mind." Klaus produced another photo. It was the same man, wearing the same hat, only now the hat had a bullet hole in it and blood was oozing down the front onto the floor where the man was sprawled. Klaus tossed it onto the desk.

Miguel seemed impressed. "Well, now we're getting somewhere." He peered over the front of his desk and said, "How many more rabbits are you going to pull from there?"

Klaus reached into the case then tossed the hat itself onto the table, crusty with dried blood. "How's that?"

Miguel made a squeamish face and poked at the hat with his pen. "I don't know...maybe."

Klaus' patience was running thin. He wanted to get this over with. He turned and gestured at the boys on the sofa. "These are your sons? Fine looking young men."

Miguel seemed please by this. "Yes, yes. The first of many," he bragged. "Boys! Come here." They didn't flinch, hypnotized as they were by the colorful images on the huge screen. Miguel threw his pen, grazing the older boy's head. "I said come here! Say hello to our guest." As the boys dragged themselves off the sofa and shuffled across the room, Miguel pointed and said, "This is Francisco and his younger brother, Ronaldo, named for his late uncle."

They approached Klaus and limply shook his hand. "Oh, this one has a firm grip," Klaus said, referring to Francisco. He pulled the boy to his side and put an arm around him while speaking to Miguel. "As you know, the Exterminator had a child as well. A daughter." He paused to let that sink in. "Of course I didn't think it wise to leave any loose ends." With his free hand, Klaus reached into the case and pulled out a sealed envelope, tossing it onto the desk. "The wife was particularly troublesome." Klaus nodded at the envelope, prompting Miguel to open it. "She made quite a fuss about the whole thing, especially when I killed her husband."

Miguel was beginning to get a queasy feeling. He opened the envelope and recoiled at the photo of a woman, covered in blood, on the floor, one leg twisted at a terrible angle. "I gave her the choice of watching her child die or having her child see her death. She struggled of course, but, well…" As Miguel looked at the final photograph, the daughter, face down on the carpet, three dark stains on her back, one hand reaching for her parents, Klaus said, "When I killed the child, the mother wilted."

"Stop it!" Miguel shouted. "Let go of my son!"

Klaus fixed his remorseless eyes on Miguel and shook his head. "I have proved my claim," he said, nodding at his phone. "I will not leave here alive without the money. And I will not die without taking someone with me."

"Whatever you want. Just do not hurt the boy."

"It is up to you."

Miguel snatched the slip of paper. He turned to his computer and logged on to his bank's website. He navigated to the fund transfer page. After a few moments he hit the "send" button, then looked at Klaus. "You are inhuman," he said. "You have the soul of a dog. You are a malignancy on mankind!"

"Yes. And you are the one who hired me," Klaus said. "So what does that make you?"

Miguel didn't respond. He just stared at Klaus' cell phone, waiting to get his son back. There was a long silence as they waited. The only sound came from an animated grasshopper saying something about how it was a bug-eat-bug world out there. When the phone chirped, Miguel flinched. Klaus, still holding Francisco, answered. "Yes?" A pause, then a hint of a smile. "Good." He flipped the phone shut, tousled Francisco's hair, and stood. "Sorry to leave so suddenly, but I have a car waiting." Klaus was halfway across the room when he stopped, turning to face Miguel. "If you announce this to the press, do me a favor. Tell them Klaus has retired. I am through."

Klaus returned to the waiting car and disappeared into the Bolivian darkness. After that, as far as anyone could tell, Klaus disappeared from the face of the earth.

Chapter Four

Corvallis, Oregon: Six years later

Klaus was hunched over the pool of blood as if to protect it. He glanced up from this vulnerable angle and said, "If you would let me use my gun, I could end this."

Bob Dillon stood ten feet away, one arm raised overhead, eyes fixed on something in the middle distance. "What makes you think I can't end this myself?"

"Because you have been waving that ridiculous thing around for the last fifteen minutes to no effect," Klaus said.

Bob feigned offense. "Ridiculous? This is the Buginator 5000, my friend." Bob held it out to admire like some sort of sci-fi tennis racket from a cheap aluminum future. "Two thousand volts of insect killing exuberance." Bob lunged sideways, taking a backhand swing. "Damn." His eyes followed the black dot as it circled the room, taunting him.

"*Musca domestica?*" Klaus asked.

Bob held two fingers in a V pointing outward from his face. "Based on those nasty red compound eyes, I'd say it's a flesh fly. *Protodexia hunteri* if I had to guess. Probably straight off a decomposing possum, or worse."

"Why do you think I am covering my plate?" Klaus had reheated leftovers from last night's lamb. Glancing down he said, "Great, I got blood on my tie." The lamb, still rare, had left a pool of it on the plate. He dabbed at the stain with his napkin and said, "If you happen to get lucky and hit the thing, I would rather it did not land in my lunch."

"Shows what you know," Bob said. "When—not if—but when I hit it, the thing will vaporize."

"Yes," Klaus said. "If by 'vaporize' you mean that the exploding insect will result in an airborne distribution of bacteria and viruses released from the gut of the fly, showering my lunch with all manner of pathogens. Perhaps this is why they warn against using them around food."

"Go put on a dress if you're so worried about it," Bob said. "I'm not stopping until I've killed it." He understood Klaus' concern for food safety but Bob's disgust for anything from the *Muscidae* and *Sarcophagidae* families, trumped all logic. He loathed flies. He swatted again and shouted, "Yes!"

Klaus shook his head and said, "No." He pointed at the target as it continued flying lazy figure-eights.

"I know I hit it." Bob looked at the face of the Buginator. "Maybe the batteries are dead."

"Maybe you should let me get my gun." Klaus sat up and resumed his lunch, confident Bob would never hit his target.

"You don't see any possible downside to discharging a weapon in a room filled with insanely expensive lab equipment that we're still paying for?"

"That's why we have insurance," Klaus said. Even after living in the U.S. for six years, his accent remained Terminator-like, though he had finally started to use contractions. "Besides," he said. "I would need only one shot."

"Do me a favor?" Bob said, as he continued stalking his prey. "Don't say things like that when Mr. Treadwell gets here." He looked at his watch. "Which should be soon. Knowing that our vice president prefers to solve problems with unlicensed firearms is not the sort of thing that inspires an investor's confidence."

Klaus shrugged. "Depends on the investor," he said. "Besides, I would not shoot the equipment. I would simply wait until the fly lit on the wall."

"And then what? Blast it with a shotgun?"

Klaus took a bite of the lamb and said, "My friend, I once shot an olive from the branch of its tree and plugged it before it hit the ground."

"Uh huh."

"With a 9mm from twenty yards." Klaus pointed at the fly, tracking it as it flew around the room. When it landed on some lab equipment, Klaus steadied his finger and said, "Bang. Dead fly."

"No," Bob said. "Ka-ching. Dead ceramic electrophoresis cooling tank."

"I would need only one shot."

Bob wagged the Buginator at Klaus, saying, "Okay, I'm thinking of a word that starts with the letter 'b', two syllables, rhymes with 'bullshit.' No wait, that's actually the word."

Klaus shrugged and looked over the top of his bifocals. "Call my friend Basil, he will tell you. He saw it."

When the fly took off again, Bob lunged around the scalable process chromatography columns that were next to, and hiding, the helium pulse regulator. Focused on the fly, Bob didn't see the regulator's hose assembly over which he tripped. "Whoa!" The Buginator crashed to the floor and shattered, revealing shoddy Chinese manufacturing. Bob ended up in a heap by the DNA electrophoresis workstation.

He lay there laughing as he reflected on how he'd ended up in the elaborate circumstance that his life had become.

Chapter Five

It all started with Bob's attempts to cross breed various members of the assassin bug family in an attempt to create a "green" alternative to chemical pest control.

A few years later, as the technologies from the Human Genome Project moved into the private sector, the world changed in strange and enduring ways. The field of transgenics guaranteed that nothing would ever be the same.

Bob and Klaus enrolled at the University of Oregon, shifting their studies to bioengineering, gene transfer techniques, molecular biology, and technical computing in molecular entomology. Using DNA mapping systems and the possibilities of genetic manipulation, they began to create transgenic assassin bugs instead of old-fashioned hybrids.

As with most entrepreneurial ventures, there were a few snags along the way, primary among which was a cash flow problem. It turned out that the lab equipment was as expensive as the science was fantastic. A quarter million dollars for a single suspension array system with performance validation tools, conversion kits, software, and the various parts and accessories to make it work. By the time they'd assembled a viable lab and hired a few qualified researchers, they'd burned through a fair chunk of their savings.

This explained why they had made inquiries with several venture capital outfits, among which was Blue Sky Capital Partners, LLC, whose president, Joshua Treadwell, was scheduled to arrive this afternoon to visit the laboratory for a demonstration of the current strains of transgenic assassin bugs.

The flesh fly landed on Bob's arm, tickling the hair and bringing Bob back from his reverie. He made a move to catch it but wasn't quick enough. "Damn." The fly was across the room now, circling near the micro-injection station. As Bob studied its orbit, a new idea formed. He looked up at Klaus and said, "Hey, do you think we could make an assassin that flies?"

Klaus eyed him skeptically. "Perhaps," he said. "But first we should…"

Bob didn't hear the objection. "No, wait a second." He slapped his hand on the floor. "Yes!" Bob scrambled to his feet, his mind fixed on new possibilities. "I mean one that actually catches insects in mid-air." He snatched at the air in front of him to demonstrate.

"Bob," Klaus said, gesturing with his fork. "You have that look on your face again." The first time he saw it was when Bob had the idea that saved their lives and led to the ten-million-dollar con. In the years since, Klaus had seen it many times, though without the subsequent profits.

"This is fantastic," Bob said as he began to calculate the potential millions of his latest idea. "Think about it!"

"Bob?"

"Something that kills flies and mosquitoes, indoors or out. And wasps! Be a huge seller during the summer." Bob crossed the room to a shelf filled with textbooks. "But what do we use?" He tilted his head to the side to read the titles.

"I think we should perfect our current bugs first," Klaus said. "What's the expression? You must learn to walk before you can run?"

"This is fantastic," Bob said. He ran a finger along the spines of the books, his head still cocked at an angle. "Got to be something with strong flight skills. Dragonflies? Ommigod, no." He snatched a book from the shelf and said, "*Promachus fitchii!*" He tossed the book to Klaus. "The giant robber fly! I can't believe we didn't think of this before. We can pitch Treadwell this afternoon."

"Bob? We don't have time to work up another presentation." Still, he looked up the insect in question.

Bob was shaking his head, deflecting Klaus' negativity. "We've got to think big! That's what venture capital's all about, right? Funding big ideas. Big buggy ideas! These guys respond to that sort of thinking. That's why he's coming here in the first place, right? Big ideas yield big returns." He pointed at the textbook as Klaus scrolled through the index. "Whaddya think? Sacken's bee hunter, what is it, *Laphria sackeni*? No, it's too small. What about *Efferia pogonias*?"

Klaus looked up the bearded robber fly. He said, "Well, it does catch prey on the wing. But the adults fly only during the summer."

"That's when you need them!" Bob grabbed a legal pad and began sketching ideas for a demonstration as he paced the room. "We'll need something big, maybe a wind tunnel, where we can test them in flight. I think the biggest problem will be keeping them in a specific area. Maybe there's a pheromone solution to that." He was passing by the lab door when it opened abruptly and whacked him in the head. "Ow!"

"Oops, sorry." Mary peered behind the door where Bob stood with a stunned expression. "You okay?" She was dressed for business in a navy blue mid-length jacket, matching skirt, and subdued floral patterned shirt with a bumblebee pin on her lapel.

Bob rubbed his head, still wide-eyed with enthusiasm. He said, "Honey, we just had a great idea. We're working on a new..."

"No time," Mary said, holding up a hand.

"What's up?"

"He's here."

Chapter Six

Bob, Klaus, and Mary walked to the small parking area outside the lab to meet their savior as he parked his rented Escalade.

Joshua Treadwell flashed a confidence-inducing smile and waved as he got out, looking like the prince of Wall Street. Starched white shirt, red tie, dark Brooks Brothers suit with a flag pin in the lapel and pants creased so sharply you could slice meat with them.

After introductions, they went into the small conference room adjacent to the lab. Bob was still thinking about how to pitch his idea for flying assassins. Klaus played the silent partner, letting Bob and Mary speak for the company while he sat there taking notes and looking like a team player. They sat at the conference table discussing the goals of their respective companies.

"My associates and I review over a hundred business plans each week and we reject at least ninety-nine of them," Mr. Treadwell said. "A few are, admittedly, hare-brained but most are submitted by serious people with serious ideas. What they lack, as far as we're concerned, is a certain…daring." He gave a squinty grimace as if to indicate the difficulty of articulating his position. "We're looking for people possessed of a willingness to consider ideas on the outskirts of reason, ideas that some might consider fantastic or beyond science fiction."

Treadwell made a sweeping gesture with one hand which he held aloft as he said, "We're looking for leaps of imagination, a willingness to visualize farther into the future than others are willing or able." He brought his hand down, balled into a fist. "We're looking for people with the vision to see the world as it will be, not as it is. People who can prophesy, if you will." He raised his eyebrows as if to indicate he believed he was looking at such people. "My partners and I think we know potential when we see it. And that is what we like about your company. Its potential."

Everyone exchanged optimistic glances and there was much nodding of heads before Treadwell said, "We foresee applications that go far beyond domestic pest management. We see large scale agricultural and industrial uses as well. And much more."

The comment hung in the air for a moment before Bob said, "What else is there?"

Treadwell brushed the question aside with a wave of his hand, saying, "Well, I'm getting ahead of myself." He turned to Mary. "Right now I'd like to address your concerns about our proposed convertible bridge financing and the rights and preferences of a proposed senior class of preferred stock."

As Mary and Treadwell discussed the financials, Bob kept thinking about the idea of flying assassins. He didn't want to distract from the bugs they were about to demonstrate, but after Treadwell's speech about leaps of imagination and the ability to think beyond the cusp of reason, Bob figured his new idea would demonstrate precisely how unconstrained he was by conventional thinking. "You know, just before you got here," Bob said, "we were talking about a great new idea."

Klaus shot him a look as if to say 'don't muddy the water,' but it was too late.

Bob continued, "We were thinking summer time and flying insects and the feasibility of creating airborne assassins."

Klaus mouthed the words in disbelief. Airborne assassins.

Treadwell looked down at his hands which were now folded on the table in front of him. He shook his head just slightly for a moment before he looked up and pointed at Bob. "See, now that's the sort of imaginative thinking we're looking for."

Bob cocked an eyebrow at Klaus, then added a little smirk. Like a pair of ten-year-olds.

After pondering it for a moment Treadwell touched his chin and said, "I take it you'd have to work with some other species?"

Figuring he'd better help to sell the idea now that it was on the table, Klaus said, "Yes. We were talking about the bearded robber fly and Sacken's bee hunter."

"And we'd want to look at some species of dragonflies as well," Bob added.

"How about your terrestrial assassins? You working with anything new there?"

"No, still using the transgenic versions of our hybrids," Bob said. "But we've put a few new species on the drawing board, like the blue-black spider wasp and the steele-blue cricket hunter." Bob cast a knowing glance at Klaus and said, "And we'd sure like to get our hands on a few African white-eyed assassin bugs, but the Department of Agriculture has turned down all requests for import permits."

"Well, that's something we might be able to help with," Treadwell said, making a note on his legal pad.

Bob and Klaus exchanged a curious glance. It seemed like a strange thing for a venture capitalist to say. They both knew that money talked, and that government officials were for sale at reasonable prices, but neither thought this was the sort of situation where that might apply.

Klaus said, "Your company has influence with federal regulatory agencies?"

Joshua Treadwell ducked his head, smiling modestly. "Well, I'm getting ahead of myself again. But, yes, that's something we could look into." He gestured toward the lab. "What do you say we go on in? I'm eager to see the demonstration."

Chapter Seven

The new lab lacked the charm of Bob's original bug room. Granted, it was fully equipped and built to code with lots of counter space but it lacked the *je ne sais quoi* that had infused the dark, cramped, rickety basement room that Bob had built with scrap lumber and garage sale shelving.

One thing the two places had in common was the smell, a vague scent that Bob thought of as his own brand of jitterbug perfume. It was an array of pheromones, insect excreta, and the tang of the assassin's digestive saliva floating on the airy essence of several thousand insects, all capped with a top note of pine disinfectant. The rooms also had a similar sound; like the sections of an orchestra, the vibes of stridulating organs, buzzing wings, and the rasping of all those curved feeding tubes resulted in a sort of new-age insect symphonia.

Bob, Mary, Klaus, and Mr. Treadwell were standing in front of a container marked, Transgenic 1. Bob slipped a heavy glove onto his right hand and reached inside. "This is the transgenic hybrid spined ambush assassin," Bob said, pulling one out. As he turned to give his potential investor a better look Bob pointed and said, "Notice the size of the rostrum." The bug made a sudden move to the edge of Bob's hand.

Joshua Treadwell took a step back. "Yes, I can see it fine from here." The bug was the size of a large man's thumb, nearly three inches long with a glistening greenish-black exoskeleton ringed with a series of sharp, rigid spines along the sides of the pro-thorax. It had disproportionately large, muscular forearms and twitchy, clubbed antennae. Its eyes were orange and rotated in their sockets with a sickening, chameleon independence, allow-ing it to look in two directions at the same time.

"As hybrids," Bob said, "these were extremely violent preda-tors. Almost as if they enjoyed killing. Through transgenics, we've turned them into more organized hunters."

"Any less violent?"

Bob shook his head. "If anything they've become almost psychotically savage but now they work in groups, like a pack of wolves. They're also extremely efficient."

"How large can you make these things?"

"Probably half again as big as this one." Bob poked at the bug with the eraser end of a pencil. It reared back on its hind legs and hissed. "But you don't want them too large or cockroaches and silverfish could escape through spaces the assassins couldn't."

"Well, now, wait a minute. Let's think outside the box for just a second," Treadwell said. "Are there practical limits to their size? I'm just trying to think of advantages and other uses."

Klaus shook his head. "Their respiratory systems limit their size," he said. "Only a few very large insect species actively ven-tilate by muscular contraction as mammals do." He gestured at Transgenic 1 and said, "These rely on diffusion of oxygen through spiracles and tracheal tubes. The process works only across very short distances, around one millimeter. A larger version of this bug would simply suffocate."

"Oh. That's too bad." Treadwell paused a moment before saying, "Maybe that's something you could work on."

Bob couldn't think of any practical reason for creating a larger version of the bug but he kept that to himself. They moved to the next container, Transgenic 2. "These are the modified masked wheel bugs," Bob said. "Far stronger and faster than the original hybrid versions." He pulled one out for show. It was a robust savage with an intimidating, muscular thorax. Fanned across the insect's back were two rust-brown dorsal ridges jutting up like the skegs of a flipped surfboard. Using its front legs, the carbon-black brute probed between Bob's fingers with enough strength to spread them apart. "This is the most tenacious bug we've made," Bob said. "Stealthy, powerful, and relentless."

"Good." Joshua Treadwell nodded. "Very good." He noticed a third box, marked Transgenic 3. "What about this one?"

Bob shook his head while Klaus held his hands up, palms out, saying, "We can't use number three yet. They are unstable and dangerous, though we have not yet determined what the problem is."

"It's a transgenic hybrid of an Eastern bloodsucking cone-nose and a thread-legged bug," Bob said. "Remarkable killers. They look like walking sticks on steroids, the body's about five inches long, like a fat pencil with legs." Bob held up his pencil and dangled his fingers below to demonstrate. "But the spined forelegs are like a mantid's, extremely quick and strong. We think the problem comes from the *Triatoma sanguisuga*."

"Tria-what?"

"The Bloodsucking conenose," Bob said.

"Also known as the Mexican bedbug," Mary added simply because it was one of the few bug facts she remembered.

"Unlike other assassins, *sanguisugas* will bite vertebrates, usually around the mouth, which is why they are sometimes called kissing bugs," Klaus said. "They have attacked us more than once while trying to handle them."

"Interesting," Treadwell said, as if entertaining an unsavory notion.

Bob returned the masked wheel bug to its bin before leading the group over to a counter where three shoe box size containers sat covered by a black towel. Removing it, Bob set off a skin-crawling scramble of tan, reddish brown, and black cockroaches. Writhing and tumbling over each other, trying to climb the slick walls and falling over backwards onto their fellow *Blattodea*. "German, American, and Oriental cockroaches," Bob was saying as he pointed at each species in turn. "The bane of the American household. We'll use a hundred or so for the demonstration."

He turned and gestured. "If you'll follow me, we'll go to the staging area."

Bob and Klaus carried the bug bins across the lab to a custom-made acrylic container about the size and shape of a refrigerator. The inside was a cutaway view of the wood frame construction of a typical American home. Electric conduit and wires ran through the wall spaces, along with water and vent pipes and ducts for heating and air conditioning.

Jutting from both sides of this was a series of shelves, each corresponding with a valved duct designed to connect to the insect containers. Bob and Klaus connected the roach and assassin boxes to the ducts. "We're going to release the cockroaches into the wall spaces," Bob said. "Then we'll introduce twenty of the assassins, ten each of the two transgenic hybrids."

"I should also explain," Klaus said. "In nature, an assassin bug would kill and eat a single cockroach and not kill again until it was hungry. But as we want them to kill all the prey they encounter, that requires that they stop eating. They simply do not have the gut space to consume that much food, so we had to manipulate the genetic design of these bugs so that killing is not merely a means to an end, but is an end unto itself."

"In order to do this," Bob continued, "we've increased the toxicity of the enzymes in their saliva, so they don't need to use as much for each kill. And we've nearly tripled its paralyzing effect as well as the potency of the amylase and pectinase they inject into their prey to liquefy the internal organs. Now they kill first and eat later." Bob looked around and said, "Are we ready?"

Treadwell looked concerned, as if he had detected a major design flaw in the demonstration. "This doesn't seem like a real world scenario," he said. "I mean, if I'm not mistaken, cockroaches aren't active in the light."

"Correct," Klaus said. "That is why we do this in the dark."

Chapter Eight

Klaus looked across the lab where Mary was poised by the switch. "Lights."

As the room went black, Treadwell said, "What?" In the darkness he kept talking, "Shouldn't we have night vision goggles or something? How am I supposed to…"

Klaus said, "You will see."

"Here we go." Bob opened three valves. "I'm introducing the cockroaches," he said.

As they streamed out, scurrying in every direction to fill the wall spaces, Treadwell's voice filled with wonder and, just above a whisper, he said, "What in the world?" The roaches glowed an eerie green in the dark.

"Okay," Bob said. "Now the assassins." It was a stunning spectacle, the transgenic killers marching into the staging area like ghostly, iridescent gladiators. "This won't take long," Bob said. "Just watch."

Then the attack began. It was the most remarkable and gruesome thing Joshua Treadwell had ever seen. He watched in awe as the masked wheel bugs seized and flipped the large American cockroaches (*Periplaneta americana*) onto their backs, holding them down with their muscular forearms. The assassins would then rear back before plunging forward, stabbing their prey with powerful mouthparts and injecting their paralyzing saliva before stalking off to the next victim.

Near the bottom of the container, where galvanized rigid conduit fed into an electrical box, a group of the spined ambush assassins had cornered several nervous looking Oriental cockroaches (*Blatta orientalis*). The assassins paused, antennae touching in silent yet complex communication. The roaches had never seen bugs like these but seemed, nonetheless, to have a good sense of what was to come. They were scrambling to get behind one another, eventually pushing the weakest among them out as a sort of offering or perhaps in the hope they could escape during the kill.

Then, as if on cue, the mercenary insects pounced. One victim after another dispatched and tossed onto a growing pile. Saved for later. In the darkness, Treadwell could see the pairs of glowing eyes searching for more prey.

One of the spined ambush assassins leapt onto the electrical box, then up to the collar of a vent pipe going through a wall stud. It had seen the scalloped end of a German cockroach (*Blatella germanica*) disappearing into a thin crevice. Just before it could escape, the hybrid killer seized the roach's sensitive cerci. A moment later, as the roach struggled to pull free, its cerci began to separate from its abdomen, taking with it the abdominal nerve ganglia and rear legs. A second assassin arrived and slipped its sharp claw into the crevice just enough to slide under the wing stubs where it got a purchase. Together they dragged the desperate, struggling German pest from the crevice and, hissing, stabbed it simultaneously. The two bugs then seemed to look at one another with the satisfied expression of men who had done their job well. For a second, Treadwell even thought he saw them nodding their heads as they swaggered off for more.

A few moments later it was over. The organized killing spree gave way to a natural calm. The ghostly shapes of the transgenic hybrids returned calmly to the piles of dead roaches and began to drain their liquified organs.

"Let there be light." Bob said with a bit of bravado. Mary hit the switch and all eyes turned to Treadwell. Klaus noticed the man's expression and wished he could have met him at a poker table. He was all tell, no bluff. This guy was impressed. Klaus felt certain they would get the funding.

Treadwell stepped toward the staging area for a closer look, craning his head to see if all the roaches were dead. Most of them lay still, but here and there legs twitched and spasmed as the nervous system fought vainly against the powerful enzymes before complete paralysis set in. Treadwell pointed at something partially hidden by a floor joist. "What's that?"

Bob looked. It was a dead and partially dismembered masked wheel bug. "Oh, yeah, that happens sometimes," he said. "They occasionally kill one another when things get in a frenzy like that. Sort of a friendly fire situation." He shrugged. "Of course we'll do a count to make sure they got all the roaches, but in any event, I think you have to agree those are some pretty impressive bugs."

Treadwell blinked once, then looked at Bob. "But how did you make them glow?"

Chapter Nine

In Linnaean taxonomy, Bob explained, organisms are classified into groups of increasing similarity, from kingdom to phylum to class to order to family to genus to species.

Notwithstanding literary creations such as the chimera with a goat's body sporting a lion's head and a serpent's tail, and the centaurs with a man's trunk and head on the body of a horse, it was universally understood that you couldn't create a ladybug the size of a Volkswagen by breeding it with an elephant. They were simply too different.

But once scientists unraveled and mapped the DNA sequences of genomes for all manner of plants and animals, it wasn't terribly surprising to discover that they were able to transfer specific traits to others within the same species, or even the broader genus or family. What was surprising (except to a few I-told-you-so types) was the discovery that they were able to transfer traits not just from one like species to another, but from utterly different types of animals, like from jellyfish to rabbits, two species you would otherwise have a hard time getting to mate.

More surprising still was the discovery that they could transfer traits from the animal kingdom to the plant kingdom and vice versa. It still wasn't possible to make an eight thousand pound ladybug, Bob continued, but scientists had taken genes from the cecropia silkmoth (*Hyalophora cecropia*) and put them into the genome of apple trees. Because the moth gene produces a peptide that attacks a variety of bacteria, the result is an apple tree resistant to fire blight and confer scab.

"The process is called zygote micro-injection," Bob said, leading the group back into the conference room where he had the relevant charts and graphs. "We took a fluorescence gene from a jellyfish…" Bob gestured at Klaus. "Actually Klaus did this part. He has very steady hands. Anyway, we modified the jellyfish gene to increase luminescence, then inserted it in a fertilized roach egg cell."

"No kidding." Treadwell looked at Mary and Klaus to see if either would betray Bob. But they just smiled at him and nodded. "That's interesting," Treadwell said. "But…why?"

"Well, we did it specifically for this demonstration. Like you said, cockroaches aren't active in the daylight. But the original idea—not ours, I might add—was to use the fluorescent marker gene to tag certain proteins or cells, like cancer cells, so surgeons would know exactly what to remove during an operation."

"Makes sense."

"It's also been done on silkworms, a chimpanzee, and a rabbit."

"Part of the same research?"

"No, the rabbit was an art project. Some guy named Eduardo Kac."

Treadwell seemed put off by the idea. "An artist made a transgenic, glow-in-the-dark rabbit?"

"Actually, he had a French biotech firm do the actual gene manipulation."

"The French." Treadwell shook his head. "Surprised they didn't use a chicken." He crossed his arms and thought for a moment before saying, "So if you can put moth genes into apple trees, what can't you do?"

Bob shrugged. "Now that the genie's out of the bottle," he said, "it's just a matter of time before we find out. We'd love to do some experiments introducing spider venoms into some of our assassins but, as you know, it's all a matter of funding." He gave Treadwell a smile.

Treadwell nodded and made a note about the spider idea. "What about control? How do you keep the assassins from leaving a building where you've install them?"

"Right now we use a pheromone system," Klaus said. "But it is an extremely time consuming and expensive process. We are hoping to find something more efficient."

"Yes, well, we can probably help with that," Treadwell said.

As Bob and Klaus exchanged a glance, Mary said, "Who is we? I mean, I'm assuming your financial partners aren't also entomologists."

Treadwell gave a sly smile and patted his hand on the conference table. "Well, the truth is, we're not interested in investing in your company for your company's sake."

"What do you mean?" Bob said with some concern.

"We're considering investing in you as part of a larger project," Treadwell said. "See, we look for companies engaged in specific areas of research that we believe we can merge into a larger idea. The Blue Sky concept is to incorporate your work with other research that we're funding. We have several different groups working on different parts of a puzzle. We believe we can integrate them into something you, perhaps, hadn't even considered."

"Okay," Bob said, sitting down across the table from Treadwell. "But you are interested in funding our research?"

"Absolutely. In fact there's only one part of your business plan that gave us any pause at all."

"Which was?"

"The environmental aspect."

He may as well have said it was the icky bugs. It was as if he had kicked Bob, Mary, and Klaus in the stomach and, for a moment, it seemed none of them could breathe. They looked at one another in disbelief before Bob said, "You understand that's one of the main selling points of the idea, right? It's what positions it in the marketplace. Don't you think? The fact that the bugs are an all-natural form of pest control."

Treadwell chuckled slightly and shook his head, dismissing Bob's concern. "Don't get me wrong, it's not that we want you to make the process bad for the environment. I mean, I'm not even sure you could unless you used locusts or something, you know, like the eighth plague in Exodus," Treadwell said. "But some of the people I work with have a negative reaction to anything that's anti-business. You know, environmental impact studies, all that sort of nonsense costs money and is based on junk science. Like the whole global warming thing."

Bob wasn't having a panic attack just yet, but he could see it from where he was. "But that's not—"

"I know, I know," Treadwell said. "Don't worry. I understand the difference. This has no impact on our decision to fund your research. Your part of this is too important."

As Klaus eyed Treadwell, trying to get a sense of his character, he suddenly had a change of heart, deciding that he was glad not to have met Treadwell at the poker table. It turned out he had been bluffing or, in any event, sandbagging. Klaus said, "There is something you are not telling us."

Treadwell took a breath and looked down at his shoes for a moment before he said, "You're right. I haven't been completely honest."

Mary perched her hands on her hips and leaned forward from her waist. "But you just said the environmental aspect wouldn't affect your decision to fund our work."

"And it won't."

"Then what is it?"

"The truth is, I'm with DARPA." Their blank expressions prompted Treadwell to say, "Defense Advanced Research Projects Agency."

Klaus shook his head. "What, exactly, is that?"

"The R&D branch of the U.S. Department of Defense."

"I don't understand," Bob said. "What do you want with us?"

"Well, Bob, we want your help in the war on terror."

Chapter Ten

There followed a silence, awkward and pregnant. The only thing threatening to make any noise was Treadwell's radiant smile.

"Did you just call me...Bob?" He tried to sound confused in an amused sort of way as he glanced at Mary and Klaus who both conjured a weak chuckle that failed to convince.

Not that it mattered.

Ever since he arrived, Treadwell had been playing along, referring to them by their aliases, the false identities Klaus had arranged six years earlier. But now he said, "I'm afraid so, Mr. Dillon." Then he smiled and said, "But don't think twice, it's all right." Treadwell chuckled as he extended his hand across the conference table and said, "Let's start over, shall we? Mary? Klaus? Pleasure to meet you." After Mary limply shook his hand, Treadwell checked his watch. "I assume Katy is on her way home from school."

"Uhhhh, who?"

"Oh, please," Treadwell said, all genial. "We don't need to play that game, do we? We know who you are. I've told you who we are. Let's just get in bed together. Make this world a safer place," he said with a wink. "Whaddya say?"

"I think you've made a mistake," Mary said feebly.

Treadwell understood the pretense but he didn't want to spend time with it. He folded his hands on the table and recited the facts. "Okay, let's see. Bob Dillon, son of Curtis and Edna Dillon, born September 12, 1963, Newark, New Jersey." He paused a moment. "Or is it October 12? We found one date on your birth certificate and the other in your Social Security file."

Bob shrugged in mock confusion. "I don't know what you're talking about," he said, though he knew there had been a typo on his original birth certificate that had been corrected when he hit the rolls at the Social Security Administration. "My birthday is May first," he lied.

"Ah, May Day," Treadwell said with a conciliatory nod before continuing with Mary's full biography, including the names of her parents, their blood types, the date of her wedding, and enough details to convince everyone in the room that he knew the truth. He turned to Klaus and pointed. "You, on the other hand, are a bit of a mystery. We found so many names in your file it's not clear which one is real. And frankly, it doesn't matter. I'll call you Mickey Rooney if you like." Treadwell tapped a spot just above his right ear. "But that scar of yours? I believe you picked that up one rainy night in Juarez when you were on the trail of that *chargé d'affaires* from the German embassy."

Klaus remembered it well, but how did this guy know about it? And what did it mean that he knew? The questions startled Klaus. His survival instincts, dormant after several years of peace, suddenly began to hum. His antennae fanned out like a European chafer beetle's (*Melolontha melolontha*), tasting the air for trouble. This was decidedly bad news. If this guy knew about them, who else did? Was he really D.O.D. or had Riviera discovered the con and sent this guy to kill them? If so, what was he waiting for? Katy? Klaus decided to err on the side of caution. He glanced around the room, looking for a weapon of any sort. There was nothing. He reached into his coat pocket and found what he needed.

Treadwell was complimenting Klaus' marksmanship *vis-à-vis* the assassination of a particularly odious African warlord some years ago when Klaus made his move. Before Treadwell could finish his thought—a regrettable pun about piercing a man's ear with a sniper rifle—he found himself pinned to the conference table, something cold and hard pressed to his carotid artery. He guessed it was a ballpoint pen.

"Klaus!" Mary shrieked at the sudden violence. "What are you doing?"

"Checking him for weapons."

Bob, who had jerked to attention when Klaus attacked their potential investor, was now holding his hands out in a calming manner. "Klaus, I think it's a legitimate question."

Joshua Treadwell tried to nod his agreement but with Klaus' forearm pressing his head firmly to the table top, it was tough going.

Klaus leaned down and said, "Who are you?"

Despite his position, Treadwell managed another bright smile. "Honestly," he said. "I'm Joshua Treadwell with the Department of Defense."

Klaus tossed the man's wallet to Bob who opened it up and said, "The I.D. says Department of Defense."

"Yes," Klaus said. "But then, what does your I.D. say?"

"Okay," Bob said, thinking of his own phony driver's license. "That's a fair point." He tilted his head sideways and squatted down, eye-to-eye with Treadwell. "How do we know you're who you say you are?"

"That's a tricky one, isn't it? Klaus is right. Fake I.D.s are easy enough, but check my wallet. What else is in there?"

Bob flipped through the contents. "Triple-A, library card, Food Town preferred customer, Home Depot credit card. All with Joshua Treadwell on them."

"Now fake driver's licenses and forged passports you could understand," the man said. "But the rest?"

Bob stood up and looked at Klaus. "A Home Depot credit card?"

Klaus thought about it, then checked the man again for weapons. Satisfied that he was unarmed, Klaus backed off, but stayed behind him in a blind spot.

Treadwell sat up, smoothed his crisp haircut and, with a laugh, said, "I know, hard to imagine. The guy with the government

is the only one in the room telling the truth." Treadwell held
up a finger. "Now let me see if I can anticipate a few more of
your questions. First of all, Bob, we've known about you and
your research ever since you did that 'extermination' work for
the C.I.A."

Bob shook his head, more frustrated than agitated. "I never
worked for the C.I.A."

"No, of course not," Treadwell replied with a nonchalant
wave. "And I didn't mean to suggest you had. But I suspect
Agent Mike Wolfe would say otherwise. That is if he hadn't
had that unfortunate…death before or during the explosion
that destroyed your house at 2439 Thirtieth Street in Astoria,
Queens six years ago." He looked over his shoulder at Klaus.
"What'd you use? C-4?"

Klaus shook his head. "Semtex."

Treadwell grinned and touched his head again as if he felt
one or two hairs out of place. "Think you used enough? They
said it blew windows out half a mile away."

"It was a last minute thing," Klaus said, a bit embarrassed
by the overkill.

"Doesn't matter," Treadwell said. "What matters is that we
found you and that we believe your research has potential military applications." He gave them a moment before continuing.
"I know, this is a lot to absorb, especially since you've been off
the radar for so long. Probably starting to feel anonymous again.
And honestly, we'd written you off. After reading the newspaper
articles we thought you'd all gone up with the house and taken
all your research with you."

"So," Klaus said. "How did you find us?"

"That's the funny part," Treadwell said. "We didn't. You
found us. When we got your proposal and saw the nature of
the research, we couldn't believe someone else was working on
it. Then we realized it was you guys. We laughed ourselves silly
when we figured out you'd changed identities and then—by
sheer dumb luck—approached us for funding."

Despite the larger implications of what Treadwell, and presumably others, knew about their identities, Bob remained fixated on the funding issue. He said, "So is Blue Sky Capital Partners really a venture capital outfit?"

"You bet we are," Treadwell said. "Though not in the traditional way."

Klaus couldn't believe he was hearing this conversation. He said, "Bob, perhaps we should focus more on the fact that our covers are blown and that our lives are once again in danger."

Bob held up a hand. "I hear you, Klaus. But I don't see any harm in listening to the man's pitch. I mean you frisked him, right? He's not going to kill us, is he?" He turned to Treadwell. "Are you?"

"Dead, you're no good to me," Treadwell said. "I need you alive and well and doing your research. Besides, killing's not my department. They're very strict about that sort of thing."

Mary folded her arms on the conference table and leaned forward. "You were saying that you're not a traditional VC outfit."

Treadwell smiled at her. "That's right. We've got an annual funding budget north of two billion dollars, and because of our structure, program managers like myself have sole discretion on who to fund."

"What do you mean, your 'structure'?"

"Oh, well, DARPA was designed to be a counterpoint to the traditional military R&D establishment, which is best described as ponderous," Treadwell said. "On the other hand, DARPA has no bureaucratic oversight to impede our progress or ability to adapt. And one of our founding principles is that we have a complete acceptance of failure if the potential payoff is substantial. In other words, we're not doing this to make our money back—hell, it's not even our money," he said with some delight. "It's the taxpayers.' As you can imagine, most venture capital outfits take a rather different view regarding return on investment."

Sensing the skepticism in the room Treadwell figured some background might help. He explained that a few years ago, the

Under Secretary of Defense for Acquisition and Technology, in conjunction with the Subcommittee of the Senate Committee on Armed Services, had worked out the Defense Acquisition Reform Act, the goal of which was to develop what they called an innovative acquisition approach for weapon systems. The result was something known as Section 845 agreements, a funding process unconstrained by the frequently inflexible government policies found in the federal government's cumbersome procurement system.

"It all stems from the Dual Use Applications Program's Commercial Operations and Support Savings Initiative," Treadwell said. "Or what we call DUAP's COSSI. What it amounts to is a smart way to leverage private sector technologies with public sector funding. So yes," he said, nodding happily. "We're in the venture capital business." He straightened in his chair, held his arms out, and said, "Questions?"

Chapter Eleven

"Yeah," Bob said. "What sort of military applications do you see with our bugs?"

"A fair question," Treadwell said, pointing at Bob. "One I'm sure you'll understand I can't answer fully since a lot of that is classified. But, for example, one project we're working on is vectoring lymphatic filariasis using mosquitoes. Properly infected, they transfer hundreds of tiny worms that eventually grow to about eight inches. They ball up in the lymph glands until the victim's legs swell up thick as an elephant's. You imagine a terrorist training camp infected with something like that? Think how easy that fight would be." He chuckled and said, "Hard to run with your legs swollen up like a pachyderm."

"That wouldn't be considered biological warfare?"

"The lawyers don't think so," Treadwell said. "Bio warfare is defined as the use of bacteria, viruses, fungi, or rickettsia. Doesn't say anything about worms as far as I know. But think back to Afghanistan. The White Mountains, the caves of Tora Bora? Those al Queda terrorists holed up so deep in those bunkers the Air Force couldn't even get 'em with those GBU-28s with 650 pounds of high explosive." He shook his head in obvious disbelief, then after a pause, he assumed a look of wonder. He held up an index finger and said, "But imagine thousands, tens, no, hundreds of thousands of your assassin bugs pouring over a ridge and slipping into those caves in search of a blood meal." His eyes grew wide at the thought of it and he counted off the advantages on his fingers as he said, "They're stealthy, they're too small to shoot, there would be too many of them to step on, and let's say your idea with the spider venom pans out…heck, with that sort of a weapon system the war might be over already."

Bob nodded slowly as he thought about it. It wasn't as crazy as it sounded. In fact, he'd seen it work six years ago, when his hybrid assassins killed the woman named Chantalle. Of course, the circumstances of her death would be somewhere between difficult and impossible to recreate on the battlefield, but perhaps there were other ways to make it happen. After a moment Bob said, "What do we have to do now?"

"Nothing," Treadwell said, apparently delighted. He pointed toward the lab with his thumb. "The presentation earlier? That's what we call an Advanced Concept Technology Demonstration. It convinced me that with further development we'll get a field-able military prototype of your transgenic assassins. It's all I need to move forward with full funding."

You could have heard the pop of a Champagne cork. It was a turn of events none of them could have imagined. At best they had anticipated protracted negotiations, a humbling loss of control over their own company, and the promise of a board of micro-managers second guessing every decision they made. But here was a man who, by all appearances, was handing them one hundred percent of their funding on a silver platter without so much as a repayment schedule. It was absolutely crazy. The one thing that made it at all plausible was that only the U.S. government would spend money this way.

"So how does it work," Mary asked. "You just cut us a check and we send updates every now and then?" She smiled to show she knew it couldn't be that easy.

Treadwell shared the smile and said, "No, I'm afraid the work has to be done under my supervision at our West Coast facilities."

Given how sweetly things had unfolded in the past hour or so Bob allowed himself to imagine the best possible scenario. "I don't suppose your lab is at OSU." He gestured in the direction of nearby Oregon State.

"No, sorry," Treadwell said. "Los Angeles."

Mary sagged like a pricked balloon, repeating "Los Angeles" in a tone usually reserved for discussions about hemorrhoids or Congress.

Bob uttered a noncommittal, "Huh."

Klaus remained mum.

A gasp of excitement caused everyone to turn. Sixteen year old Katy was standing in the doorway, her big brown eyes like the O's in the Hollywood sign. "We're moving to L.A.?!" Her head tilted back and she said, "Coooool!"

Chapter Twelve

Joshua Treadwell left them with a DARPA brochure, information on DOD subsidized housing, and his business card. He said he'd like to hear from them as soon as possible.

Mary looked up from crunching the numbers, tapping her pencil on the legal pad. "If everything he says is true, it's a good deal."

"Good?" Bob said. "If everything he says is true, it's unbelievable!"

"Yes," Klaus said, peering cautiously out the window. "Unbelievable is the word that comes to mind."

"Who caaaares," Katy said. "It's, like, El Aaaa! Hell-oooo." Katy looked at her pale arms and legs and imagined how hot she'd be with a tan. "Anywhere has got to be better than this place. Especially, like, a planet with, I dunno, a suuun. I mean look at me. I've got, like, the complexion of tofu."

They were each right in their own way. For Mary, the numbers told the story. In addition to the funding, Joshua Treadwell said they'd be able to control any resulting patents relating to commercial applications of their insect research. But even if there were no patents, that the funding was essentially a grant instead of a loan made accepting the deal a no-brainer.

For Bob, it was more than the money. A best friend from childhood, Ricky Molloy, keeping the family tradition, joined an engine company in Manhattan. Charged into the north tower that day, his last. The possibility that Bob's work might result in some sort of weapon that could be used in the war against terrorists had powerful appeal. Bob was a New Yorker born and bred. And, despite his litany of complaints when he lived there, he loved the city and its people. He missed it—they all did—but their unusual circumstances dictated the move west.

Life in Oregon was fine, but Bob would never forget New York, nor the images of the attack on it, nor his feeling of powerlessness as he watched the events unfold from three thousand miles away. And he would never forgive those responsible. He wasn't naturally hostile, but after 9/11 Bob wanted to inflict terrible violence on everyone who had conspired to see those events come to pass. And now, against all odds, the government had come offering him the chance. In his mind Bob could see an army of his assassins—hundreds of thousands of them—transgenically altered into ruthless and unforgiving soldiers being brought to bear against a wicked and malignant enemy. He couldn't wait to get started on his airborne assassins.

For Klaus it was simply unbelievable that Bob and Mary were so nonchalant about what had just happened. Despite the assurances of Joshua Treadwell, Klaus knew their names were out there somewhere—on a memo or an email or in a phone call—and it was just a matter of time before the wrong people found out.

Chapter Thirteen

C.I.A. Headquarters: Langley, Virginia

Agent Nick Parker didn't join the CIA to get rich, which was good since he would never make more than fifty-one thousand a year. He joined because he believed in the CIA's vision, mission, and values. He longed to be part of an organization that provided the knowledge and was willing to take the actions necessary to ensure the national security of the United States and the preservation of American life and ideals.

In other words, he fell for the recruiting pamphlet. Now, nearly a decade later, Agent Nick Parker had serious questions about the wisdom of his career choice. After several years in the field, he now worked for the Directorate of Intelligence, the branch responsible for analyzing all the information gathered by the other branches, from human intelligence to satellite imagery to signals and communications intel, which consisted largely of intercepted radio transmissions, e-mails, and telephone conversations.

Whereas the CIA has fewer than five thousand case officers skulking around the globe trying to recruit, bribe, or blackmail locals into poking their noses into sensitive places, they have well over thirty thousand eavesdroppers who generate a staggering pile of transcribed communications, all of which must be reviewed and summarized. Most of these are of no consequence to the security of the United States. But every now and then an analyst stumbles across something that makes the skin crawl.

It was just after lunch. Agent Parker's eyes were nappy as he sat staring at his computer screen, his left hand absently spinning the American flag pinned on the lapel of his dark suit. His right hand clicked the mouse, and his eyes moved slowly across the screen. Click, scan, nothing. Click, scan, nothing. Click, scan, huh? The flag was upside down when it stopped spinning. Agent Parker paused for a minute before muttering, "Un-be-leave-able." He scrolled up and down the screen, taking in all the information, making sure he had it right. Was this possible? His jaw opened slightly before he said, "Jesus." His head began to move slowly back and forth. "I don't fucking believe it."

"Don't believe what?" It was Agent Hawkins standing at the entrance to Parker's cubicle, a manila folder in one hand.

Parker turned. "How long have you been there?"

Agent Hawkins shrugged. "I didn't put a watch on it." He slapped the folder against his leg and asked again. "Don't believe what?"

"See for yourself," Agent Parker said, nodding at the screen.

Hawkins stepped into the cubicle and looked. His expression dissolved from mild intrigue to utter disbelief. He turned to look at Agent Parker. "Five hundred sixty thousand?"

"You believe it? For a damn two-bedroom, one-and-a-half bath down near Dumfries."

"Dumfries?" Hawkins shook his head. "I wouldn't pay five-sixty for that piece of crap if it was on Pennsylvania Avenue."

"Roger that."

Owing to a combination of his meager salary, poor fiscal discipline, and a housing bubble, Agent Parker was still living in a dismal condo complex in Spotsylvania, Virginia. Every day he was forced to inch up the I-95 corridor at the speed of drying paint to what was known as the Mixing Bowl, a ludicrous array of exits and on-ramps, merges and lane shifts, unfinished bridges and clueless drivers that was the interchange with the Beltway. On average, Agent Parker's commute was two and a half hours each way. He'd calculated it once, twelve hundred hours a year in his car, crawling to and from a job that had betrayed him. A job he once believed offered him an endless array of possibilities for adventure, advancement, and a better address. A job that now seemed only to limit his possibilities.

Ten years ago things weren't so bad. Just as he had swallowed the recruiting pamphlet, Agent Parker had believed the Realtor who told him what a great investment the condo was and how, in a matter of just a few years—thanks to the miracle of equity—he'd be able to move into a fine house of his own in the D.C. metro area. That, it turned out, was the first of many betrayals that had been gnawing lately at Agent Parker's soul.

At one end of the spectrum the betrayals seemed minor upon examination. But in the same way that each drop of Chinese water torture is minor, the betrayal of the media with each inaccurate traffic report, and the treachery of his fellow drivers with every unsignaled lane change had a cumulative effect that was beginning to take a toll. Even his hair, once thick and luxuriant, had turned on him with an unfortunate balding pattern that had him considering plugs that he couldn't even afford.

At the other end of the spectrum, the betrayal he endured lacked the subtlety of slow torture. From the internal betrayal of Aldrich Ames, Robert Hanssen, and others to the external betrayal of his own party with the outing of a covert CIA agent by some vindictive SOB with a partisan agenda—it was enough to make a man rethink where he placed his loyalty.

Agent Parker gestured at the folder Hawkins was holding. "Is that for me?"

"Oh, right." Hawkins opened the envelope and, looking down, said, "Didn't you work with Mike Wolfe when you entered on duty?"

"Yeah, why?"

"We picked up some chatter," Hawkins said. "A couple of cell calls up in Oregon." He flipped through the file until he found what he was looking for. "Looks like they originated from a D.O.D. phone."

"We had a warrant?"

Hawkins gave him a you-gotta-be-kidding look and said, "What do you think?"

"You don't want to know what I think."

"Fine. Anyway, the recognition software flagged a couple of key words—names, actually—that came up in the conversation."

"And one of them was Mike Wolfe?"

"Actually, no. But the names that did come up were linked to one of Wolfe's old case files. We figure they were assets he was working."

"Okay," Parker said. "What're the names?"

"One was a first-name-only, guy named Klaus. The other one's kind of funny. It's Bob Dylan. You know, like the singer."

The names triggered enough visceral jolt to blow a twenty-amp fuse, but Agent Parker offered only a blank nod. "Vaguely rings a bell," he said as he recalled every detail of that night in Queens when he'd gone looking for Mike Wolfe. The lights of the emergency vehicles playing on the smoke and steam rising from the burned out shell of a house. The improbable smell of what turned out to be tens of thousands of roasted insects. The paramedic pulling back the sheet on the gurney to show Parker what looked like a large and badly burned pork roast, which turned out to be part of someone who had been in the house when it exploded.

Agent Parker feigned indifference as he pointed at the file and said, "So what's the gist of this conversation?"

"Something about the D.O.D. offering these two guys a contract."

Another jolt. "You don't say."

"Fits their profile, according to Wolfe's info anyway. So you have to assume they're talking about a wet job."

Parker shrugged. "Any target named?"

Hawkins shook his head. "I don't think so. The only other names appear to be the alias I.D.s they used."

"Used? What tense are the verbs?"

"What do you mean?"

"In the conversation," Parker said. "Maybe they were talk-ing about a contract that was executed years ago. You know, reminiscing about the good old days."

Hawkins looked at a few pages of the file. "No. It's all pres-ent tense."

"Well, there you go."

Hawkins saw the gears turning in Parker's head. "You got a theory about this contract?"

"Who knows," Parker said. "Maybe D.O.D. signed Dylan to a recording deal."

Agent Hawkins pinched off a sarcastic smile and said, "Yeah, that's a good place to start your investigation."

"What?" Parker looked up, feigning annoyance. "Oh, come on," he said. "Don't do me like that. I'm too busy as it is."

"What, house-hunting?" Agent Hawkins smiled again and said, "Next stop, Corvallis, Oregon." He tossed the file onto Parker's desk and gave him a wink. "You're gonna make me lonesome when you go."

"I don't believe you. Can't you dump this somewhere else?"

"You know the rules," Hawkins said. "If Wolfe was still around, he'd get it. But since he poofed, and since you were with him when he opened this file, it's your baby. The D.O. wants to know what these guys are up to." Hawkins stepped out of the cubicle then turned and said, "Oh, be sure to pack some flannel." He walked off humming a bar of "Tombstone Blues."

Agent Parker stared at the file for a moment. The odds that the names Klaus and Bob Dillon would show up in conversa-tion regarding a contract, on a D.O.D. phone no less, were too slim to believe. It had to be them. He opened the file, read the transcript. By the time he finished, every one of Parker's previous assumptions about what had happened six years earlier had flown out the window, leaving open a whole new world of possibilities.

Chapter Fourteen

"I can't believe you're doing this to me! I hate you!" Katy stormed from the kitchen, where the family had just finished discussing the pros and cons of Joshua Treadwell's offer. A moment later, Katy's door slammed. Then, for good measure, it slammed again.

This melodrama in one act followed closely on the heels of the list of reasons Mary had given Katy for why she wouldn't be moving to Los Angeles with her father.

The list wasn't based on personal experience or in-depth research so much as it was completely improvised based on things Mary had heard over the years, things that she believed served her current purpose. She began by explaining that the Los Angeles school system was among the worst in the country, that the classrooms were virtually run by gangs. Quality-of-life-wise, she said the air in Southern California was literally brown with carcinogens and the sunshine everybody touted was simply melanoma waiting to happen. And, she continued, if you go to the beach and actually make it to the water without stepping on a used hypodermic, you're likely to get one of those antibiotic-resistant infections from all the sewage they dump into the ocean.

Katy stared at her mother, momentarily stunned by the catalogue of horrors flowing from her mouth.

During the ensuing silence Mary took the opportunity to fabricate statistics about the amount of time people spent stuck in traffic and the number of citizens who died every week during random freeway shootings. She said that the only time traffic seemed to move at all in Los Angeles was during the daily high speed chases resulting from car-jackers and escaping bank robbers, since it was a well established fact that Los Angeles was the bank robbery capital of the U.S.

Here, Bob added that it was also the nation's porn capital which brought Mary's speech to a momentary halt during which Bob explained that it was just a fact he'd heard somewhere and he could be wrong and, just, never mind, forget he'd said anything.

Mary resumed by saying that the justice system in Southern California was as broken as everything else, ticking off a long list of celebrities who had gotten away with murder, child molestation, and making films like *Gigli* and *Dukes of Hazzard*.

"The people down there are complete idiots," she said. "For God's sake, look at who they elected governor. I don't want you exposed to all that."

Katy said, "But you're letting dad go?"

"He'll have Klaus to protect him, sweetie."

"Hey, I can hold my own," Bob said, thinking back on how he'd helped the once famous assassin survive the streets of New York without a gun.

"Besides," Mary said, "you don't want to live in a place where the only cultural advantage is that you can turn right on red." She held up her hands to forestall any further argument. "That's it," she said. "You're staying here with me."

That's where Katy declared that she would rather be killed in a drive-by shooting than to live in Corvallis, Oregon, for another minute, where she was more likely to die of mold and mildew. She continued by saying that her parents were massively lame for ruining her life and that she hated them and would, like, for the rest of eternity.

After the door slammed for the second time, Bob looked at Mary and said, "You really think that line from *Annie Hall* is going to convince her she doesn't want to move to L.A.?"

"I had to say something," Mary said, somewhat agitated. "You certainly weren't helping."

"Hey, I added the porn statistic," he said. "Besides, until you started with the anti-Chamber-of-Commerce speech, I didn't know you and Katy weren't moving with us."

"I'm not moving down to that cesspool."

"You've never even been there."

"I know, but it's…Los Angeles. It's a big ugly, sprawling mess filled with pretentious, preening, image-obsessed, surgically altered nitwits. And it's not where I want Katy going to high school. There are too many temptations and she won't have any friends and that'll just make it more tempting to do the wrong things to be accepted." Mary went on to admit that she liked living in Oregon. She loved how green and peaceful it was. Besides, she pointed out, the D.O.D. funding was only for a year at a time. She didn't want to move down there and then have to move back in a year. "That," she said, "would be nuts."

"What is nuts," Klaus said. "Is that the two of you do not seem to realize the significance of what has happened. Our covers are no longer viable."

"I know," Bob said. "But Treadwell said they'd provide new ones."

"Yes," Klaus said. "But they will generate paperwork in the process. And someone else will find that paperwork. And it will leak. And they will come looking for us." After everything that had happened over the past six years, Klaus found it incredible that Bob took at face value the representations of any U.S. government official.

"Why would anybody believe it?" Mary asked. "Everyone knows you collected the bounty six years ago. There's nothing in it for anyone anymore."

Klaus propped his elbows on the kitchen table, closed his eyes, and began to rub his temples. He could not believe these two. He had been their best friend for the past six years and yet it was as if he had just met them, had no idea how these people thought. He couldn't believe Bob and Mary had forgotten how easily they had been found and how close they had come to being killed in New York when all the wrong people knew who they were. Apparently six years of calm and prosperity had dulled whatever edge they had honed during those frenzied days when they were targets of some of the world's best assassins. Finally Klaus put his hands on the table and said, "We must obtain new identities."

Mary reached over and patted his hand. "You do whatever you think is best."

"Thank you." Klaus pulled his cell phone and punched in a number. A moment later he said, "Yes. I am having an identity crisis. I was hoping you could help." Klaus listened for a second before a look of surprise crossed his face. "No kidding?" He put his hand over the phone and looked at Bob. "He has a website now." He turned his attention back to the call. "It is secure? Yes, PayPal is fine," he said as he grabbed a pad of paper and a pencil. "All right, www dot what?" A moment later he flipped the phone shut and went to the computer.

As Bob and Mary resumed their discussion about the move to L.A., Klaus navigated the website. At the low end of the product line was a do-it-yourself option which allowed you to download templates of birth certificates and driver's licenses from various states. At the other end was the Gold Member option. It was expensive, but the work came with a money-back guarantee. Clicking there, Klaus was taken to a screen where he could choose the number of identities needed, the genders and age of each, and the names. A drop-down menu allowed him to select first from ethnic groups. Thinking about the move to L.A., Klaus selected 'Hispanic.' This took him to a second drop-down menu. He scrolled through it then turned to Bob and said, "What do you think? Gonzalez? Recendez? Something like that? Be in the majority?"

Before Bob could answer, Katy appeared in the doorway holding several pieces of paper. She cleared her throat as if standing in front of a class about to give a report. "Okay, first of all," she said, "based on per-student spending, Oregon schools aren't any better than California's. Second, I'm four times more likely to get addicted to crystal meth living in Oregon." Flipping to the next page she said, "It's true that the five counties with the worst air quality in the country are in California, but Los Angeles county isn't one of them. And according to the Department of Transportation, the average commute time in Los Angeles is twenty-eight minutes, not three and half hours." She gave Mary a how-do-you-like-them-apples look before continuing. "You're right that it's the bank robbery capital of the world, but 94 percent of the high-speed chases that follow end with no injuries to bystanders." Katy turned to look at Bob. "Sorry, Dad, but I couldn't confirm that L.A. is the porn capital."

"That's okay, sweetie, thanks for trying."

"But even if it's true, it's irrelevant. What is relevant," Katy said, her accusing eyes turned back to Mary, "is the fact that if Dad moves down there and we stay here, this will be a single-parent household, which quadruples the likelihood of my becoming a pregnant, drug-addicted, high school drop-out."

Mary looked at Katy with amused annoyance, and not for the first time.

"It's a fact." Katy waved the sheets of paper. "Children from single-parent homes drop out of school, get pregnant, sniff glue, and become prostitutes at, like, twice the national rate. Do you want to hear the facts about cocaine and heroin use?" She hoped Mary's answer would be no since most of what she was saying wasn't supported by her documents, but she figured she'd bluffed her mom before and it was worth a try.

After taking a moment to absorb Katy's presentation, Mary said, "Your grades would be so much better if you put this much effort into your school work." She shook her head. "By the way, where'd you get all that? Some bogus Internet site?" She reached for Katy's documents.

Katy refused to hand them over. Instead she said, "Guh. At least I'm not quoting from dumb old Woody Allen movies."

All Mary had to say was, "You're not going."

"Katy?" Klaus said. "Sorry to interrupt, but would you prefer to be Liliana, Blanca, or Rosa Martinez?"

Katy looked at Klaus with all the contempt a sixteen year old could muster. She said, "Guh. You guys are so laaaame." She rolled her eyes and left.

Klaus turned back to the computer and said, "Rosa it is."

A moment later, Katy's door slammed again.

Chapter Fifteen

Miguel DeJesus Riviera was surprised to hear that someone from the CIA was on his way up to see him. Miguel had lost touch with most of the guys at the Agency after the Iran-Contra thing blew up in their faces. But he still had fond memories of shipping large quantities of product through Ilopango Air Base in El Salvador where the CIA maintained their logistical support center for the Contras. That it was all done with the winking approval and string-pulling of folks in the White House basement just made the memories that much sweeter.

Miguel smiled at the thought of how much money they had made selling all that coke to the gangs in South Central Los Angeles, and the nutty story that the whole thing was a CIA plot to introduce crack into poor black neighborhoods to bring about genocide when in fact it was just a clumsy attempt to get around the Boland amendments and the U.S. arms embargo against Iran. Ahh, the good old days, Miguel thought. Still, he wondered why the Agency would be paying a visit now. Perhaps they had another brilliant scheme up their covert sleeves.

The door opened and a man carrying a laptop stepped into the room. He wore a dark suit and a darker expression. He took his time, gazing disparagingly at the decor as he crossed the floor toward Miguel and his antique Victorian writing table.

"Come in, come in." Miguel smiled and gestured grandly at the African chieftain's chair. "Please, sit," he said.

Placing the laptop on the table, the man ignored the invitation. He looked at the ridiculous chieftain's chair, put his hands into his pockets and said, "I'll pass." He'd been sitting on planes for the past eleven hours and wanted to stretch his legs. Not that the man was going to explain this. He just wanted to keep his host off balance, make him wonder why the CIA had sent this ill-mannered asshole in the first place. He roamed, looking at each piece of furniture as if he were a surly antiques appraiser, now and then issuing derisive snorts and shaking his head. He paused at the Spanish Colonial Revival bronze floor lamps and said, "Who's your decorator? Helen Keller?"

Miguel forced a smile. Obviously this wasn't a friendly social visit. So, he wondered, what was it? "What can I do for you, Agent...?" He held his hands out asking for help.

"Parker."

"Agent Parker." Miguel gave a courtly nod despite being offended by the man's demeanor. Still, he knew of no good reason for pissing off the CIA, so he asked again how he could be of help.

"I'm doing some follow-up," Parker said. "About your brother."

"Ronaldo? What about him?"

"His unfortunate death," Parker said.

Miguel screwed up a mournful expression and said, "Yes, well, it was a shock and a tragedy, to be sure. But after so many years, I've managed to put it behind me." Miguel crossed himself, saying, "May the blessed Virgin have mercy on his soul, but I prefer not to dwell on the past."

"That's very touching," Parker said. "But we're going to dwell for just a moment, if you don't mind."

Uh-oh, Miguel thought. Not good. Conjuring a smile and an appeasing tone he said, "Always happy to assist my friends from Washington."

"Good answer." Parker pointed for Miguel to sit. And he did. "Now, you offered a nice little bounty for the head of his killer, am I right?"

"Of course," Miguel said, acting as if he had chosen to sit on his own. "It is bad business for a man in my position to let such things go unpunished. So, yes, I put money on the table and the call was answered."

Parker nodded. "You're talking about that business in Queens, yes? The explosion? All that?"

"That's right." Miguel was getting suspicious and worried about where this was going. "Why do you ask?"

"And the bounty was collected?"

"Of course," Miguel said. "And, not to be too blunt, but I suspect you know by whom."

Agent Parker smirked. "If you're going to tell me it was the man they call Klaus, I've got a bridge I'd like to sell you."

"Is that so?" He could feel his blood pressure rising.

As Agent Parker pulled a laptop from the case, Miguel thought back to that night when Klaus showed up with the Exterminator's baseball cap, crusty around the bullet hole where the blood had dried. Miguel said, "You can keep your bridge, my friend. I saw the proof. The Exterminator, his wife and his child, all killed before the house was blown up."

"Uh-huh," Agent Parker said. "But what would you say if I were to tell you that Klaus and the Exterminator are alive and well and still accepting contracts?" Parker hit a few keys on the computer, launching a program.

Miguel thought about it for a moment before he forced a smile. "I would say, *eso es un cuento chino!*"

Parker paused as he translated. "A Chinese story?"

"It is an idiom," Miguel said. "A Chinese story is what you would call…a tall tale."

"Ah," Parker said, glancing down at the computer, then back at Miguel. "I do enjoy the colorful use of language."

"Do you?" Emboldened by irritation, Miguel said, "Well, another colorful expression I might use would be to say that you are full of shit."

Parker chuckled. "I've always like that one myself," he said. "But having just spent two days in a car with a Nikon D1H and a 300-millimeter lens with a 2X extender, I'm here to tell you that particular expression doesn't apply in this particular situation." He ducked his head slyly and said, "Would you like to see the slide show?" He hit 'enter' and spun the laptop around for Miguel. As the photos came up, Agent Parker narrated.

"That's the view from the front of their property," he said, as he came around the table to stand next to Miguel's chair. "A nice two-story Craftsman with a couple of acres." The next photo appeared on the screen. "Now this is farther back on the property," he said, pointing at the image of a large steel frame prefab building. "Turns out that's a laboratory full of all sorts of DNA sequencing equipment and insects." Parker looked at Miguel, shrugged, and said, "A guy needs a hobby, I guess."

"Yes," Miguel said between clenched teeth. "I suppose he does."

"Now comes the fun part." Agent Parker gestured at the screen. "That's the daughter, Katy, getting off the school bus. Sure has grown up, hasn't she?" Next photo. "And Mary, the wife, outside cutting flowers." He turned to Miguel and, nodding, said, "She really does have a green thumb. Beds filled with trillium and red baneberry. It's quite nice, if you go for that sort of thing," Parker said.

"I prefer tropicals," Miguel said dryly.

"Yeah, I noticed that on the way in," Parker said. "And by the way, you have some big ass cockroaches out there, you might want to call Orkin." Miguel stared at him blankly before Parker directed his eyes back to the laptop. "Now I'm sure you recognize our next guest." The screen clicked automatically through a series of photos. Klaus coming out of the lab. Klaus talking to Mary holding a bunch of flowers. Klaus tousling Katy's hair as she passed by after getting off the bus. Parker noticed Miguel's silence and his sullen expression. He gave him a gentle elbow and said, "You still with me?"

The Bolivian gave him a nasty look. He didn't like where this was going.

"Okay," Parker said. "Here comes the money shot." The next picture was a pickup truck with a crew cab pulling into the driveway—on the roof, a large fiberglass bug. The truck door opened. Parker said, "Wait for it." Then Bob getting out, facing straight toward the camera, waving at the others. Agent Parker hit the pause button and said, "Now, who does that look like to you?"

Miguel's expression grew darker than Parker's suit. He leaned in for a closer look at the Exterminator's face, taunting him with a smile.

Agent Parker took a couple of steps back. He figured Miguel was about to embark on the Machismo Express, throwing furniture, breaking windows, and vowing violent retribution. A real man's tantrum, something in the neighborhood of Mel Gibson. And who could blame him, Parker thought. Being made the fool was no small shame in Miguel's world. So a tantrum would be a good release. Then, after he'd smashed some things up and calmed down, they could discuss Parker's proposal. But Miguel did none of these things. In fact he seemed chillingly calm and quiet. Perhaps he wasn't convinced, Parker thought. So he said, "Now before you start talking about Photoshop and that kind of crap, let me assure you, this is all legit."

Miguel didn't hear the last comment because of the ringing in his ears and the sudden, crushing headache that had rendered him virtually blind. The simultaneous dizziness he could handle, since he was already seated, but the increasing intracranial pressure had him thinking that his head would explode at any moment.

Miguel knew he had no one to blame but himself. Having ignored his doctor's advice for years, Miguel's chronic, untreated high blood pressure had just been upgraded to an acute hypertensive episode, pushed over the cliff by the smiling face of Bob Dillon and all that it implied.

Agent Parker grew concerned. He didn't want his gravy train derailed. So he moved around the table to look at Miguel. He had developed a body tremor and a facial tic to boot. "Take it easy there, cowboy," Parker said. "Nothing we can't fix." Looking closely at the whites of Miguel's eyes, he saw blood vessels bursting like a tiny red skyrockets. "Whoa." Parker turned, looking for the bar. "You want a drink?"

Miguel either nodded yes or his tremor had changed directions.

As Agent Parker went over and poured a glass of scotch he said, "I understand your reaction, Miguel. I mean, not only is the man you blamed for your brother's death still alive after you paid all that money to his alleged killer, but it turns out the two of them were in cahoots all along. That's gotta hurt." He set the bottle on the table and handed the drink to Miguel who downed it at once.

"And now? Hell, you look like a serious pussy who can't even avenge his own brother's death, and worse," Parker continued, "you look like a dupe, conned out of ten million bucks." He shook his head as he lowered himself into the African chieftan's chair. "When word gets out—and you know it will—your reputation is going to suffer."

The drink seemed to help. Riviera grabbed the bottle and poured another. "I cannot afford that," he said, followed by a second shot of whiskey.

"No, I don't think you can."

He poured a third. "I assume you have a plan of some sort?"

Parker smiled. "What do you think?"

"I think both of them must die."

"I think you're right," Parker said. "But it won't be easy." He paused, looked at his fingernails and said, "Or cheap."

"No, it never is." Then, knowing that he couldn't lower his price from the last time, Miguel said, "Ten million for each."

Agent Parker put his hands together and pointed them at Miguel. "As it turns out, that's exactly what I was thinking. All I ask for is an exclusive on the contract. No competition."

Miguel downed another drink. "For how long?"

"Six months?"

"Two."

"Four."

"Done."

Chapter Sixteen

Paris, France

For over twenty years Marcel Pétain had run the most successful boutique employment agency in Europe. Marcel's company offered what he called specialized staffing and professional service solutions. However, unlike most employment agencies, Marcel's job placements were never for permanent positions. These jobs, by definition, were temporary.

Marcel had been putting assassins to work since 1979.

He had established a sterling reputation by hiring only the best and by matching the needs of the employer with the skills of available service providers. Unfortunately the business took a serious downturn after the third quarter of 1998, when many of the world's best killers were permanently and involuntarily retired while pursuing the same target in New York. Since then, the level of expertise available for hire had sunk to all-time lows. Sure, Marcel would say, there were a few good people still around, and there were some promising up-and-comers, but it was a simple supply-and-demand situation: it being a world where there were more people wanting to hire good killers than there were good killers to be hired.

Or, as Marcel's trusted and fashion-conscious assistant, Jean, dryly put it, "It's so hard to find good help these days."

They were sitting around the office one afternoon watching television when Jean shook his delicate fist at the flat screen and shouted, "*Avoir le timbre fêlé!*" He turned to Marcel. "*Yoyoter de la touffe!*"

Marcel was too engaged with his pastry to respond with anything more than a lazy nod.

They were watching the induction ceremony of fashion designer Dominique Molymeux into the National Order of the Legion of Honor, rank of chevalier. Cultural protectionists that they are, this was the sort of thing that passed for good television en France. When the French minister of culture said, during his introduction, that Dominique's "daring use of rayon made her terribly feared but totally respected," Jean, who for years has been telling anyone who would listen that her work was thematically derivative and philosophically irrelevant, shook his fist and accused the man of having a cracked bell, which was roughly akin to being touched in the head. To underline his point, Jean had continued by saying the minister was yodeling from the rooftop.

Which is when the phone rang, sparing the minister of culture from further insulting idioms. Since the majority of their employment opportunities came from foreign countries, Jean was pleased to see the international area code for La Paz, Bolivia on the caller I.D. He answered as he always did, "Specialized staffing and professional service solutions," because, as it turns out, like air traffic control and maritime communications, English was the official international language of the trade. Jean listened for a moment, then, with a certain excitement in his voice, he said, "But of course!" He put his hand over the receiver and said, "It is for you."

Jean muted the television so Marcel could take the call while he could continue hurling psychic insults at the Minister of Culture. Marcel set his pastry down, wiped his mouth and, assuming that the French was close enough, said, "*Allô?*" For the next five minutes, he listened as the caller explained his situation. Now and then a word or phrase would catch Jean's ear, diverting his attention from the cultural travesty that was unfolding at the Opéra Garnier, phrases like: "How ironic." "It will be difficult." "Twenty million?" "No problem."

After a few more minutes, Marcel said, "Consider it done." Then he hung up, looked at Jean and said, in all seriousness, "We will need three."

"Three? We are lucky to find one these days. And you promised him three?"

Marcel pushed himself up from the sofa which seemed to gasp for air as his massive buttocks arose. "These days we will promise anything for a fee. *N'est-ce pas?*"

"Fine," Jean said, tossing off an existential gesture. "What are the details?"

As Marcel waddled over to his desk he said, "Two targets in the States. A job I would have thought perfectly suited to Chantalle." Here he dipped his head and looked at Jean. "If she had not already failed at it." He smiled slyly, waiting for his assistant to get the point.

It took a moment but then Jean's mouth dropped. "No."

"*Oui!*"

Marcel stuffed another pastry into his mouth then smacked his forehead with the palm of his hand. "Ha! I have one," he said, raining flaky crumbs onto this desk. "I ran into Leon last week. He told me he had been taken off his latest project and was available." Marcel peered into the pastry box. "*Trés bien!* We have our first."

Not to be outdone, Jean said, "What about the Pakistani? Fareed Ghulam Abbas? He has talent."

Marcel shook his head. "He also has a room at Abu Ghraib."

"Ah, how about Nicolas Olszewski?"

"That old Polack's in a wheelchair," Marcel said uncharitably. "He is finished, I'm afraid."

"All right then, perhaps Azacca Volcy, the Haitian?"

"He would be perfect," Marcell said. "If only he were alive."

"He's dead?"

"His wife killed him."

"No."

"Caught him with another woman out in their garden. Knocked him out with a shovel. Castrated him with hedge shears. Bled to death."

Jean considered that for a moment, then said, "Perhaps we should hire her."

Marcel gave him a sideways glance. "I'd say she is too volatile." He snapped his fingers. "Now, come. More names." He reached into the box to select another treat.

"How about Sergio Esparza?"

Marcel shook his head. "I'm afraid this case is beyond his skill level."

Jean knew that Marcel would reject the next name that came to mind. But after several minutes of silence he said it anyway, "What about…the Mongoose?"

Marcel was about to sink his teeth into a Savarin pastry cream when he stopped cold and deliberately set it down. "Please. You know he retired."

"It would be worth a try," Jean said. "What is the worst he could say?"

Marcel seemed astounded by what Jean was asking him to do. "You expect me to call the Mongoose and try to lure him back for one last big job? It hurts just to say the words. Do you have any idea how hackneyed that sounds?"

"Of course." Jean shrugged. "But twenty million dollars goes a long way toward soothing the pain of committing such a cliché."

Chapter Seventeen

Los Angeles, California

The Defense Advanced Research Projects Agency laboratory was located in a light industrial area of the San Fernando Valley, near the Van Nuys Airport. The lab complex consisted of four nondescript, cream-colored buildings, three floors each, with blacked out windows, all sitting on two acres behind a tall wrought-iron fence.

Dressed in his dark suit, white shirt, and red tie, Joshua Treadwell gave Bob and Klaus the nickel tour. He pushed through a door marked MAV and, speaking over his shoulder, said, "It's all about amplifying military flexibility. We can no longer afford weapons research with long-term time horizons." He shrugged and shook his head. "That's pre-9/11 thinking. What we need are near-term, specific deliverables."

Bob nodded, already on board with the program. "And that's what you call your 'quick reaction' projects?"

"Exactly," Joshua Treadwell said. "And your transgenic assassins fit the model."

Klaus was thinking it was far too early to reach such a conclusion but he kept that to himself. Bob and Joshua Treadwell were engaged in a like-minded love-fest that was far more faith-based than fact-based, so Klaus knew the introduction of logic into the discussion would only be met with disapproval and possibly with accusations of treason. He glanced back at the door and said, "What is MAV?"

"Glad you asked," Treadwell said as they approached two men wearing lab coats. "It's the research group I thought of when Bob mentioned your airborne assassin idea." He pointed at the pair of MAV researchers and jokingly said, "You might just put these guys out of a job." Treadwell introduced everyone before finally answering Klaus' question. "MAV stands for micro-air vehicle. The original idea was to create tiny flying robots to carry monitoring devices to the enemy's side of the battlefield. Something so small they couldn't be seen, let alone shot down. But now that we're fighting an enemy too scared to line up on the other side for a face-down, we're trying to engineer them into a weapon system." He pointed at one of the MAV researchers and said, "Show them what you've come up with."

The man led them over to a large magnifying glass held by a C-clamp. Brightly lit underneath was a tiny winged device tethered to a magnesium coil. It looked like the nymphal offspring of a shuttlecock and a fly fishing lure. He explained how they had solved the seemingly impossible issue of lift, which turned out to spring from a micro-scale vortex at the leading edge of the machine's narrow wing. "But," he said, "programming the exact wing stroke to maintain lift in variable conditions has proven to be difficult code to write."

"Power's another problem," Treadwell said as Klaus leaned in for a look. "Batteries are too heavy for the limited lift MAV's can generate so they're working on a reciprocating chemical muscle for power. And if you add any sort of weapon system…" He shook his head to finish the sentence. "Things were looking grim for the MAV project until a couple of weeks ago." Treadwell pointed out the window toward another building. "One of our research groups finally delivered a new technology we've been waiting on." He held up what looked like an impossibly thin sheet of white plastic. "Nanotube sheets," he said. "A fundamentally new material, stronger than steel, self-supporting, able to turn sunlight into electricity. Miraculous stuff."

"We think we can use it to create artificial muscles," the MAV researcher said. "If that works, and we can solve the wing stroke issue, we might have something."

"Still," Treadwell said, nodding at Bob and Klaus, "these guys are ahead of the curve since all they have to do is weaponize something that already flies and is capable of carrying a payload." He led Bob and Klaus back to the hallway. "We'll leave you two to your work," Treadwell said. "But you better hurry or my bug boys might just take all of your funding."

Klaus wanted to say something about the obvious problem of controlling and directing insects in a close, contained environment, let alone on the wing from miles away but since irrational exuberance was the currency of the moment, he said nothing.

As Treadwell led them across the quad in the center of the complex, he talked about the work of the other research groups. "We're close to breakthroughs in several areas, including swarm technology and intelligence and remote control of nanobots using GPS. And as I said, we hope to bring all these technologies together somehow to create something that is more robust than the sum of its parts."

They arrived at another building. "Here we go," Treadwell said. "Your new office." He pushed open the double doors to reveal three thousand square feet of gleaming instrumentation.

Klaus couldn't believe the scale of the thing. The room was equipped with top-of-the-line pulsed field gel electrophoresis systems, lipid transfection monitors, eukaryotic and microbial gene pulser units, thermal cyclers and everything else necessary for the creation of transgenic assassin bugs and God knows what else. For the first time since meeting Joshua Treadwell, Klaus contracted a small case of enthusiasm. He pointed in wonder at a bank of sleek machines across the lab. "Are those Bio-Plast 545 sequencers?"

Treadwell smiled his reply.

"But they are still on the drawing board," Klaus said in disbelief.

"We make things happen a little faster here." Treadwell clapped his hands once and said, "Oh, I got you a little present." He turned and pointed toward a large gift-wrapped box on one of the stainless steel work tables. "Go ahead, open it."

Bob walked over and plucked the bow from the top of the package before tearing off the shiny gold wrapping paper. He looked at the contents for a moment before he said, "No way." Klaus stepped closer to see for himself. It was a terrarium heaving with bizarre, angular insects. "African white-eyed assassins?" Bob looked at Treadwell. "You shouldn't have."

"Perhaps," Treadwell said. "But the way we see it, what the Department of Agriculture doesn't know can't hurt 'em." He gestured for Bob and Klaus to follow him to the back of the lab. "I also got you some spiders," he said. "I want to see if the venom idea is viable."

There were a half dozen more terrariums, each with a nameplate of the arachnids housed within. On the top: the Brazilian huntsman (*Phoneutria fera*); the Sydney funnelweb (*Atrax robustus*); and the black widow (*Latrodectus hesperus*). "Got these from a Professor Harmon down at U.C. Riverside, does work on how venoms disrupt synaptic transmission." The bottom row held the brown recluse (*Loxosceles reclusa*); the tropical spitting spider (*Scytodes longipes*); and the South African six-eyed sand spider (*Sicarius Hahnii*).

"I tried to get Professor Harmon to join the project, but he declined based on the commute. Said he'd be glad to consult, though. So if you have any questions, he's the guy to call."

Treadwell leaned close to one of the terrariums, inviting Bob to join him as he admired the beautiful and deadly creatures. "Look at the articulation of the legs. The complexity and dexterity and perfection when they move. It's humbling," he said, turning to look at Bob. "Don't you think?" He leaned even closer, his nose almost touching the glass. "I can't see how this could be the result of some undirected process, you know? The elegance of the design is just awesome."

"They're pretty remarkable," Bob said.

Treadwell stood and smoothed the front of his suit coat. "We're blessed to have them at our disposal," he said, giving Bob a slap on the back. "Well, you guys poke around, find out where we've put everything and start settling in." He pulled two magnetic security key cards from his pocket and handed one to Bob, the other to Klaus. "The keys to your new kingdom," he said as he sneaked a glance at his watch. "Late for a meeting. Welcome aboard." He gave a salute with his index finger off the corner of his forehead, turned and left.

After the doors closed behind Treadwell, Bob looked as if he might start giggling. He had the expression of a kid who just got locked inside an adult book store. He held his arms out wide and said, "Can you believe all this?"

Klaus looked around suspiciously. "It is impressive," he said.

Failing to notice the skepticism in Klaus' voice, Bob said, "A dozen Bio-Plast 545 sequencers? Hell, we could make dinosaurs with this stuff." He aimed his thumb at the door and said, "Notice how he keeps bringing up the airborne assassins? I told you he liked it." He caressed a $65,000 high-throughput fluidics system and said, "This is unbelievable."

"Yes." Klaus looked around the sterile room and said, "Nothing about this bothers you?"

"What do you mean?"

"What was he talking about, the elegance of design and undirected processes?"

Bob shrugged it off. "Yeah, I don't know what that was all about, but take a look around." He made a sweeping gesture reminiscent of a game show host. "What a great opportunity. I mean, think of the possibilities!"

"I think the greatest possibility is that someone will find out we are still alive and try to remedy the situation."

Bob shook his head. "Jesus, Klaus. You know what your problem is? You thrive on negativity. If you don't have any troubles, you go looking for some. That's one of the reasons I like Treadwell. He's always so positive." He went to Klaus and put his arm around his shoulder. "I wish you could see this for what it is and—"

Just then a man came through the doors carrying a box. "Hey, this got delivered to the wrong building. I think it's yours." He opened the box pulled out what looked like a high-tech handgun, which he pointed at Bob.

Klaus dove behind a counter, yelling, "Get down!"

Bob cracked an embarrassed smile. He leaned over and said, "Uhhh, Klaus, that's an adjustable helium pulse gene gun."

Chapter Eighteen

The Puget Sound

Richard Mills never set out to find a nickname, or earn one, or have one bestowed upon him. He was simply a professional doing his job. But after he killed the leader of an outlaw motorcycle gang—a large and violent piece of white trash that went by the moniker King Cobra—certain people began to call Richard Mills the Mongoose. He didn't refer to himself that way but others did. He didn't care. He just wanted to do his work, get paid, and go home.

After fifty-six assassinations, Richard Mills bought a small island in the San Juan archipelago and retired. It was twelve acres of fir trees, towering rock cliffs, and a 360-degree view half a mile off the coast of Washington. The Olympic Mountains to the south, Mt. Baker and Rosario Straits to the east, Lopez Sound and Orcas Island to the north. He enjoyed the serenity and beauty of the place, but he bought it for the security. It was not the sort of place you could sneak up on, which was exactly the point.

Richard Mills thought he was done with killing, but Marcel had given him twenty million reasons for making a comeback. So now he was on a ferry, heading south to Seattle.

As the boat chugged across Elliot Bay, Richard Mills noticed the cruise ship docked at the Bell Street Cruise Terminal, Pier

66. Good. That meant the Pike Place Market, where he was headed, would be packed. He liked crowds, he could disappear in them. They made him feel safer.

The ferry docked at Pier 50. Richard Mills picked up the duffle bag he'd brought, secured with a small padlock, and stepped onto the mainland. He walked north to Pier 54 and the Seattle Aquarium. He crossed the road and the street car tracks, heading for the base of the Pike Hill Climb. He paused at the bottom of the stairs and looked up. This, he assured himself, would be the last time he climbed these stairs. Michael Jordan might come out of retirement twice, but not the Mongoose. Once would be enough.

As he climbed, he found himself counting the stairs. He was in good shape for a man of fifty-eight but he was winded after he'd counted eighty-two steps. He paused to catch his breath, then continued toward the top. 153...154...155. His heart was pounding when he reached the top. He liked how it felt as the blood pressed against the walls of his veins and arteries. The stairs delivered him to the heart of the famous Pike Place Market, a thriving, bustling farmer's market and vast warren of shops selling everything from magic tricks and jade products, to brilliantly colored produce, flowers, spices, and seafood.

Breathing heavily, taking in the smells, he passed between All Things Lavender and Baja Bath Salts, with its polished silver bowls filled with a rainbow of colored salts on display. The place was cheek-to-jowl with tourists. There was a noisy crowd around the Pike Place Fish Company where the fish mongers played to the throngs by tossing twenty-pound king salmon from the market floor over beds of cracked ice and stacks of crabs and into the waiting hands of a partner who caught the slippery silver fish with the greatest of ease. The crowd loved it, cheering louder with each throw.

Richard Mills slipped unnoticed through the crowd with his locked duffle bag and walked out under the big red Pike Place Market sign, heading for Second Avenue. He passed an ad hoc kiosk with an overhead sign that read, "Are you a good person?"

The guy manning the booth held out some literature and said, "Take the test?"

Without stopping, the Mongoose shook his head and said, "I already know the answer."

He turned right on Second Avenue. Half a block down, between Ghengis Khan Chinese Restaurant and Check Masters Check Cashing was a pawn shop called Palace Loans. Displayed in the window was a pile of hocked jewelry, a set of bongos, and a vast array of folding knives. Richard Mills pushed through the door, triggering an electronic beep. He stopped and looked around. Straight ahead, a desperate musician was negotiating to sell his guitar. A fat, black dog was asleep in the corner. In the back of the shop a sign hung from the ceiling. "Loan Desk." Under the sign and behind the counter was a large, bearded man, looked half Arab, half Samoan. Impassive of stare, swarthy of complexion.

As he approached, Richard Mills and the man exchanged a mumbled greeting and a nod, like this wasn't the first time. Mills placed the duffle bag gently on the counter along with two hundred dollars, the price of no-questions-asked on this stretch of Second Avenue. The man slid a ticket across the counter in return. Richard Mills slipped it into his pocket and said, "It won't be long." The man didn't seem to care. He just nodded and put the duffle bag under the counter.

Richard Mills walked out of Palace Loans and checked his watch. His train didn't leave for several hours. He decided to return to Pike Place Market for lunch, perhaps some fresh salmon.

He took his time, wandering around the market, looking at the menus posted outside the restaurants, just waiting for something to strike him. What was he in the mood for?

Just behind him, the crowd in front of the Pike Place Fish Company let out a roar as one huge salmon after another flew through space, only to be snagged out of mid-air by a guy using butcher paper like a catcher's mitt.

Richard Mills stopped at the top of a flight of concrete stairs to let an elderly couple come up. While he waited, he looked down and saw the brown, six-sided tiles that covered the market floor. One of those fund raiser things where people buy tiles with their names on them. "Crissy." "Don Dicky." "Zac and Lizzy Albert." He noticed a small crack in one of the tiles.

What he failed to notice was that, about twenty feet away, by the Pike Place Fish Company, the larger of two severely tattooed and pierced teenagers lurched out of the crowd in an alcohol-and-weed induced fashion. He plunged his hands into the icy fish display, grabbing the largest salmon he saw. Twenty-six pounds worth of king.

Some in the crowd wondered if this was part of the show.

With ice under his dirty fingernails and a row of ants tattooed crawling across his face, the kid turned to his equally inked and inebriated buddy and said, "Like, go long!"

The second kid, skinnier than the first, started moving backwards, shouting, "Hit me! Hit me!" as his friend reared back—underhanded with both hands—to toss the big fish.

"Hey!" The guy from the Fish Company couldn't get there in time to stop the throw.

The ant-faced kid heaved the huge, oily salmon. The crowds' eyes followed the arc of the slick fish wiggling slightly as it soared overhead, as though swimming upstream for one final spawn.

The skinny kid never had a chance to catch the thing. The heavy salmon shot through his fingers like twenty-six pounds of greasy eel, hitting Richard Mills squarely in the head just as he was taking his first step down the stairs.

The mass and velocity of the flying salmon knocked him wildly off balance. He knew in that instant that he was going down. Time slowed to a crawl. He reached for the handrail but missed in a long, looping grab. Then, for just a moment as he began to tumble down the stairs, Richard Mills found himself looking up at the ceiling and the green and white neon restroom sign pointing down the concrete stairs. Pointing down to Hell. Pointing at him.

Then things went black.

Chapter Nineteen

Father Paul Anik was a dedicated, unpretentious man in his early sixties. Every Friday afternoon he sat in the same hard plastic chair in the hospital's waiting room, elbows on his knees, reading the paper. There was a cushioned sofa nearby but, in a typical act of self-abnegation, Father Paul chose the discomfort that only injection molding can provide. Shifting in the hard seat, his arthritis reminded him that rheumatology was just three floors up, tempting him with pain-relieving hip replacement. But, preferring the self-discipline that came with suffering and the possibility that it offered insight into the nature of God, he quietly endured.

Father Paul was a volunteer. After completing his weekly duties at St. Martin's, he came to visit the sick and the elderly, to offer the sacraments and whatever comfort he could. With silky white hair and blue eyes serene as tiny mountain lakes, his soft, jowly face conveyed a welcome serenity.

On finishing the headline story, Father Paul took a thoughtful breath and calmly folded the newspaper in half. He let the breath out slowly, trying to maintain his composure. Then, in a fit, he ripped the paper in half — and half again—and threw the damn thing to the floor. In the calm that followed, he looked at the newsprint on his hands and wondered what Jesus would do.

It seemed as if there was a new story every day. Actually, it was the same story over and over played out in a different city, a different diocese, a different country. And with every story Father Paul grew angrier. He'd been sold out again and again, as if by Judas, but for more than forty pieces of silver. Fifty million dollars paid out in New Mexico, three times that in Dallas, unknown sums in Boston, Philadelphia, Los Angeles, and virtually every other diocese in the country, and many other countries in the world. And that money wasn't coming from Vatican City. Instead, they were fleecing the flock.

It wasn't just that the abuse happened that angered Father Paul so—those in power couldn't prevent that, at least not the first time. It was the cover-up. And there was always a cover-up. But it was even more than that. It was the tenacity with which the crimes were denied and hidden and perpetuated. How the blame was shifted. And it was the galling church policy of intimidating anyone who came forward with the truth about what they had been subjected to as children.

Pedophiles were moved around like chess pieces in a terrible game played at the expense of children. And of those responsible, some were actually promoted to the Vatican, moved out of harm's way and into sinful luxury. Father Paul thought of St. Peter when he said, "Lord, which is he that betrayeth thee?"

Sordid and corrupt, it was the sort of thing one had come to expect from businessmen and politicians, shameless cons who declared all indictments politically motivated and who struck deals admitting no guilt, just to get the thing behind them so they could all move forward and let the healing begin. But this wasn't business or politics—or perhaps it was both.

It was bad enough when it happened elsewhere, Father Paul thought, but now this. His own dioceses. Caught with its pants down, so to speak, as they tried to sweep another one under the rug. And he knew who would be made to pay. And it wasn't the guys in the miters. The parishes would have to pony up, literally paying for the sins of the fathers. It left Father Paul torn between outrage at the perfidy and worry about his ability to do his job. As it was, he didn't have the resources necessary to do the Lord's work.

And now?

Perhaps this was a test of his faith. He would pray and hope the Lord would speak to him.

"Father Paul?"

That was quick, he thought. He looked up and saw a nurse standing there, her eyes alternating between the shredded newspaper and the priest. He gave a rueful smile as he picked up the shreds. The nurse said, "Father? Someone wants to see you."

Chapter Twenty

Katy was in the kitchen on her laptop when Mary walked in with some groceries. "Hi, hon."

Katy glanced up long enough to register her disdain for all things civil, like saying hello. So far she'd managed to nurse her grudge for a week, never saying anything more than absolutely necessary to coexist with her mother, including the occasional grunt and her favorite utterance of vexation, Guh!

Mary knew Katy was still pissed about having to stay in Corvallis and figured the best way to deal with the pouting was to let it exhaust itself. It was annoying, but privately she was impressed with Katy's ability to maintain this degree of sullenness. It showed an admirable degree of commitment to a position, even if the position was less than noble.

Crossing to the pantry with several cans of tomatoes, Mary passed behind Katy. She paused and glanced over her shoulder and said, "Whatcha working on?" Before Katy could flip the screen down in a rush of outrage, Mary saw what looked like a string of typos: BHOF, DETI, and X-I-10. The only combination of characters that formed an actual word was PIMP.

"Guh! Excuse me. Uhhh, private." The word came out in three syllables as puh-ri-vate.

"Pardon me," Mary said as she put the cans on the shelf. "But I'm curious about your use of the word 'pimp.'"

Katy couldn't believe the nerve of this woman. "Do I read your e-mails?"

"I don't know, do you?"

Katy tilted her head at the proper angle to indicate how stupid the question was. "Uhh, nooo."

Mary gestured casually at the computer with a package of dried spaghetti. "I couldn't help but see the word."

"You could if you didn't snoop," Katy said. "Besides, it's not a word."

"Sure it is. A pimp is a guy who—"

"I know what it means." She rolled her eyes. "Guh."

Mary started putting a dozen eggs into the refrigerator's egg tray. "The reason I ask is I was thinking back to your research about how children in single-parent homes are more likely to become drug-addicted prostitutes."

"Right, mom. I'm ordering from pimp-dot-com right now."

"Eww, try to get one who doesn't beat you too much. Even if it costs extra, it's worth it."

"You are so not funny. PIMP is IM shorthand. It means pee in my pants."

"Oh, acronyms."

"Duh. Like MYOB means mind your own business. Or POS for parent over shoulder."

After the last egg was in, Mary said, "Honey, technically those aren't acronyms. I think the letters have to spell something you can pronounce like a word. Like scuba or radar."

"I didn't say they were acronyms. You did."

"No, when I said 'oh, acronyms,' you said 'duh,' indicating that I was obviously right." Mary was doing this to annoy and, based on the stare Katy had fixed on her, she was succeeding. Mary smiled and said, "Well, just remember, it's hard out there for a pimp."

Katy just stared at her.

"I'd love to stay and chat," Mary said. "But laundry calls."

"Guh. What. Ever." Katy kept staring until her mom was gone. She resumed typing. "Sorry, POS. WW I?" As in, where was I?

A moment later, her friend responded, "YR BIG SHHHH!"
Katy typed, "OK. R SECRET?
"Y!"
"GOING AWOL 2 LA."
"N!"
"Y!"
"COOL!"

Chapter Twenty-one

The name had been changed, but not to protect the innocent. The innocent had nothing to do with it. In fact the entire exercise was pointless without the guilty. Some called it penance, others confession. The Church had taken to calling it reconciliation, which to Father Paul's ear made the holy sacrament sound about as spiritual as balancing a checkbook.

In his thirty-five years as a priest, Father Paul Anik had heard thousands of confessions. Some were entertaining, many were depressing, others infuriating. He hated first confessions most—innocent children made to feel guilty over nothing at the age of six, herded into the box where they tried to convince themselves and the priest that they deserved to burn in Hell if they didn't properly beg forgiveness.

Some of the people who came were just scared and lonely, parishioners who didn't have anyone else to listen to their problems. They simply wanted someone to assure them of God's love in a heartless world.

Then there were the argumentative sons-of-bitches who wanted to split hairs and plea-bargain. "That's not coveting! Look, I know a priest over at St. Anthony's who only charges two Hail Mary's for that kind of shit."

Every week Father Paul heard people confess things that made him doubt Genesis, things that made him think Darwin must have been right because only something evolved from apes could be this depraved and then have the nerve to ask for and expect forgiveness. If this was intelligent design, he wondered, where was the intelligence?

He had listened as championship sinners casually reeled off grocery lists of abominable behavior with no contrition in their voices, hoping to get the whole thing over with in five minutes as if it was some sort of spiritual oil change. Others came to ask questions, to probe in secret the limits of sin and morality to find out what they could get away with in the eyes of God. And many of them went on to win re-election.

But of all the penitential circumstances, Father Paul most looked forward to the death-bed confession. People who knew the end was nigh tended to take it seriously, tended to get down to brass tacks. They were sincere in their contrition and in their belief of what God could do for them. Faith tended to firm up when you were staring into the eye sockets of death.

Father Paul was standing in the corridor, his ink-smudged hands clasped softly behind his back, listening as the doctor talked about the sinner at hand.

"He has a high cervical injury, spinal cord partially lacerated around C3," the doctor said before glancing at her watch. "By now he's got secondary damage from the arachidonic acid cascade and inflammation." She continued by saying something about the release of excitatory amino acids and lipid peroxidation of cell membranes by various forms of oxygen free radicals. She referred to her chart. "Oh, plus he chipped a couple of teeth."

Father Paul looked up with sorrowful eyes. "Nothing you can do?"

"Nothing anybody can do," the doctor said as if her credentials had been questioned. "Not in this life."

"Does he know?"

"Yes."

"Can he talk?"

"He's fine from the chin up."

"How much time does he have?"

A professional shrug. "Tonight, tomorrow, early next week. Impossible to say, but no question he's *in articulo mortis*." The doctor didn't see too many people who understood Latin. She figured an older priest would appreciate it.

Father Paul gave a solemn nod. "He asked for last rites?"

The doctor shook her head. "He was unconscious when they brought him in. Fell down some stairs at Pike Place Market, landed square on his occiput," she said, tapping the back of her head. "Came to about an hour ago, said he'd seen some sort of sign about going to Hell and wanted to make a confession. We assumed he wasn't talking about the cops." She held her hand out, palm up, ushering Father Paul into the ICU.

There were six beds separated by curtains. Richard Mills was the only patient in the room. Stainless steel screws anchored an alloy halo to his skull and large bore needles were embedded in his veins delivering fluids. His face was bruised and swollen. He looked as if he were being subjected to the tortures of a modern-day Inquisition.

Father Paul kissed his violet stole and draped it around his neck, then pulled a chair to the bedside. The ventilator huffed and hissed as the priest laid his hand gently on Richard Mills' shoulder and leaned close to his ear. He caught a faint whiff of fish as he said, "I am here, my son." His voice was soothing and offered reassurance, though his breath left something to be desired.

Richard Mills had a trach with a speaking valve so he could talk during what were sure to be his last hours. His voice was scratchy and hoarse as he uttered a thought that had never entered his mind until he saw that restroom sign as he began to tumble down those stairs. He said, "Forgive me father, for I have sinned."

Father Paul said he understood and he encouraged the man to clear his conscience.

Richard Mills had murdered dozens without a moment of remorse but now he could see the face of every person he'd killed. A grim parade, marching through his mind, haunting him, crushing him with guilt, demanding that he seek forgiveness. "In my life," he said, "I killed forty-eight men."

Father Paul had started to nod, the way he always did during a confession, a sign that no matter what sin was confessed, it wasn't unforgivable. But when "I killed forty-eight men" finally registered, his head jerked back and he said, "What?"

Richard Mills felt a great relief as he repeated his statement. A tear rolled out the corner of one eye.

Father Paul wondered if the man was delusional. The doctor hadn't said anything in that regard so Father Paul looked for another explanation. Perhaps he'd been a soldier. The man looked old enough to have been in Vietnam where Father Paul, then private Paul Anik, had found his calling. Perhaps this man had served his country and seen and done the terrible things required of him in such a circumstance. Father Paul tried to recall church doctrine on when "thou shalt not kill" didn't apply. After a moment it came to him. Augustine's "Just War" theory. Wanting to give the man the benefit of the doubt, Father Paul said, "You were in the military?"

"No," the man said, wishing he could still shake his head. "An assassin. I killed for money."

"Oh." So much for the benefit of the doubt. Father Paul knew the church had some extremely sophisticated theology that allowed a wide range of egregious misbehavior under certain circumstances, but he didn't think the church's situational ethics stretched quite this far. He'd have to conjure some forgiveness.

Once Richard Mills began to confess, he couldn't stop talking. He explained that he'd retired five years ago. Money in the bank, set for life. Then he got lured back for one last job.

Father Paul couldn't believe it. Lured back for one last job? Like an inciting incident in bad movie. In fact it brought to mind several films he'd seen recently featuring that tired plot point. Still, he felt compelled to ask, "Have you done this last job?"

"On my way," he said. "Two men, and not good men either. Killers like myself."

In his halting, scratchy voice Richard Mills told Father Paul the whole story, how the Frenchman had contacted him and told him about the twenty-million-dollar bounty to kill Bob and

Klaus. "You must warn them," he said, wanting to grab Father Paul's arm to make his point, but unable to do so. "Tell them, others are coming." His eyes turned to look at his bedside table. There was a plastic bowl with a watch, a slip of paper, a small key, and other personal belongings. "That ticket? Take it to Palace Loans on 2nd Ave. They will give you a duffle bag in return. Everything you need is in there. Keep the money or give it to the church, I don't care. The other things you must throw in the ocean. It's up to you now. Warn them. Others will be coming."

Richard Mills closed his eyes. The steady beep-beep-beep of the heart monitor became a steady tone. A flat line. Father Paul bowed his head and began to pray when a team of doctors and nurses rushed in, displacing him to the hallway.

Removed from the commotion, he stood there thinking about what the man had said. Not about the people he had killed or his guilt or his need for redemption or that he should warn the men that others were coming.

But about the twenty million dollars.

He bowed his head and began to pray, "Lead us not into temptation."

Chapter Twenty-two

Bob and Klaus had been putting in ten-hour days, but their work was going on around the clock. Three eight-hour shifts of highly qualified microbiologists loading the DNA fragments of insects and arachnids onto microscopic-gel-beads treated with illuminating reagents so the DNA sequence could be visualized by hyper-spectral imaging systems, chemiluminescence detectors, and computer controlled digital microscopes that recorded the color changes onto a light-sensitive chip. Fourteen million beads at a time packed into an area the size of a dime, checked by fluorescent chemical probes. Bob loved the irony that the beads signaled these sequences by activating luciferase, the light-producing enzyme found in fireflies (*Photuris pennsylvanicus*).

"It's unbelievable," Bob said. "The progress, the pace…it's, it's like playing God." He cradled the phone in the crook of his neck as he continued to work. "But I guess that's to be expected when you put a dozen Bio-Plast 545 sequencers into the hands of people who know how to use them."

"You know, that technical talk used to get me sooo hot," Mary said, "but right now I'd rather be in the hands of someone who knows how to use them." She paused before lapsing into Lauren Bacall saying, "You do know how to use them, don't you?"

Absorbed in his work, Bob wasn't listening as closely as he should have been. He said, "Use what?" Then he stopped what he was doing and said, "Whose hands are you talking about?"

"Yours, you knucklehead. I miss you." Mary could see him now, his nutty professor hair trying to keep up as he darted from one corner of the lab to another, bursting with energy and passion, although not the sort of passion Mary had in mind.

"Oh, I miss you too, sweetie. Sorry, I'm trying to fractionate some proteins."

"Yeah? Well, why don't you come up sometime, and fraction-ate me?" This time as Mae West.

Bob smiled as he indulged an impure thought or two. "I promise I'll be all hands next weekend when I see you. Well not all hands, of course, but…" Bob heard a clearing of the throat. He turned and noticed a disapproving glance spilling over the top of Klaus' bifocals. "Well, 'nuff said."

"Hubba hubba," Mary said. "So tell me, what's it like play-ing God?"

"It's pretty cool," Bob said. "Klaus and his team are sequencing the DNA for the spiders and it looks like we'll be able to transfer the venom to the transgenic assassins. And I think it's safe to say you would not want to be overrun by a hundred spined ambush assassins loaded with sydney funnelweb spider venom."

"What about gender distribution?"

"Are you kidding? Other than the breeders, this is boys only. Can't take a chance on uncontrolled reproduction," Bob said. "We've also started to sequence the giant robber fly for the airborne assassins. So the next big step is figuring out how to control and direct them. We're meeting with some of the other research groups about that tomorrow. Treadwell's pleased with the progress so, like I said, it's all good. How's Katy?"

"Pissed off."

"What now?"

"I wouldn't loan her the five hundred bucks she wanted."

"Five…for what?"

"Ticket to LA. She wanted to run away but she didn't have the cash. Said she wasn't about to take the bus, which was the only thing she could afford."

"She was just going to show up and call for a ride from the airport?"

"Not our little princess," Mary said. "A hundred bucks was for a car service."

Bob laughed. "That's not running away. That's an all-expense-paid vacation."

"Yeah, she didn't want to hear that either. When I told her if she wanted to go she'd either have to take the bus or hitchhike, she looked at me like I'd blown a jellyfish out of my nose."

"How is she other than that?"

"Hard to tell from those grunting noises she makes," Mary said. "But I don't think she misses you as much as she hates both of us and our guts now and for the rest of time. Klaus too."

"Still?"

"You know how stubborn she is."

"Yeah, I wonder where she gets that."

"Listen here, Science Boy, why don't you just run a wad of your DNA through one of those fancy sequencers of yours. I bet it spits out a stubbornness gene the size of golf ball."

"I'm persistent," Bob said. "She's stubborn."

"Oh," Mary replied. "You didn't tell me you were using electron microscopes."

"To fractionate proteins?"

"To split those tiny hairs."

Bob had another impure thought. He lowered his voice and said, "I'll split your tiny hairs."

"Bob! You dirty little entomologist."

"You started it. Say something else."

Mary giggled for a moment before asking a question. Bob turned to Klaus and said, "Mary wants to know if you're still paranoid about our identities."

Klaus looked up from what he was doing and removed his bifocals. "Let me speak with her." He walked over and took the phone. "Mary," he said. "There is an old saying. Just because a man is paranoid does not mean that people are not after him."

Chapter Twenty-three

Though unaware of it, Nick Parker grew up in search of a father figure more masculine than the one life had dealt him. His own father was a college professor who believed intellectual strength trumped the physical, that chess was a superior form of competition than any contact sport. And had Nick Parker been reared on the upper east side of Manhattan, that might not have been the worse thing to happen to him. But, as it was, he grew up in central Ohio, where real men liked football and hunting.

His father was the type who was inclined to say things like, "That we live in a region where the notion of 'real men' not only has traction but goes unquestioned, tells you all you need to know about the level of sophistication of the local populace."

Nick Parker never considered any of this a betrayal on his father's part. Such things weren't the result of conscious processes. He simply rejected most of his father's values and found himself seeking a different type of mentor, gravitating toward football coaches and the fathers of friends who would take him into the woods to kill and gut deer.

The one thing Nick Parker did take from his father was a love of books. A voracious reader, he consumed everything from military history to biography to fiction. This gave his father hope. Every time he saw Nick's nose buried in a book, he dreamed his son would pursue a career in academia or perhaps the law. But after reading G. Gordon Liddy's autobiography as a gullible high school student, Nick Parker decided to pursue a career, not in the law, but in law enforcement.

At Ohio State, Nick's blind and youthful exuberance developed into a more nuanced respect for the one-time Watergate bungler. After graduating with a degree in criminology, Nick Parker joined the CIA, where he hoped to bring to his job the same steely willpower that G. Gordon Liddy had brought to his.

But a decade in the trenches removed his blinders. And the five years after that hardened any soft edges that remained. Political reality and access to information forced him to re-evaluate his tenets. With every intelligence failure, the CIA faced another purge and another feckless stab at reform. Agent Parker watched good people get drummed out of service, only to be replaced by political appointees and other hacks. In the course of his career, the intelligence community in general, and the Agency in particular, had become dysfunctional jokes, more adept at undermining one another for political advantage than keeping the nation safe. Vital information went unshared. Directors came and went. Books were written and published. Secrets were revealed for personal gain. And no one was held accountable for any of it.

To Agent Nick Parker, the message was loud and clear. It was every man for himself.

And, while he wasn't proud that it had come to this, he also wasn't so naive as to pretend things were otherwise.

So, after visiting Miguel Riviera, Agent Parker returned to Washington and immediately contacted another agent, one of the real estate variety. He wanted to see what five or ten million would buy in the D.C. market. It turned out that kind of money still counted for something, even in Georgetown. After a couple of open houses, Agent Parker knew he had to go through with it, but not without a good plan. This wasn't tiddlywinks. If he failed, he'd end up in a windowless condo six feet under.

Chapter Twenty-four

The Department of Defense maintains dozens of fully furnished apartments in complexes throughout Los Angeles. Bob and Klaus each had a two-bedroom unit at the Avondale Oaks in Woodland Hills, a corner of the San Fernando Valley that had been transformed from walnut and orange groves into post-war housing and malls. Avondale Oaks was a sprawling, gated apartment community dotted with tennis courts and swimming pools all nestled among towering eucalyptus trees.

Bob and Klaus were scheduled to give Treadwell an update in the morning, so they took a couple of beers down to the pool to draw up an outline for the presentation. Bob scooted to the edge of his chair. He peeled off his socks and stuffed them into his shoes. He dropped his feet into the water, opened his beer, and said, "All right, Transgenics one and two are weaponized. Three is still unstable. And we're making progress on the airborne assassins. So, it seems our main focus for the presentation is on how to control their movements and behavior. And part of that is making sure they hunt humans instead of insects."

Just out of sight behind some tall shrubs, there was a clang as a metal gate closed behind someone entering the complex. Klaus sat up suddenly, his hand darting under the towel folded on the table beside him. A moment later a neighbor walked by with groceries.

Bob smirked and gestured with his beer can. "See? You did it again."

Klaus made a show of rolling his shoulders, wincing as if in pain. "No, I was uncomfortable," he said. "My back hurts." He leaned back in his seat gingerly.

"Bullshit," Bob said. "Every time you hear that gate shut, you jump like a squirrel."

"You are exaggerating."

"You reach for a gun every time your back hurts?"

Klaus fixed Bob with stern eyes. "Someone needs to be prepared to defend us."

"Against groceries?" Bob pulled his feet from the water and pressed them onto the warm flagstone, wiggling his toes. "As far as we can tell, nobody knows we're alive. And even if they did—and assuming your forger is a trustworthy fellow—they don't know to look for Mr. Javier Martinez and Mr. Juan Flores." Bob felt a tickle on the bridge of his foot. He reached down and brushed away an Argentine ant (*Iridomyrmex humilis*), the most common ant in California. "So," Bob said, "take your hand off the gun, put it on your beer, and relax so we can get this presentation together."

Klaus was reaching for his beer when the automatic pool light clicked on. He knocked the can over as he went for the gun, spilling beer and drowning a couple of ants. He mumbled "shit," then set the can back on the table and took a deep breath.

"Your back?"

Klaus ignored him. He looked around, the pool light illuminated everything a cool diamond blue. He turned to Bob and said, "Perhaps I am a little tense." He took a pull on his beer and leaned back, looking up at the light shimmering on the eucalyptus leaves. "But at least one of us should be."

"You know," Bob said, wagging his finger at his friend. "I still think you ought to introduce yourself to that fashionista up in four-oh-two. I saw her at the mailbox the other day. She wasn't wearing a ring or a bra and I gotta tell you…"

Klaus smiled. "Perhaps you are right."

"Of course I'm right," Bob said. "You need to get laid."

Despite his years in the States, Klaus still maintained his old world sensibilities as much as his Austrian accent. Bob's coarseness caused a stammer, "Yes, well, I, uh…"

Bob gripped the arms of his chair and began to thrust his hips lewdly, the chair scooting forward with each comical lunge. "You gotta get you some, Klaus. Lay a little pipe, you know? Get your ham bone boiled."

"I get your drift."

"Spear the bearded clam," he said.

"Bob?"

"Strike the pink match."

"Bob, I believe you may be projecting your own needs."

"Well, thank you, Dr. Freud." Bob paused, smiled sheepishly, and said, "What do you expect? I haven't seen Mary in nearly a month!" He reached down to brush away another of the tiny ants, this one tickling his ankle.

"I understand," Klaus said. "And I sympathize."

"Thank you."

"By the way, her name is Audrey."

Bob looked at Klaus, confused for the moment. Then he pointed and said, "Up in four-oh-two?"

Klaus raised his eyebrows in victory.

"You dog!"

"She is a costume designer. Speaks three languages. Delightful company."

"I don't believe it," Bob said. "So Thursday night isn't health club night?"

"Well, it is exercise," Klaus said. "Now, our report."

"No, I want details."

"Of course not." Klaus sipped his beer.

"Please?"

"It would be improper," Klaus said, shaking his head.

Bob was about to say something else when he felt another tickle on his foot. He looked down at the line of ants going about their business. "Okay, fine" he said. "Back to the bugs."

Picking up a legal pad of handwritten notes, Klaus flipped a page and said, "We agree that pheromones are the key to controlling their movements and behavior," Klaus said. "So we must figure out how to control the pheromones."

Bob nodded. "And part of that is finding how to make the assassins hunt humans instead of insects."

"I was thinking perhaps a genome from the *Sanguisugas* could help with that. But the trick will be getting them to distinguish good guys from bad guys, and that is an extremely subtle control issue."

Bob nodded as he reached down to let a couple of ants climb onto his hand, staring at them as he rooted around his brain for some relevant tidbit. He knew it was in there, somewhere, but where? And what was it?

Klaus talked about the problem of collecting significant amounts of pheromones and the process for determining which compounds did what. "We are making progress on the mandibular gland secretions of the spined ambush assassins," he said. "But perhaps we should focus on the binding proteins that bring pheromones to receptors in the first place." Klaus looked up and saw Bob mesmerized by the ants. "Are you listening?"

"Yeah," Bob said as he watched the ants scuttling over his hand. "Yeah, you're right about all that. But I just had an idea about how to get the bugs to hunt humans."

"Okay. What is it?"

He held his hand out toward Klaus and said, "Siafu."

Chapter Twenty-five

The man behind the desk at Palace Loans didn't ask any questions. Wasn't his business. He just took the ticket and gave Father Paul the duffle bag.

A bus returned him to the rectory, where he set the duffle bag on the floor in a corner of his small office and tried to ignore it. The bag was heavy and its weight made him both curious and frightened. But the fear outweighed the curiosity so he couldn't bring himself to open the thing. He just stared at it, day in, day out, wondering what to do.

Some days he sat there for hours, fingering the little key, the man's words echoing in his mind. "You must warn them. Others are coming."

He wondered, am I morally obliged to open the bag? Does the notion of *ought* obtain in this situation? Had he wandered into categorical imperative territory? Who came up with that, Kant? Was he Catholic? What was his point? That when conscience dictates action, one is morally obliged to act accordingly? Something along those lines. But what if the conscience dictates evil? Was that dealt with in a footnote? If there were something in the bag that could save lives, ought he use whatever it was to save those lives? Was that church doctrine or just philosophy?

On the one hand, Father Paul wanted to know what was in there. On the other hand, as long as he didn't know, he wasn't on the hook for anything. Or was that willful ignorance? Conscious disregard? Was that a sin or just a legal concept? Or both?

On the third hand, if he opened it, well, Pandora's Box came to mind.

Father Paul was pretty sure there was a sort of necessity imposed on his will to do what was good and avoid what was evil and that his will was, by its own nature, inclined toward the good in general and thus he couldn't wish for what was evil unless it presented itself to him under the appearance of good. Beyond that, things got blurry.

Father Paul had always been more of a pastoral priest than a philosophical one, more concerned with feeding, clothing, and teaching than in splitting theological hairs. But this heavy bag and the man's dying words were forcing him to think back on doctrinal lessons long forgotten.

He looked again at the bag. Was this a test?

The dying man's words continued to echo. "Twenty million dollars." No, Father Paul thought, those are the wrong words. He had to be concerned with the other words. Was he obliged to warn anyone about anything? Could he do so without violating the seal of the confessional? How could he know if there was any truth to the confession? For that matter, how could he know if there was truth in any confession? He'd never spent time thinking about that. He just offered forgiveness, issued penance, and said "next."

Lacking, as he did, sufficient confidence in his philosophical grounding, Father Paul turned to his dusty bookshelf. Where would he start? He turned at random to Cardinal Newman's letter to the Duke of Norfolk hoping it might shed some light. He skimmed the words. Divine law, the rule of ethical truth, sovereign, irreversible, absolute. The Fourth Lateran Council, "*Quidquid fit contra conscientiam, aedificat ad gehennam.*" The rule and measure of duty is not utility, nor state convenience, nor fitness, order, or beauty. Yes, Father Paul thought, that's all good and well but do I have an obligation to—

Father Paul almost jumped out of his skin when the phone rang.

He'd been expecting the call. It was inevitable, but he was so immersed in his quandary that the sudden ringing gave him a start. It was the bishop. He said they needed to increase the diocesan assessment to cover expenses incurred by recent lawsuits. Cost of doing business, you know. Effective immediately. "Get the kids on the car washes and the parents on the spaghetti suppers," the bishop said. "Oh, do some raffles too," the bishop said with what might have been construed as contempt. "They love the raffles."

Father Paul thanked the bishop for his call and hung up. What would Jesus do?

He crossed the room and picked up the duffle bag then set it heavily on his desk. He pulled the key from his pocket. He slipped the key into the lock. He hesitated. It wasn't too late.

Twenty million dollars. No, not that. Others are coming. You must warn them. That.

He looked at the thick, khaki canvas, brass grommets, the strong, wide zipper. He turned the key and the latch popped. Now the zipper was all that stood between him and God alone knew what.

Warn them. They love the raffles. Others are coming. Twenty million dollars.

Father Paul pinched the zipper between his finger and thumb. He opened the bag and saw the dull reflection of light off gun metal gray. There were weapons and documents and two thousand dollars in twenties. Among the documents were pictures of two men—two killers according to the confession, along with an address in Corvallis, Oregon, and instructions on how to collect the bounty when the job was done.

It was all he needed to save these two men. Or many others.

Chapter Twenty-six

"Siafu?" Joshua Treadwell flipped through the document Bob had given him when he and Klaus arrived to give their report. "I don't see that in here," Treadwell said. "Am I missing a page?"

"No, sorry," Bob said. "That's not part of the presentation. It's something we thought of last night."

"Siafu."

"Yes," Klaus said. "It is the Masai name for African driver ants (*Formicidae dorylinae*), sometimes called army ants. They live in huge colonies, up to twenty million members. With those numbers, they quickly exhaust the food supply wherever they are, so they move to new territory every day or two."

"And when they do," Bob said enthusiastically, "they kill everything in their path."

"Interesting." It was the first time that morning they had seen a smile on Treadwell's usually cheerful face.

"You should see it," Bob said as if describing a lurid work of art. "Like a stream of bloody oil, reddish black, five inches wide, flowing across the ground. Twenty million ants, blind as bats, communicating via scent pheromones."

Intrigued, Joshua Treadwell said, "They can kill humans?"

"I suppose they're capable," Bob said. "But it's not likely a human would stand still long enough. Frogs, rats, insects on the other hand are small enough that the ants can overwhelm them before they can escape."

"I'm not sure I follow," Treadwell said. "If they don't kill people…" He raised his hands in curiosity.

Bob smiled. "We think they might be useful for how they recognize prey."

"You say they're blind?"

"Yeah, they sense their prey's carbon dioxide."

"Insects emit carbon dioxide?"

"Yes," Bob said. "But not nearly as much as humans, obviously. And one of the issues we're dealing with is how to get the assassins to hunt humans instead of their natural prey. So we'd like to sequence siafu DNA, see if we can isolate the genome that allows them to detect CO_2 and then transfer it to the assassins."

Treadwell scratched his head, then smoothed his hair back into place. "Don't all mammals emit CO_2?"

"Yeah, that's an issue," Bob admitted.

Treadwell sat back in his chair. "I mean I can see how that might work if you're fighting in the desert where there are fewer animals, but if you release something like that, say, in an urban warfare situation, I mean that's a target-rich environment in terms of insects and larger animals like rats, possums, dogs. Won't they get, I don't know, confused about what to kill?"

"We think we'll be able to get the assassins to hunt whatever emits the largest amount of the gas. But that's just speculation at this point."

Treadwell thought about it for a minute before he pointed at Bob. "See? That's what I like about you. Always thinking 'what if'? I think it's an idea worth pursuing," he said. "Good job."

Like a child receiving the approval of a parent, Bob seemed to stand a little straighter at the words. Treadwell's relentless positivism always seemed to give Bob a boost.

"Now, how are we doing with these bad boys?" Treadwell gestured at the two jars Klaus had put on his desk earlier. Each contained one of the two transgenic hybrids. Something caught Treadwell's eye and he leaned in for a closer look. "Are these bigger than they used to be?"

"Yeah," Bob said. "About 30 percent larger. It's a phenom-enon known as hybrid vigor. This is probably as big as they'll get, though, given the respiration issue."

Treadwell slowly turned the jar holding the transgenic spined ambush assassin. An awful creature, glistening greenish-black exoskeleton, spined and menacing. The bulging muscles of the forelegs, like Popeye the Insect Man. As the jar turned, the insect's disturbing orange eyes rotated to keep the men in sight. Its clubbed antennae constantly tapped the glass, trying to learn more from whatever was in the air. Treadwell lifted the jar to see the underside. The bug's sharp, piercing beak throbbed like a knife with a heartbeat. When Treadwell put his hand on the lid, Bob said, "I wouldn't do that."

He paused. "No?"

Bob and Klaus shook their heads.

Treadwell set the jar down gingerly. "So what's the status with these?"

"I think the term you guys use is 'fully weaponized,'" Bob said with a boyish grin. "After testing the toxins of the different venoms we found a component of the Sydney funnelweb's to be the most efficient." Bob glanced at his report. "Robustoxin is a protein, 4854 D, forty-two amino acids, a presynaptic neurotoxin that interferes with neuronal transmission, causing cardiovascular disturbance, pulmonary edema, severe acid base disturbances, and intracranial hypertension."

"According to the literature," Klaus said, "envenomation leads to a complex multisystem crisis involving the central, peripheral, autonomic, and neuromuscular nervous systems."

Treadwell looked up with disappointment, or maybe disbelief, on his face. "According to the literature? You mean you haven't tested it?"

"Yes and no," Bob said. "The venom doesn't effect standard lab animals, but previous data shows an astonishing sensitivity in primates, especially man."

"Something on the order of fifty to a hundred times more sensitive," Klaus added.

"How do you know the assassins carry the toxin?"

"We milked them," Bob said. "But we can't test how well the envenomation mechanism works on, uh, military targets. Because, obviously, the best subjects would be, well, people."

"We can get around that," Treadwell said with remarkable nonchalance. When he noticed Bob and Klaus exchanging a look of disbelief, he hardened a bit and said, "This is military research. Not a place for the squeamish. We'll find a way." Treadwell tapped the report again and said, "This is good stuff. I'm pleased with the progress."

"You want us to get working on the control issue?"

"No need," Treadwell said. "The boys in nanotech are way ahead of you." He glanced at his computer screen. "First test is next week."

Chapter Twenty-seven

Beverly Hills, California

Leon walked into the Polo Lounge as if he owned the place; at least, that was the thought that crossed Lauren's mind. She was on her cell phone and, before she finished her thought, she said, "I'm going to call you back." She flipped it shut and thought, Who is that man?

He was wearing a suit that would have worn lesser mortals. He had the look of assurance that, in Hollywood, usually came with gross points and a forty-million-dollar opening weekend. But she knew everyone who got gross points and he wasn't one of them. He crossed the room, not bothering to look around to see who was there. He was there and that was all that concerned him at the moment. He went to the bar and ordered a drink. A double from the looks of it. Whiskey.

She was watching him over the lip of her martini glass when someone said, "Lauren?" She looked up. It was her meeting. A young writer with a hot script. She smiled and gestured for him to join. The kid said there was interest in his script at Paramount and Fox and that a certain unnamed star would attach if the right director was involved. Lauren gave every appearance that she was not only listening but keenly interested and able to get a green light.

But she never lost track of the man at the bar. He ordered his second drink at the same time they did. He glanced at the bar menu. There was a woman on his left, drinking champagne. He didn't speak to her.

Eventually Lauren reached across the table and touched the script. "This is, without question, the edgiest, most original thriller I've read in years. I would love to put it into the hands of the right director. If you would let me." She would get him associate or coproducing credit and wanted him involved in everything from casting to locations, because he had such an incredible eye for character and setting. And so forth.

He insisted she was the only producer who understood the depth of the material and that her previous films proved his point. And when the mutual masturbation portion of the meeting was finished, the only surprise was that the script had no stains on it. She said she was having dinner with the perfect director later in the week, though she wasn't at liberty to say his name. The writer said he was off to talk to a hot young actor about a supporting role. They agreed to do lunch, and he was gone.

She quickly flagged down her waiter and sent a drink to the man at the bar. When it was served, the bartender leaned in and said something. Leon turned. She smiled an invitation. He accepted. As he crossed the room she scooted further into the booth, revealing expensive shoes at the ends of athletic legs.

"Hello," he said, arriving at the edge of the table.

"Join me?"

He did.

"I don't usually buy drinks for strangers," she said.

"But?" He had an accent she couldn't place.

"You're different." She lifted her glass and with a sly arch said, "Bottoms up."

Smiling at her tone, he touched his glass to hers. Leon had seen a lot of women, but this one would never escape his mind. A dangerous mouth, and eyes somewhere between English royalty and East German secret police, desirable in a ruthless sort of way.

"Different how," he asked.

"You tell me. What do you do?"

"I'm a consultant." A half-truth he'd told a million times.

She studied the olive in her glass. "That covers a lot of ground."

"All right, security consultant."

A slight squint and she said, "You sell burglar alarms?"

"Not exactly." Keeping things cool. "What about you?"

"Producer."

"Of?"

A quick smile. "You're not from here, are you?"

He shook his head. "Paris."

"Films," she said. "I'm a movie producer."

"Good films or popular ones?"

She pulled the olive from her drink. "They can't be both?" She popped it in her mouth.

"They usually aren't." He glanced at the script on the table. "Is that going to be one of your movies?"

"It might be."

"Any good?"

She smiled again and said, "There's an old joke about a producer talking to an agent. The producer holds up a script that the agent sent him and says, 'This the worst script I've ever read, unless DiCaprio is attached."

"Attached?"

"Agrees to star in it," she said. "See, producers don't make movies, we make deals. Directors make the movies. Producers make the deals necessary so they can make the movies. And making deals is about gathering the elements."

"Like earth, wind, and fire?"

"Sort of. A star, a director the studios want, that sort of thing."

"The script doesn't stand on its own merits?"

"Maybe in Paris. Nobody goes to the movies to see a script. They go to see the stars."

Leon spun the script around and looked at the title page. 'Killing Machine.' He said, "A love story?"

"Political thriller. Rogue CIA agent turns assassin."

Leon gave a nod. He understood. "They always get things wrong in those."

She looked up from her martini. "And you would know… how?"

"I told you."

"Oh, right." Using her fingers for quotation marks, she said, "Security consultant."

"Don't believe me?"

"You've given me no reason to," she said.

He moved closer, touching her hand as he did. "Our secret?"

She crossed her heart as she studied the lines in his face.

He took a slow sip from his drink before he lowered his voice and said, "I kill people for a living." He loved saying that, loved the reaction it got. And he said it so genuinely people usually had to take a moment to decide how to respond.

But not her. She just smiled as if she not only believed him, but liked the idea. And him too. She said, "Rogue CIA?" Again with the arch tone.

He shook his head. "General Directorate for External Security," he said.

"Should I know them?"

"French Foreign Intelligence." He ducked his head a bit and shrugged. "Although I am allowed to freelance now and again."

"Is that why you're here?"

"Can't say."

"Ahh." She finished her martini and said, "Ever thought about writing your story?"

It took him a moment. "What, a script?" He looked at the one on the table.

"Sure," she said. "Get things right for a change. Tell the story only you can tell."

He looked away, intrigued by the idea. "Never crossed my mind."

"It's not as dangerous as your current job." She gave him a wink. "No one shoots back."

He smiled. "No one shoots back now. How does it pay?"

"Depends on the script."

He pointed at 'Killing Machine.' "How about that one?"

"No one's bought it," she said. "But it could go for a million, maybe a million five."

"That's not bad. I might have to consider it."

"I could help," she said.

"I'd like that." As it happened, Leon had some time on his hands. So far all he knew was that Bob and Klaus were somewhere in Los Angeles. He was waiting on a couple of local contacts, one to get more specific information on the whereabouts of his targets, and another for his weapon. "By the way, I didn't get your name."

"Lauren," she said, extending her hand. "Lauren Carneghi."

He kissed just above her knuckles. "As in Carnegie Hall?"

She shook her head. "Spelled different, G-H-I instead of G-I-E. And you are?"

He sipped his drink before he said, "Mysterious."

She was laughing when her phone rang. She looked at the caller ID and muttered something underneath her breath. "Excuse me," she said. "Got to take this." She flipped it open. "Hey, I'm stuck in traffic but I'm on my way. God-damn 405." She holstered the phone. "I have to go." She handed Leon her card as she got up from the booth. "Call me."

Chapter Twenty-eight

Bob and Klaus each carried a container of the transgenic, venomized assassins as they crossed the parking lot at the DARPA labs. Joshua Treadwell pointed to a Hummer and said, "I'm right over there."

As they approached the thing, Bob couldn't help but wonder why a guy whose job was to help protect the country had gone so far out of his way to support OPEC. Bob suggested they take his car but Treadwell wasn't having any of it. "Nah," he said. "Let's drive over there like big boys."

Ignoring them, Klaus casually looked for vanity plates, the deciphering of which had become a hobby since moving to Los Angeles where vanity had long been considered not just acceptable, but a competitive sport. Most of the messages were clever, if obvious—the urologist with UP4ME; the actress-model with 26E4U; the surfer with NDLSMR—others were so abstruse as to be indecipherable without knowing more about the driver. This was the category into which Joshua Treadwell's message fell. At first Klaus hadn't even noticed it was a vanity plate, it so closely adhered to the DMV's standard format of a number followed by three letters followed by three numbers. But no matter how he pronounced various combinations of letters and numbers, G1V2628 (Give to six to eat?) didn't become any word or phrase Klaus could think of.

Ten minutes later they arrived at Van Nuys Airport where the DOD maintained a couple of hangars, one for the maintenance of visiting aircraft, and one for experiments requiring more space than their labs allowed. Treadwell led them inside where some workers were putting the finishing touches on a 1:10 scale model of what looked like a small Middle Eastern city on the edge of a mountainous desert. The rectangular set was two hundred by one hundred feet of rolling hills dotted with cacti and boulders. At one end of the desert was what looked to be the outskirts of Kabul or maybe Kandahar. The entire thing was surrounded by a ten-foot-high plexiglass wall.

"It's like a sound stage," Bob said. "You guys built all this for the test?"

"Nah." Treadwell shook his head. "Bought it from one of the studios. It's from some war picture set in Afghanistan." He pointed. "But if you ask me, those brown humps over there look more like Granada Hills than the White Mountains." He shook his head. "Hollywood."

From across the hangar a man called out, "Hey! Are you the bug guys?"

Treadwell led Bob and Klaus across the building where several men were gathered around some crates and a work bench. When they were ten feet from the men something scurried out from between two of the crates. Someone pointed. Bob looked and was shocked to see one of his assassin bugs. He nearly dropped his box. "Shit! Look out!"

The men all stepped back, looking down at the insect. One of them said, "What the hell is it?"

"A venomized transgenic," Bob said. "Extremely poisonous." He checked his box to see if he'd sprung a leak but it was sealed tight.

The bug turned and charged toward Bob. Another man said, "Get it!"

Bob went to step on it but every time he got close, the thing would turn and scoot away. Bob looked closer at the thing. Something strange about it. The bug wasn't moving right. Bob looked at Klaus and said, "What are you grinning about?"

Klaus nodded in the direction of a guy holding a radio remote control. Bob looked down and saw the insect doing figure eights corresponding with the movements of the joy stick.

Treadwell chuckled and gave Bob a clap on the back. "We call it a Ro-bug," he said as he turned to make introductions.

Two of the men were from RUR-FX, a Hollywood special effects company, specializing in small robots. They had designed exact fiberglass replicas of the exoskeletons of Transgenic Assassins One and Two, down to the finest detail of their antennae. "The leg movement was the only thing we couldn't replicate," one of the men said. "It's a very complex pattern."

"But we don't think that's going to matter." This was one of the two men from DARPA's nano-technology group. He picked up the Ro-bug and unsnapped the exoskeleton. "Check this out." Sitting in the palm of his hand was a sleek carbon fiber chassis on which were mounted a pair of tiny cylindrical tanks. "They hold synthetic pheromones," he said. "One will get your bugs to follow, the other makes them attack whatever we paint with it." He looked at Treadwell and smiled. "At least we hope that's what happens."

"I got the idea from you," Treadwell said to Bob.

Some weeks ago Bob had told him the story about the French killer, Chantalle. Just as she was about to kill him, six years ago, Bob had sprayed her with a cockroach pheromone and spilled assassin bugs all over the floor. Before she could say *sacre bleu*, she had wheel bugs attacking the soft tissues of her eyes. They punctured the sclera and gnawed into her corneas. The piercing mouthparts of the jagged ambush bugs delivered a flood of digestive enzymes that liquified surface muscles and nerve endings under her skin.

Bob looked a bit embarrassed. "Actually, we don't know if the bugs killed her. She might still have been alive when Wolfe shot her."

"You're too modest," Treadwell said.

Klaus looked closely at the pheromone tanks. He said, "What is the dispersal rate?"

The nano-guy smiled. "You know what an angstrom is?"

"Smaller than a micron."

"Boy howdy. The wavelength of red light is a little shorter than a micron. The smallest atoms are about two angstroms in diameter, about 1/5,000 of a micron." He pointed at the narrow end of the cylinders. "These puppies have flat micronozzles etched out of silicon with a throat width on the order of eighty-five microns. We can damn near squeeze that stuff out by the molecule." He pointed at the front of the Ro-bug. "The eyes are cameras, left for daylight, right for night vision. It's got a 128 K ROM processor, differential GPS with wide area augmentation system, and five days of power." He touched the rubbery track wheels at the bottom. "We've tested it in all sorts of terrain. It'll go anywhere a real bug can, and faster."

"What if it flips over?"

The guy placed it upside down on the work bench then pushed a button on the remote control. A tiny arm immediately flipped the Ro-bug upright.

"Cool," Bob said.

"And of course the bug is bugged," Treadwell said. "Along with everything else, it can monitor everything from conversations to the data on a wireless computer network."

Bob pointed at something. "What's that little ball around the thorax area?"

"Plastic explosive," Treadwell said. "Can't let anyone get their hands on this technology."

"If they did," the nano-guy said. "They lose the hand." He pointed at the covered self-destruct button on the remote control unit.

Bob shook his head. "That's a helluva bug."

Klaus agreed. He was suitably impressed by the technology, but he still wondered how Treadwell planned to test their assassins' envenomation mechanism on what they were still euphemistically calling 'military targets.' He was about to raise that question when the hangar's big roll-up door began to clang open, followed by the beep-beep-beep of a panel truck backing into the building. The logo on the side of the truck said *Atypical Resources, Inc.*

Treadwell clapped his hands once and said, "Ah, here we go."

Listed under several categories in the phone book, including Laboratory Equipment and Supplies, Atypical Resources was a privately owned company whose business was satisfying unusual requirements for military research, testing, and operations. By demonstrating a willingness to cross into gray (and black) legal areas, they earned a steady stream of contracts from the Department of Defense, the Pentagon, and the CIA.

The driver got out of the truck. He was an angry, tick-faced creep name of Lloyd. He took a parasitic drag on his cigarette before flipping it to the ground. He saw the group of men approaching and said, "One of you a Mr. Treadwell?"

"That would be me. You want me to sign for it?"

Lloyd shook his head. "I was never here."

"Excellent," Treadwell said.

Lloyd walked to the back of the truck and threw the doors open.

Bob and Klaus craned their necks to get a look. They stared at it for a moment to be sure, then they exchanged a nervous glance. From their vantage point, the only thing they could see in the dark cargo bed was a cage large enough to hold a man.

Chapter Twenty-nine

Father Paul nibbled on his cracker. It was stale, but the salt dissolving on his tongue was delicious. It was his first food in two days. He felt a twinge of guilt as he swallowed, and he prayed it wouldn't derail the process. He needed all the help he could get.

Fasting has long been acknowledged as a way to help believers make difficult decisions, to receive God's instructions. It slowed the physical functions so that the mind could be more in tune with Christ. But it was a lost spiritual discipline in an age of fast food, abundance, and self-indulgence. It had occurred to Father Paul that decisions reached during a fast—decisions assumed to be divinely inspired—might simply be the result of swings in blood sugar. Still, he had to do something. Ever since opening the duffle bag, he'd been struggling to receive God's instructions. He hoped fasting would open his heart to the right path.

It was a Hobson's choice or worse. Should he warn these two men—two killers according to the confession—that others were out to kill them? If he did and they were, in fact, assassins, then they would be free to continue killing and that would be blood on Father Paul's hands. The alternative was to kill the two men. The upside here was that he would be saving the lives of all of their future targets and he'd collect $20 million with which he could do a lot of good.

He was sitting in his car across the road from the address he had found in the duffle bag along with the dossiers on Bob and Klaus. In the past forty-eight hours, he'd seen a woman and a teenage girl come and go from the house, but neither of the men seemed to be around. Based on the files, Father Paul assumed the females were the wife and daughter of the man named Bob. If that was true, and if the men weren't there, Father Paul figured there was no point in waiting any longer.

He got out of the car carrying the duffle bag. He opened the trunk, set the bag inside. He was about to slam it shut when he had a thought. He unzipped the bag and pulled out a .45. He looked at it for a moment then snugged it into his waistband, covering it with his shirt tail. He closed the trunk and headed for the house.

Father Paul never noticed the man watching from the other car.

Katy was in the kitchen when the door bell rang the first time. Whoever it was would have to wait at least twelve more seconds. The bell rang again at the same time as the microwave. A few moments later Katy opened the door. She was holding a freshly nuked beef-and-cheese burrito. Standing there, waiting for the man to say something, Katy peeled back the plastic wrap and let the steam waft away. She looked him up and down as she took a bite of the burrito and chewed.

Father Paul felt the squeeze of his salivary glands. He flexed his jaw as he stared at the bitten end of the burrito, soft pinto beans in a beefy brown sauce with orange streaks of cheese. He caught himself licking his lips as he made eye contact with Katy and said, "Hello, I'm Father Paul."

She took another bite of her lunch, rolled her eyes, and said, "Whatever." She turned and yelled, "Mom, there's, like, a priest or something at the front door." Then she walked away, leaving Father Paul standing there, his stomach grumbling.

Mary came in from the backyard wearing jeans and a work shirt, soiled from gardening. When she saw the priest, she figured he was soliciting donations. She pulled off her gloves and said, "Can I help you?"

"Yes, hello, I'm Father Paul." He hesitated, not sure what to say. "This is difficult. I hardly know where to begin." He swayed a bit.

"Are you all right?" He was rather pale.

He closed his eyes briefly, nodding. "I haven't eaten in two days."

"Oh." Mary smiled awkwardly, then gestured toward the kitchen. "Would you like something?"

He shook his head. "I'm fasting."

"Oh. All right." He was a large man, a bit jowly. Perhaps it was a diet, she thought.

"It's a way to help one make difficult decisions, to receive God's instructions, to be more in tune with Christ."

"I see." Even though she really didn't. She had agnostic leanings. Mary stepped back and gestured him in. "Would you like to come in, maybe sit for a minute?" Father Paul followed her into the living room and sat on the sofa. Mary brushed something from the back of her pants and sat across from him in an armchair. "Now, is there some way I can help you?"

"Yes," Father Paul said, glancing around the room. "There is something I must tell your husband."

Mary smiled in curious way. Bob had never mentioned knowing any priests. "He's not here," she said. "But I can give him a message."

"I'm afraid I can't tell you." Disappointment in his voice.

"You can't."

He shook his head. "It's confidential."

"Well, I'm his wife," she said cheerfully. "He trusts me. So can you." A sincere smile coupled with an affirming nod.

"No, I'm afraid it's a matter of priest-penitent confidentiality. The sacramental seal is inviolable."

Confusion replaced Mary's curious smile. She shook her head. "We're not Catholic."

"No, it was someone else's confession, you see, but it concerned your husband and I've been struggling with how to convey the information without risking *latae sententiae*."

"Of course." She had no idea. It said so, right on her face.

"Automatic excommunication."

"Oh."

"On the one hand I think your husband would want to know what I have to tell him but on the other hand, if I violate the seal of the confessional…"

"You could be fired."

"Worse," Father Paul said. "Excommunicated. That's why I've been fasting." He sniffed the air for the burrito.

They sat in a reverent silence for a moment before Mary said, "Here's an idea." She leaned forward with a smarty-pants expression. "Couldn't you just tell me and then go to confession about it?"

Father Paul looked up at the idea, momentarily hopeful. "I hadn't thought of that." After thinking about it he said, "No, you can't commit a sin with the intention of seeking forgiveness for it." He smiled sadly, shaking his head. "That would be too easy."

Mary smiled back in sympathy, nodding. "They think of everything."

"They have nothing else to do."

"Well," Mary said. "Do you mind if I just ask a few questions?"

"No, go ahead." Father Paul hoped she could find some way to get the information from him, to lift his burden without any cost to him.

Mary thought for a moment, then chuckled. "I'm not sure what I should ask."

A man's voice came from behind, startling Mary. He said, "I'd ask him about the gun in his pants."

Chapter Thirty

Lloyd, the queasy, tick-faced driver, got a couple of guys to help him pull the cage from the truck. It had long poles attached on each side and the men lifted the cage onto their shoulders, like African porters in some old jungle movie.

It came as a surprise to both Bob and Klaus that inside the cage was what looked like a small, hairy cowboy. At first he was slumped against the bars, as if sleeping off a bender, but when they brought the cage into the light, he looked up. His big ears stuck out like jug handles under a smutty Stetson. Bob wasn't sure if he was relieved it was a chimpanzee instead of a man, but that's what it was. A chimp dressed in a tattered old cowboy outfit, complete with a holster and a pair of tarnished six guns. He tilted his head back and blew a raspberry in their general direction.

"His name's BeeBo," Treadwell said. "Apparently they got him from an old theatrical agent. Had a client did animal acts passed away and left him the chimp, two ponies, and a flatulent lion." He pointed at BeeBo. "According to the agent, that's the last chimp to appear on the Ed Sullivan show. Did a few commercials after that but…" He shook his head. "He's too old to work now. Apparently they get nasty and don't obey too well after a certain age."

"Sounds like my daughter," Bob said.

The cage was too wide to fit through the door into the test area. Lloyd was standing there, trying to figure the best way to get BeeBo into the arena when it hit him from behind. It took only a moment for Lloyd to figure out what it was. A fistful of stink, dark brown and still warm, sliding down the back of his neck, foul beyond words. "Goddammit!" Lloyd sprayed obscenities as he moved in a herky-jerky circle trying to shake the shit off his skin. "You stupid fucking ape!"

BeeBo was jumping up and down with a shit-flinging grin on his little cowboy face. He shrieked in joy and blew another raspberry, this one aimed at Lloyd.

The guys from the special effects house were doubled over. The others were doing their best not to laugh, for Lloyd's sake.

But it was too late. Lloyd already felt the hot blood of embarrassment in his ears. He turned in a fury and jammed a cattle prod into the cage. BeeBo shrieked again, this time in pain, and withdrew into the corner, nursing the sore.

"I didn't move to Los Angeles to be a goddamn chimp wrangler," Lloyd thought. "I did Shakespeare in the Fucking Park. I had that national toothpaste spot last year. [He was the "before tartar control" teeth.] But now, just because of that stupid thing at that stupid club on Sunset that night—hell, that was months ago—nobody's returning my calls. And now I'm just the guy with chimp shit in my hair."

Someone tossed Lloyd a roll of paper towels as he stormed off toward a restroom.

Bob felt a sense of unease at what was to come. He turned to Treadwell and, lowering his voice, said, "Is it legal to use chimps for…experiments like this?" By which he meant is it legal to kill one?

"It is for us," Treadwell said. "DARPA's funded through the DOD, not the NIH, so we're not regulated by the Animal Welfare or Health Research Extension Act or any of that nonsense. Believe it or not, Congress occasionally passes laws more concerned about people than animals." Treadwell waved a dismissive hand in the air as he continued, "We're supposed to file something with the Office of Laboratory Animal Welfare, but why bother?" He made a vague gesture toward the ceiling. "Higher authority," he said with a wink. "Let them have dominion over every creeping thing that creepeth upon the earth. I'm pretty sure that includes monkeys."

As Treadwell walked off to speak to the nano-tech guys, Klaus nudged Bob and said, "Dominion over every creeping thing?" He was incredulous. "Is he serious?"

"I think he's serious about this test," Bob said, looking around, not sure for what. "It looks like BeeBo here is about to be subjected to some post 9/11 thinking."

Lloyd returned from the washroom, still fuming, and resumed trying to figure out how to get the cage into the enclosure, finally deciding to use a hydraulic lift to lower it in.

Bob stepped closer and looked at BeeBo. Their eyes met and they held one another's gaze briefly. In that moment, Bob thought about all the people he'd known with less intelligence behind their eyes and, ironically, with less humanity. The evolutionary kinship was obvious, undeniable, even humbling. Except to some. He turned and walked toward Treadwell. "You can't just kill him," Bob said.

Before Treadwell could respond, Lloyd snorted a reply over his shoulder. "Shit, give me five minutes with that stupid monkey and I'll kill him." He jammed the cattle prod into the cage again but BeeBo dodged it.

Treadwell folded his arms while narrowing his mind. "Like I said last week, Bob. This is military research, not a place for the squeamish."

Bob looked at BeeBo, then back at Treadwell. "Squeamishness isn't the issue."

Treadwell turned on him and said, "You have a better idea, Bob? You told me yourself the venom doesn't work on standard lab animals. What should we do? Use people?" He paused a moment, suddenly disappointed that he hadn't thought to make inquiries about getting some 'detainees' from the military prison at Guantanamo.

"Of course not," Bob said. "But there's bound to be a better way."

As a matter of fact, Treadwell had approached the Governor of Texas about using death row inmates for this sort of thing but the talks didn't get very far for reasons Treadwell was still unclear about, especially since it was the Governor of Texas. He said, "Look, we can't send a weapon into theater without testing it. We can't put troops in danger like that. It's very simple. Winning the war against terror is more important than this run-down old monkey."

Klaus didn't care much for Treadwell's dismissive characterization of a primate as fine as BeeBo, but he could see his point. Why spend millions to research and develop a weapon if you weren't going to test it at the end?

Bob used his thumb as if gesturing at their conversation last week. "When you said you'd find a way to test the bugs, I assumed you meant computer modeling or something on the cellular level. Not this. This is barbaric."

Treadwell put on some exasperation now. "Ask yourself this question," he said. "You think anybody on those airplanes or in the World Trade Center would have objected to this test?" Treadwell shook his head. "I'm surprised at you, Bob. I mean you jumped at the chance to work on this project. You knew you were designing weapons, and now you're upset about this? You told me you stood in your own home and watched your bugs kill two or three people."

"They were trying to kill us," Bob said.

"What do you think the terrorists are trying to do?"

"I don't think BeeBo's with al Qaeda."

Treadwell squeezed off a smile. "If you don't have the stomach to watch, by all means don't." He turned and walked away saying, "I've got a daughter like that. Loves her hamburgers but gets all teary about the slaughterhouse."

Bob saw no point in responding to the cheap shot about his masculinity. He was more concerned about what he could do to forestall the experiment. But he had to hurry. They were lowering the cage into the enclosure. The nano-tech guys transferred the venomized assassins into containers with remote control doors, then placed them at the far end of the miniature desert.

A bullhorn squawked and someone said, "We're hot! Everybody out!"

The workers left the area and locked the small door behind them. Bob knew if he was going to do anything, he needed to do it before they released the bugs.

Lloyd was hovering overhead in the basket of a cherry picker, ready to open the cage door. The guy on the bullhorn looked up and said, "Ready?"

"Yeah," Lloyd said, thumbs up. "Let's do this." With a little too much relish.

"No." Calmly at first, Bob moved toward the guy with the remote control, waving his hands, then shouting, "Whoa! Hold it!"

Already aware of the futility of Bob's protest, Klaus smiled and shook his head slowly in admiration. He stood ready to help, one way or the other, depending on how things played out.

"Test's off," Bob said. "Everybody stop!" He tried to take to the remote control from the nano-tech guy but he pulled it out of Bob's reach.

Everybody looked toward Joshua Treadwell for direction.

He circled his finger in the air. "Go!"

Bob pointed sternly at the remote control guy. "Don't do it," he said as he turned and ran for the test area. He jumped, barely getting his hands over the top of the thick plexiglass wall.

Klaus smiled more broadly now and looked skyward before heading over. He wasn't sure if he was going to help Bob get over the wall or just help him get down. He'd have to play it by ear.

With his grip tentative and his shoes slipping against the slick walls, Bob continued yelling, "Stop! Don't release them!"

Klaus thought it was a commendable, if pathetic, effort. But his friend looked like a four-legged bug squirming on a windshield. In the annals of protest, this wasn't going down with Rosa Parks or the guy blocking tanks in Tiananmen Square.

Treadwell looked up at Lloyd, pointed at Bob, and said, "Get him down!"

Lloyd began to steer the bucket of the cherry picker over to where Bob was hanging on the wall. He waved the cattle prod. "I ain't afraid to use this," he said.

Klaus reached up and grabbed a pants leg. "Bob, come down before you get hurt."

Bob tried to kick at him but, lacking leverage, it was a feeble attempt.

Hanging there, his face pressed to the plexiglass, Bob saw BeeBo, hands high on the bars of his cage, as if mimicking his would-be savior. He put his lips together thoughtfully as if to blow a kiss, but blew a raspberry instead.

Klaus got a better grip on the pants and pulled. They came down. Boxers. Bob came down next. "Good try," Klaus said. "But it's all over now."

Chapter Thirty-one

"Who in Christ's name are you?" Mary turned to Father Paul and said, "Oh. Sorry."

"No." He waved her off. "It's a good question."

"I'm Agent Parker." He flashed his identification. "CIA." He was standing in the doorway between the living and dining rooms, his gun trained on Father Paul.

This is about the point when most people would express some skepticism about a man who had broken into the house and claimed to be with the CIA. But Mary wasn't most people. Bob and Klaus had told her the stories about the redoubtable CIA Agent Mike Wolfe, who had tried to kill them only to be done in by some African leaf beetles (*Diamphidia simplex*) in what would best be described as unlikely circumstances.

It dawned on Mary at this moment that Klaus had been right. Just because a man is paranoid doesn't mean people aren't after him. Mary held her hands out for an explanation. "What are you doing in my house?"

"Don't worry," he said. "I'm here to help." Parker wagged his gun at the priest. "Let's go, padre. Real easy, just put it on the coffee table there."

Father Paul's arthritic hip pained him as he reached behind and pulled out the .45. He set it gently on the table then leaned back in the sofa, calmly raising his hands.

Mary looked at Father Paul, betrayed. "You had a gun?"

"I'm sorry," he said. "I'm not sure why I brought that." Which was true. Standing at the trunk earlier, he'd had some vague notion of the possibility of running into trouble and as long as he had a sack full of weapons, well, it had seemed prudent and vaguely thrilling at the time.

"Right," Agent Parker said. "Had nothing to do with plans to kill Bob and Klaus."

"What? No! That's nonsense." He had to say something.

"You've never crossed the Agency's radar," Agent Parker said as he picked up the .45. "So, who are you? Really?"

Hand up as if taking an oath, he swore, "I'm Father Paul Anik. From St. Martin's Catholic Church in Seattle."

Agent Parker shook his head and said, "Lying's a sin, father."

"I can prove it." His arthritis grabbed as reached for his wallet. He froze when Parker brought both guns his way. Wide-eyed, he said, "I have identification."

"Oh, I know you've got identification," Parker said with a laugh. He walked back to the doorway between the two rooms. He leaned over and picked up the duffle bag which he'd left on a dining room chair. "You're lousy with identification. And weapons and cash too." He unzipped the bag to show the evidence. "Although I think it's germane to point out that none of the passports were issued by The Holy See." He pulled a Bible from the bag. "But this is a nice touch."

"I can explain all of that." He paused, conflicted. "No, actually I can't."

"Of course you can. No point in making up a story if you don't tell it later."

Mary pointed at the duffle bag. "Where did all that come from?" she asked.

"Found it in his trunk," Parker said.

"What about you?" Father Paul pointed at Agent Parker. "We should believe you're with the CIA just because you have a gun and a cheap suit?" It was the hunger talking; he wouldn't normally make derogatory comments about anyone's clothes. Wasn't his style.

Agent Parker looked at his suit, a little rumpled maybe and certainly not expensive, but he didn't think it deserved the insult. He looked at Mary who seemed to want a good answer to the question. So Parker said, "Who're you going to believe, the guy with the duffle bag full of forged passports and a priest costume or the guy with a gun and a badge?"

Mary gestured at the bag, then looked at Father Paul. "You have to admit, it looks funny."

He shrugged and said, "*Nimium ne crede colori.*"

"What's that?"

"Latin," Father Paul said. "Uh, more or less, appearances can be deceiving."

Agent Parker squinted his way. "Probably not your best idiom at the moment, padre."

"No, probably not, but who speaks Latin?" He pressed his hand to his chest. "Priests."

"I got a friend who can quote Cicero," Agent Parker said. "Doesn't make him the Pope."

The priest pointed at the phone. "Call St. Martin's, ask for Father Paul. He won't be there."

"So you know a church with a Father Paul who's on vacation." Agent Parker laughed. "Or better yet, you actually are Father Paul. Perfect cover," he said. "And it's not as if you'd be the first priest to commit a federal crime. Hell, you probably wouldn't be the first priest this week."

Father Paul closed his eyes and thought about the most recent headlines. Minors across a state line. Immoral purposes. He sighed. His hip hurt. "Don't remind me." He didn't need this kind of grief.

Mary wasn't sure she wanted the answer, but she had to ask, "But why would he come here in the first place?"

"Well, we've picked up some chatter recently and reread some old files and here's what we know for sure," Agent Parker said, taking a seat. "After he'd paid good money to have Bob killed, Miguel DeJesus Riviera..." he paused, then said, "...you remember him, don't you?"

Mary nodded.

Parker continued, "Miguel was understandably upset to learn recently that Bob was still alive. So he took out a new contract on Bob and another one for the guy who took the money in the first place." He looked at Mary to see if she would admit knowing anything.

She played dumb.

"That would be Klaus," Parker said. "We suspect Miguel is going through Marcel Pétain to recruit a few assassins." Agent Parker was, understandably, angry with Miguel for failing to honor his word about giving him an exclusive on the contract and next time he saw the toot kingpin, he'd let him know about that. Meanwhile, he pointed at Father Paul and said, "I think the fact this guy is here tends to support my theory."

"I can explain," Father Thomas said. Some words tried to escape but he was suddenly struck mute. "No, I can't say anything more." Though it was riddled with faults, he loved the Church too much to risk excommunication.

Mary was thinking about the last time this happened. Klaus having to kill that cowboy from Oklahoma and the others. This wasn't a game. She said, "What are we going to do?"

"We're going to get out of here pronto," Parker said, glancing out the window. "If someone I've never heard of…" He pointed at Father Paul "…like the pistol-packing padre here, has tracked you down, others are certainly coming. We're not safe here."

Father Paul touched his finger to the tip of his nose as if to say, that's what I was going to tell them.

"I'm calling Bob," Mary said, moving for the phone.

"No." Agent Parker blocked her path. "Too dangerous. Your line could be tapped and, trust me, cells are easy to monitor. Simplest way for someone to find where they are. We don't want that. You'll just have to take me to wherever he is."

"Drop it!" Everyone turned to the voice. Katy stood in the doorway, leaning forward from her waist in a strong Weaver stance, a Walther P99 in her hand. "Now!"

Agent Parker could tell by her posture that she'd fired the gun before. In fact she gave the impression of being a good shot. He doubted she'd ever fired at a live target but, with this family, he decided not to test it. He squatted and laid the gun at his feet, then stood with his hands raised and said, "You must be Katy."

She looked past him and said, "Way to go, Mom. I see you're being real careful here."

"Honey, now is not the time." She took the .45 off the coffee table. She kept it on Father Paul as she moved toward Agent Parker.

"So," Katy said. "Wanna tell me what's going on?"

Mary picked up Agent Parker's gun and said, "We're going to L.A."

"Really?" Katy smiled. "Cool!"

Chapter Thirty-two

Lloyd steered the cherry picker back to hover above BeeBo's cage. He reached down with a long gaffing hook, opening the door to let BeeBo out.

It was as if the curtain had gone up. The moment seemed to transport BeeBo back to his glory days on the variety show circuit. He gathered himself and stood as tall as he could. He hitched up his holster and walked out of the cage, swaying side to side like John Wayne, into the desert.

One of the nano-tech guys tested the Ro-bug. Left, right, forward, backward. He turned on the camera and, looking at the monitor, he saw things from the Ro-bug's point-of-view. He zoomed in and out on BeeBo's face. "It's all good," he said. "We're set."

His partner triggered the hatchways on the assassin containers. They flipped open like angry garage doors. When BeeBo saw that, he did a back flip and drew his six shooters. Then he blew another raspberry.

The transgenic assassins stalked out of their containers like soldiers. Big bugs. Half were greenish-black, spined and muscular, with those rotating eyes; the others were stealth gray with ruby red markings and those cog-like half-wheels splayed on their backs. Both had the razor sharp rostrum tucked underneath, ready to pierce, inject, and suck. Ready to kill.

The bugs moved in all directions, probing their environment, paying no attention to the Ro-bug as it crisscrossed and circled in front of them.

Treadwell pointed at them and said, "They're ignoring it."

"Hang on." The nano-tech pushed a button to release the first pheromone. It worked like a magic trick. The scattered insects suddenly scampered over to form an agitated group behind the machine. The guy said, "Ewww…nice." He moved the joy stick forward and the insects followed. He led them around cacti, through tunnels, and over rocks.

Treadwell looked on approvingly but didn't speak.

Unlike ants following a pheromone trail, single file and orderly, the assassins, who weren't social insects, traveled in a broad pack behind the leader. Whenever a few of the transgenics would begin to stray, nano-guy released more pheromone and they immediately rejoined the pack.

"Fantastic," Treadwell said. "Now…the other test."

BeeBo took a keen interest in the tiny parade that was now heading his way. Despite having spent his entire his life in Hollywood, there was something buried deep in BeeBo's brain stem that warned him about things with the color and movement of these six-legged creatures. As they came closer, BeeBo began to bark and threat slap the ground. Bad! No! But they kept coming. So he bared his teeth and let out a fearsome scream. Bad!

The bugs showed no interest in the noisy primate. They were simply in lockstep behind their false leader. This calmed him somewhat. The Ro-bug grew closer and BeeBo, being a curious creature, leaned down to look at it, wondering if, perhaps, he'd misjudged.

That's when they released the second pheromone.

BeeBo didn't know what it was, but he didn't like it. He screamed and took off his hat, slapping it on the ground near the Ro-bug. Bad! The pheromone was all over him and the assassins were suddenly alert to the scent of Oriental cockroach (*Blatta orientalis*). They spread out, forming two groups according to species. Something about these movements frightened BeeBo and he leaped on top of the cage, barking, threat slapping his hands, and swaying side to side.

Lloyd was watching from his perch in the cherry picker. "No sir," he said. "You ain't getting off that easy." He lowered the basket to shoo BeeBo back to the ground. He didn't want to get close enough to use the cattle prod—he wasn't that stupid—so he swung the gaffing hook.

BeeBo didn't see it coming. It pissed him off when it hit him, but it didn't knock him down. Lloyd reared back and swung it again but this time BeeBo caught it in a firm grip.

No one was more surprised than Lloyd to discover that a chimp the size of BeeBo has the strength of four or five large men. When BeeBo pulled, Lloyd tumbled out of the basket like a ball of yarn, landing next to BeeBo who punched him once in the chest then jumped on him, ass first.

"Jesus!" Bob said, "Stop the bugs!"

The nano-tech guy looked at him, a little embarrassed. "Uhh, we don't have, like, a stop pheromone. That wasn't part of the contract."

No one noticed the tiny smile as it crossed Treadwell's face.

"Lead them away," Klaus said. "Quickly!"

The guy sprayed the first pheromone and directed the Ro-bug away from the cage as fast as it would go. What they learned was that hunger and the drive for food trumps the drive to run away from food. The assassins began to circle the cage, a silent and relentless army.

"Now what?"

Treadwell walked away from the others, pulled his cell phone, and punched a preset number. He had a short conversation before disconnecting and returning to watch the experiment.

Klauss went to the cherry picker to see if he could help. But Lloyd, on his way out of the basket, had inadvertently over-ridden control by the ground operator. Klaus turned and headed for the coffee room. Perhaps there was some Raid under the sink.

Bob pointed at the test area and said, "If we don't stop this, that man's going to die."

Treadwell threw up his hands. "What can I do? Your bugs didn't follow the leader." He looked at Lloyd and shrugged. "The guy fell. Call OSHA; they'll tell you, accidents happen. And we can't send anyone in without putting them in danger."

"This is crazy. We've got to do something." Bob pulled his cell phone. "I'm calling the police."

Treadwell grabbed his arm and said, "No you're not. I've already called the proper authorities." He nodded toward the door where half a dozen men were coming in, serious men in dark suits.

"Those aren't cops."

"This is a highly classified project," Treadwell said. "City police don't have the necessary security clearance."

The hungry venomized assassins were climbing the bars of the cage. As far as they knew, there was a meal up there. A big one.

Lloyd scrambled to his feet, begging for help, while BeeBo slapped him with his cowboy hat, inadvertently transferring the essence of cockroach. When the first assassins grappled over the top of the cage, Lloyd began stomping them frantically, one at a time, with his work boots. But there were too many. As he tried to defend himself from one direction, he was attacked from the other. He'd spin and stomp and spin again.

BeeBo knew it was time to go. Something about those colors warned him. With Lloyd providing cover, BeeBo grabbed the gaffing hook and latched it onto the bucket of the cherry picker. He pulled himself up effortlessly and climbed in.

Lloyd, seeing himself encircled, tried to follow, but he didn't have that sort of strength. His grip weak, he slipped slowly toward his fate, pleading and whimpering all the way down.

With his work boot dangling a foot above the cage, the first assassins leapt up and quickly scurried under his pants leg, everyone in the room stared fixed in fear and fascination. Unable to look away, some held a hand to the mouth, others were slack-jawed and horrified, yet all of them moved closer for a better look.

Up in the cherry picker, BeeBo pulled his six guns and fired them in the air, a demented Old West sheriff from the Planet of the Apes.

Treadwell watched impassively—a middle manager considering a presentation before taking it to the boys upstairs. He folded his arms across his chest and watched as the bugs went about their work.

The numbness started around Lloyd's mouth within seconds of the first bite on his leg. His tongue spasmed, and he started to drool and sweat profusely. With more bites came severe abdominal pain and acute gastric dilation as his stomach filled with a frothy gas. The vomiting and severe lacrimation were beyond his control. After a dozen bites, tears streamed from their ducts as if from a turned faucet. Lloyd collapsed onto the cage, paralyzed muscles unable to twitch left him more-or-less vibrating. The bugs wasted no time finding their way to Lloyd's head and into his open mouth and sinuses, injecting their predigestive enzymes. His withering face began to resemble a generous piece of dried fruit. Lloyd was silent now, his pupils dilated, his lungs struggling, then his heart finally stopped.

The assassins grew still, their razory mouthparts sinking into skin, sucking the remaining life out of the man.

Once it was done, Treadwell walked over to Bob who was standing a few yards away, stunned by what he'd seen. "Congratulations," Treadwell said. "I'd say they work." He pointed at the serious men in the dark suits and lowered his voice. "They're going to want to talk to you now."

Suddenly BeeBo came swinging down from the cherry picker. He hit the floor of the warehouse and charged out the door. Treadwell shook his head and pointed after him. He said, "Somebody wanna go get that monkey?"

Chapter Thirty-three

After ushering Bob and Klaus into a small conference room at the edge of the hangar, the head man from the DoD said, "This won't take long." He tossed a document onto the table. It slid to a stop between Bob and Klaus. "That's the contract you signed for the DARPA funding." He gestured at it and said, "Page fourteen, section twenty-four, paragraph three."

Bob flipped to the page even though he had a good idea of what was there.

"Those are some of the penalties provided by statute for anyone who in any way breaks any law pertaining to national security."

Bob looked at the paragraph about prison time and fines. "Some of the penalties?"

"Not everything is put in writing." He looked at Klaus. "I'm sure you understand."

Klaus shrugged. "Actually, I do."

Bob pointed to the interior of the hangar. "We just saw a man killed in there."

"Yes," the DoD guy said. "And a tragedy it was. But let's not compound the matter and see anyone else die as a result of misinformation, for example, leaking to the press."

"How about real information?"

"It's all the same," DoD said. "Equally dangerous, especially to you."

Bob looked at Klaus, then at the DoD guy. "You're threatening us?"

"What you saw and, more to the point, what you participated in, was a classified military experiment. That it didn't play out as planned is immaterial. The Department of Defense takes these matters very seriously and will conduct a thorough investigation. On that you can rest assured. You will be called to testify at a hearing at some point. In the meanwhile, anyone who says anything about it publicly will face the full wrath of the federal government." He leaned across the table onto his knuckles. "And that, my friend, is shit so deep you'll need Jules Verne to help you navigate."

Chapter Thirty-four

Leon walked into the coffee shop on West Sunset Boulevard. He was meeting a friend of a friend. Ex-army, rifle platoon, became an expert sniper, then retired. Moved to Southern California, worked on his tan and became a weapons consultant for the studios as well as several local law enforcement agencies. On the phone he told Leon that he'd be in uniform, waiting in the booth farthest from the door.

At first Leon wasn't sure it was the guy. He was dressed in khakis, deck shoes, and a blue guayabera. Leon said, "That's your uniform?"

The guy smiled. "Hollywood armed forces," he said with a wink. "Only uniform I wear these days."

Leon sat down, made small talk, ordered a club sandwich. After the coffee came, the guy said, "I'd go with the Tango 51, same as I recommended to L.A. County Sheriff's S.E.B."

"Special Enforcement Bureau?"

He nodded, showing Leon a picture of the thing. "It's based on the Remington M700, blueprinted to Tac-Ops specs. Custom precision-ground recoil lug. Most accurate thing I've ever fired. Even in heat with opticals and mirage. You won't believe it."

"Threading for a suppressor?"

"Optional."

"I'd like that."

"You got it."

"How much?"

"Five thousand dollars, and worth it."

They did the deal. The Tango 51 would arrive in a few days.

When he left the coffee shop, Leon drifted down Sunset Boulevard until he came to the Samuel French Bookstore. The window display featured several books on script writing. Why the hell not, he thought. He went in and browsed the titles, finally settling on a copy of *How To Write A Screenplay in 30 Days*.

He stepped outside and sat on the bench in front of the store and began to thumb through the book. Looked simple enough. Three acts, plot twists, reversals, conflict. Maybe the producer was right. Maybe he should put his story on the page, do it right for a change, pick up some easy money. Turning to another chapter, he read what he considered a dubious assertion about character development, so he pulled his cell phone and punched a number from the business card in his pocket.

A young man answered, "Lauren Carneghi's office."

"Is she in?"

"She's in a meeting," he said. "Can I take a message?"

Leon realized he had never given her a name, real or otherwise. He said, "Tell her the security consultant called."

"Excuse me?"

"She'll know."

"Can you hold a moment?" The kid didn't wait for a reply, just put Leon on hold, so he held.

A moment later Lauren came on the line. "I was wondering if you were ever going to call."

"I thought you were in a meeting."

"It's just something we say."

"Okay." He paused before saying, "Let me ask you a question."

She laughed quietly. "Why don't you?"

"Do you think a character has to change in the course of a story?"

She laughed again, more throaty this time. "You mean have an arc?"

"Yeah, if that's the word. All these books say the main character has to change."

"Yeah, well it's —"

"It's stupid," Leon said. "I mean, take *The Maltese Falcon*. Bogart doesn't change."

"You mean Sam Spade."

"Yeah, his character. He's cool, hard, strictly business when the story opens and that's how he is at the end when he sends what's-her-name to jail."

"Brigid O'Shaughnessy."

"Right. He doesn't go all soft on us. He doesn't start weeping and try to save her. That's why we like him. He's the same guy at the end as he was at the start. He's consistent." Lauren didn't respond at first and her silence derailed him. He thought she would argue the point or agree wholeheartedly or something. So he said, "I'm not saying a character can't change but—"

"I think I see where you're going," she said.

"Do you?" He didn't know what she was talking about. "Good."

"Assassin noir." The words came out slow and sexual. "I like it," she said. "You're thinking, what? Uh, *Day of the Jackal* meets what, *This Gun for Hire*. That's good. Your killer is tough, man of few words. But he likes cats."

"What?"

"It doesn't have to be a cat. I'm just thinking out loud. Anyway, I'm glad you called. I talked to Brad Pitt's people last night, told them about the idea."

"What idea?"

"Your script idea."

"I don't have a script idea," Leon said. "I was just reading this book and wanted to ask you about the character thing."

"They say he'll be intrigued. They want to meet you. They think he'll love the noir angle."

"What are you talking about?"

"Lunch. Thursday at the Ivy. I'll pick you up."

Chapter Thirty-five

"Hit me!" Bob held out his glass.

Klaus filled it with scotch, then topped his own. Following the experiment, Bob had needed a little something to settle his nerves. Halfway through the bottle he and Klaus were sharing a feeling of well being, a sensation of warmth, and a minor impairment of reasoning and memory.

Gruesome as Lloyd's death had been, it hadn't bothered Klaus so much. He'd seen a lot of men die, most by his own hand, and all deserving it, at least by his measure. In Klaus' view, Lloyd hadn't deserved to die despite his cruelty toward the defenseless chimp. He may have deserved a few jolts from the cattle prod, maybe a good thrashing, but not death. Besides, as Treadwell had pointed out, accidents do happen, and what they had seen was purely accidental. So Klaus was simply enjoying the scotch and the camaraderie that such lubrication tended to encourage.

They were back at the Avondale Oaks, sitting by the pool in their lounge chairs, debriefing one another on their debriefing. "I'd say that last thing was definitely a threat," Bob said, making the point that the phrase 'twenty thousand leagues under the shit' didn't sound like an invitation to a tea party.

Klaus held out a fist, then opened it, palm up, and blew across it. He said, "We would disappear." He took a sip of his drink and added, "Listen, my friend, when the milky-eyed goons in the dark suits begin to invoke national security, the best recourse is to listen and nod."

"I s'pect you're right." Bob pulled his cell phone and hit a preset.

Klaus looked over the top of his glasses and said, "Thank you."

Bob kept the phone to his ear for a while before disconnecting and trying another preset. A minute later he flipped the phone shut.

There was something funny going on. Klaus could feel it in the air. He said, "Still no answer?"

Bob shook his head but showed no concern. "They probably went out to a movie or something, forgot to turn the cell back on afterwards. She'll call when they get home, hear the messages." He held out his glass. "Hit me!"

Klaus stared at him. After all these years, he still couldn't believe Bob's ability to look at the burning fuse of a bomb and comment only on how pretty the sparks were. As he poured, he said, "Bob, you know I have always found your optimism to be one of your more endearing qualities but it sometimes clouds your judgment."

"It's only been three hours," Bob said. "She'll call."

Klaus wondered if Bob really believed it or if he was simply too terrified to admit that something seemed wrong. That was the problem when dealing with people who clung to a philosophy that demanded blind faith in the existence of silver linings, that sort of belief being impenetrable by the light of disproof, or whatever the phrase was. Klaus said, "Bob, you cannot address a problem by insisting it does not exist."

"What problem? I don't see any problem."

Klaus pointed out that Katy, owing to teenage rebellion, wouldn't be caught dead going to a movie with her mother. "I have heard her say as much," Klaus said. He also made the point that the only time Mary turned her cell off was at night. "She puts the phone on vibrate if she goes to a movie so she will know if you or Katy is calling."

Bob shook his head. "Klaus, I swear, you could find weeds in the Garden of Eden."

"Only if they were there," he said. "Besides, what is the alternative? Pretending they are not?"

Bob fished an ice cube from his glass using his tongue. He said, "It must be hard living with that perspective. Always finding the negative."

"I wouldn't know," Klaus said. "I do not find something wrong with everything because not everything has something wrong with it."

"Oh, please," Bob said. "You're Chicken Little. Always insisting that the sky is falling. What you need is a brighter outlook." He waved his glass at Klaus, spilling some on his pants. "Damn."

"I hate to be the one to tell you," Klaus said. "But you cannot make the world turn out the way you want simply by insisting that things are going to be wonderful. I believe that is what they call magical thinking."

Bob pretended to shield himself from above. "Oh, no, the sky's falling, the sky's falling!"

"All right," Klaus said. "If it will be easier to get your tiny drunken brain around it, we can talk about this in terms of children's stories."

Setting his drink down, Bob put his fingers under his arm pits and flapped his wings while doing his chicken imitation, "Bach, bach, bach."

Klaus ignored it. "There is an Aesop's fable in which I suppose I would be the ant preparing for winter, for the worst, for the cold weather when food would be scarce. That would make you the optimistic grasshopper insisting that there was no need to work and worry about the future because there is nothing unpleasant happening at the moment. Does that help?"

Bob thought about it for a moment before he said, "I don't think that's the point of that story."

"No? Well, how about that song from *Pinocchio*?" He hummed a few bars before the lyrics caught up with him and he began to sing, "'Like a bolt out of the blue, fate steps in and sees you through.' That is how you see the world, is it not? You just wish upon a star and whistle while you work and everything comes up roses?" Klaus shook his head and took another slug of the scotch.

"I think you've got your cartoons mixed up," Bob said.

"The thing I cannot figure out is whether you subscribe to that Disneyland philosophy because you really believe it or because the song was sung by a cricket."

Bob nodded like a sage and held up a couple of fingers. "Two things," he said. "First, you have a lovely singing voice. Secondly, I'll say this for you and all your negativism: at least your stories feature insects. That's a good thing." Bob held out his glass. "To bugs!"

Klaus tipped his glass toward Bob's. "Bugs."

"Now, what were we talking about?"

"Your mania for insisting that all is well when things are going badly."

"What about it?"

"You are telling me that you are not in the least worried about Mary and Katy?"

Bob looked at Klaus as if he were crazy. He laughed and said, "Remember when Katy broke that guy's arm?"

"It was his wrist," Klaus said. "And he should have stopped when she told him to stop."

"Hey, I agree," Bob said, holding one hand up. "No means no, especially when my little girl says it. My point is that with all you taught them, I think they can take care of themselves."

After narrowly escaping from New York, Klaus had instructed the entire Dillon family on the basics of Krav Maga, the Israeli hand-to-hand combat system that was pure self-defense, not a martial art, designed simply to end a fight as quickly as possible. Katy first got to try it out when a young boyfriend got caught up in a moment of hormones and heavy petting.

"It's a good thing you hadn't given her that P99 before she went on that date," Bob said, thinking about how Klaus had also taught them to handle weapons.

Klaus shook his head again. "My friend, there is a difference between lusty teenage boys and professional killers."

"She'll call," Bob said. "Now, shouldn't we be celebrating?"

"Celebrating what?"

"Our bugs! They work!"

Klaus waited a moment before saying, "A man died."

"I was there," Bob said. "I know that. What's your point?"

"I am simply saying you seem to have recovered from the shock."

"The liquor helps," Bob said, only slightly insulted by the insinuation that he lacked the appropriate sympathy. He drank some more, lowering his judgment to the point that he said, "Tell you the truth, I almost feel bad saying this..." He looked around, drunk enough that he was about to say something he wouldn't ordinarily, though not so drunk that he didn't care who heard him say it. "But let's face it, not only did poor old Lloyd die, he died fast and completely."

Klaus nodded. "There is no question the insects are lethal."

Bob mocked him, speaking in his exaggerated Klaus accent, "There is no question the insects are lethal." He laughed and said, "Face it, the bugs rock!"

"Yes, they do," Klaus said. "And now that you have done your part for your country, we have to consider disappearing again. Our lives may be in danger."

Bob looked at his friend with sympathy. "I haven't seen you this gloomy in years." He tilted his head. "You haven't stopped taking your antidepressants, have you?"

"You know I stopped three years ago," Klaus said. "This is not depression. This is paying attention. I have said this from the beginning. Our names are out there. And now that we have spent time with the dark suits and their additional paperwork, the odds that Miguel DeJesus Riviera will discover the truth falls in his favor." Klaus sat up and looked at Bob. "And how do you think that will make him feel?"

Chapter Thirty-six

The four couples sitting in Joshua Treadwell's living room that night were scrubbed pink and pure and they gave off the fresh mountain scent of a quality fabric softener. The wives were soccer-mom dressy, lightly tanned, and perky. The husbands were new-country-club-member casual, earnest, and they all managed to look as if they had come straight from the barber.

Mrs. Treadwell, a chipper blonde with platinum highlights, served tea, fruit juice, and the high-fat, low-carb snacks everyone loved.

It could have been a book club gathering and, in a way, that's exactly what it was.

One of the men, Charles Browning, touched his finger to a line on a page of his book and said, "So I think we all agree that the seven heads of the beast refers to seven hills." He looked at everyone to receive the affirmation he desired, then continued, "But the hills aren't literally hills." He held his finger up to make the point. "They're nations."

Joshua Treadwell smiled and said, "Exactly."

Everyone nodded as a happy murmur of consent spread through the room.

Mr. Browning counted the nations on his fingers. "Syria, Lebanon, Iraq, Iran, Libya, Jordan, and Egypt." More nodding ensued, prompting the man to continue, "And of course the ten horns are ten kings, one each for the seven nations plus the three who were subdued by Arafat."

"The little horn," someone added. "The eleventh king."

"Of Palestine," one of the men said as he also wrote something in the margin of his Bible.

"Yes."

"And his death brought us that much closer to the Rapture," Mr. Browning said.

"Wait, wait, let's back up," a woman named Cynthia said. She turned to a different chapter and verse. "I'm sorry, the covenant of Daniel 9:27 was between Arafat and Rabin, right? That was the Oslo Accords?"

"Yes," Mrs. Treadwell said, smiling like a saint.

"Okay," Cynthia said. "I'm with you now, go on."

It was like this every Wednesday night when the Treadwells met with half a dozen of their closest friends, men and their wives with whom they attended services. But they all agreed this was their favorite night of the week. It was an evening of fellowship, prayer, and lively discussions about Scripture. They belonged to the United Family of Calvary Church, a booming congregation of some fifteen thousand. And, like everyone else in the United Family of Calvary Church, the Treadwells and their friends also belonged to a smaller group from the congregation.

None of them would have been able to say where the idea started, but they would all agree that the small group dynamic worked. One of the problems for large organizations—corporate, military, political, or religious—is how easily they can lose control over the rank and file. If you're simply one of a group of ten thousand, it's very easy (and tempting) to freeload. And for organizations that depend on the financial participation of its members, freeloading can be a killer. What large organizations needed was a way to compel and enforce participation in everything from tithing to volunteering, and what they found was that having lots of small groups within the larger group accomplished this.

The theory is that while it's easy to hide in a crowd of ten thousand, it's impossible to hide in a group of six. The success of this small group theory has been proven over and over, from communist and terrorist cells to AA. In short, it turns out that forming tightly knit groups of like-minded people, in pursuit of a common goal, and having them meet in one another's homes where they can find acceptance in their ideas and friendship among peers turns out to be a powerful way to control people and direct their actions.

No one understood this better than the folks running the United Family of Calvary Church. They'd jumped on the small group bandwagon years ago and flourished. The United Family of Calvary Church was a dispensationalist congregation that embraced the doctrine of nineteenth-century Irish-Anglo theologian John Nelson Darby, who proposed that a literal reading of the Bible offered "rediscovered truths" and a detailed chronology of the impending end of the world.

"If I just might add something," Mrs. Browning said, nibbling on one of the low-carb treats. "When the Lord speaks of the Abomination of Desolation in Matthew 24, he isn't referring to Daniel 9:27."

"Right," Mr. Browning said. "That's just a play on words."

"Exactly. But my point is that the Abomination does not fall within the seven years of Daniel 9:27."

The discussion over the meaning of the seven hills and the eleven kings seized their imaginations for another ten minutes before they agreed that those nations collectively composed the beast of Revelation 13, at which point Joshua Treadwell read verse 16, "And he causeth all, both small and great, rich and poor, free and bond, to receive a mark in their right hand, or in their foreheads."

"Wait, I'm lost again," Cynthia said with an embarrassed smile. "Sorry. If we're saying that the second beast of Revelation 13 is Mahmoud Abbas, what's his mark?"

"The mark of the false prophet," Mr. Browning said. "The one who maintains the legacy of Arafat. The mark came during the election for president of the Palestinian Authority when voters were forced to put their right thumbs in the indelible ink that lasted forty-eight hours."

Treadwell offered a reassuring nod and said, "It was applied to all, no matter what economic status they held, right? So both small and great, rich and poor, free and bond, to receive a mark in their right hand. See?"

"Oh, sure, of course. That makes sense," Cynthia said. "How did I miss that?

"And," Mrs. Treadwell added, "a vote for the false prophet, or the second beast, brings eternal damnation."

"In effect, such a vote is akin to selling one's soul."

"Got it."

Joshua Treadwell glanced at his watch. "It's getting late." He shared a smile with them and said, "What do you say we pick it up here next week?"

Chapter Thirty-seven

If you create an insect nearly four feet long, weighing eighty-five pounds, and capable of speeds in excess of a hundred miles an hour, people will stare in amazement. If you attach a machine gun to four of its six legs, they'll point and tell others about it, especially if sparks shoot from the barrel and it smokes. And that was the idea. You had to look at such a thing, and when you did, you saw "B&K's All Natural Pest Control" along with the 800 number in bold lettering down the insect's abdomen.

The truck wouldn't have been Mary's first choice but Bob had taken the Volvo to L.A., Agent Parker had rented a compact at the airport, and Father Paul's Impala had 169,322 miles on it when the odometer gave out a year ago. So Mary figured that the truck with the big bug perched on the crew cab was the best way to get the four of them down to Los Angeles.

Standing in the driveway with the gun in her hand, Mary was dealing with some anger management issues. She was furious for having put herself and Katy, and, by extension, Bob and Klaus, in danger. She gestured angrily with the P99 and said, "Make sure that knot's tight."

Father Paul was too weak to struggle as Agent Parker tied his hands with the nylon cord. Still, he protested, "I am not an assassin."

"Padre, you can sing that song until Jesus comes back," Agent Parker said. "But that duffle bag we found in the trunk of your car tells a different story."

Father Paul leaned against the truck for support. "I can only tell you the truth. I cannot make you believe it."

"That's what I keep saying," Agent Parker said, nodding at Mary. "I'm with the CIA. That's the truth, but it's a hard thing to prove. You can't just call my office and have them confirm it." He shrugged. "I was in her shoes, I'd be suspicious too." Parker figured it was best to play along with Mary, since all he wanted was to be taken to Bob and Klaus in the first place. This just made it easy. This way he wouldn't have to hold Mary and Katy hostage to make Bob and Klaus show themselves, which had been one of the possibilities he'd been forced to entertain.

Katy locked the duffle bag in the truck's tool box. "We don't have enough rope for him," she said, glancing at Agent Parker.

"Use those plastic cable ties in the garage."

"You don't have to tie me up," Agent Parker said. "I'll be a good boy."

"Hey." She wagged the gun at him. "It's just as easy to pretend you're with the CIA as with the church."

After Katy zip-tied Agent Parker, Mary took his phone and punched in a number. "Hi, honey, it's me. Oh, I borrowed somebody's phone. No, everything's fine. Yeah, got your messages. Sorry I didn't call sooner but listen, we're coming to L.A. Hmmm? Oh. Well, something's come up."

Chapter Thirty-eight

It was two in the morning when Joshua Treadwell steered the black van off Los Feliz Boulevard up into the Hollywood Hills where the skinny winding streets were the only things crazier than the price of real estate. Four-thousand-a-month dog kennel apartments next to million-and-a-half-dollar handyman's dreams too low for a view. Snaking through all the street-parked cars, (garages long ago having been turned into desperate third bedrooms) Treadwell passed two-million-dollar 1,800-square-foot magical writer's retreats and three-million-dollar custom entertainer's delights. Closer to the top were the five-million-dollar trophy properties and finally, at the end of the road, the seven-million-dollar gated Spanish style estate he was looking for.

Treadwell circled the cul-de-sac and pulled to the curb, facing downhill for an easy exit. He killed the engine and sat in silence for a few minutes, looking down on the twinkling lights of the L.A. basin. He thought about II Kings, Chapter 19, Verse 35: "And it came to pass that night, that the angel of the Lord went out, and smote a hundred fourscore and five thousand: and when they arose early in the morning, behold, they were all dead corpses."

Treadwell's goal tonight was modest by comparison, intending to smite just one instead of 185,000. But he felt like an angel of the Lord, and he believed in his heart that if the experiment worked outside the controlled lab environment, smiting 185,000 was well within his grasp.

His will be done.

Treadwell moved to the back of the van and opened one of the lock boxes, removing a Transgenic One Ro-bug. He powered it up and set it aside. He slipped on a pair of heavy duty gloves before opening a second lock box from which he removed a plastic container about the size of a shoe box. Inside were fifteen weaponized spined ambush assassins.

A moment later a hatch next to the transmission opened under the van and a small ramp extended down to the asphalt. The Ro-bug moved quietly down the ramp followed closely by the glistening green-black insects, hissing and muscular, the rigid spines circling their prothorax, each with a dark red ring at the base.

Treadwell eyed the monitor inside the van as he toggled the remote control. All systems were go. When the insects began to wander off in different directions Treadwell pushed a button on the remote unit, releasing a few molecules of the follow-pheromone. The effect was instantaneous; the transgenic insects twitched and hopped, returning to the pack, seeking only direction. The Ro-bug whirred over to the dry gutter, then turned and led his platoon of assassins up the cul-de-sac.

At first the only sound picked up by the bug's listening device was the pulsing chirp of field crickets (*Gryllus pennsylvanicus*). But twenty feet up the road it picked up the soft padding sound of something approaching. Treadwell turned the Ro-bug and saw a coyote creeping across the street. It came to investigate, mangy and curious. The coyote stopped suddenly about two feet away, bared its teeth with a low growl then turned and trotted back into the hills.

Thirty feet later, the thumb-sized bugs turned up a paver-stone driveway, crept under the security gate, and on toward the house. There was a half moon and the skies were clear. The monitor displayed a Lynchian vision of the world as the bugs entered a patch of turf grass, dew droplets forming on the blades, refracting the moonlight. A moment later they emerged onto a flagstone patio that looked like the surface of Mars. Treadwell rotated the

Ro-bug until it faced the sliding glass door, wide open, gauzy white curtains lilting in the breeze like a soft southern accent.

When a few of the assassins began to wander in different directions again, Treadwell released more of the pheromone, bringing them quickly back to the pack, their muscular forearms twitching with obedience. The Ro-bug navigated the tracks of the sliding door, leading the pack onto the cool sherbert-orange saltillo tiles of the living room.

Inside the house the sensitive listening device picked up new sounds. Animal sounds. Grunts, groans, and coarse breathing.

Treadwell rotated the joystick for a 180-degree scan. A moment later the Ro-bug turned to move down the hall. The bugs followed like a pack of eight-legged wolves, hungry and unafraid.

At the doorway to the master bedroom Treadwell stopped the Ro-bug and scanned the space. Seeing movement, he zoomed the lens until the sins filled the screen. He couldn't tell who was who or what was what or even if it was hetero or homo. But it didn't look like the sort of behavior intended to make children. This was pure self-gratification. Action not serving a higher purpose. Deviant. He disapproved.

Still, Treadwell lingered, waiting to see what abominations these people were capable of, what they might do next, from what angles they would do it, what sorts of sounds would they make as they did it. How deep a grave would they dig?

He watched until he was satisfied. The LED of the clock on the bedside table glowed 2:48 A.M. as the couple writhed on the California-king-size mattress perched on a sleigh-bed frame, three feet off the floor.

Treadwell guided the assassins to the side where the sheet reached the ground.

The Ro-bug's treads couldn't gain traction on the steep incline, so Treadwell directed it away from the bed, raised the abdomen to a 45 degree angle, and triggered the cockroach-pheromone release. The transgenic assassins alerted, their chameleon eyes turning all at once toward the sweaty congress, itchy with anticipation. It was time to eat.

Their spined tarsi easily grabbing the fabric, they climbed. On top, they spread out, circling the writhing bodies. They waited until, a few moments later, the pair collapsed in exhaustion. They crept forward in the heat and musk that followed. Their twitchy clubbed antennae hovered and swayed over pulsing skin, seeking the blood closest to the surface.

"Oooo, that tickles," a woman said.

"Hmmm?"

"Ouch! That hurt!"

"What the…Jesus!"

"Ohmigod, get 'em off!"

Treadwell could see the bodies moving again, desperate and frightened. Heard their screams choke off as the venom swelled their throats to gagging, then to death.

After the bodies grew still and the bugs gorged themselves, another release of pheromones called them back to the floor where they found their leader and followed him back into the California night.

Chapter Thirty-nine

Father Paul thought the effects of the fasting were upon him. He heard the voices of angels, or perhaps saints, telling him what he must do. You must wait, they said. Wait. Then he heard another voice and realized it was his own, saying that he had to pee again.

Agent Parker shook his head. "You got a bladder the size of a cannelli bean."

"I'm an old man," he said. "Just wait, you'll see."

Mary glanced in the rearview mirror. "Can't you hold it? We're only an hour or so from L.A."

Glancing down at his lap Father Paul shook his head sadly.

"Out of curiosity," Katy said, "isn't it hard to be an assassin if you have to pee every thirty minutes?"

They pulled into the rest area at Castaic Lake. As Mary instructed, they did the same drill every time. The two men went together into one restroom while either Katy or Mary waited outside with the gun. Katy went in this time. Mary was standing by the water fountain reading the California Department of Fish and Game's warning about rattlesnakes when she felt the sure grip of Agent Parker's hands on her arms, pinning them to her side. "Easy now," he said, quickly reaching around into her open purse. He took the gun and stepped away. "Just relax."

Looking past him, Mary saw the only other car in the rest area pulling back onto I-5. It was pointless to scream, so she said, "How did you get loose?"

"I told you, I'm with CIA. Cable ties aren't that tough, trust me."

"Trust you? The last guy who said he was with the CIA tried to kill my husband."

Thinking about the various betrayals he had suffered at the Agency Agent Parker said, "Yeah, well, I understand your skepticism."

Father Paul stepped out of the restroom wearing a deeply satisfied look. He walked toward Mary and Agent Parker but stopped when he saw the gun. "What's going on?"

Before anyone could answer Katy came out of the other rest room and saw exactly what was going on. "Guh," she said. "Way to go, Mom." She rolled her eyes and shook her head.

"Not now, Katy."

Agent Parker gestured with gun. "Everybody back to the truck. We'll be in L.A. soon."

"No," Mary said, holding her ground. "This is as far as we go."

"Mom," Katy said. "I don't want to die at a rest stop. How gross would that be?"

"Mary, let's not waste time on this. We're going to L.A."

"No. You just want to kill Bob and Klaus for the money."

"Well, you're half right," Agent Parker said. "I do plan to kill them. And guess what?" He pointed the gun at her. "You're going to help."

Chapter Forty

Bob was at the kitchen table with a headache, a cup of coffee, and a bowl of Lucky Charms. He turned on the TV to catch the morning news as he enjoyed the magically delicious cereal.

Anchorman Todd Hererra hardened his face to give the impression that he was a man familiar with the darker side of human nature but no longer surprised by it. He said, "Shockwaves are rippling through Hollywood this morning as word spreads that Oscar-nominated director Peter Innish and an as-yet-to-be-identified young woman were found dead just a few hours ago at a house in the Hollywood Hills. Innish, whose latest film, *Pole Position*, has been described as the 'gay NASCAR movie,' reportedly received numerous death threats from motor sports fans after the release of the film. For the latest on this rapidly developing story, let's go to our own Traci Taylor who is on the scene."

Traci, an angular brunette with a smile like a meat slicer, held a microphone in one hand while pointing over her shoulder with the other as she said, "Todd, as you can see, I'm standing in the shadow of the famous Hollywood sign." The camera followed Traci as she turned to say, "And just across the street from another famous sign in Hollywood…crime scene tape."

Behind her, the end of a cul-de-sac and a uniformed cop guarding the gated driveway as moon-suited CSI techs scoured the grounds for forensic evidence and grey-suited detectives talked to the housekeeper and made notes.

"Celebrities and murder," Traci said as she walked slowly toward the scene. "Here in Los Angeles, they go together like Will and Grace, Law and Order, Sex...and the City." She glanced at the sky. "And so once again we find the hills are alive with the sounds of emergency vehicles and news helicopters. Todd?"

"What have you learned so far, Traci?"

"Police aren't releasing any details publicly but someone close to the investigation tells me that despite the fact there were no signs of a struggle, they consider the deaths...highly suspicious."

Todd donned a weighty expression and leaned toward the camera. "Have you been able to find out why they're saying that?"

Traci nodded as if she'd seen the question coming. "Todd, my source tells me the medical examiner ruled out natural causes almost immediately." Here she raised her eyebrows and the specter of nefarious activities simultaneously. "Since there hasn't been time for an autopsy—indeed, since the two bodies haven't yet been removed from the house—I asked how the medical examiner reached that conclusion. I was told off the record that there was something about the condition of the bodies that makes them suspicious."

There was a quick knock at the door to Bob's apartment, then it opened. Klaus came in with a newspaper folded under one arm. Bob looked up from the TV. "Hey, how's your head?"

Klaus shrugged as he poured a cup of coffee. Then he said, "Have you heard from Mary?"

"Yeah, she called about an hour ago, said they were making one last stop up at Castaic." He glanced up at the clock. "Should be here pretty soon."

Klaus leaned against the counter, snapped open the paper and began reading.

Bob gestured at the TV with his spoon, spilling a marshmallow clover. "You seen the news?"

Klaus peered over the top of the front page of the LA Times, gave it a shake.

Bob shook his head and pointed at the TV. "No, I mean today's news."

From behind the paper, Klaus said, "Peace in the Middle East?"

"Better," Bob said. "Celebrity death under mysterious circumstances. The guy who directed that gay NASCAR movie? Found dead in the sack with a young woman, the good money says aspiring actress." He pointed at the television just as Traci was promising a special report in which she would deliver exclusive, shocking developments in the Peter Innish Murders.

"Thanks, Traci," said Todd. "We'll check back with you later in the newscast." Turning to camera one, Todd's pliable face swapped grave concern for amused disbelief. He even gave the impression of suppressing a chuckle before saying, "Southern California drivers had a real monkey-wrench thrown into their morning commute today when an unusual hitchhiker appeared on the 405. The Highway Patrol confirmed reports of a chimpanzee dressed in a cowboy outfit dashing into traffic and pulling his six guns, causing a multi-car pile up and snarling traffic for five miles."

Bob looked at Klaus who was peering out from behind the paper. "You think it's…"

"I think it is unbelievable they call this news," Klaus said before reaching over to turn off the television.

Bob pointed at the black screen. "But, BeeBo…"

"Bob, do you remember last night when Mary called to say she was holding a gun on two men, one of whom claimed to be a CIA agent, the other an apparent assassin with our photographs? Does any of this sound familiar?"

Bob muted the television. "I was drunk," he said. "But I wasn't that drunk."

"So you remember the part about Miguel DeJesus Riviera offering twenty million for our deaths?"

"Mary said she had it under control."

"So any concern about the assassin part of the story is unwarranted?"

"You taught Mary and Katy all they need to know. I have full confidence in you."

Klaus stared at him for a moment before saying, "Your optimism troubles me."

"Uh oh, the sky's falling again." Bob took his bowl to the sink and said, "They're an hour north of town, what's to worry about? Besides, what can we do from here?"

"We could be packing," Klaus said. "I predicted this. I told you word would get out and people would come for us. And it has, and they have, and so we have to disappear again."

"Let's talk to Treadwell, see if the DOD can help us out."

"They are the ones who got us in trouble to begin with."

"Perfect," Bob said with a clap of his hands. "So they owe us."

Not long after that there was a knock on the door followed by Mary saying, "Bob?"

"See? There they are." Bob cinched his belt tight around his bathrobe as he crossed the apartment. When he opened the door he saw Mary, Katy, and a man in a priest outfit standing in front of another man who, apparently, had the gun.

"Hi, honey," Mary said. "We're home." She had the chagrined look of someone who'd had the tables turned on her.

Katy said, "Hi, Dad. Guess what Mom did?"

Agent Parker nudged Mary in the back and said, "Inside. Let's go."

Standing in the living room, assessing the situation, Bob sounded more surprised than disappointed or accusing. "Sweetie, you said you had things under control."

Normally Mary wouldn't have said what she did, but for the past hour or so Katy had been giving her relentless and snarky teenage grief for letting Agent Parker get the gun back. By now Mary was sick and tired of all the Monday-morning quarterbacking, so when Bob said "Sweetie, you said you had things under control," she couldn't help but say, "I did, Bob, but shit happens."

"That would be me." The man in the back of the group waved his gun in the air. "Agent Nick Parker, CIA. You knew my boss, Mike Wolfe?" He passed his free hand over his head. "Crazy old white-haired coot."

"Hard guy to forget," Bob said.

Agent Parker looked past Bob and spoke louder. "Klaus? I assume that's you in the kitchen." He held the .45 in the air again and pulled the hammer back. "Hear that? It's a big gun, Klaus. So why don't you just put down the knife or the can opener or the zester or whatever it is you planned to kill me with, and come on out. There's a lot at stake here, and I don't intend to let this opportunity slip away."

Klaus eased out of the kitchen with his hands raised in loose fists.

Agent Parker took a step back, extending his arm, bringing the gun up, aiming at Klaus. "What's in your hands?"

"Nothing," Klaus said. "Relax."

"Open 'em up. Now!"

"Calm down." Klaus kept moving toward Parker, his hands still closed.

"I said stop!"

Chapter Forty-one

If he hesitated another second, it would be too late. He would be the one killed. So he squeezed the trigger. The bullet exploded through the heart. He was still alive when he landed on his knees. You could see it in his eyes. But he was dead before his nose crunched on the floor.

Leon sat back and let out a long breath. He read the words again. "Now that," he thought, "is an opening action sequence." He hit the "save" button and stretched to one side until something in his neck made a noise and felt better. "It's not perfect, but it sets the tone."

For the past few hours Leon had been working the keyboard on his laptop like Scott Joplin playing "Maple Leaf Rag." A blinding torrent of notes, becoming words, rendering character and action and plot. He hunched over the thing, hammering like a man possessed. On the desk next to a cup of coffee, *How To Write a Screenplay in 30 Days* was splayed open, the spine already cracked from constant reference. The room service tray with breakfast was almost untouched.

The night before, thinking about what Lauren Carneghi had said about writing a killer's story the way it really was, Leon had watched some pay-per-view, a couple of action movies that had been big hits. One was cops and gangstas, the other was special agents and terrorists. They were all gasoline explosions, machine guns, and death with no soul. As he watched these violent spectacles, Leon couldn't help thinking that a man with his experience, a man who had done the things he had done, could do a lot better than these innocent screenwriters. All he had to do was tell the truth.

He thought about all the close calls he'd had, the near disasters, the way things could go completely wrong in the blink of an eye. The perfect shots, the lucky ones, and that one about which he had regrets. His world was complex, morally ambiguous, and cinematic. And the more he thought about that, the more his pulse quickened. He had never thought about his life's work; he'd always just done it. But now he was thinking. He was thinking Lauren was right. He was the guy to reveal the truth. He would be the guide into the underworld only he knew. Writing the script would be like planning a job, the only point at which he had total control over everything that happened, what went right and what went wrong.

He started working on the opening action sequence and before he knew it, the idea of writing a movie about the ways of the assassin had seized him whole.

In the quiet of his hotel room, the only sound was the hum of his computer. Leon was so caught up in the process, so immersed in the world he was creating, that he jumped when the phone rang. He looked at it for a moment before answering. Only two people knew he was there, the man he'd hired to locate Bob and Klaus, and the producer. He was surprised to find himself hoping it wasn't the man with the information that would send him down the other road. He was too excited about this script, about meeting with Brad Pitt, about suddenly, and improbably, being a Hollywood screenwriter.

Sure, Leon knew he could make twenty million for the murders, but that assumed he wouldn't get killed trying, something for which there was no guarantee, given that Klaus had been one of the world's best assassins in his day. And even if he didn't get killed, he ran the risk of getting caught after the fact. So there were two strikes against, on the one hand. And on the other, there was the mystique of the movie business, the draw of the magic, the lure of the stars that was spreading throughout his body like a cancer.

He picked up the phone and the young man on the other end said, "I have Lauren Carneghi for you."

A moment later she came on the line blurting, "Can you believe this shit with Peter Innish?"

Her voice brought a smile to his lips. "No," Leon said. "It's unbelievable."

She paused when it dawned on her. "You don't even know what I'm talking about, do you? Don't you watch the news?" She laughed.

"I'm working on the story," he said.

"You are? That's great," she said. "That's why I'm calling. The whole Innish thing—"

"Wait, who is this person?"

"Wrong tense," she said. "He was a director. Did the movie *Pole Position.*"

"What is he now?"

"Dead. And suffice it to say, the shit has hit the Hollywood fan. We had to reschedule the meeting with Pitt's people."

"His people?"

She heard the disappointment in his voice. "We'll meet with Brad eventually," Lauren said. "He's shooting right now. But the Innish thing derailed a huge project they had going. They're scrambling to find another director to keep it alive. But they love what they've heard so far. They said Brad's totally crazy about the project. He absolutely loves the noir angle. Said he wants it to be his next picture."

Leon smiled. "Really?" More disbelief than excitement.

"Absolutely! So, listen, I'll reschedule the lunch ASAP. You just keep writing."

"By the way," he said, "I never told you my name."

"You can tell me next Sunday."

"Next Sunday?"

"You're my date."

"Where are we going?"

"The Academy Awards."

Chapter Forty-two

As Traci was finishing her segment, she noticed the housekeeper skirting the herd of reporters that had stampeded into the hills on the scent of fresh blood. It looked as if she was trying to get away before someone asked about the status of her citizenship but she stopped, lurking on the edge of Traci's peripheral vision.

"Reporting live from the Hollywood Hills, I'm Traci Taylor, *Eyewitness Action News.*" She held her expression until Ronnie, her cameraman, killed his lights and headed toward the driveway, said he needed to shoot some more B roll.

Traci hung back, said she was going to check with the medical examiner to see if he had anything new, but she was curious about the housekeeper who kept inching in her direction, looking over her shoulder every few seconds. Finally she said, "Excuse me?"

"Yes?" Traci looked up from her notepad.

She kept looking around as if expecting the INS to swoop in and cart of her away at any moment. "Can I talk with you?"

"Sure. What's your name?"

"Blanca."

"You're the housekeeper, right?"

"*Sí*, yes." She nodded, still obviously nervous.

Traci was used to people being nervous when they approached her. Even the minor celebrity of a TV field reporter had surprising impact on some viewers. Traci smiled, hoping to put the woman at ease. "What did you want to talk about?"

"I am the one who found the bodies," she said.

Traci knew this already. She nodded sympathetically. "That must have been terrible."

Blanca nodded in agreement but didn't speak for a moment. She looked at her shoes as if her next words might be down there. Finally she said, "But that is not all I found."

"Oh?" Traci wondered what else there could be. Two dead bodies was a pretty good find. Still, whatever it was, Traci's instincts told her it was news. Possibly big news. Her heart began to race. Was this a scoop, an exclusive, the Holy Grail? If it was, she wondered why Blanca had approached her instead of any of the other two dozen reporters on the scene. Then she wondered why she was looking a gift horse in the mouth. She said, "What did you find?"

Blanca nodded toward the *Eyewitness Action News* van. "Can we talk over there?"

She assumed Blanca didn't want the police to see her talking to a reporter about whatever she had found, which just made Traci that much more excited about the possibilities. She led Blanca to the other side of the van, out of sight. Blanca looked around one more time before she pulled a small videotape cassette from her pocket. "I also found this," she said. "I didn't want the police to find it."

Traci struggled to keep her jaw from unhinging and dropping to the asphalt. The tape was like a magnet pulling on her eyes. Felt like a retina might detach at any moment. She couldn't look away. Whatever this was had local Emmy written all over it. The videotape found at the death scene. She couldn't tell if Blanca was simply being loyal to her former employer or if she had something more profitable in mind. Not that it mattered. Traci wanted the tape, and she figured she would go to whatever lengths were necessary to get it. She pointed at the cassette, all nonchalant. "What is it?"

Blanca seemed embarrassed when she said, "The camera was in the bedroom." She looked uncomfortable with the insinuation. "I didn't think—" She shook her head. "He was a nice man."

Traci gave a sympathetic nod. "It was in the bedroom?" She could hardly speak. "Where the bodies were?"

"Yes. I put the camera away and took the tape." She shrugged and dropped her head, as if she wasn't sure she'd done the right thing.

"You did the right thing," Traci said, putting her hand on Blanca's shoulder. "The police don't know about this?"

Blanca shook her head.

"Did you look at it?"

"No."

It took all of Traci's strength and self-control to keep from ripping the tape from Blanca's hand, possibly taking the hand with it. Did it show the killer? If so, why would the killer leave it? Maybe the camera was hidden. The killer didn't know it was there. Maybe the woman didn't know it was there either. But then how would Blanca know? Or maybe the tape didn't show the murder at all. Maybe it was just a sex tape. Just? What was she saying, just? A sex tape made on the night of the murders would be just fine. The problem, however, was obvious. Traci knew she couldn't use the tape without getting into deep shit with LAPD. So how was this going to play out?

As if she was reading Traci's mind, Blanca said, "You will have to give it to the police, sooner or later."

"Yeah, I don't see any way around that," Traci said, reaching for the tape.

Blanca pulled it out of Traci's reach and said, "Do you have children?"

"No. And I certainly wouldn't show this to them if I did," Traci said, misunderstanding the point of Blanca's question.

"I have a daughter," she said. "She starts college next year. She wants to be a TV reporter, and she says you are the best in the market. She wants to go to USC, just like you."

"Does she?" Traci was beginning to get the drift.

"This morning? I called my daughter and told her what I had found. She told me I could trust you to do the right thing."

"Well, I'd be happy to write a letter of recommendation for her. I know the dean of the school of cinema and television. It's a great program."

"Yes." Blanca nodded. "And very expensive."

"Ohhh." Traci said, "You know, as a matter of fact, I've been thinking about funding a scholarship for deserving young women."

Blanca smiled and handed the tape over. "My daughter said you might want to make a copy of this before we give it to the police."

Traci took the tape and said, "She's a smart girl, your daughter. She'll go a long way in this business."

Chapter Forty-three

"I said stop, and I mean it," Agent Parker said.

Klaus stopped. "Okay, relax."

"I'm as relaxed as I need to be." Parker gestured with his gun. "Now what's that in your hands? Pepper or something? What do you think, this is like a Roadrunner cartoon? Just drop whatever it is, so we can get on with this."

Bob looked at Katy and saw the fear in her eyes. He also saw more eye makeup than he thought she should be wearing, but for now he'd have to let that go. Most teenage girls weren't equipped to deal with this sort of situation. But Katy wasn't like her peers and Bob knew it. For all her guhs, duhs, and what-evers, Katy was smart and tough when the situation dictated. She was resourceful and her motor was always running. Bob flattered himself by thinking she got that from him. So he wasn't surprised to see that, in addition to being frightened, she was also calculating, trying to figure her best response under the circumstances. After their narrow escape from New York, Klaus had drilled the Dillon family in a variety of defensive tactics and escape strategies in case anything ever happened. Bob made eye contact with Mary. She nodded, then looked at Katy.

Klaus could see they were evaluating and considering their options, so he kept his hands up and said, "Think this through, Agent Parker. It will be difficult killing five of us in a confined space like this. One of us is bound to get to you before you have finished. And every one of us, even Katy, knows how to kill bare-handed. I trained them." He nodded at the gun. "And if you somehow manage to shoot us, without suppression on that .45 someone will hear something. Like the unemployed gun nut two doors down or, even worse, the cops could show up and start shooting. It will be a mess."

Out of nowhere, Katy let out a blood-curdling scream, shocking everyone in the room.

Agent Parker jerked so violently that he just about fired the gun. "What are you screaming about?"

"Put the gun down," Katy said, moving to her left. "Or I'll do it again."

Mary said, "Somebody's bound to hear it too." She began drifting to her right.

Father Paul began moaning and he started to wobble, as if he understood what they were doing. He listed into Agent Parker who pushed him back to an upright position. The priest's eyelids began to flutter unnaturally. His mouth opened and, in a ghostly voice said, "Isaiah."

"What's wrong with him," Bob asked, pointing at the priest. "He doesn't look so good."

"He's been fasting," Mary said. "Hasn't eaten in three days, I think." She moved toward the kitchen. "I'll get him something."

"No! Don't worry about him." Agent Parker waved the gun around while pointing at the couch with his free hand. "Everybody just sit. Klaus, let's see what you got. Don't mess with me. I don't want a bunch of cayenne in my eyes."

"Bob's right," Klaus said, nodding at Father Paul. "The man looks ill." He wondered who this guy was and what he was up to. Did he know what the rest of them were doing? Was he trying to help? Or was he a killer, like Parker said, trying to get his own advantages?

Katy put her hands on her hips and said, "Isn't somebody going to do something?" She headed for the phone. "I'll call 9-1-1."

"No!" Agent Parker kept the gun on Klaus while stabbing a finger toward the couch. "Everybody just sit!"

Father Paul's eyelids stopped fluttering and he began to hyperventilate.

"He's going to faint," Mary said, now heading for the stairs. "I'll get a cold compress."

"Get back here!" Agent Parker sensed he was losing control of the situation, but he didn't want to fire the gun, let alone shoot anybody since, even in Los Angeles, that would very likely draw attention. He was about to yell something else when he noticed the priest.

Father Paul's eyes appeared to fix on something floating in the middle of the apartment. He seemed to be reaching for it with his bound hands. He looked like some mad character escaped from a Goya painting as he said, "Son of Amoz."

"Seriously," Bob said, "I think there's something wrong with this guy." He pointed at the phone. "Katy, 9-1-1."

"No!"

"I'll get the compress."

"Don't move!"

Father Paul's eyes rolled up into his head. He began to pitch and jerk as if he'd suddenly contracted a religious fever more befitting a Pentecostal than a Catholic. "Isaiah," he said, still reaching into space. "Fifty-eight, verse six."

Agent Parker gave him a bewildered glance. "What?"

"Guh. He's talking about the Bible," Katy said, now drifting toward the door.

"I know that!" He waved the gun again. "Now sit!"

Seized by this sudden palsy, Father Paul's bound hands twitched and quivered in front of him as he said, "Is not this the fast that I have chosen?" He showed the nylon cord tied around his wrists. "To loose the bonds of injustice and to let the oppressed go free?"

Agent Parker turned and said, "You, shut up!"

With his hands already extended, Father Paul struck like a snake, expertly grabbing Agent Parker's wrist, twisting upward, aiming the gun toward the ceiling. He groaned as he made an effective, if arthritic, move with his right leg, taking Agent Parker to the floor on his back. The .45 landed softly on the carpet a few feet out of reach.

Now, Father Paul thought, if I can just reach the gun…

The sudden, unexpected violence caught Klaus off guard and sent adrenaline pouring into his system. Who was this old guy in the priest collar? It now appeared he had been feigning his illness to distract Parker long enough to disarm him. This went a long way toward confirming the notion that he was an assassin here to kill them. Klaus figured he had to do something, and fast.

As the older man tried to get past Parker to reach the gun—a series of moves rendered slow and painful by arthritis—Klaus yelled, "Father!"

Father Paul looked automatically when the title was invoked. He saw Klaus throwing something just before he was hit by what felt like two dozen little punches in the face. Father Paul dropped the gun as he put his hands over his cheeks. "Ow! Jesus!"

Agent Parker got a rug burn as he scrambled across the carpet to his gun. Spinning up on one knee, he aimed at Klaus, then Father Paul, then Klaus again. "All right," he shouted. "That's it! No more bullshit!"

Everyone froze for a moment, waiting to see what he would do.

Father Paul looked like he had come down with the measles, a pattern of red welts covered his face. "What the hell was that?" he asked, peeking between his fingers.

Klaus shrugged. "Pie weights, I think."

Father Paul looked at Bob and, in a tone that seemed to call into question Bob's masculinity, said, "You have pie weights?"

"I bake sometimes," he said. "It keeps the crust from—"

"Enough!" Agent Parker grabbed Mary by the hair and put the gun to her head. "If every one of you doesn't sit down right fucking now, I might actually have to kill somebody!"

Chapter Forty-four

The television announcer slipped into his tabloid voice and said, "The entertainment industry was stunned when Academy Award-nominated director Peter Innish was found dead in his Hollywood Hills pleasure palace with actress Ashley Novak. But is there more to the story? Did Innish and Novak have something in common with Rob Lowe, Pamela Anderson, and Paris Hilton? Find out tonight on *Eyewitness Action News* at Ten when Traci Taylor files her exclusive report with shocking new developments in the case."

The promo was a sleazy montage of shamed celebrities intercut with shots of Traci Taylor posing at unnatural angles while projecting authoritative disapproval. As the urgent soundtrack faded, they cut to Todd Herrera at the anchor desk, nodding seriously at the monitor where he'd just seen what his viewers had. After the moment that was the traditional compromise between showing adequate respect for the deaths of two human beings on the one hand and the needs of television news on the other—about a second and a half—Todd turned to camera three and broke into a bright smile. "But right now, let's go to the Beverly Wilshire Hotel where our own Dan Butler was on hand to see the unveiling of the Academy Award swag bags. Dan?"

They cut to Dan, a short bug-eyed sycophant, standing in front of a backdrop featuring the repeated D/S logo of Distinguished Selections, a marketing outfit specializing in entertainment marketing and corporate gifting. They were most famous for assembling the swag bags for the entertainment industry's major award events. With their specialized knowledge of celebrity needs and their access to cutting-edge products and services, Distinguished Selections got away with charging firms upwards of thirty thousand dollars to have their products or services included in their gift baskets to the stars.

Dan Butler grinned at the camera and said, "Thanks Todd, we're here in the grand ballroom, where just moments ago, the best kept secret in Hollywood was finally revealed." Dan cast his glance down and to the side, inviting viewers to join him in watching what had happened five minutes earlier.

They cut to footage of a man on a stage in front of the same D/S backdrop. He was standing behind an extravagant table covered by a billowing silk tablecloth, flanked by a pair of security guards. Centered on the table was a large glossy pink bag with silk rope handles and the D/S logo on the front. Spread across the table, a hundred thousand dollars worth of products the man had pulled from the bag so far, items ranging from a Rolex Oyster and grand suites for a world cruise on the QMII, to a designer suede-lined leather clutch, matching suede sandals, a cashmere throw, a bottle of Krug Clos du Mesnil, a Baccarat crystal lighter, and a full line of exclusive skin products for men and women, including a lip gloss containing ground diamonds.

Finally there was only a single item left in the bag. The man suddenly assumed the expression of someone about to award the Nobel Peace Prize. He paused to heighten the tension before he reached into the bag and said, "And now the moment you've been waiting for. This year's fragrance is…" He pulled out an elegant jeweled bottle of satin-finished crystal capped by a stylish metered pump of white gold. Holding it aloft like the Holy Grail, he said, "Ladies and gentlemen, Rapture by François!"

The flashing cameras exploded like fireworks on the Fourth. The half-blinded crowd ooohed and aaahhhed and pressed in toward the stage. Others turned to look toward the back of the ballroom where, in a scene that made Zoolander seem understated, oddly angular models came streaming through the doors spritzing themselves with the fragrance before mingling with the crowd while making their necks, wrists, and cleavage available for the sniffing.

Returning to live coverage, Dan Butler stared in wonder at the camera and gushed, "What a moment that was! And with me now, the man who made it all happen, the president of Distinguished Selections, Mr. Charles Browning."

The camera pulled back to introduce the man who had presided over the event. In his mid-fifties, Charles Browning had artificially whitened teeth, weirdly rosy cheeks for a man his age, and the severely disciplined hair and dark suit of a senator or a television packaging agent. Something about him gave the impression that if he hadn't yet sold his soul to the devil, he'd certainly worked out a good deal on a lease.

Dan Butler made a sweeping gesture around the ballroom and said, "What an incredible scene this is," he said. "A galaxy of stars from the world of film, television, hip hop, and rap. You must be very pleased with the turnout." He thrust the mike at Charles Browning.

Mr. Browning broke into a dazzling smile. "It's wonderful, isn't it? We're truly blessed and very excited about this year's gift bag. We think it's our best ever."

"Now, I've got to ask," Dan said. "Four straight years of celebrity fragrances, and now this. What made you go with a concept fragrance instead of a celebrity scent?"

"We just felt the timing was right," Mr. Browning said. "As you know, we do a lot of market research and what we found was that a progressive, tolerant fragrance like Rapture was the perfect match for this year's event."

"Absolutely," bug-eyed Dan gushed. "Now, I've heard the scent described as having an open-minded spiciness with notes of sage and leather. While others are saying it's more of an appeasing blend of evergreen, Moroccan Tangerine, and a hint of gay naughtiness."

"Well, François is the world's leading perfumer, and we asked him to create a scent that satisfied the most rugged libertarian leading men while still luring the free-thinking ingénue. And I think everyone agrees, he captured it."

Dan was nodding like a bobble-head doll. "Mr. Browning, thanks for talking with us. We're already looking forward to next year's gift bags as much as we're looking forward to the Awards."

Mr. Browning leaned in with a wink and said, "Tell you the truth, Dan, I'm looking forward to the after parties. I hear just about anything can happen."

Chapter Forty-five

Agent Parker was the first guy to put a gun to Mary's head in six years. Last time was when that cowboy caught her at the house in Queens, trying to retrieve that piece of her mother's jewelry. Now, with Parker holding not only the gun, but a good shock of her hair, she was unable to turn around when she said, "What do you mean, actually kill somebody? That's what you said you were going to do."

Agent Parker shoved Mary toward the couch where the others were already sitting. He looked at Bob. "Is she always this literal?"

Bob shrugged. "It's one of her charms."

"Wait," Mary said as she rubbed her head. "What do you mean, literal?"

All of the sudden and—to everyone's surprise—Klaus sat back on the couch and laughed as if he suddenly knew everything was going to work out all right.

Mary shot him a stern look. "What is so damn funny?"

Klaus gave a wise squint and a tilt of the head, "Perhaps Agent Parker was being more figurative when he spoke of killing us."

Parker bowed slightly and said, "Thank you." He holstered his gun and took a seat opposite the couch. "And why not? It worked once, right?"

Bob was the next one to get it. "Ohhhh."

"Ohhh, what?" Mary said.

"Duh." Katy rolled her eyes the way she did. "He wants to con that drug lord guy again."

Mary said, "Ohhh." She paused for a moment. "Why didn't you just say so from the beginning?"

"Couldn't take the chance," Parker said. "First of all, you'd have no reason to believe me, right? I mean, I tell you my idea, you tell Bob and Klaus that some guy claiming to be CIA has a proposal. They'd have to be suspicious. Be crazy not to. They'd have to assume I was just some guy out to collect the original bounty, so you'd all disappear. I couldn't take that chance. I needed you to bring me to them. And now, here we are. None the worse for wear."

Father Paul made a grunting sound. His wrists hurt from the nylon cord. His hip ached and his face was covered by red welts.

Mary was still rubbing her head where Agent Parker had grabbed her. She ran her fingers over her scalp and was shocked by how much hair came out in her hand. She leaned over to Bob and said, "Do I have bald spot?"

"Look, it's very simple," Agent Parker said. "I can either kill you and collect all twenty million or I can take the low-risk approach and learn to live on ten. The only difference is a little belt tightening." He smiled. "It's up to you."

Klaus said, "A fifty-fifty split?"

"Seems fair," Parker said. "Neither of us can pull it off without the other. But we've got to move fast. Riviera promised me a forty-five day exclusive to do the job." He gestured at Father Paul. "But five days later, St. Francis of Assassination here showed up, so I suspect Riviera hired Marcel to put the word out. Once it gets around that you're in L.A. and you're worth twenty million, there are going to be more mercenaries in this town than starving actors."

Klaus pointed at Bob. "What did I tell you?"

Bob held his hands up in surrender. "Okay, you were right. I admit it." Then, in more of a mumble he said, "Of course if you assume the worst about everything, sooner or later you'll be right about something."

Klaus stared at Bob briefly, shaking his head. He knew there was nothing to be gained by arguing, so he returned his attention to Agent Parker. "Exactly how do you propose to kill us?"

"Well, now, that's the big question," Agent Parker said. "And I'm open to suggestions. You conned the guy one time, but, what's the expression? Fool me once, shame on, uhhh, shame on you. Fool me, uhhh, can't get fooled again.'"

"Yeah, something like that," Mary said, having made the same mistake in the voting booth.

"This time we'll need more than a few Polaroids and a hat with a bloody hole in it." He held his hands out and looked at everyone. "Any questions or suggestions? Comments? No? Well, that's it. First we've got to relocate you guys and avoid getting killed by whoever else is after you and second we have to figure out how to convince Riviera that both of you are dead and that I'm the one who made you that way."

"Actually, we have a third problem," Klaus said. He looked at Father Paul, sitting silently at the end of the couch. "What do we do with this guy?"

Chapter Forty-six

Father Paul had slipped into a state of contemplation. He sat there, quiet as the proverbial church mouse, his bound hands clasped in his lap. He stared into space, lost in ecclesiastical thoughts.

He believed his prayer had been answered. The fasting had slowed his physical functions to the point that his mind was more in tune with Christ. His heart had bloomed like a flower opening to the righteous path, and he was filled with a sense of divine understanding that made him believe he was ready. He experienced such clarity and resolve as he never thought possible. He had achieved a state of actual grace and the ability to receive God's instructions.

This guidance lifted a mighty burden from his shoulders. He had done the thing he was morally obliged to do. Actually, he hadn't done it, Agent Parker had, but in any event, it was done. These men had been warned of the danger they were in. It was up to them to seek forgiveness for their sins and to abandon their evil ways. It wasn't Father Paul's job to change them. That would interfere with His plan, whatever it was. That Father Paul didn't understand the plan was of no consequence. Only the arrogant believe they can grasp such things.

So he was free to go, free to return to St. Martin's and continue his own work.

Transported by this state of grace, Father Paul found himself deeply troubled by the fact that he had entertained the notion that he might kill two men for money. He was afraid of what this said about him, and this led him to reflect on the nature of temptation and its ability to stir the lower powers of the soul. God, he knew, never intended temptation; he merely allowed it as an opportunity to practice virtue and self-control; such a great God was He.

Satan was the source of the temptation. He had dangled the twenty million in front of Father Paul as a test. Being good at what he does, Satan had made the temptation even more powerful by presenting the two men as murderers and the money as a way to help those in need. A moral win-win, so to speak. This way Father Paul would have to struggle even more with the choice. Upon realizing this, Father Paul felt truly blessed that the Lord had permitted Satan to test him this way, as such an event could be considered evidence that God wanted to show Father Paul that he had the strength of faith necessary to overcome temptation to which lesser mortals would succumb.

This revelation resulted in a great sense of relief for Father Paul. He had passed the test. He had not given in to temptation. Notwithstanding the fact that he had never actually had an opportunity to kill Bob and Klaus, Father Paul convinced himself that he had held firm, handing Satan a defeat. He could feel the light of God in his soul. His troubles, resolved. His burden, lifted. He breathed deeply and gave thanks.

But then Klaus said, "What do we do with this guy?" And all eyes turned to him.

And it was at this moment that Father Paul realized his quandary hadn't been solved so much as it had been transformed into something much, much worse.

Chapter Forty-seven

"What do we do with this guy?"

"Good question." Agent Parker considered it for a moment before he said, "What if we turn him over to Homeland Security with his duffle bag, try to sell him as a terrorist?"

Klaus seemed dubious. "Unless you can arrange a terrorist background for him, the story will not hold very long."

"True," Parker said. "And if the story doesn't hold, they'll kick him loose pretty quick."

"Yes, and what do you think his first order of business might be then?"

"That's a fair point. We don't want that."

"Also," Bob said, "wouldn't he just tell them what we're up to?"

Parker dismissed that concern with a shrug and a chuckle. "So? If he tells Homeland Security the CIA is out to fake the deaths of two guys from the DOD in order to run a con on a Bolivian drug lord, they'll either figure he's nuts or it's just us doing our job." He tapped the side of his head as if it was a no-brainer. "In fact that's exactly what we'd say. It's just part of the War on Drugs. They'd swallow that."

Katy came back into the living room. She and Mary had been on the computer in Bob's room looking for a new place to live. "Hey," Katy said. "You ought to see this place we found in Malibu! It's totally pimped! Mom wants to know how much we can spend."

"I don't know yet," Bob said. "I'll talk to my boss tomorrow." He hesitated before saying, "How much is it?"

"It's right on the beach!"

"How much?"

She shrugged. "Like twenty thousand a month or something."

Bob stared at Katy for a moment to see if she was joking.

She kept a straight face and said, "What?"

"Keep looking," he said. "Inland."

Klaus wanted to consider more extreme options for Father Paul. He said, "What about your agency's program, what do you call it, extraordinary rendition? Can you have him shipped to the Saudis or somewhere for 'interrogation?'" He made the quotation marks with his fingers.

"I like the way you think." Parker chuckled again before he said, "An ex-case officer I know, old Bob Baer, said if you want a serious interrogation, you send a prisoner to Jordan. You want them tortured, send them to Syria. You want 'em to disappear, send them to Egypt."

"Egypt, huh?"

"Yeah, but tell you the truth, these days it's hard to get anybody on a rendition flight unless they're a confirmed, hard-core Islamic fundamentalist."

Everybody looked at the jowly, white-haired Father Paul. Bob shook his head. "Even with this administration, I think that would be a tough sell. He looks too much like Santa Claus."

Father Paul looked up glumly. "Maybe you could convince them it was part of the War on the War on Christmas." But no one seemed to be listening.

Klaus said, "What does that leave us with?"

Agent Parker rubbed his chin and said, "We either keep him like a pet for the rest of his life or we exterminate."

No amount of God's light in the soul could keep this from sounding like bad news to Father Paul. But what could he do? So far the truth hadn't worked and he couldn't think of any lies that would do any better. So he stuck with his story. "I'm not what you think I am," he said.

"You're not a killer?"

"I am a priest."

"You've never killed anyone?"

Here, Father Paul paused. He couldn't start lying now. Well, he could, but he decided not to. "Yes, I have killed."

"Ahhh, the plot thickens," Agent Parker said.

"I was in Vietnam. During that misguided war." He paused, as if he couldn't believe so many years had passed. "I was a tunnel rat."

"Ewww." Agent Parker seemed impressed. "The Cu Chi complex? That was some serious hand-to-hand shit. No wonder you took me down so easily."

"Yes, I was trained," Father Paul said. "It was terrible, nerve-wracking business, crawling around in those stifling black holes with a knife, a pistol, and a flashlight. That's all you had, nothing else. When you came across the enemy, it was kill or be killed." He shook his head, sadly, as he thought back on things he had done. "A man can do awful things if the circumstances are right. After what I did, I wanted to atone. That's why I became a priest."

"That's very touching," Parker said. "Any of it true?

"Check my military records," Father Paul said.

"Oh, I will," was Parker's reply. "But if it's true, it just proves you're not only a trained killer but an experienced one." He reached down and gave Father Paul a pat on the shoulder. "You might want to work on a better story."

"Yes, I see your point. But it's my past and I'm stuck with it."

Klaus looked at Agent Parker and said, "Are you sure Egypt is not an option?"

As they continued discussing his fate, Father Paul realized that even if he told the whole story about Richard Mills' deathbed confession, there was no way for him to prove it was true, nor was there any reason for them to believe him. And to complicate matters further, no one knew that Richard Mills was 'The Mongoose.' In the end Father Paul sat mute. He decided it wasn't worth violating the seal of the confessional if it didn't get him off the hook.

The irony, of course, was that the whole mess resulted from the fruit of people's beliefs. Father Paul believed Bob and Klaus were professional killers. Bob, Klaus, and Agent Parker believed the same thing about Father Paul. Both sides were wrong in their beliefs, but neither knew it, and, given the nature of faith, no amount of truth-telling would change anyone's mind. Given all this, Father Paul suddenly felt as if he was back in the tunnels, rounding a corner, face-to-face with the Viet Cong. And he reached the only available conclusion.

Once again, it was kill or be killed.

Chapter Forty-eight

Agent Parker and Father Paul followed Klaus back to his apartment. They locked the priest in the second bedroom. Parker took the fold-out sofa.

Back at Bob's place, Mary was soaking in a hot bath.

Katy was in the guest bed with the blankets pulled up to her chin when Bob knocked on the door and stuck his head in the room. "Hey, Doodlebug, can I come in?"

"Daaad," she said in a sweet, exasperated tone. "I'm too old for that nickname."

He stepped in. "Sorry," he said, sitting on the edge of the bed. "Old habit. You've always been Doodlebug. Want me to start calling you Antlion?"

"Guh, be serious," Katy said.

"All right," he said. "I'll work on it." He gave her a pat on the leg. "You okay? Got everything you need?"

"Yeah, I guess."

He looked at Katy's freshly scrubbed face, relieved to see it free of all the make up she'd started wearing, apparently since he'd moved to L.A. He realized that his objection to all the eyeliner and eye shadow wasn't that it made her look trashy, just older. He was constantly surprised to discover how hard it was to let his little girl grow up. But he knew better than to talk about that so he said, "Pretty exciting day, huh?"

Katy played it teenage cool with a dismissive frown. "Better than average," she said.

"You think you'll be able to sleep?"

"Yeah, why not?"

"I know your adrenaline kicked in during all the chaos. That stuff's worse than caffeine, keeping you awake, even after you think it's worn off." Bob brushed the bangs from Katy's forehead and said, "I just wanted to tell you how proud I am of you. You did really good back there." He broke into a big smile. "I especially liked the blood-curdling scream. I think that really threw him."

"Thanks." Katy seemed simultaneously embarrassed by the praise and eager for more. "It seemed like a good idea at the time, don't you think?"

"Yeah, and your mom said you were great back at home. Said your Weaver stance was perfect."

"She did?" Katy seemed more surprised at her mother's approval than pleased by it.

Bob gave a serious nod. "Most kids wouldn't be that composed in a situation like that, drawing down on an armed man."

Katy hunched her shoulders and said, "Most kids haven't been trained by a world-class assassin."

"Yeah, well, Klaus is proud of you too." He pinched the tip of her nose. "He told me to tell you that."

She smile broadly at that, then, after a second, her face slipped into concern. "What do you think's going to happen? Are more assassins coming after you guys?"

"It's a definite possibility." Bob cocked his head and his eyebrows and said, "You got your gun?"

She rolled her eyes like it was a dumb question asked one time too many. "In the drawer, safety on."

"That's my girl."

Katy looked over to the window. "Is that locked?"

Bob got up, checked the latch. "Yeah, even has one of those rods in the track to keep it from sliding open. Just in case."

"Good. Can't be too careful."

Bob crossed back to the bed, leaned over and kissed her on the forehead. "You scared?"

Her bravado made her say, "No, not really." But that wasn't entirely true. She was afraid the truth sounded too childish, so she didn't say that she was scared of losing him and Klaus. Instead she said, "It's just kinda unreal that, you know, a bunch of assassins or whatever are out there looking for you. You know?"

"Yeah, I know, but listen, it's going to be fine. We've got our own personal CIA agent. Plus Klaus, the three of us, and the Department of Defense. What's there to be scared of?"

Chapter Forty-nine

Mary and Katy spent the next day looking for a new place to live. They got home half an hour before Bob and Klaus returned from work with Thai food.

Agent Parker was on the computer. Father Paul, hands still tied, fast still unbroken, was sitting on his bed drifting in and out of delirium or something close to it while watching *Entertainment Tonight*'s coverage of the deaths of Peter Innish and Ashley Novak.

Mary poked her head into the guest room and said, "Sure you won't join us?" She looked at Father Paul with remarkable sympathy given that she believed he wanted to kill her husband.

Father Paul looked up with sunken eyes, shook his head. "No, thank you. I must continue my fast." He turned his attention back to the perky host of *Entertainment Tonight*.

In the dining room Bob pointed across the table. "Katy, pass me the *gang ped,* would you?" He spooned a heap of the red curry and chicken onto the jasmine rice. He looked at Mary and said, "So, I talked to Mr. Treadwell about the housing allowance. He tried to get us to move to another one of their places but I told him…"

Klaus cleared his throat and looked at Bob as he dipped his *satay* in the peanut sauce.

"…Klaus told him that we didn't want them to have our address on file given that both the CIA and our friend, the priest, had already tracked us down in Corvalis. He said he understood. He okayed three grand a month."

Katy's fork clanged onto her plate. "Guh! Three grand?" She looked at Bob as if he'd told her to sleep in a wet dumpster. "What sort of cheap outfit do you guys work for? You can't get a decent one-bedroom for three grand, let alone a place for all five of us." She pointed at the legal pad on the table next to the *pad prik khing*. "We did the research."

Mary looked at her notes. "Well, we won't be moving to Brentwood, that's a fact. Three grand puts us in Tarzana, Canoga Park, or farther north in the valley."

"Somebody just shoot me," Katy said, before attacking her *pad see ew*.

Agent Parker was fanning his face after accidentally eating a chili. He gulped half of his Thai iced tea and said, "You should know that I confirmed that there is, or was, a priest calling himself Father Paul at St. Martin's in Seattle. The woman I spoke with there said he'd been missing for several days." He drained the rest of his tea before saying, "And my friend at the Pentagon confirmed that a private Paul Anik—that's what our man in there claims to be his name—served in Vietnam. B Company, 1st Battalion, 50th Infantry."

"So he's telling the truth?"

"Well, that's a leap," Agent Parker said as he segregated the rest of the chilies on his plate. "All we know for sure is the guy in the priest outfit knows these things are true. Whether he's the same guy, we won't know until we run his prints through the Pentagon database."

"So," Klaus said, "it would be premature to send him to Egypt?"

"For now."

"Here's what I think," Katy said, pointing her fork at Bob. "Just tell your boss you need at least 5K a month, otherwise you're outta there."

"We'll see, sweetie."

Mary asked how the research was going on the airborne assassins.

"Great," Bob said. "Turns out the giant robber flies are exactly what we—"

A loud knock at the door froze everyone for a moment. Then, with a flurry of hand signals, they pushed silently away from the table and ripped into action, scattering in different directions, arming themselves, taking defensive positions, and dousing the lights.

Another loud knock was followed by a woman saying, "Here's a hint. Don't turn the lights out if you're pretending not to be home."

Bob thought he recognized the voice. Being nearest the door, he looked out the peep hole. He recognized her immediately and sounded oddly pleased when he said, "Oh, my God." With his gun behind his back, he opened the door and stood there smiling like a guy who expected to be told that he'd just won the Publisher's Sweepstakes. He turned on the light, pointed at her and, blanking on her name, said, "It's...you."

Traci Taylor, impressive in a fitted black linen suit with pale pink pinstripes, smiled at the recognition and said, "Why, yes, it is."

Watching unseen from the shadows of the kitchen, Mary sensed an unacceptable level of familiarity between Bob and the attractive and slightly younger visitor. She stepped into view with a gun in her hand and said, "Bob, who is this woman?"

He turned, revealing to Traci the gun behind his back. Bob looked at Mary in disbelief. "Uh, honey?" His tone seemed to suggest she wasn't supposed to be using his real name.

From behind the sofa came: "Guh, way to go Mom." Katy stood up, her gun in plain sight, her eyes rolled back for effect.

In her years as a reporter, Traci had interviewed the leaders of notorious street gangs, organized crime figures, and dangerous gangsta rappers without seeing this many weapons. She held her hands up. "I'm Traci Taylor," she said, leaving off the *Eyewitness Action News*, assuming her name and face would be enough to trigger recognition. When that didn't seem to impress the pistol-wielding woman with the jealous tone, she said, "I don't know this man."

"He seems to know you," was Mary's response.

"She's on TV every day," Bob said. "She's a reporter."

"Really?" Katy pointed her gun at Traci's outfit and said, "I love what you're wearing."

Hands still in the air, Traci said, "Okaaay, thanks. Anyone else behind the sofa with a gun?"

"No, just me," Katy smiled.

"Is there something we can do for you?" Bob asked.

"Not if your name is Bob," Traci said. "I'm looking for Javier Martinez and Juan Flores."

Bob just kept staring at her. She assumed he was star-struck. In truth he'd forgotten his new identity, though the two names did sound familiar to him.

Finally, Klaus stepped out of the darkness of the hallway, gun in hand, and said, "I am Juan Flores."

Chapter Fifty

Traci looked at the handsome man with the European accent and said, "You're Juan Flores?"

Klaus produced an awkward smile which he hoped would convey a south-of-the-border flavor.

Traci looked at Bob. "And that would make you Javier Martinez?"

"We were adopted," Bob said, unconvincingly.

"Both of you."

"*Sí.*" Bob smiled. "By different families. Obviously."

"Obviously." She looked at Katy. "So let me guess, you're little Maria Flores?"

"Nope. Rrrosa Marrrrtinez," Katy said, rolling her R's excessively. She nodded toward Mary. "Mi madrrrre, Senorrrra Lucida Marrrrtinez."

Bob glared at Katy, then turned back to Traci. "What can we do for you?"

She assumed this guy wasn't going to explain why the Lucinda woman had called him Bob, so she said, "I got your names—and by that I mean Juan and Javier—from a Professor Harmon at UC Riverside."

"Harmon?" Bob looked at Klaus who gave a convincing shrug. He looked back at the reporter, shaking his head. "Doesn't ring a bell."

"He told me you two are entomologists working at the DARPA facility in Van Nuys."

"No, I think you've made a mistake. You know, there are a lot of Martinezes in Los Angeles. Flores too. We're in landscaping."

"Uh huh." As Bob continued spinning his landscaping story, Traci looked around the apartment. On the bookshelf to her left she noticed some titles that she read aloud. "*Perspectives in Urban Entomology; Breeding Habits of Phymata Erosa; Invertebrates of North America.*" She turned to Bob for his explanation.

"Oh, yeah," he said. "Landscape work is a lot more than just mow-and-blow these days. You need to know your pests."

The bullshit was knee deep at this point. Traci had no idea why and she didn't particularly care as long as it turned out they knew about bugs. She leveled her eyes at Bob and said, "Okay, Juan, as long as you've got a professional interest in insects, I think you'll want to see this." She pulled out the video tape, then pointed at Katy. "But I wouldn't let her watch."

"Guh," she said, managing to wedge a tone of betrayal into the syllable.

Katy retired to the guest room where Agent Parker was keeping Father Paul from yelling for help. The others sat at the dinner table where Traci Taylor explained how she'd ended up at their place.

"The medical examiner told me—off the record—that Innish and Novak died of acute spider venom poisoning. That led me to UC Riverside where I talked to Professor Harmon, a venom specialist I know from a black widow story I did last year. He said the DOD was doing what he characterized as interesting invertebrate research through the DARPA program, said they'd offered him a position which he'd turned down because of the commute, though he did a little consulting now and then and even supplied a few varieties of spiders. When I asked who was running the project he told me it was Juan Flores and Javier Martinez. So here we are." She snapped her fingers over her head once and said, "Cha, cha, cha."

"That's all very interesting," Bob said, "But you know, spiders are arachnids, not insects."

"Exactly," Traci said. "More interesting still is that the venom that killed Innish and Novak came from a spider that not only isn't native to California, it's not even native to this hemisphere."

"That's bizarre, but—"

"Oh, I haven't even gotten to the bizarre part yet," Traci said. "After seeing this video, Professor Harmon said the spider venom was delivered by insects." She held her hand up, palm out to forestall objections. "Wait," she said. "There's more. And not just any insect. We're talking about insects bigger than any found outside the Amazon River Basin. Insects Professor Harmon said he'd never seen, or heard of, before." She leaned forward onto her elbows and said, "Now, you two wouldn't happen to know anything about that, would you?"

There followed a pause after which Mary pushed one of the Styrofoam containers toward Traci and said, "Would you like some *pad thai*?"

"Maybe later." She stood and gestured toward the living room. "Right now, what do you say we just watch the video?"

Chapter Fifty-one

There were no close-ups, dolly shots, or special effects. Just a continuous wide shot of an actress trying to move her career along. Traci had the tape cued past most of the foreplay which consisted of a tedious exercise involving fresh produce which she assumed was an homage to Mr. Innish's first feature-length film, "How Green the Zucchini."

It made Klaus think of Audrey and their time in and around the bedroom. Unfortunately she'd been on location in Spain for a couple of weeks, leaving Klaus itching for her.

A minute into the action, Traci pointed at the screen and said, "Now watch the side of the bed." On cue, a series of dark images crept in from the bottom of the frame. Traci hit the pause button and pointed again. "Obviously the focus was set for the middle of the action, but these things climbing up the bedspread are clearly not spiders."

She noticed Bob and Klaus exchanging a look which she interpreted as what-the-Hell-are-those-bugs-doing-there? Then she hit Play and the action continued.

As Innish and Novak came down the backstretch of their zesty union, the bugs spread across the bed, forming an irregular circle around the couple. "He's almost done," Traci said, managing to refrain from a joke about submitting the video for Best Short Feature.

A moment later, the lusty on-screen couple collapsed in apparent satisfaction (his real, hers less so). For a moment the only sound on the tape was heavy breathing and a car alarm going off somewhere in the distance. Then the woman said, "Oooo, that tickles."

"Hmmm?" Innish replied, already half asleep.

"Ouch! That hurt!"

He sat up and said, "What the…Jesus!"

"Ohmigod, get 'em off!"

Bob, Klaus, and Mary watched as the bodies began moving again, this time frantic and desperate as they grew tangled in the sheets. But the frenzy was short lived. The paralytic venom disrupted their synaptic transmissions in a few terrible moments. In the stillness that followed, Traci pointed out how the bugs were apparently feeding on the couple. "Professor Harmon said they looked like some sort of new or mutant species of assassin bug injecting a predigestive enzyme into its prey. But he pointed out that the prey was usually another insect, not humans."

Traci popped the tape from the deck. "They feed for a while before climbing down from the bed and disappearing. Of course the camera's static so we don't see anything else." She wagged the tape at Bob and Kluas. "So, now what do you have to say?"

"We are not at liberty to discuss our work," Klaus said. "National security."

"And the boys at the DOD don't take that lightly," Bob added. "I wouldn't mess with them if I were you."

"Those goons don't scare me," Traci sneered. "The only thing I'm afraid of is ending up as the noon anchor in Modesto. This story is huge. It's my career, and I'm not going to let that slip away."

"How do you even know about the DARPA facility?" Mary asked. "Isn't that classified?"

"They don't make a secret about who they are," Traci said. "Just about what they're up to inside. That's why I need your help. Now I don't think you two had anything to do with the deaths of Innish and Novak, but I suspect you know something that will help me break the story."

"We'd like to help," Bob said. "Really would, but the penalties for breaching national security are…unpleasant. I've seen a partial list."

"I understand," Traci said in her most conciliatory tone. "Really do." She rubbed her forehead and gave it a moment's thought. Finally she took a deep breath and said, "Okay. Juan, Javier, Juanita—"

"Lucinda."

"Sorry. Lucinda." She offered a sympathetic look and said, "You guys are obviously hiding something. Maybe you're just hiding yourselves. Maybe you're in witness protection on top of working for DARPA. I don't know. I don't care. But you know more about this than you're letting on and I want to know—I have to know—what it is. So here's the deal." Her look of sympathy dissolved into something more reptilian. "If you don't help me find the connection between DARPA and the deaths of Innish and Novak, I'll see to it that your faces are splashed across every television screen in the world. After that, you'll find it extremely difficult to hide from anybody."

Chapter Fifty-two

Traci Taylor left them to nibble on cold Thai food while considering her offer.

"It's a lose-lose," Bob said for the benefit of anyone not paying attention. "If we don't help her, every assassin on earth is going to know where to start looking for us. And if we get caught helping…" The sentence was too depressing to finish.

"Okay," Agent Parker said. "If you're sure the things in the video are your bugs, then the first obvious question is who took them out for a spin. The second question is why Innish and Novak?"

"Treadwell seems to be the obvious answer to the first," Klaus said. "He is the only other person with access to the transgenics, the Ro-bugs, and the controlling pheromones."

"And the only one with security clearance to remove them from the labs," Bob added.

"But what's his motive? Why Innish and Novak?"

"Maybe he didn't care who he killed," Parker said. "Maybe he was just field testing the weapon."

"In the middle of Hollywood?"

"Why not?"

"That's crazy," Mary said. "Why would he endanger citizens?"

Agent Parker looked at her as if she were a child. "I take it you not familiar with DOD directive 5141.2."

Mary shook her head.

"Directive 5141.2 states that one of the duties of the Director of Operational Test and Evaluation within the DOD is to designate selected special interest weapons, equipment, and munitions as major defense acquisition programs. And every time somebody proposes a potential weapon, someone else has to go test it."

"But on U.S. citizens?"

"Three words for you," Parker said. "Tuskegee syphilis experiments."

"Oh, yeah," Mary said, remembering only vague details. "But that was a long time ago."

"Went on for forty years," Parker said. "Didn't stop until the early 1970s, and then only because they got caught." He ticked off some of the other examples: the Jewish Chronic Disease Hospital case, the Willowbrook studies, and the BZ tests.

"All that was military research?"

"Ultimately," Parker said, "everything is military."

Chapter Fifty-three

Based on personal experience and a cursory review of the past few years, it didn't take the group long to reach the conclusion that professional hit men in pursuit of twenty million dollars were far more likely to get their shit together and cause trouble than the U.S. intelligence community, so Bob and Klaus agreed to do some poking around at the DARPA labs.

The only problem was they didn't know what they were looking for. Traci Taylor said she wanted to know about the various projects Treadwell was funding, hoping something might help her develop a theory to connect to the Innish and Novak murders. "But," she said. "I don't want you to reveal anything that might be considered a threat to national security. Just tell me if any of the projects seem out of the ordinary."

To which Bob had said, "As compared to transgenic insects that follow robots around and deliver deadly spider venom?"

She flashed her meat-slicer smile and said, "It's like pornography. You'll know it when you see it."

At lunch the next day, Bob and Klaus marched into Joshua Treadwell's office without an appointment. Bob held up an official-looking document and said, "We need a minute."

Treadwell glanced at his watch. "That's about all I've got." He pointed at the document. "What's this about?"

"Office pool," Klaus said.

Treadwell looked at his calendar. "It's too early for the basketball tournament, isn't it?"

"Academy Awards," Klaus said.

Bob pointed at the form. "We're just doing the top seven categories. Best film, actor, actress, director, supporting roles, and best original screenplay. Ten bucks a head. Whoever gets the most right wins the pot or splits it. You in?"

"Sure, what the heck." Treadwell slipped ten out of his wallet and traded it for the form.

Klaus put the cash in an envelope and said, "Get that back to us before Sunday."

They spent the rest of the afternoon collecting money from the other researchers while checking out their projects. They started in Unit D, their own building. In addition to the lab where they created the transgenic assassins, there was another for breeding the bugs. So far they had nearly a thousand of each type. There was another lab used for the large-scale manufacture of synthetic pheromones. Unit D also housed the Micro-Air Vehicle project, as well as related research programs, including the nanotube sheets and the artificial muscles.

Next door, in Unit A, was a research group dedicated to advanced tactical high-energy chemical lasers, and the platforms to house battle management and beam control subsystems. Two floors up from that was the Pulsed Energy Projectile Project.

After kicking in ten bucks apiece and complaining about *Star Wars* losing to *Annie Hall* in 1977, the researchers explained that they were looking into the sensory consequences of electromagnetic pulses emitted by laser-induced plasmas. "It's designed to produce pain and temporary paralysis," one of them said. "It's an electromagnetic pulse produced by the expanding plasma which triggers impulses in nerve cells. We're looking for the optimal pulse parameters to evoke peak nociceptor activation." No amount of thoughtful nodding could hide the dumb-as-a-sack-of-hammers expression on Bob's face, so the scientist said, "In other words, to cause the maximum pain possible."

Unit B was known as the Directed Energy Project, a group working on explosively pumped flex compression generators, or more simply, a device that fired man-made lightning bolts.

The thing was designed to take the energy of high explosives and convert it into bursts of electromagnetic energy sufficient to disrupt electronic devices.

Unit C was home to several projects related to the creation and application of what they referred to as metamaterials, substances designed to bend electromagnetic radiation, radio waves, and visible light. Stealth fabrics engineered at the submicroscopic scale so they neither reflected light nor cast a shadow. Several of the labs in Unit C were clean rooms, so Bob and Klaus had to don the requisite white coveralls before passing through the air locks. It was like stepping into an olfactory void. The highly filtered atmosphere was constantly recirculated through high efficiency particulate air and ultra-low penetration air filters so there were virtually no odors in the labs. It took forty-five minutes to collect two hundred dollars in this hyper-clean environment, after which they removed their coveralls and stepped back outside with a member of the metamaterials research team who was taking the rest of the afternoon off.

After nearly an hour of olfactory deprivation, Bob's sense of smell was keen. He sniffed the air and noticed Klaus doing the same. The metaresearcher smiled and said, "Oh yeah, you'll be hypersensitive for a little while. Never realized the valley had this many smells, did you?"

"I'm only getting one thing right now." Bob sniffed again and looked at Klaus. "Do you smell…livestock?"

"If by livestock you mean manure, yes."

"Oh, that's the basement project," the meta-researcher sneered. "It's more like a 4-H club than serious science, if you ask me. We don't associate much with them."

"What are they doing?"

"Tell you the truth, I don't even think they know. They converted the bottom level of the underground garage into a breeding facility and brought in a load of hay and some cows."

Bob looked at him curiously. "Cows?"

The researcher nodded and said, "Mooooo."

Chapter Fifty-four

As Leon put on his tux—an Italian one-button notch Loro Piana—he had no way of knowing that what would happen that night at the Academy Awards would make all of Hollywood forget about the deaths of Peter Innish and Ashley Novak. And he certainly didn't know that something would happen after that to make an even wider audience forget about both events.

What Leon did know was that his local contact had tracked Bob and Klaus to a corporate apartment complex in the west end of the San Fernando Valley. He also knew that Lauren Carneghi was picking him up in twenty minutes and that neither Hell nor high water was going to keep him from attending the Academy Awards. Besides, there was no hurry. It wasn't as if he planned simply to knock on their doors and gun them down. He would have to spend days or even weeks on surveillance before making a move. There was too much at stake to be hasty.

He stepped into the cool California night under the dark awning in front of the pink hotel, feeling like Humphrey Bogart. A limo waited. The back window gliding down released her voice. "Hello, handsome," she said. Leon ducked into the back seat where Lauren handed him a crystal tumbler with one cube of ice and two fingers of the whiskey he liked. She was slinky and shimmering in an elegant peach and mauve beaded gown by Ferretti, a simple pearl, gold, and coral necklace, and Christian Louboutin satin bow shoes.

"You look extraordinary," he said.

Peering over the top of her glass with a devilish glint, she replied, "You ain't exactly chopped liver." As the driver pulled out to Sunset Boulevard, Lauren reached over and tweaked the angle of Leon's bow tie. "So," she said. "Who do you like for best picture?"

He looked unsure. "What are my choices?"

She laughed, slapping his arm playfully without spilling a drop. "Do you know what some people would pay to go to the Academy Awards?" She shook her head. "And you don't even know the nominees of the big category. You're a Philistine."

"I'm kidding," Leon said before taking a sip of the whiskey. "I know everybody keeps saying *Pole Position* is going to sweep, and I really like *Please, Mrs. Henry*, but my money's on *Drifter's Escape*. The WGA liked it and I think it would have won the Golden Globes except for all the ad money the studio poured into the trades. Plus I have the feeling that the Academy wants to make up for not nominating his last film, which I think they know was a mistake."

Lauren leaned closer as if to examine something she'd never seen before. "Who are you? Two weeks ago you didn't know a treatment from an outline and now you know how much the studios are spending on Oscar campaigns."

"I'm a quick study," Leon said. "How about you?"

"I'm a pretty quick study too. *Please, Mrs. Henry* is good, but I like *Buckets of Rain* for best picture," she said. "It's got the sort of scope the Academy tends to go for. Plus it did great on the festival circuit, and it won the SAG award."

"How about *Altar Ego*?"

Lauren shook her head. "First of all, comedies never win best picture."

"What about *Annie Hall*?"

"Okay, they rarely win. And it's not that *Altar Ego* is a bad movie, but the whole twin brother, identity-switch thing is so, I dunno, so Patty Duke. Plus they released it too early in the year. I don't think it has a chance."

"It's a funny story, though," Leon said. "Great casting and deftly directed. Feel good picture of the year."

"Listen to you."

They spent the rest of the drive discussing their predictions for the top categories. They also talked about some of the second act problems Leon was having with his script. Lauren had some ideas Leon thought were interesting, and she said she loved what he'd come up with so far, and she swore Brad Pitt would, too. When they pulled up to the theater, Lauren leaned close to his ear and whispered, "Just think, a year or two from now? You'll be walking that red carpet with a nomination for best original screenplay."

And, as he looked out at the paparazzi and the velvet ropes and the bright lights, he allowed himself to believe it might be true.

Chapter Fifty-five

Over the past few weeks the buzz for *Pole Position* had spiked. *Variety* and *Hollywood Reporter* predicted it would take at least six of the top awards out of its eight nominations. So everyone in the auditorium was stunned each time the presenter said, "And the award goes to…" without following it with the words, "*Pole Position*."

The crowd gasped louder with each loss as if every voting member in the audience thought they were the only ones who had said they were voting for it but had done otherwise in the privacy of the voting booth. It came as a complete shock to those in the business that, with the exception of Achievement in Sound Editing, *Pole Position* was shut out of the Academy Awards.

The surprise winner was *Altar Ego*, a wildly popular identity-switch-romantic-comedy featuring twin brothers, one of whom was a priest, the other a self-centered ad executive. They showed a clip from the film, the scene where the priest has just returned from Africa with an unknown illness. He was talking to his twin.

"If I knew what it was," the priest said, "I wouldn't need to see a doctor to find out."

"You'd still be asking for money though, for medicine or surgery or something."

"I'll pay you back."

"How? You took a vow of poverty!"

The crowd roared with laughter. In the end, ad exec loans insurance card to brother. Brother dies leaving a $400,000 hospital bill. Ad exec is forced to put on the priest outfit, after which he falls for a woman pretending to be a nun, after which he has a spiritual awakening that resonated with movie goers to the tune of $235 million in domestic box office. *Altar Ego* went on to win Best Film, Best Director, Best Actor and Actress, and best adapted screenplay, based on the original novel.

Most of the audience was so stunned by this turn of events that they forgot about Peter Innish and Ashley Novak. But they were reminded during the brief eulogy the producer felt obliged to include at the last minute because there hadn't been time to re-edit the annual *In Memoriam* film montage. The actor who played one of the gay race car drivers in *Pole Position* gave the eulogy for Peter Innish. He wrapped up by saying, "He died far too soon."

At which point Lauren leaned over to Leon and said, "Hell, he died about two weeks too late. If he'd died sooner, he might have won Best Director out of sympathy."

Chapter Fifty-six

The A-list after-parties are held in a stretch of West Hollywood known as Oscar Alley. Several venues in close proximity. Opulent tents pitched to expand capacity for extravagance. High security, celebrity chefs, and more stars than the sky.

Leon and Lauren would attend a party held in one of these sprawling tents, 80 feet by 160, its interior dressed to convey Hollywood dreams. Tables draped with white Ultrasuede, elaborate ice sculpture and waterfall centerpieces, and a special effects projection that transformed the ceiling into the aurora borealis with planets and stars drifting overhead so convincingly you'd think you were lost in space.

The tent was pitched by a professional crew from Hollywood EvenTents. That afternoon, as the electrical system was installed, a man from the company arrived. He had a dozen white metal containers, each the size of a hat box. He attached these with a wire to the one-inch carbon steel tent stakes, explaining to the curious security guard that they were electronic monitoring devices to let them know if any of the stakes were tampered with or were otherwise losing stability during the event. An hour later, under the big top, the same man was installing several other devices in the tent's overhead framing when the security guard approached and said, "Hey, what's that?"

The man climbed down from the ladder and showed him. "Automatic aerosol dispensers." He pushed a button, sending a fine mist drifting toward the guard. "One of the sponsors wants their fragrance in the air during the event."

The guard sniffed the air. "That's nice. What is it?"

The man opened the container. "Something called Rapture by François."

◇◇◇

Eight hours later, Leon found himself taking it all in, conscious of maintaining nonchalance. He considered himself worldly, not easily impressed. He'd been to lavish parties in the capitals of Europe. He'd rubbed shoulders with royalty, international sports stars, and political leaders—he'd even killed a few—but none of that prepared him for Hollywood.

It wasn't the insane crush of screaming fans and the paparazzi shouting the names of the celebrities as they made their way up the red carpet into the tent. A loud and tacky exhibition of idol worship, unexpected in its ferocity, perhaps, but without any emotional impact. What took Leon by surprise was the curious and powerful force that true movie stars emitted like radiation. The effect was weirdly intoxicating. The high difficult to resist.

The true meaning of presence and magnetism hit Leon when someone bumped him from behind and he turned to find himself face-to-face with Lauren Bacall.

Lauren Carneghi, who had stopped to air-kiss a director she was courting, missed the exchange with Ms. Bacall. But a moment later, as they ordered drinks, Leon recalled the moment for her. He said, "She looked me over as if I was something she might purchase. Then she said, 'My, but you're a handsome devil.' In that voice of hers. Then she narrowed her eyes and said, 'From now on, watch where you're going.'"

"What did you say?"

Leon's face went blank. "I don't remember. I don't know if I said anything. I was—"

"You were star-struck," Lauren said, smirking.

"That voice," Leon said, with a dreamy look about him. "I mean, it was her. Talking to me."

"You'll get over it."

A jazz quartet on the round stage in the middle of the tent was playing "I'll Remember April." Clint Eastwood was nearby, nodding his approval. Leon escorted Lauren through the crowd, past Jack Nicholson, Angelica Houston, Will Smith, and Jennifer Aniston, all of whom seemed to notice Leon, as if they sensed something about him, as if he had a presence too. Or at least that's what Leon led himself to believe.

A moment later Lauren got a mischievous look in her eyes and she said, "Let me ask you a professional question." She looked around the tent, then ducked her head toward him and whispered, "Would this be a good place to kill someone?"

Leon seemed momentarily confused, as though she had asked about something outside his area of expertise. "What? In here?" The look on his face changed as he surveyed the space, looking over the heads of the crowd, considering options, measuring distances, and conjuring circumstances. After a moment he said, "First. Hard to get a gun past security. And harder getting back out after using one." He nodded toward one of the food stations. "You could take one of those knives, hope to get your target alone but that seems unlikely in here. And messy."

A passing waiter stopped, offering a tray of hors d' oeuvres. Lauren took one, Leon didn't. The waiter moved on. As Lauren lifted the appetizer to her lips, Leon said, "Barbados nuts."

She covered her mouth to say, "No, I think this is a *gougere* with potato and herbs."

"No." Leon smiled. "You come in with the caterer. You bring Barbados nuts. Very tasty, but their oil inhibits protein synthesis in intestinal wall cells. Kills in fifteen or twenty minutes by which time you're long gone. Of course the trick is making sure your target eats the right appetizer."

Lauren wasn't sure whether to believe him. But then she looked in his eyes and saw that he was telling the truth. Something about this dangerous man appealed to her. She did her best Lauren Bacall as she said, "Well, just so you know, I think you could talk me into putting just about anything into my mouth."

Chapter Fifty-seven

At midnight, the doors on the white metal boxes silently opened. The bugs, hungry and agitated after so long without a meal, made a tentative move to the outside world, their antennae probing the air for cues to a food source. Inside, the overhead aerosol dispensers released a fine mist of the fragrance. Pssst. The molecules instantly set antennae to twitching and the bugs advanced quickly on the tent, slipping under the flap by the hundreds from every direction, seeking the source.

Leon and Lauren were on the dance floor, about fifty feet from an actor by the name of Lawrence Roberts who was lurking in a shadow against the far wall. He gulped a double vodka hoping to dull the words of his famous, Oscar-winning, father. But they still echoed and stabbed like an ice pick, going on about how Lawrence didn't have what it took to make it in film, or anywhere else for that matter. And tonight's failure to win Best Supporting Actor was further proof. From the start, Lawrence had seen the nomination as akin to being hoisted in the air like a pinata—lifted up only so he could be beaten more publicly. And now, five full years after his death, his father was still swinging the stick. Lawrence thought about leaving, finding a bridge and taking the leap. Finally ending it.

While this wasn't the first time Lawrence had entertained suicidal notions, it was destined to be his last. Because as he was standing there in his pool of self-loathing he felt an odd tickling sensation around his ankle.

And a moment later, the bug bit him.

The venom wasted no time before interrupting his synaptic network. As he stood there, trembling and weeping uncontrollably, not sobbing or, indeed, making any noise whatsoever, just tears flowing uncontrollably down his face, Lawrence's agent approached and, seeing how utterly distressed his client looked, gave him a hearty pat on the back and said, "Don't worry, Larry, it's not the end of the world."

As foam began to issue from Lawrence's mouth, the agent offered a cocktail napkin and said, "C'mon, Larry, try to keep it together. You're not the only one who—"

The sting of the bug's bite made the agent jerk as if he'd received an electrical shock. He looked down and didn't know what to make of what he saw; dozens of huge strange-looking insects—the transgenic masked wheel bugs with their muscular mantis-like forearms and the raised dorsal ridges—streaming past his black patent leather Guccis like an army. The tingling sensation he felt around his mouth came with a spastic paralysis that prevented him from speaking. He went into acute respiratory distress at the same time as Lawrence. They collapsed into one another, went to their knees together, then to the ground. From a distance, they looked like maudlin drunks.

Pssst.

Similar scenes began to play out all around the perimeter of the sprawling tent as the spined ambush assassins and masked wheel bugs found their way up pants legs and under designer gowns to perfectly pedicured toes. In a matter of minutes, dozens of people began to exhibit reactions to the envenomation. Laryngeal edema, bronchospasm, pulmonary edema syndrome, hypoxia and acidosis from intercostal muscle spasm and pain, respiratory arrest, neurologic and autonomic dysfunction from alteration of sodium and calcium ion transport.

Within five minutes there were eighteen dead.

The reason there was no stampede at first was that there was nothing obvious from which to run. There was no fire, no gunshot, no screaming. In other words, no galvanizing cue to trigger flight. The people near the perimeter didn't understand what was wrong and the people in the rest of the tent didn't know anything was.

Pssst.

The initial reaction for most upon seeing someone collapse was to back away a respectful distance and hope someone else would do something. This would soon became problematic as it was happening from all directions simultaneously, creating a crush in the center of the tent.

Leon noticed it first. People backing onto the dance floor from three sides, hands over mouths, someone in another part of the tent calling for help. He scanned the room and said, "Something's wrong." Being European, Leon had attended enough soccer matches to know that they didn't want to be caught in the middle of a panicked crowd. So he pulled Lauren off the dance floor, moving toward the perimeter, fighting for a way out.

When the aerosol dispenser released another round of the fragrance, the bugs became more aggressive still. Their hard wing-casings opened, powerful thorax muscles pulled the wings forward, and the bugs took flight, awkwardly, like June bugs (*Phyllophaga* spp.) around a porch light, bumptious and without control, crashing into people's faces and getting caught in their hair.

That's when the screaming began, which in turn started the stampede.

There weren't enough exits to handle the rush. Everything bottlenecked at the doors, and with the panicked crowd pushing from behind, it wasn't long before the crush was so awful you could actually hear plastic surgery coming undone.

Lauren was smart enough to be scared but also smart enough not to panic. She turned to Leon and said, "Got any ideas?"

"Grab the back of my coat and don't let go," he said. He knew better than to swim against the current, so he cut sideways across the flow of the stampede. His goal was to reach the food station with the roast beef. There he grabbed a carving knife and continued pushing sideways, heading for the tent wall. By now Leon had seen enough to know that these huge bugs were the problem. He suddenly thought of Lauren's satin bow shoes and her exposed feet. He stopped abruptly, turned and picked her up, slinging her over his shoulder before she knew what was going on. He charged for the nearest wall, swinging the carving knife like a machete when he got there, slashing a huge hole in the canvas and getting free of the tent.

Outside, he put Lauren on the ground and pointed toward Santa Monica Boulevard. "Run! And watch where you step. Don't let those bugs near you."

"What are you doing?"

But he was gone. Back to the tent, slashing open entire panels of canvas so others could escape. Then he raced inside looking for Lauren Bacall.

Chapter Fifty-eight

Traci Taylor was at a bar in Santa Monica watching a replay of the Clippers game when her cell phone rang. She looked at the display. It was Ronnie, her cameraman, no doubt calling to concede defeat after his Oscar-wagering fiasco. She flipped the phone open and said, "I told you *Altar Ego* was going to clean up. You owe me fifty—"

"Get your ass down to Oscar Alley!"

"You know I don't do entertainment," she said. "Especially after midnight."

"How about possible terrorist attacks?"

"What?" She looked up at the television, Clippers were up five. She said, "Bullshit. I'm watching TV now, there's nothing on!"

"Listen, the 9-1-1 system nearly crashed they got so many calls. Reports of a lot of deaths, some as high as a hundred."

"What?" Traci threw a twenty on the bar and ran for the door. "Give me some fucking details!"

"There aren't any fucking details! That's what you're for! Meet me at La Cienega and Fountain in five."

"On my way."

The story would have broken already but for the fact that many of the entertainment reporters were killed by the bugs or crushed in the stampede while others had either abandoned their equipment or had it destroyed in the chaos.

Most of the people at the party had no idea what had happened, otherwise they might have used their cell phones to report it. One minute everything was completely normal, at least by Hollywood standards, then someone appeared to faint or pass out, also not unusual in a crowd with this many substance abusers, but then some bugs began flying around and all Hell broke loose.

It was a classic example of crowd psychology, with a few members of the group exerting a disproportionate influence over the others, leading to collective suggestibility as a contagious emotion swept the room. Otherwise rational individuals lacking adequate information abandoned reason in the face of some unknown danger. People who—under normal circumstances—would engage in helpful behavior, suddenly assume an every-man-for-himself strategy. This becomes a circular problem as one feeds the other, amplifying the sense of panic and danger, driving people toward irrational and deadly action, not unlike the ways some films get made.

Traci was speeding up Santa Monica Boulevard, flipping from one news radio station to another, trying to find information. But none of them seemed to have reporters on the scene. The announcers were saying only that something had happened, sort of accident had occurred and they were trying to gather details, stay tuned for the big story. Frustrated by lack of details, Traci turned to her police scanner. "Code 13. Multiple 10-52," the dispatcher said. "This is a 10-99, repeat, 10-99." Traci knew enough radio code to decipher this as a major disaster activation, a call for multiple ambulances, an emergency for all units and stations. And sure enough, every few blocks another cop car, ambulance, or fire truck went racing past her, apparently heading for West Hollywood. She hadn't seen anything like this since the North Hollywood bank robbery or the Northridge earthquake.

As she sped through Century City, the dispatcher called a multiple 905 which Traci didn't recognize. She pulled a cheat sheet from her glove box. Nine-oh-five was a vicious animal call.

Multiple vicious animals? Traci looked at the scanner and said, "This is now officially weird."

When she got to La Cienega and Fountain, Ronnie broke the bad news. "Cops won't let anybody within a mile of the scene." He pointed at a row of emergency vehicles in the background. "Best shot we can get is you doing a stand-up with the flashing lights behind you."

Traci was trying to decide how to frame the shot when she heard something coming down the hill. Sirens and somebody leaning hard on a car horn. She turned to see six big, black SUVs with orange emergency lights on the dashboards, hauling ass down La Cienega Boulevard. The cops at the road block hustled the barricades out of the way, letting the caravan pass without slowing down. The doors were marked with the official seal of the State of California. Below that, words that left Traci momentarily baffled. She turned to her cameraman who looked equally confused. She said, "Did that say 'Department of Agriculture'?"

Chapter Fifty-nine

Traci ran her fingers through her hair and adjusted her blouse, then gave a nod that she was ready. The camera lights popped on and Ronnie counted it down. "Three…two…one." He cued her.

"I'm near the corner of La Cienega and Fountain, at the edge of West Hollywood," she said. "Authorities won't allow us any closer to the scene of whatever has occurred at the Academy Awards after-parties. But whatever it was, it has drawn a massive response. In the past five minutes we've seen emergency vehicles from the Los Angeles police and fire departments, LA County Sheriff, and the California Highway Patrol along with dozens of ambulances. I've been told that representatives from the Federal Emergency Management Agency and the Department of Homeland Security are on their way to the scene."

Traci didn't mention the Department of Agriculture as their name conveyed neither urgency nor danger, though it did give her an idea of what to do next.

"Right now," she said, "all we're getting from anyone is a strict 'no comment.' So, for now, all we have are questions and speculation. Was it a mass shooting or a suicide bomber? An angry studio executive or an act of terrorism? Are there hostages? And how many are dead?" She shook her head sadly. "We simply don't know." She looked to the sky and pointed, the camera following to the buzz of a dozen helicopters hovering above the scene. "But our eye in the sky is overhead trying to find the answers. Let's go to Ted in the *Eyewitness Action News* copter."

"And we're out," Ronnie said, killing the lights. "Now what?"

"Now we're going to the valley."

"What's in the valley?"

"A couple of landscapers who are going to help us break the story."

"Landscapers?" He looked at her skeptically. "How many beers did you have?"

"Trust me."

Since there didn't seem to be a cop left anywhere outside of West Hollywood, Ronnie didn't worry about speed limits. As they raced over the Sepulveda Pass, they heard the police dispatcher trying to raise someone from the Department of Parks and Recreation. Traci looked at Ronnie. "What the hell are they gonna do?"

"Let's find out." He picked up the mic and keyed it. "Roger that. What do you need?"

"Insecticide," the dispatcher said. "And lots of it."

Traci slammed her palm on the dashboard. "I knew it!"

"Knew what?"

As they sped down the Ventura Freeway toward the Topanga Canyon exit, Traci told Ronnie all about the bugs—from the video Blanca sold to her, to Professor Harmon, the DARPA labs, and the two Anglos calling themselves Juan and Javier.

"Why didn't you break the story about the bugs killing Innish and Novak? That's a local Emmy right there."

"I know," Traci said. "And I almost did. But when Professor Harmon told me about the DARPA experiments, I held off. I needed some proof, something to connect the bugs to DARPA. All I had was the video, which, I'll grant you, would make some good TV. I mean, c'mon, mutant killer bugs with spider venom? But the real story is the government connection," Traci said. "That's a Pulitzer, not a local Emmy. If I went with the deadly bug story, it would tip off the DOD, they'd lock down, destroy evidence, and intimidate witnesses. We'd never get what we need. So I persuaded 'Juan and Javier' to do some snooping for me. Now it's time to see if they found anything useful."

Ten minutes later Ronnie was hoisting Traci over the gate at the Avondale Oaks, followed by his camera, and then himself. "By the way, don't make any sudden moves around these guys," Traci warned. "Even the daughter carries a gun."

"What? Who are these people?"

"I'm not sure, I'm just saying." She held her hands out in a calming manner. "Be cool."

The lights at Bob's apartment were off. Traci knocked. "Juan? Javier?" She waited a few seconds before she gave the door a couple of good kicks with the toe of her shoe. "Wake up! It's Traci Taylor."

A moment later Bob's groggy voice came from the other side. "It's two in the morning."

"That's right," Traci said. "And if you don't open the door, every television household on earth will know your faces by six."

The door opened, revealing a sleepy-eyed Bob in a pair of boxer shorts decorated with ladybugs (*Hippodamia convergens*). He rubbed his face and squinted at her. "We took your threat seriously the first time," he said. "Can't this wait until after breakfast?"

"Turn on your TV."

Something about the way she said it sent Bob shuffling back into the apartment. He did what he was told, and a few seconds later Traci and Ronnie heard him say, "Uh oh."

Chapter Sixty

Trying to get his pants on while simultaneously calling Klaus, Bob was hopping around on one leg with the phone cradled between his ear and shoulder. "Get up, get dressed, and turn on the television." He paused for the question. "Because something happened with the bugs and Traci Taylor is back threatening us again." Another pause. "No, we're coming down to your place so we don't wake Mary and Katy."

Klaus and Agent Parker were standing in front of the TV when Bob and Traci walked in. Ronnie, bringing up the rear, walked in a moment later with his camera aimed at everyone, causing Klaus and Agent Parker to spin and draw on him.

Ronnie nearly dropped his gear. "Whoa, it's cool. I'm cool. No sudden moves."

"Don't shoot him," Traci said. "He's my cameraman."

Ronnie closed the door behind him and everyone turned their attention back to the news. A CNN reporter was saying, "Authorities are still very tight-lipped about exactly what happened. Survivors interviewed at area hospitals said there was a panic of some sort that led to the stampede. A spokesman for the coroner's office was unable to confirm or deny rumors that there might be as many as three hundred dead. Homeland Security officials have not ruled out the possibility of a terrorist connection and—"

Traci walked over to the coffee table and picked up the TV remote. She hit the mute button then gestured at Agent Parker with the remote as if she might turn his volume up. She said, "Pardon me for asking, but who are you—their pal Pancho?"

Parker was confused for a moment before it dawned on him. He smiled and said, "Oh, that's right, the whole Juan and Javier business." He looked at Bob and Klaus, then pointed at the television. "You know, now that the, uh, cat's out of the bag, so to speak, I don't see much point in trying to maintain the landscaping ruse. Why don't we just put the cards on the table?"

"Yes," Traci said. "Why don't we?"

Bob and Klaus exchanged a glance followed by a why-not shrug.

"Okay, then, I'll start. I'm Agent Nick Parker, CIA. These are my friends Bob and Klaus. Klaus is one of the world's best professional killers."

"Was," Klaus said, looking at Traci. "I retired six years ago."

"Sorry, was," Parker said. "Still, I'd stop threatening him if I were you. People come out of retirement all the time. And Bob here was an entomologist working in the private sector until he took some DARPA funding and started developing insects as weapons for the DOD, ostensibly for use in the War on Terror." He glanced back at the tube. "Though it would appear now that some of what they told Bob might not have been entirely true."

Traci gave Agent Parker a skeptical squint and said, "You know, when you say that, the whole landscaping story sounds more credible."

"Ain't that the truth," Agent Parker said. "But again, here's something that strikes me as funny. If you tell somebody you're an accountant or an attorney, they never doubt you, never ask for proof. But say you're an assassin or you're CIA and nobody believes it." He pulled his ID and showed it to Traci.

"All right," she said. "For the sake of argument, let's say I buy the whole CIA assassin thing. What are you doing with an entomologist?"

"Long story," Parker said.

She aimed her meat slicer at him and said, "Shorthand it for me."

Agent Parker pointed at Bob. "Entomologist breeding assassin bugs for environmentally friendly pest control is mistaken for killer known as The Exterminator," he said. "For reasons not worth going into, Bolivian drug lord puts a ten-million-dollar bounty on his head. Many assassins go to New York to kill Bob, Klaus among them." He pointed at Klaus. "Sequence of unlikely events leads Klaus to befriend bug guy." He pointed back at Bob. "Together they kill a dozen assassins, including my former boss, then fake Bob's death, con the drug lord out of the ten million, and disappear. Six years later, drug lord discovers he was conned, puts a twenty-million-dollar bounty on Klaus and Bob at about the same time the DOD lures them to LA to create deadly insects. Then you walk in."

Traci stared at Parker for a moment before she said, "That's the most ridiculous thing I've ever heard. You expect me to believe that?"

"You asked," Parker said. He looked at the others, feigning disappointment. "See?"

"Hey!" Bob pointed urgently at the television. "Turn up the sound." A grainy photo of one of the spined ambush assassins was superimposed over the shoulder of the CNN anchor.

"This exclusive photograph was taken with a cell phone camera by someone attending one of the after parties. According to reports, swarms of these extraordinarily large insects descended on all three of the major parties in West Hollywood following the Academy Awards. One witness described it in Biblical terms, saying it was like having a plague of locusts visited upon them. Meanwhile, officials with the Federal Emergency Management Agency say they are working to come up with enough buses to evacuate the entire city of Los Angeles."

Everyone in the room paused to wonder how long it would take to evacuate five million people in busses on freeways that rarely moved. When the moment passed Agent Parker looked at Traci. "You were saying something about the ridiculousness of our story?"

Chapter Sixty-one

They flipped through the channels, riveted by the resourcefulness of television news departments. The stations that hadn't received the photo of the bug were forced to trot out some of the more familiar and terrifying alternatives for which they already had a good graphics package.

First was footage from the aftermath of the 1995 Tokyo subway attacks. The reporter was saying, "According to unofficial reports, the FBI is looking at the Japanese religious cult AUM Shinrikyo, or Supreme Truth, the group accused of perpetrating a poison gas attack in the Tokyo subway, killing twelve and injuring thousands by releasing the deadly nerve gas Sarin into the tunnels. But what's the Hollywood connection? For more on that, we turn to our own Kiku Terasaki."

On the next channel they saw a familiar visual, the magnified film footage of a rapidly multiplying bacteria. Tubular, gram-positive sausages of death. "We're getting reports from inside sources this may have been an aerosol anthrax attack. Far more deadly than cutaneous, pulmonary anthrax is nearly one hundred percent fatal. It's unknown how the infection, which usually takes days to kill, acted so quickly, but experts say this suggests a virulent new strain of weapons grade—"

Flipping again, they came to a reporter holding a handful of small brown beans. "Ricin is an extract of these innocuous looking castor beans. The toxin is considered twice as deadly as cobra venom."

Traci understood more than the others. She knew that at this stage, the stations were just grasping for straws and viewers without regard to the facts. She hit mute again and turned to Bob and Klaus. "What about you two? Find anything at the DARPA labs that might shed some light?"

They told her about the high-energy chemical lasers, pulsed energy projectiles, the sensory consequences of laser-induced plasmas, the directed energy project, and the stealth meta-materials, but she remained unimpressed. "Nothing unusual there," she said. "That's it?"

"Well, there was the underground garage project," Bob said. "But it hardly seems military."

"What makes you say that?"

"It involves cows."

Traci looked at him as if she wasn't sure she'd heard correctly. "As in bovines?"

"As in," Bob nodded. "Said they were trying to breed a pure red heifer."

"A pure red heifer?"

Bob and Klaus both nodded. "Mooo," Bob said.

Something clicked in the back of Traci's mind. "Did they say why?"

Bob shook his head. "Said they were getting paid enough not to care or ask. But they were quick to admit that it seemed like a strange project for the Department of Defense."

The words 'plague of locusts,' 'Biblical,' and 'pure red heifer' danced around on Traci's brain until the synapses finally connected and the answer came to her. She looked at Klaus and Agent Parker. "I need a Bible."

The two men shared a wry smile before Agent Parker said, "You're in luck." He went to the guest room and returned a moment later with Father Paul and a Bible which Parker handed to Traci.

She couldn't help but notice that Father Paul's hands were bound with nylon cord. She looked at Ronnie. He shrugged, saying, "Hey, it's not even the weirdest thing we've seen tonight."

"Right," Traci said. "I won't ask why you've got a priest tied up in your apartment."

"Actually we offered to untie him," Agent Parker said. "But he refused. He's way off into the whole self-abnegation thing. Hasn't eaten in days, as far as we can tell. Says he's fasting, you see, trying to help him make an important decision."

"All right," Traci said, surrendering to the madness. "Then I'll ask. Why was he tied up in the first place?"

"We have reason to believe he is an assassin," Klaus said.

"Sent by Opus Dei?" Traci looked at Father Paul. "Are you really a priest?"

Father Paul looked at Traci with his sunken eyes. "Yes, my child."

"Great." She held up the Bible. "Isn't there something in here about a pure red heifer?"

Father Paul held out his hands, taking the Bible from her. Without opening it he said, "The Book of Numbers, chapter 19, verses one and two." And handed it back.

"Thanks," Traci said. "Allow me." She flipped to the appropriate page and started to read, "'And the Lord spake unto Moses and unto Aaron, saying,' yada, yada, yada, 'Speak unto the children of Israel, that they bring thee a,' here it is, 'bring thee a red heifer without spot, wherein is no blemish, and upon which never came yoke; And ye shall give her unto Eleazar the priest, that he may bring her forth without the camp, and one shall slay her before his face.' Yada, yada, yada." She closed the book and said, "Okay, what's that supposed to mean?"

Father Paul used his thumbs to point at himself. "It means nothing to me, I'm Catholic. But it's a passage of great eschatological importance to certain sects of Protestantism."

Traci put one hand on Father Paul's shoulder, the other on her chest. "Look, Father, I'm the liberal media elite, okay? Essentially an agnostic with atheist friends. I don't subscribe to *Eschatology Monthly*. What's the red heifer got to do with anything?"

"Many evangelicals believe that the Temple Mount is the sight of the first Temple of the Hebrews, destroyed by King

Nebuchadnezzar and later by the Romans. They believe Jesus will return to earth only after the temple has been rebuilt. But religious Jews aren't allowed on Temple Mount because it's been defiled by war for so long. The only way around this, and therefore the only way to get the temple rebuilt, according to The Book of Numbers, is to be purified by the ashes of a pure red heifer."

As he said this, Traci had started to nod slowly. "Now I remember," she said, slapping the scriptures in the palm of her hand. "There was a story on this a few years ago, pre-millenialist cults. In Texas, a bunch of Christian Zionist cattlemen in cahoots with fundamentalist Israelis, trying to breed one of these things. I thought they'd done it."

"So did they," Father Paul said. "But it started sprouting white hairs and the rabbis declared it wasn't pure. So it was back to the drawing board."

"Which is apparently in an underground garage in Van Nuys," Bob said.

"And they need the red heifer before they can build the third temple?"

"Yes."

"So Jesus can return?"

"Right. So He can do battle with the Antichrist on the plain of Armageddon."

"And they're in a hurry for this to happen?"

"Oh yes. Certain evangelical Christians and fundamentalist Jews believe it is their solemn duty to do whatever they can to speed the Apocalypse. That's why they're trying to create this pure red heifer. To help bring about the end of the world."

There was a long, uncomfortable, silence as everyone considered the implications of the U.S. government and or the military working toward such a goal.

Finally, Bob said, "Holy cow!" All eyes turned slowly toward him. He gave a weak shrug. "Somebody had to say it."

Chapter Sixty-two

The reading from the Book of Numbers reminded Klaus of something. On a hunch, he picked up the Bible and opened it to the beginning, where God created the heaven and the earth without form, and void and darkness was upon the face of the deep. His eyes skimmed silently over the words as he tried to get at the thing hiding in his mind.

Meanwhile, Traci was pacing the room, trying to put the puzzle together. Her instinct told her the pieces connected, but failed to say how. Perhaps she just needed to rotate them until they lined up and fit. She said, "Now, this Joshua Treadwell, is he just your boss, or is he in charge of the whole shebang?"

"I suspect he reports to someone at the Pentagon," Bob replied. "But he's the guy in charge of all the projects we know about, from acquisition to funding to termination if he doesn't like how it's working out. That's the thing about DARPA. It's designed to have one guy in charge, no bureaucratic oversight, so they can deliver what they call 'quick reaction' projects."

"What do you know about the guy?"

"Well, he sucks at picking the Academy Awards," Bob said. "He was oh-for-seven in the office pool. He drives an SUV the size of this apartment, with an American flag sticker in the window, a support-the-troops ribbon on the bumper, and one of those adhesive fish symbols—"

"The ichthus," Father Paul offered.

"Right," Bob said. "The ichthus with 'truth' written inside, eating the fish with 'Darwin' written on the inside."

"All right, so he's a Christian conservative," Traci said. "What's his background? His schooling? Does he have hobbies? I mean, who is he?"

"We've never socialized with him," Bob said. "Just seems like a pretty strait-laced family guy. But I'll say this; it looks like he gets his hair cut two or three times a week."

"Ahhh," Traci said. "The Eagle Forum look. Hair so done you can stick a fork in it." She nodded. "Okay, I'll run a background on him."

"Wait a second," Bob said. "This isn't about Treadwell per se, but you might want to look into the death of a guy named Lloyd. Worked for a company called Atypical Resources."

Traci's head snapped back like she'd been hit by Tom Sizemore. "What?" Said in a mixture of disbelief and frustration. "Lloyd who? How did he—? When?"

Bob looked at Klaus. "Hey, did you get Lloyd's last name?" Klaus, still reading Genesis, shook his head absently. Bob looked back at Traci. "He was killed by the bugs. It was an accident, unless you think a chimpanzee can have intent."

Traci wasn't sure if it was the newly revealed death of the man named Lloyd or the vague reference to the potential culpability of a lower primate in the matter that got her there, but at that moment she reached the end of her rope. She took a deep breath and turned to Father Paul, who was having a silent conversation with St. Eramus, the patron saint of abdominal pains, who was disemboweled in Formiae, Italy, around the year 303.

"Father, forgive me," Traci said. "But I'm about to sin."

Without really looking her way, Father Paul waved his hand in the sign of the cross and said, "Whatever."

Traci turned and punched Bob in the chest. "Goddammit!" she said. "What other little secrets are you hiding?" She punched him again, advancing on him as he reeled backwards. "How many deaths have there been? How many more species are you going to introduce to your narrative?" She faked one more punch, just to make him flinch, then stood there pointing a finger at him so hard it looked like her nail might pop off.

"Sorry," Bob said, rubbing his chest. "I forgot about Lloyd until just now." He explained what had happened that day in the hangar up to and including the stern talking-to administered by the men in the dark suits.

"Okay, that's it," Traci said. "I'm going public with the story that the military is behind the bugs and the deaths. And you're going to help."

Bob's hands shot up in protest. "You want us to be whistle-blowers?" He shook his head. "No way. If we come forward with what we know, we end up in prison, or worse. Right?" He looked to Klaus for agreement but he was still lost in scripture.

"And if you expose them," Agent Parker said. "You'll screw up my chances to con Riviera. Now, I've never lost ten million dollars before, but I suspect it's the sort of thing that would make me want to kill. You, specifically."

"No, you're right," Traci said, untroubled by the death threat. "Besides, we're better off if they still have access to the DARPA labs as this goes forward." She began pacing again. "Okay, I'll go back to Professor Harmon, get him on the record about the bug research, the job offer, and his comments on the Innish tape. But we've got to find something that connects your boss to all of this."

Finally Klaus put his finger on a line of text and read aloud: "And God said, Let us make man in our image, after our likeness: and let them have dominion over the fish of the sea, and over the fowl of the air, and over the cattle, and over all the earth."

"What?" Agent Parker said, "You think there's a connection between dominion over the cattle and the red heifer thing?"

"No," Klaus said. "Something else. A connection to Treadwell. His personalized license plate. G1V2628. Genesis, Chapter 1, Verses 26 and 28."

"He's a dominionist," Father Paul said.

"A what?"

"Christian reconstructionist," Father Paul said. "Similar to the dispensationalists in many ways. If I understand it correctly, they want to end the separation of church and state, replace democracy with a theocracy ruled by literal readings of the Old Testament, and abolish all government social programs and regulatory agencies. They believe Christ will return only when they have prepared the world for him."

"Prepared it how?"

Father Paul said, "Perhaps you should ask him."

Chapter Sixty-three

The first thing Traci thought when she saw the police cars parked in front of Boyce Hall was that Professor Harmon was being questioned about the bugs. She figured that someone, somehow had already made the connection. The good news was that she didn't see anyone else from the media, so it looked like she still had the scoop. But there was bad news around the corner in the form of the ambulance and the coroner's wagon, only one of which would be needed.

There was a cop standing at the door. He was shooing away the gawkers but seemed to be allowing other students into the building. Traci stopped and opened her satchel. She pulled a rubber band and put her hair up in a bouncy little pony tail that was enough to let her pass as a graduate student. She talked her way past the cop at the door and made a beeline for the stairs at the far end of the hall. Professor Harmon's office was on the third floor. She emerged from the stairwell and fell in behind a group of undergrads who were talking in urgent whispers as they walked down the hall. One girls said, "I heard it was the Brazilian huntsman." The others let out a collective, "Ewwww."

Traci peeled off the group as they went into one of the labs. She continued down the hall to Professor Harmon's office. She saw the EMTs from the ambulance leaving empty-handed, which gave her some hope. She approached the beefy guy from Campus Security who was guarding the door. She stuck her chin toward the commotion and said, "What's going on?" She tried to look past him but he side-stepped to block her view.

He said, "Can I help you?"

"Yeah, I'm supposed to meet with Professor Harmon about my thesis." She hoisted her satchel as she tried to remember the titles of the books on Bob's shelf. "*Perspectives in Urban Entomology.*"

The guard pointed down the hall behind Traci. "You need to speak with the department chair," he said. "They're taking care of all that."

"Why, is Professor Harmon sick or something?"

"Or something," the guard said.

"Oh, my God, what happened?"

The guard lowered his voice. "From what I've heard, the professor got a little careless with one of his experiments."

Traci put her hand to her mouth with a convincing gasp. "He got bit?"

The guard nodded.

"Is he going to be all right?"

The guard shook his head just as the medical examiner wheeled the gurney out the door, sheet over the head.

Chapter Sixty-four

In a town built on hero-worship, Leon's status as an honest-to-God action-hero was currency Lauren wanted to spend quickly. His cool fearlessness in the face of danger and the rumors about his past as an honest-to-God assassin for a foreign government—rumors spread by Lauren—had him at the top of everyone's must-meet list. That he was said to be writing the most original and authentic screenplay ever about a professional killer was the cherry on top.

Lauren and Leon arrived at Paramount Studios two days after the Academy Awards. Everything seemed to be business as usual, except the guard at the gate said they could park in any of the reserved spaces on the sheet of paper he gave them, a list of the studio executives and the stars with deals on the lot who hadn't survived the parties.

They were meeting with Vicki Roberts, the head of the studio, a tall, energetic brunette who had worked with Lauren years ago at Creative Artists and later at Warner Brothers.

Vicki stood when Lauren walked into her office. "Oh, Lauren," she said, coming out from behind her desk for a shoulder hug and an air kiss. "I was so glad to hear you were okay. I was— Oh." She looked past Lauren at Leon, apparently startled by his good looks. She smiled, gave a little nod, then looked back at Lauren. "I thought you were bringing the writer."

"This is the writer," she said. "Leon, Vicki. Vicki, Leon."

Vicki took in a sharp breath. "Oh!" Her eyes grew wide and she took Leon's hand in both of hers, holding it warmly. "My God, it's a pleasure to meet you," she said. "I'm honored. What you did was remarkable, so incredibly brave. The studio thanks you." She put a sincere hand over her heart. "I thank you."

Among the many people Leon saved two nights ago was the young star of a $175 million-dollar action picture based on a breakfast cereal icon, Sir Chock-a-Lot, a medieval knight who spewed hot chocolate from his lance while in pursuit of fair maidens. It was a project Vicki had championed from the start. Had the star died at the party—3/4 of the way through shooting—and they'd had to reshoot, it would have been with a bullet through the studio's head.

Vicki turned to Lauren and said, "You didn't tell me he was so...gorgeous." The last word squeezing out from between mock-clenched teeth.

Leon felt his ego getting hard as she stroked it. While mildly embarrassed by the flattery, he was mostly falling for it. Even after the dramatic events of two nights ago, he found himself in an odd state of wonderment to be on the lot of a major Hollywood studio, a lot where everyone from Cecil B. DeMille and Mary Pickford to Eddie Murphy and Tom Hanks had done work. To find himself the center of attention in the offices of the head of the studio was intoxicating stuff.

Leon went to move for the sofa but Vicki stopped him. "No, stay there." She kept looking at him, moving around him, framing his face with her fingers now and again. "Before writing and your...other job," she said, "did you model? You must have."

Leon smiled modestly. "No, I'm afraid not." He cut his eyes to catch his reflection in the window.

"Please, forgive me for staring," Vicki said, gesturing for them to sit. "But you must get this sort of thing a lot."

"Same reaction I had, first time I saw him," Lauren said. "When he walked into the Polo Lounge, I nearly took a bite out of my martini glass."

Leon and Lauren made themselves comfortable on the leather sofa. Vicki sat on the edge of an armchair, leaning forward. "Listen, I appreciate your coming in light of everything that's happening. This whole thing is so surreal. I mean, they found another eighteen people dead this morning in the Hills, and all of them in the business. It's just awful, unless you're looking for work."

Lauren nodded gravely. "I heard there's not a can of Raid on a shelf for three counties."

"These bugs," Vicki said, "whatever they are, they're scary as hell. And we've lost so much great talent." She sighed and shook her head. "Still, as they say, the show must go on. In fact, I think we have to go on; otherwise it's like letting the bugs win, isn't it? And that's a terrible message to send. So!" She clapped her hands and said, "Onward and upward."

This seemed to be the philosophy at all of the studios. There were already seventeen killer bug projects in active development around town.

"So, Leon," Vicki said. "Lauren has told me all about your script. And I can't tell you how excited everyone is about the project; the buzz is incredible. I understand Brad is absolutely crazy about the noir angle." She looked to Lauren. "What did you tell me he said?"

Lauren launched into a fantastic fable. She quoted Brad praising the screenwriter's refusal to compromise his vision, how the script had integrity and elegance and an economy of dialogue on par with Mamet. She wrapped up with a whopper about Brad proclaiming that the story had more depth of character and stunning realism than anything he'd ever read.

Leon was so taken by the glorification of the script and his writing skills that he forgot that he'd written only about eighty pages, half of which was clichéd beyond repair, while the other half was a jumble of page-length speeches taking ham-handed exposition to a new level. But he saw no advantage in bringing this up, so he just gave a modest smile and said, "Who am I to argue with Brad Pitt?"

Vicki laughed at that and seemed poised to ask a question about the sequel possibilities. And all the while she kept studying Leon's face. She seemed completely taken by some idea she hadn't yet expressed. There was a long silence before she said, "I'm sorry to change the subject, but do you have another meeting within the hour?"

"Nothing we can't change," Lauren said. "Why?"

"Would you indulge me? I would never forgive myself if I didn't take Leon down for a little screen test."

Chapter Sixty-five

The story got out despite the best efforts of municipal authorities. Concerned that news of two species of deadly insects swarming over Los Angeles might have a negative impact on the local economy, the heads of the Department of Tourism and the Chamber of Commerce brought to bear all the pressure they could on the media outlets, trying to get them to kill the story, or at least soften it, but as the head of the Tourism Council was overheard saying, "Keeping this out of the news was like trying to keep the panties on Paris Hilton."

The story broke like the Seventh Street Canal Levee, flooding the world like the Ninth Ward. The cell phone image of the assassin bug was seen by nearly two billion people in the first twenty-four hours. Newspaper circulation spiked and the only thing rising faster than television ratings of the news channels were the ad rates.

There wasn't much to go on, but what there was was fabulous if you were in the news business. Over three hundred dead, all of them connected one way or another with show business. And more were being killed every day as the bugs spread further into the crevices of the Hollywood Hills.

The fact that there were more questions than answers only improved the story. There were few things in the news business juicier than pure speculation. How many bugs were there to begin with? How many are still out there? Where did they come from? Where are they now? What can be done to stop them? Were terrorists involved? Is there a conspiracy to cover up the truth, whatever it is? The Big Story: Target Hollywood. Stay tuned for exclusive coverage and shocking new developments.

Down in Orange County, the conservative stronghold just south of Los Angeles, two members of the Board of Supervisors took the opportunity during a press conference to suggest that the plague of deadly insects was proof that God was fed up with Hollywood's constant promotion of abortion and the homosexual lifestyle.

Some of the media's fair-and-balanced crowd opted to play the terrorism card, as it seemed to have the most traction with their audience, no matter what the underlying story. Others tailored their reports to the more spiritual of the demographic, seizing on the phrases "almost Biblical" and "like a plague of locusts." The CGI departments were working on graphics packages to help frame the story. Ominous flames and symbolic imagery along with a doom-laden soundtrack and the words, "Apocalypse Now!"

The well-organized faithful at Rapture Readiness had started a nationwide email campaign reaching out to all who believed, urging them to come from all corners of the nation, to meet in Los Angeles to celebrate the end.

Though no one saw it coming, this ultimately would ease concerns about a slowing tourist trade. First came the swarm of worldwide media, descending upon Los Angeles in such fevered numbers as to make coverage of the O.J., Simpson, Michael Jackson, and Robert Blake trials seem like a slow day in traffic court. After that, Christians of every Protestant variety began arriving by the church busload. Everything from Pentecostals, Anabaptists, and Calvinists to Charismatics, Premillenialists, and Two-Seed-in-the-Spirit Predestinarian Baptists.

As hotel occupancy rates raced past 90 percent, the tourism and commerce folks began to see the whole thing as more of a blessing than a curse. This silver lining to an otherwise gray cloud, prompting airlines, hotels, and rental car agencies to begin marketing and promotion campaigns appealing to the end-time demographic. Hallelujah and take a coupon! End-time rates and travel packages! All tastefully done of course.

A survivor from one of the parties had smuggled the carcass of a spined ambush assassin past the cops and, after some torrid negotiations, had sold it to one of the cable news channels. Entomologists were universal in their pronouncement that it was a species never before seen. But that's all they could say. They didn't know about the transgenics or the venom.

That was a bomb Traci Taylor would get to drop.

Chapter Sixty-six

Bob and Klaus were summoned to Treadwell's office with an early-morning call. As they left for the DARPA labs, Mary and Agent Parker, posing as a Mr. and Mrs. Smith, went to put a deposit on a four-bedroom in Tarzana. Katy went along as the petulant daughter; Father Paul passed as the aging and slightly demented uncle.

The first thing Bob and Klaus noticed when they walked into Treadwell's office were the three large American flags standing behind his desk, creating a furled backdrop of red-white-and-blue-stars-and-stripes-I'm-more-patriotic-than-you'll-ever-be. Treadwell offered no explanation and they didn't ask. He just steepled his fingers and said, "As I'm sure you know, there are rumors that some sort of exotic insects were responsible for many of the deaths after the award show."

Bob and Klaus exchanged a look of "Rumors?"

"I've seen the photo," Bob said. "It looks like more than rumors."

"Yes, that cell phone image, I've seen that." Treadwell shook his head. "It's troubling, very troubling. It looks an awful lot like Transgenic One, doesn't it?"

Klaus said, "I would say it is a Transgenic One."

"Yes, but…" His shoulders hunched in feigned confusion for a moment. "But how is that possible? Their containers are secure. We've had no break-ins. It just doesn't make any sense."

He tapped the top of his desk a few times with his index finger, then held his hands out for an answer. "I mean, how would you explain it?"

Bob and Klaus had assumed this would be Treadwell's opening gambit, and they agreed it was best to play along with it, first acting surprised at the accusation, then pledging complete cooperation with whatever Treadwell had in mind. Bob went for vaguely incredulous when he said, "What are you suggesting?"

"Well, they're your bugs," Treadwell said. "You're the only ones with access and an understanding of how they work. But for the life of me I can't imagine any motive."

Bob put a hand to his chest. "You think we had something to do with this?"

Treadwell narrowed his eyes. "You understand I have to ask."

"Absolutely," Klaus said. "It is just part of your job."

"Thank you. It's nothing personal," Treadwell assured them. He was just going through the required motions. "I'm sure you had nothing to do with it. Still, we'll have to announce we're conducting a thorough investigation."

"Of course," Bob said. "We'll take a polygraph if you'd like."

Treadwell acted as if the suggestion insulted him. "No, that won't be necessary," he said. "The investigation's mainly CYA. I'm likely to get some heat from Congressional oversight people. Nothing unusual. I'll assure them you've both taken and passed the test, that you're cooperating fully, et cetera."

Bob leaned forward, all the sincerity and concern of a good team player. "We'll do whatever you need us to. We're behind you a hundred percent."

Nodding, with a big smile, Treadwell said, "I'm glad to hear you say that. Really, I know I can trust you. If those jackals in the press get wind of this, we'll have to show a united front, deny everything, and stick to the talking points."

"Just give us the script," Bob said.

"Atta boy."

"You know, I was just thinking," Bob continued. "However it happened, the bugs are out there. Perhaps we should do something to stop them before they spread too far."

The idea hadn't crossed Treadwell's mind before now. He gave it a moment's thought before saying, "You think that's possible?"

"I have no idea," Bob said. "But it seems like something we ought to consider."

Treadwell sat back, warming to the idea. "Come riding in like the calvary, to save the day?"

"I think you mean cavalry," Bob said. "But yeah."

"That's good," Treadwell said. "I like it." He pointed at Bob while looking at Klaus. "That's what I love about his guy. Always thinking: what if?" He tapped the side of his head. "I'll write a press release that says we're working on something to help stop these things. It's a good PR move, shows we're part of the solution, not the problem. Makes us that much harder to attack in case the press stumbles across something that leads them to our door. Meanwhile, if you're approached by anyone asking questions about your work?"

Bob pointed at him and said, "Deny everything."

Chapter Sixty-seven

At six o'clock sharp, the urgent and orchestral *Eyewitness Action News* theme blasted from televisions across Southern California. The logo swirled onto the screens as the announcer intoned, "Here, with an *Eyewitness Action News* Special Report, is Traci Taylor."

The logo dissolved to a medium shot of Traci standing in the midst of a vast sea of flowers, candles, teddy bears, and handwritten notes—the shrine to the celebrities killed by the bugs. Traci walked slowly toward the camera with her no-nonsense gaze as she said, "It was a story-line straight out of a horror film, only this time it wasn't made *by* Hollywood, it happened *to* Hollywood. Over three hundred killed by two new species of deadly insects. The question on everyone's mind: Where did they come from? The answer is both complicated and terrifying."

Cut to Traci standing on a sidewalk on the southern edge of Van Nuys airport, facing away from the camera. In the background, she watched a Gulfstream 400 touch down on the runway before she turned to face the camera and said, "The story begins with a man by the name of Lloyd Thursby, a part-time actor and full-time driver for a company called Atypical Resources. According to his agent, Norm Robinson, Lloyd disappeared several weeks ago while making a delivery here, at the Van Nuys Airport. Lloyd's car was found at his apartment. The delivery truck was returned to the company. He was not admitted to any area hospital. So what happened to Lloyd Thursby? The answer may shock you."

Cut to a location in the Hollywood Hills. Traci, standing at the end of a familiar driveway. She said, "A few days after Lloyd Thursby went missing, I was here reporting on the mysterious deaths of director Peter Innish and actress Ashley Novak. Police say the cause of their deaths is unknown and still under investigation. But according to high-level sources at the coroner's office, while the cause is known, it remains hard to believe."

The camera pulled back to a medium shot of Traci holding a video cassette. "Like many celebrities before him, Peter Innish secretly filmed his bedroom activities. This video was taken the night he and Ashley Novak were killed. We must warn you, this is graphic footage. Children should not be allowed to watch."

Cut to the video of the lovers collapsing in bed after sex. Using a Telestrator, Traci highlighted the transgenic assassins as she narrated, "Here we see something crawling up the bedspread. This is the first known footage of the so-called assassin bugs. Watch as they surround Innish and Novak. Ashley is the first to feel something."

As the sound was somewhat muffled, their words were captioned on the screen:

"Oooo, that tickles."

"Hmmm?"

"Ouch! That hurt!"

"What the…Jesus!"

"Ohmigod, get 'em off!"

As the couple began to thrash in the bed, the image froze, then squeezed into the upper left corner of the screen, revealing Traci Taylor sitting behind the anchor desk on the *Eyewitness Action News* set. "After obtaining this video, I showed it to Professor Zac Harmon, an entomologist at the University of California, Riverside. He told me these things appeared to be a new or mutant species of predacious insect known as assassin bugs. But Professor Harmon was unable to explain what prompted them to attack humans, let alone how they were able to kill. While the first question remains unanswered, my source at the coroner's office says they were able to kill because these insects apparently did the impossible. They delivered the venom of a spider that lives only on the eastern coast of Australia. The Sydney funnelweb."

The insert shot changed to an overhead close-up of what looked like a black tarantula.

"So how is it that an insect can transmit spider venom? For that, we turn to the world of biotechnology and transgenics."

Aided by some graphics, Traci gave an overview of the science and how it allows the transfer of traits from jellyfish to mice and from moths to apple trees. They cut back to Traci at the anchor desk with Professor Harmon's photo over her shoulder.

"When I asked about this, Professor Harmon acknowledged it was theoretically possible to transfer traits from arachnids to insects. In fact he told me about a project on which he had consulted involving both assassin bugs and the Sydney funnelweb spider. The project, he said, was run by the Defense Advanced Research Project Agency, a branch of the Department of Defense that maintains facilities—among other places—in a hangar at the Van Nuys Airport where Lloyd Thursby was last seen."

Even without watching, you could tell Traci's eyebrows had arched.

Cut to a medium shot of the entrance to the University of California, Riverside. "After the attacks at the Academy Awards parties, I went back to see Professor Harmon."

Cut to footage of the sheet-draped gurney being wheeled out of Boyce Hall as Traci's voice-over continues, "Only to find him the most recent victim of a suspicious death, the result, we're told, of alleged carelessness with the venomous spiders he has worked with for a decade without a single mishap. Ironic coincidence? Our investigation has uncovered shocking connections between all of these events, connections that suggest this was more than mere happenstance."

Cut to Traci walking through the parking area of a nondescript office park. She stopped in front of a building with the words Atypical Resources on the door.

"The connections begin with Atypical Resources, the company Lloyd Thursby worked for before his mysterious disappearance. A company spokesperson would say only that they were in the business of satisfying unusual requirements for military research and testing operations. But is that all they do? A search of public records shows that Atypical Resources is also a holding company for two other businesses in completely unrelated fields."

Cut to insert shots of legal documents with the pertinent language highlighted. "Among the companies Atypical Resources has acquired in recent years is Distinguished Selections, a niche marketing firm specializing in branding opportunities in the entertainment industry and best known for assembling the so-called swag bags for events like the Academy Awards. Another recent acquisition is Hollywood EvenTents, the company that provided the tents for the A-list after-parties where the bugs attacked. In our search of public records we uncovered several other intriguing, and troubling, facts. First: the CEO of all three of these companies is a man named Charles Browning. Second: a surprising address where copies of all corporate correspondence were mailed. The third fact, we'll get to in a moment."

Cut to a split screen showing (1) the bland front of Atypical Resources, (2) The Rodeo Drive entrance of Distinguished Selections, and (3) the light industrial exterior of Hollywood EvenTents. "First we spoke to the people who run the day-to-day operations at these companies. None of them had heard of Mr. Browning. So we pursued our next lead, an address in the sprawling suburbs north of Los Angeles where copies of all corporate filings were sent."

Cut to a long shot of what looks like a small college campus. "This is the United Family of Calvary Church, one of the new breed of so-called megachurches. It is also where Charles Browning works as full-time legal council. When we contacted his office regarding an interview for this story, we were told Mr. Browning would have no comment."

Cut to the home page of the United Family of Calvary Church website.

"So, what sort of congregation is the United Family of Calvary Church? While their website reveals plenty about the amenities offered to church members—a fitness center, a Christian values shopping mall with food court—it reveals very little about the tenets of their faith. So I spoke to Dr. Karen Watson, a professor of comparative theology at USC."

Cut to a medium shot of a pigeon-faced woman in her fifties, sitting in front of a book-lined wall. Professor Watson answered the question with expert matter-of-factness. "They're an apocalyptic, fundamentalist Protestant congregation whose members believe in one of the many variations of end-time doctrine. They hold that Christ will return only when they—evangelical Christians—have prepared the world for Him, a process that involves the 'Christianizing' of America. One of the first steps toward this end is doing away with what they consider the secular entertainment industry, which they believe has a corrupting influence on the nation. This is the same mind-set reflected in legislatures where elected officials pass anti-environmental laws under the logic that there's no point in trying to stave off environmental collapse if the Rapture is imminent. In fact, many of these legislators are actually on the record saying that the sooner we achieve ecological collapse, the sooner Christ will return. Of course there are other evangelical groups who dispute this interpretation of scripture, saying God intended man to be good stewards of the earth." She shrugged and said, "It's an interesting schism."

Cut back to Traci standing by the side of a delivery truck marked with the Atypical Resources logo. "All of this raises the question: Why would a company specializing in fulfillment of unusual contract requirements for military research acquire a niche marketing firm and a party tent supplier? The answer to this was the third intriguing fact we came across in the public records."

Cut to shots of new legal documents with highlighted language as Traci continues in voice-over, "Documents reveal that Distinguished Selections, Hollywood EvenTents, and Atypical Resources are all controlled by the same company. That company is Blue Sky Capital Partners, ostensibly a venture capital firm based in the San Fernando Valley."

Cut to a wide shot of the DARPA complex. Traci walked into frame holding what looked like a thin phone book. "The Southern California directory of venture capital firms says Blue Sky Capital Partners is headquartered in this complex of buildings in Van Nuys. But the sign at the gate tells a different story."

The camera zoomed in on a small sign by the front pedestrian gate. It reads: D.A.R.P.A.

"DARPA," Traci said, ominously. "The Defense Advanced Research Project Agency, an agency whose sole charter is radical innovation and the development of new and unusual weapons technology for the U.S. military. We called Blue Sky Capital Partners to confirm this as their mailing address. We then called the public information officer at the Department of Defense and were told that these DARPA labs are run by a man named Joshua Treadwell, the same man listed as the CEO of Blue Sky Capital Partners. The name rang a bell," Traci said. "I had seen it before…at the website for the United Family of Calvary Church."

Cut back to the website. "Here, on the back pages is a listing of the church's board of directors and various church committees. And here, listed as a board member and as the head of the finance committee was the name Joshua Treadwell."

Cut back to Traci at the anchor desk, the Department of Defense logo keyed in over her shoulder.

"It all adds up to a series of troubling questions," Traci said. "Why is an agency of the Department of Defense pretending to be, or acting as, a venture capital firm? Is it a mere coincidence that they control the three companies with direct connections to the deaths of Lloyd Thursby and over three hundred celebrities? Is it possible the mutant bugs are actually weapons created by DARPA? If so, how and why did they end up at the A-list after-parties in West Hollywood? Was Lloyd Thursby killed in an experiment gone awry at the DARPA facilities at the Van Nuys airport?"

The graphic changes to the U.S. Constitution.

"Given what Professor Watkins told me about the imperative of the faithful at the United Family of Calvary Church to do all they can in their private and public lives to help bring about the Second Coming, it also raises terrifying questions about the flagrant disregard for the establishment clause of the First Amendment, the separation of church and state. Is it conceivable that a few men with strongly held religious beliefs of this nature—men like Charles Browning and Joshua Treadwell—are using these deadly insects in an attempt to 'Christianize' America by doing away with the entertainment industry?"

Flames began licking at the Constitution.

"We offered Mr. Treadwell the opportunity to address these and other questions, but he refused our interview requests, leaving us to wonder what he might be hiding…For *Eyewitness Action News*, I'm Traci Taylor saying good night, and good luck."

Chapter Sixty-eight

Joshua Treadwell and Charles Browning met at the food court at the United Family's shopping mall to discuss perception management options in response to Traci Taylor's special report.

Treadwell's normally rosy cheeks were pulsing with a shade of boiling blood as he struggled to keep his voice down. "You're the lawyer, you tell me. What sort of public records and legal documents led that bitch to our door?"

Browning shot some mustard into his paper basket. "She made it up," he said. "Out of whole cloth. There aren't any public records—well, there may be a couple—but there's no way she'd ever find them. That's how they operate. Public fishing expeditions. They tell lies and half-truths until the whole truth somehow gets uncovered. Then they print a correction after the indictments have been handed down." He dipped his corn dog into the mustard and took a bite.

Treadwell nibbled on a freedom fry and said, "Then that's our angle. We disprove her assertions now."

"No point in that," Browning said. "The toothpaste is out of the tube. The public's seen the documents on TV. That makes them real enough. Besides, it's true."

Treadwell surrendered the point. "All right, so we hold a press conference. Say we conducted an internal investigation that uncovered Bob and Klaus as, I don't know, some sort of terrorist infiltrators." He pointed at Browning. "That's it, a couple of guys who joined the jihad, like that John Walker Lindh kid."

"The new American Taliban."

"Exactly. They infiltrated DARPA and released the bugs into Hollywood as part of some radical Islamic plan to destroy the Godless entertainment industry because…no, I guess that's too close to…never mind."

Browning shook his head while dabbing his lips with a napkin. "Press conference is no good. Can't come directly from you. Looks too defensive," he said. "We need someone else to do this. Independent third party. Maybe one of those think-tank whores with a regular column."

This seemed to put an ounce of starch back in Treadwell's spine. "All right, how about we leak it to William Cooper? He's always happy to play ball for the team. And cheap too. Give him the worldwide print exclusive, all the facts we want put out there. A couple of former mercenaries, men with bounties on their heads, big-time traitors, that sort of thing."

"That's a good place to start," Browning said. "But we don't want it just coming from the right. It'd be nice to see something in the *Times*. We know anybody who can sell them a freelance story?"

Treadwell seemed skeptical. "Two leaks seems a little obvious, don't you think?"

"No, just pay somebody to write an 'investigative' piece like they were on the trail separately. An independent story that fingers these two with a variation of the evidence."

"Judy Rendon's a possibility."

"She's perfect," Browning said. "We give her a 'highly placed source in the Pentagon' or naval intelligence that Williams doesn't get, something like that. The story looks stronger coming from two directions." Browning pushed the bottom half of the corn dog to the top of the stick, dipped it in the mustard and slipped it into his mouth.

"Hey, what about Winston Archer? Can he be bought?"

"Sure," Browning said. "But it's a dumb way to spend money."

"He's already drinking the Kool-Aid?"

"Hell, he's stirring in the sugar."

"God bless him," Treadwell said. "Maybe we could get him to Swift-Boat this Traci Taylor."

"You read my mind."

"Yeah, the usual hates-America, aid-and-comfort-to-the-enemy sort of thing."

Browning pointed his corn dog stick at Treadwell and said, "If it ain't broke, don't fix it."

"Yeah, and if you're not with us, you're against us."

Browning finished his cola and said, "Think it'll work?"

"You kidding? I got two words for you: Mission Accomplished. This is nothing."

Chapter Sixty-nine

Father Paul was at one end of the sofa, his bound hands resting in his lap. Katy was in the middle. Mary was at the other end with the remote, surfing from one news report to another. Agent Parker was standing behind them, eating a lamb shawarma that he'd picked up at a nearby Middle-Eastern take-out joint. From the corner of her eye, Mary noticed Katy passing a hand in front of Father Paul's face. Mary turned and said, "What are you doing?"

"I'm worried about him," Katy said. "Every now and then his lids close and his eyes move around like he's having a dream, but I don't think he's asleep. Half the time he does it with his eyes open." She tilted her head sympathetically. "He kind of reminds me of Granddad."

In fact, the smell of the onion, lamb, and hummus had Father Paul drifting in and out of a vivid hallucination about the torture and death of St. Lawrence, the patron saint of cooks who, after irritating the prefect of Rome in August of 258, found himself strapped to a large grill and laid over a bed of hot coals without the benefit of so much as a dry rub. After being adequately browned on one side, legend has it that St. Lawrence made his famous and cheerful remark, which Father Paul now uttered, "It is well done," he said. "Turn it over and eat it."

"Guh." Katy moved away from him slightly and said, "What-*ever*."

"Just leave him alone." Mary hit the remote again and came across the *Winston Archer Report*. "Oh," she said. "This ought to be good."

Winston Archer had a large radio and cable television audience, a fan base known collectively as Archer's Army. It consisted primarily of bumper-sticker-logic white males over sixty-five, though it skewed slightly younger and with more female appeal among the NASCAR demographic. Their catch phrase, repeated *ad nauseam* by his studio audience and those who called in to his radio show, was "Amen, Archer!"

Wearing his costume of red tie, white shirt, and blue blazer with the flag pin on the lapel, Archer was alternately avuncular and contemptuous as he delivered the news of the day. "Looks like those killer bugs got another dozen last night in La-La Land," he said reading from a sheet of paper. "What do we have here, five actors, four agents, two set designers, and another director." Archer pumped a fist before shaking his head as if contractually obligated to show some degree of humanity, even for those in the entertainment industry. He put the paper down and said, "Is it just me or has anyone else noticed that the only people getting killed seem to be Democrats?"

The studio audience chuckled in anticipation of the punch line.

"I mean, it's uncanny. It's like these darn bugs can smell a lib-brull from a mile away!"

Now they laughed and yelled, "Amen, Archer!"

"Mary?" Bob called from the dining room table. "Could you turn that down?" He gestured at the stacks of entomology textbooks. "We're trying to work here."

Klaus pushed one of the books across the table to Bob and said, "What about pirate bugs?

Bob put a hand across one eye and said, "Arrrgghhh, *Orius insidiosus*." He read about the bug's life cycle and feeding habits.

"They can eat thirty spider mites a day," Klaus offered somewhat desperately. "Perhaps—"

Bob pushed the book back to Klaus. "Way too small," Bob said. "Their beaks probably wouldn't even penetrate the assassins' exoskeleton." Bob grabbed another book and said, "What about the hunting wasps?"

"Perhaps," Klaus said, reaching for the *North American Field Guide to Wasps.*

There were several species to choose from, but they focused on the ones that preyed on shield, wing bugs, stinging the victim to deaden, but not kill it, before laying an egg inside the prey, sealing it in a nest, and letting the larva eat its way out.

"But we'd have to design them to hunt the assassins," Bob said. "I don't think we have that much time."

Klaus nodded. "I still believe the best approach is to bait traps with the cockroach pheromone. If nothing else, it would reduce the numbers and buy us some time."

Agent Parker finished his shawarma as Winston Archer began his interview with a U.S. congressman who, in addition to evading taxes and engaging in mail and wire fraud, had steered deals to a defense contractor in exchange for two million dollars in bribes. He said, "So, Congressman, what's your reaction to what's been happening in Los Angeles?"

The man offered a wry smile. "Winston, I think it just goes to show that even if big government couldn't do anything to fix Hollywood, God sure could."

Winston replied with a wink and a nod before he said, "Now, Congressman, let's talk about this indictment of yours." He paused to sniff the air. "If you ask me, it smells like nothing but partisan politics."

Once again the audience called out, "Amen, Archer!" followed by sustained applause.

Agent Parker reached over the back of the sofa and took the remote from Mary. He turned off the television and said, "Guys, I think we've lost our focus here." He pointed the remote at Bob and Klaus. "Now, I know you're busy trying to save L.A., but there's twenty million dollars on the table and we need to put our heads together and figure out how to make it ours."

"Yes!" Katy slapped her thighs and jumped up. "I was starting to wonder if I was the only one thinking about that." Katy figured her cut was in the neighborhood of five million, and it had been burning a hole in her pockets since Agent Parker revealed his plan. "I've been working on some ideas," she said. "But I've got a question." She looked at Agent Parker. "Like, what kind of proof is he looking for? I mean, he can't expect you to bring the bodies to Bolivia, right? And I doubt he'd come up here, since he could get arrested. So how are we going to prove they're dead? Like you said, Polaroids and a crusty hat probably aren't going to cut it this time."

"No, you're right," Agent Parker said. "That's why we need to—"

"I was thinking either fingers or teeth," Katy interrupted. "If we can prove the fingerprints really belong to them, and I don't know how we'd do that, I'd leave that up to you guys, but if we hand over the fingers, that might work, except he might suspect we just cut them off and they're not really dead, right, they just have fewer fingers." She pointed to Agent Parker. "Hey, do you know if it's possible to transplant fingerprints to other fingers?"

"Katy, we're not going to cut off your dad's fingers," Mary said. "Or Klaus'."

"Guh. Well then you're probably going to shoot down my teeth idea, too."

"Try me."

"I was thinking if we got the jaws of a couple of dead guys, we could phony up some dental records, and how's he going to argue with that?"

"Where do think we're going to get human jaws?"

"Guh, I don't know. It was just an idea."

Chapter Seventy

When the Treadwell-Browning version of the story broke a couple of days later, Winston Archer jumped on it like a scarlet-and-green leafhopper (*Graphocephala coccinea*).

"As good soldiers in Archer's Army, you'll recall the other day I was telling you about that lib-brull wacko, Traci Taylor, trying to blame Christians for the nearly four hundred and fifty deaths in Los Angeles. I'm not making this up, folks, she says God-fearing Christians are at the bottom of this thing. Can you believe it? Now, I've pointed it out before, but this is just more proof that part of the lib-brull press agenda is to demonize people of faith. It's scandalous. BUT, there's good news." He held up a copy of the *Times* along with a glossy news weekly, pointing at the front-page and cover stories. "Fortunately, there are still a few journalists in the mainstream who still go out and investigate to get to the truth. Judy Rendon is one of them; William Cooper is another."

"This story will chill the blood of patriotic Americans," Archer said, waving the articles. "It's absolutely unbelievable, but here it is in print. While that lib-brull chowderhead was out fabricating her Traci-in-Wonderland story, insinuating some sort of insidious plot and slandering two good men, Judy Rendon and William Cooper were out gathering facts. I know, we shouldn't let facts get in the way of a blame-America-first narrative, but, according to these two thoroughly researched articles, the facts are these: the Department of Defense—you remember them, don't you? The men and women who protect this great nation from those who would destroy us—you remember 9/11, don't you? Well, long before the lib-brull press was conjuring their fairy tale, the Department of Defense was conducting an internal investigation into the possible infiltration of one of their agencies by illegal enemy combatants. I'm not making this up, folks. I'm not even sure I could. Don't ask me how these guys got hired in the first place, probably some equal-opportunity requirement. I'm just surprised one of them isn't a black Jewish lesbian."

"Amen, Archer!"

"But in any event, the DOD investigation yielded results. And I'm here to share those results with you. So take a good look, my friends," Winston Archer said. "Here are the faces of the enemy."

Chapter Seventy-one

Within an hour of publication, every news organization on earth was airing the allegations and the photos of Bob and Klaus that were in the articles.

In Bolivia, the story was picked up by *Globo Rural,* though that's not where Miguel DeJesus Riviera saw it. He had his satellite dish aimed at CNN International for several reasons. First because his fellow Bolivians were far more interested in *Padre Coraje,* the telenovela of handsome young Coraje, who moved to Cochabamba from places unknown and, for mysterious reasons, disguised himself as a priest and started working in a local church where he met beautiful Clara Guericco and her wheelchair-bound sister, Ana. He immediately fell in love with Clara, while Ana fell in love with Coraje. In a recent installment revolving around a baptism, Coraje slipped on some holy water, hit his head on the font, got amnesia, and left the nation in a tizzy of anticipation. And *Globo Rural* wasn't about to interrupt that for killer bugs or anything else.

Miguel also preferred CNN because they had so far delivered the news about the insect attacks with a lurid pizzazz he found enticing and, because they had an entertainment bureau in Los Angeles, there was a constant stream of interviews with surviving celebrities.

Miguel had been glued to the tube ever since the killing spree began, sprawled on his sofa staring at the plasma screen. He was so fascinated by the story that he failed to make any connection between these deadly insects and his nemesis, the Exterminator.

But that changed as soon as the photos of Bob and Klaus popped up on the screen.

"These two men," the CNN announcer said, "have been identified by senior intelligence officials as Bob Dillon and Klaus Müller, also known as Bob Landy and Kurt Schickling, and as Javier Martinez and Juan Flores. They are believed to be armed and dangerous and living in the Los Angeles area. Arrest warrants have been issued by the FBI and Interpol."

Miguel leaned forward, his blood pressure already rising. He mumbled, "*Hijo de puta.*"

When his rivals saw this, they would know Miguel had not only failed to avenge his brother's death, but also that he had been conned out of ten million dollars. He would be the laughingstock of Latin America. It was virtual castration. His reputation as a man, ruined.

Feeling a sudden stiffness in his neck, Miguel pushed himself off the sofa, heading for his bar. His phone began to ring, sending a wave of nausea rolling over him. He looked at it but refused to answer. After a few rings, it stopped. As he reached for the scotch, one of his men came into the room and said, "Sir, Hernando Varela is on the phone."

Miguel knew there was but one thing that would damage his reputation more than his apparent inability to exact revenge on his brother's murderer. That would be to exhibit cowardice in the face of the inevitable taunting at his failure. Miguel mustered all the machismo he could, snatched the phone, and barked, "What do you want?"

Hernando laughed and said, "*Ir por lana y volver esquilado.*" Then he started to make some clucking noises.

Miguel felt the intracranial pressure creeping toward a hypertensive crisis. It might well kill him, but he wasn't going to sit quietly and be told he had gone out for wool and come back shorn. He pulled a spicier idiom from his repertoire, saying,

"*Chinga tu madre com pan y vinigre!*" Even though he had never understood what the bread and vinegar had to do with anything.

Hernando stopped clucking, paused a moment, then shouted, "*Concha de tu madre!*"

Between each insult, Miguel, who loved his mother, but not that way, took another slug from the bottle. Scotch dripped from his chin as he screamed, "*Come verga, pendejo!*"

Hernando, who had no intention of eating any such thing, countered with "*Vete a la mierda zorra!*"

Miguel collapsed on the sofa and took another slug. His chest tight, his skin moist and clammy. He said something about having the fire of the sun in his pants and being as hard as a stick before vowing to kill Hernando and his family as soon as he had taken care of Bob and Klaus. He slammed the phone back in the cradle then took another slug before using his cell to call Marcel Pétain.

The Frenchman said he, too, had seen the news and, sensing how upset Miguel was, suggested that he should see it as a mixed blessing. "It's true, your secret has been exposed," he said. "But at least now we know where they are. So I think we should—" He paused, hearing the interruption for call waiting. "Do you need to take that?"

Miguel's mouth was dry as chalk dust, and his chest was squeezing like a vice. But he managed to say, "*Mama pinga.*"

Marcel, whose grasp of the romance languages stopped at the French border, said, "I'll take that as a no." He could almost hear the tiny blood vessels bursting in the whites of Miguel's eyes. "In any event, I assume our friend the Mongoose will see this on the news and that should be the end of that."

"He has had enough time," Miguel said. "I am tired of waiting. It is now an open contract."

Chapter Seventy-two

"I think it's safe to say we're now officially screwed," Bob said.

They'd been watching the news on the latest death toll and the troubling increase of end-of-the-world religious fervor while simultaneously discussing how they might stop the transgenic assassins from spreading and how they might pull the con on Riviera, when Katy nodded at the television and said, "Uh oh."

Their faces splashed across the screen accompanied by the news that they were now wanted as terrorists.

Treadwell had been meeting with reporters to confirm the stories while at the same time going to great lengths to say how disturbed he was that this information had been leaked in the first place. "My office will conduct a thorough investigation to find out who was responsible for it," he said.

"I can't believe I ever trusted this guy," Bob said.

Klaus looked at his credulous friend. "You were the perfect mark."

"The what?"

"He conned you," Klaus said.

"He's right," Parker said. "He knew your weak spot and he hit it. Terrorists attacked your home town, killed people you knew. You wanted to fight them. He appeared to offer you that opportunity in exchange for your expertise and your loyalty. But he wasn't going to get that wearing Birkenstocks and Hawaiian shirts. He had to look the part. The respectable suit, the excessive grooming, the pin in the lapel. All designed to inspire con-fidence."

Klaus said, "He dressed right, said the things he knew you wanted to hear, and he promised a big payoff in the end."

"Of course, the con's usually for money," Parker said.

"Or votes," Mary added, still bitter about previous elections.

"But in this case, the big payoff was the notion that you could actually help fight the war against the terrorists."

"You wanted to believe," Klaus said with a shrug.

Agent Parker gave Bob a slap on the back. "And I'm sure it's just a coincidence that con happens to be the first syllable in conservative," he said. "But we're getting off track. Now that the con's been exposed and Treadwell's put in the fix to forestall any legal action you might have taken against him, we've got to figure our next step."

"We have to disappear," Klaus said as if to end the discussion.

"Worse thing we could do is leave this house," was Parker's response. "Landlord thinks it's me, Mary, Katy, and Uncle Joe. Nobody knows you're here. This is as disappeared as you're going to get."

"Besides," Bob said. "We have to be here if we're going to do anything about the bugs."

Klaus looked at him in disbelief. "Are you under the impression that we will be allowed back at the DARPA labs?"

"We'll figure something out," Bob said.

"In the meanwhile," Agent Parker said. "Let's put on our thinking caps, see if we can't come up with a nice neat con of our own."

With a scheming glint in her eyes, Katy said, "Isn't there, like, some drug that, like, paralyzes you and slows your heartbeat and your breathing so you look like you're dead? What if you, like, went to Bolivia, gave them this drug and—"

Agent Parker shook his head. "I think we'd have problems with airport security, what with your dad and Klaus being wanted terrorists."

"Guh." Katy slumped on the sofa, then just as suddenly she brightened up. "Okay, what if we did like a cool disguise, like, I dunno, like, oh, like Mrs. Doubtfire!"

"Yeah," Mary said doubtfully. "Nobody would notice that."

"Hey, guys, take a look at this." Bob was pointing at the television. A helicopter shot above the intersection of Wilshire and Santa Monica. Tens of thousands of people clogging the wide boulevards for half a mile in all directions.

They cut to a reporter on the ground in the midst of it, "At first glance it looks like a protest march, but these people aren't protesting or even marching so much as simply gathering and testifying. It all started about an hour ago when a small earthquake shook central Los Angeles. Caltech seismologists say the 4.5 magnitude temblor was centered at the north end of the Newport-Inglewood fault."

"Earthquake?" Bob looked at Mary. "Did you feel anything?"

She shook her head as Agent Parker shrugged. "I sure didn't notice."

"I thought I felt something," Katy said.

The reporter continued, "With the death toll in the wake of the killer insects passing six hundred and fifty, and with Protestant religious leaders preaching that the end of time is upon us, the 4.5 quake was all it took to unite these believers on the streets of Los Angeles."

Cut to footage of the crowd with people carrying signs:

"Repent Now!"
"One World Government = Antichrist!"
"Rapture Ready!"
"Jesus Is Coming! Looking Busy Won't Cut It"
"UPC Barcodes = Number of the Beast!"

Cut to an interview with a guy in his thirties, neat and trim, wearing an Amen, Archer! T-shirt. "It's all right there in Revelation," he said with a perky smile. "The four horsemen shall be given power over a fourth of the earth to kill by sword, famine, and plague, and by the wild beasts of the earth. Now I don't know if these insects are a plague or wild beasts, maybe they're both, but it seems pretty clear the prophecies are coming true. Isn't it fantastic?"

The reporter continued, "But it's not all doom and gloom out here. The spiritual fervor that has gripped thousands has also unleashed the spirit of entrepreneurial Angelenos."

The report went on to show savvy merchandisers hawking T-shirts with catchy slogans: "The Rapture IS an Exit Strategy." "Someday Soon, My Prince Will Come." and "Revelation 6: 12-14...Told ya!" Impromptu food booths had popped up as well. Lamb o' God Ka-bob plates and Jesus' All-You-Can-Eat Old Fashioned Endless Bread and Fish Baskets.

They cut back to the reporter saying, "Still, while some are trying to keep the tone light for the apocalypse, others prefer sticking to the classics, offering up good old fire and brimstone."

Cut to a wild-eyed, sweat-soaked, preacher with his sleeves rolled up, waving the Bible and screaming, "The day is coming that the graves will ex-pa-lode as their occupants soar into the heavens!"

Cut back to the reporter nodding at the camera with a grin, saying, "You'll want to be sure to have your camcorder ready when that happens! For *Eyewitness Action News,* I'm Gary Rockwell. Back to you in the studio."

Chapter Seventy-three

Bob was standing by a map of central Los Angeles that was tacked to the wall. The red push pins indicated where the transgenic assassins had killed. Starting with the cluster in West Hollywood, the pattern radiated mostly north into the hills where it began to spread westward more than east. There were a few outliers in Hancock Park but the concentrations were primarily in Beverly Hills, Beverly Glen, and Coldwater and Benedict Canyons. There was also a line roughly along the spine of the Santa Monica Mountains that corresponded with Mulholland Drive.

Bob said, "So we've ruled out aerial pesticide spray, natural predators, and—" He noticed Klaus daydreaming. Bob snapped his fingers a couple of times. "Klaus? You still with us?"

He was staring out the window, unable to concentrate any more on the bugs or the con or anything else, save Audrey, whom he hadn't seen in weeks. Turning to look at Bob he said, "Sorry, what?"

"I was saying that after we rule out these alternatives, the only solution that seems to make any sense are the cockroach pheromone traps, so we need to start talking about design."

Klaus nodded and said, "I need to call Audrey." He reached for the phone. "She needs to know what they are saying about us is not true."

"No can do." Agent Parker pinned Klaus' hand to the table. "Her line's bound to be tapped. We'd be dead or in jail before the five o'clock news."

Klaus pulled his hand free, stood, and put on his jacket. "Well then, I will go see her."

"It'll have to wait," Agent Parker said. "You can't expose yourself now. Someone will see you and—"

"I am willing to take that risk." Klaus crossed the room as if to leave.

"Don't open that door."

Klaus was reaching for the handle when he heard Parker rack one into the chamber of his gun. Without turning, Klaus said, "It would be foolish on several levels to pull the trigger."

"Back away from the door."

Klaus turned in a smooth motion, simultaneously drawing his own gun, aiming at Parker. "If you kill me without proof," Klaus said. "You lose ten million. It would be a waste for things to end that way."

"Doesn't have to," Parker said.

"I need to see her."

"Won't hurt for her to think you're a bad *hombre* for a few days."

"I think it's more than that," Bob said, thrusting his hips to and fro. "He hasn't seen her in a while, if you get my drift."

Parker watched Bob's lewd act for a moment before he turned to Klaus with a look of disbelief. He said, "You'd risk your life just to crash the custard truck?"

Unfamiliar with the idiom, Klaus said, "Crash the custard truck?"

That's when it dawned on Bob. He slapped a hand to his forehead before slowly wiping it down his face. "It's one of the primary drives."

"Of course," Klaus said, as he lowered his gun. "After food and water." He shook his head. "What were we thinking?"

"Well, I know what you were thinking," Bob said. "And it wasn't about bugs."

Agent Parker looked back and forth between the two men. "What did I miss?"

"The solution to the assassin problem."

"Sex?"

"The smell of it," Bob said.

Klaus smiled. "A few molecules is all it takes." He told Parker about a study in which a single caged female pine sawfly (*Neodiprion sertifer*) attracted more than eleven thousand males from the field in four days.

"I knew a girl like that once," Agent Parker said with a smirk. "Think it'll work with your bugs?"

"I know it would work," Bob said. "Only problem is, we need access to the lab to collect the pheromone."

Knowing he wasn't going to make any progress on the Riviera scam until Bob and Klaus dealt with the bugs, Agent Parker pulled his CIA identification and said, "Trust me, that's not a problem."

Chapter Seventy-four

Watching Leon as he lay there in the bed, Lauren couldn't help but think about how dreamy his eyes were as they opened. "Hey," she said in a tender whisper. "How you doin'?"

Leon blinked, slowly, trying to bring her face into focus. "Still a little woozy," he said.

Lauren nodded. "It's going to take a while to wear off. But the doctor said everything went great. Said without any complications, the bandages will come off in a few days."

Leon tried to smile but the muscle relaxants hadn't worn off yet, so he was still partially paralyzed. There was also a slight tingling sensation in his jaw resulting from some damage to a motor nerve during the surgery.

It turned out that while Leon's screen test had gone well, it had revealed a slight imperfection that left him, in the words of Vicki Roberts, half-a-chin shy of George Clooney.

So, after some discussion with Lauren, and a consultation with one of the best plastic surgeons in Los Angeles, who suddenly found himself with a lot of openings on his schedule, Leon had agreed to have a little work done. At the suggestion of a leading casting agent who was a friend of Lauren's, Leon decided that as long as they were doing the chin augmentation, he might as well get the cheek implants and have a little laser skin resurfacing done.

Lauren picked up an ice pack and held it to the side of Leon's face. "For the swelling," she said.

He aimed his bandaged chin at the television. "What's going on?"

"Oh, well, let's see. They identified two guys who they said released the bugs." She flipped channels until she came across the photos of Bob and Klaus. "Here we go."

"Authorities are still seeking these two men…"

Leon just about popped his stitches. "That's them," he said, sluggishly.

"Yeah, that's them all right," Lauren said. "Depending on the newscast, they're either unlawful enemy combatants or innocent citizens framed by the Defense Department in a cover-up."

"No, those are my targets," he slurred.

"What?" She looked at the television, then at Leon. She figured it was just the drugs talking. "You just relax, handsome" she said, her hand tender on the side of his bandaged face. "We're going to make you into a star."

Chapter Seventy-five

Nobody heard the car pull into the driveway. But they heard the door slam shut, launching them into a fiercely choreographed dance, taking positions with guns drawn. Father Paul, being the exception, remained still and mute on the sofa, unfazed by the frenzy.

Klaus took the hall closet, giving him a clear shot at anyone coming in the front. Agent Parker, to the kitchen, covering the rear from behind the fridge. Bob defended the door from the garage. Katy had a concealed spot where the stairs turned and Mary had her back, covering the upstairs hallway in case anyone tried a second-story entrance.

When the knob of the front door began to rattle, Klaus drew a bead. If it was a killer, he thought, it wasn't a pro. Probably some yahoo, saw them when they moved in, like the cable guy, recognized them on TV later. If he came through the door, Klaus had him cold. He adjusted his stance, and slowed his breathing. He was so focused on his aim that he didn't notice, until it was too late, that Father Paul was on his way to open the door. "Hey, stop!"

But it was too late. Father Paul opened it and stepped calmly aside, allowing the intruder to pass. "Padre, how ya doin'?" Traci said as she breezed into the house.

Father Paul offered a weak smile, closed the door, and shuffled back to the sofa, awaiting God's instructions.

Klaus stepped out of the closet, gun down by his hip. He called out to the others, "False alarm!"

"*Hola, Juan, cómo está?*" Traci walked past Klaus with a paper sack in one hand, a large manila envelope in the other.

"You may want to consider calling ahead in the future," Klaus said, holstering his weapon.

"I take it you haven't heard about the government's eavesdropping programs."

The others came into the room one at a time. Traci tossed the paper sack to Bob and said, "I figured it out."

"Figured what out?"

"Why the bugs are attacking people."

Bob pulled from the sack a bottle of Rapture by François. "Is this for Mary?"

"Not unless you want her dead," Traci said.

Klaus took the jeweled bottle from Bob, admiring the satin-finished crystal. He removed the cap and gave it a cautious sniff, thinking it could be a topical poison like chloramine-T or chlordane in a solution. "What is it?"

"Insanely expensive, for one thing," Traci said. "There was a bottle of that in each of the swag bags they gave to the celebrities."

"Let me guess," Klaus said. "It contains pheromones?"

"Bingo." Traci smiled. "Eau de cockroach." She read from the report, "*Blattella germanica* to be specific. All the tents had overhead aerosol dispensers, misting the crowds with the stuff."

"Explaining why Treadwell needed Distinguished Selections for this whole thing," Bob said.

"They assembled the swag bags," Traci said. "Everything in the bag was a pre-existing product except for the Rapture, which, according to François, was made under contract and with specs and ingredients supplied by Distinguished Selections. When François refused to share the specs with me, I took the fragrance to a lab for analysis."

"Beautiful," Agent Parker said. "So that solves everything, right?" He looked at Bob. "You don't have to bother with the traps now."

"What traps?" Traci asked.

After explaining the sex pheromone idea, Agent Parker pointed at Traci and said, "So now you do a product recall story, get the news out that Rapture is a bait for the killer bugs. In the process, you nail Treadwell and get your Emmy. Congratulations. Meanwhile, we collect and haz-mat the stuff before finally move on to relieving Senor Riviera of his money." He clapped his hands together and began thinking of five thousand square feet in Georgetown.

"Actually, no," Bob said, causing Agent Parker to fix him with a stony glare. "We still have to deal with the bugs that are out there."

"Whoa," Agent Parker said. "If they don't attack people without the cockroach pheromone and if we recall all the Rapture, what's the problem? I mean, bugs don't have much of a life span, do they? Won't they just die in a few days or weeks?"

"We don't know if they're capable of breeding with existing assassin bugs," Bob said. "And if they are, we don't know what traits they might hand down."

"There could be another problem," Klaus said. "Treadwell may have released both males and females. They could be breeding already."

Chapter Seventy-six

Resigning himself to the fact that no one was going to help plan the Riviera con until the bugs were under control, Agent Parker decided to help speed that process. He tracked down one of Professor Harmon's former associates who was now teaching at U.C.L.A. After explaining the hows and whys of his former associate's murder, Professor Julius Lang signed on.

Given that Bob and Klaus were wanted men and that driving around in a truck with a big bug on the roof might draw unwanted attention, Agent Parker rented a cargo van and stuck the two fugitives in the back. The three of them drove to U.C.L.A., grabbed Professor Lang, then headed for the DARPA lab. On the way, Bob and Klaus explained their idea for the sex pheromone trap.

"No reason it shouldn't work," Lang said. "All we have to do is isolate and sequence the pheromone-binding protein. Then, based on the pattern of the binding protein expression in the bugs, we produce a compound of one or more pheromones. Whichever ones bind to the protein can be eluted, analyzed, and chemically reproduced."

"You've got the equipment for this?"

"Oh, sure." He looked at Bob and Klaus and said, "Now based on the news reports, I assume we want the traps to kill, not just collect, the bugs."

"Yeah," Bob said. "And I've been trying to think of some way to use giant robber flies in the process, but I can't think of a practical way to do it."

The professor gave Bob a sideways glance. "Nearly a thousand dead and you're thinking about using robber flies?"

Bob held up both hands. "No, forget I mentioned it."

"I will," Professor Lang said. "From what I've heard, I think you want to go with something robust from the inorganic category. A contact insecticide, probably some sort of neurotoxic, acetylcholinesterase compound."

"I would think so," Klaus said.

A minute later Agent Parker pulled to the curb in front of the DARPA labs. He told Bob and Klaus to sit tight. Then, with Professor Lang in tow, Parker CIA'd his way into the bug lab.

Watching as Professor Lang collected the female transgenic assassins from the breeder cages, Agent Parker said, "How do you get them to excrete the stuff in the first place? Free drinks and credit cards?"

After a moment Professor Lang said, "You might want to consider seeing a professional about your...issues."

"Nah." Agent Parker waved him off. "That's a can of worms best left unopened."

Chapter Seventy-seven

Traci figured that breaking her news to a national audience would improve her chances for a book deal and a Pulitzer. So she took her latest scoop to MSCBN, one of the cable news channels that functioned as an outlet mall for political punditry with lots of brand-name commentators selling analysis on the cheap.

The highest-rated show on the channel was *HardHeads,* with Matt Christopher. He was a former presidential speech writer who came from enough family money not to have to care about anything beyond his shiny forehead and whether he had spinach between the teeth. He hosted the show with a combination of Ivy League swagger and a sense of entitlement.

"Welcome to *HardHeads,*" he barked coming out of the show's intro. "My guest today is investigative reporter Traci Taylor, who recently broke a huge story alleging a connection between an agency within the Department of Defense, a fanatical sect of Protestants, and the deadly insects responsible for nearly a thousand deaths in Hollywood." He turned toward camera two and said, "Traci, let's start with the recent comments from the majority leader, who suggested that your actions were traitorous and essentially threaten national security."

"Well, first," she said, "I think we should keep in mind that this is the same majority leader who, in his capacity as the chairman of the Senate Subcommittee on Disaster Prevention and Prediction, also recommended that the citizens of Los Angeles stock up on duct tape and plastic sheeting as a means of protecting themselves from these deadly insects."

Matt slapped the desk top. "Oh, that's right," he said, breaking into a wide grin. "I'd forgotten about that already."

"Don't beat yourself up about it," Traci said. "It's impossible to keep track of all the nutty things these guys say on the Senate floor."

"Ain't that the truth," Matt said. "So, Traci, tell us about what you've uncovered on this whole bug thing, because I know one of the complaints the Senator made about your earlier story is that it insinuated connections between certain people and events without having what he called a 'smoking gun.'" He pointed at the lab results and said, "I take it that's what you've got there."

"That's right, Matt. In my initial report, I showed the connection between Blue Sky Capital Partners and the company called Distinguished Selections," Traci said. She then proceeded to connect the dots between Distinguished Selections and Rapture, and finally between Rapture and the bugs.

When she finished, Matt looked like a guy who had just found out about Rock Hudson. "I never would have guessed," he said, shaking his head. "That is wild. Cockroach pheromones, of all things, blended into a fragrance. The way these guys think! You know, it reminds me of something Jackie Kennedy said, at least I think it was Jackie who said people will wear just about anything if it's exclusive enough." He paused, confusion on his face. "Was that Jackie or someone else?"

Traci shrugged.

"Well, doesn't matter," Matt said. "Anyway, given that you made your case, and this sure seems like the so-called smoking gun, are you expecting an apology from the majority leader?"

Traci smiled and said, "No, I've learned to keep my expectations extremely low for the Senator and his esteemed colleagues. What I would like to see, however, is an investigation, a special prosecutor or someone looking into whether an agency of the U.S. government is testing weapons on U.S. citizens. To find out if this was an institutional failure or if there are rogue elements within the DOD who need to be singled out and prosecuted."

"Like this Joshua Treadwell and the other guy, Browning."

"I'd say those two are a good place to start."

"I think that's what the majority leader would call 'playing the blame game,'" Matt said.

Traci shrugged and said, "He only calls it that because he can't rhyme 'accountability.'"

"Ha! Good point. So, anyway, now that we know this stuff is bug bait—and you gotta love that they called it Rapture, don't you? I mean you've got to give them points for cuteness on that—but, anyway, what's everybody supposed to do now—what's the plan? Is FEMA involved in this?"

"No, the folks at FEMA are still drafting press releases blaming state and local officials for their failure to prepare for this eventuality."

His head jerked back and he said, "Get out!"

"I'm kidding, that's a riff on the whole New Orleans thing."

"Oh, right."

"Seriously," Traci said. "I understand L.A. County Hazmat is setting up collection sites in the Beverly Hills, Hollywood, Century City areas so people can bring the stuff for safe disposal."

"This is great," Matt said. "Just great investigative reporting. First and, I guess most important, is that now we know how to keep from being attacked by these bugs. Second, this would seem to clear the two former DARPA employees whose names were leaked to the press and wrongly linked to terrorist groups. Oh, and you gotta love that one of them is named Bob Dillon. I mean, how bizarre is that?"

"Further proof that truth is stranger than fiction," Traci said.

"Now, what about the arrest warrants?" Matt said. "Have they been revoked or quashed, or whatever happens in a case like this?"

"It's my understanding that the issuing court plans to consider this evidence, but until then, they're still wanted men."

Chapter Seventy-eight

"Even if the warrants are withdrawn," Klaus argued, "It does not change anything."

"Sure it does," Bob said. "Then we wouldn't have to worry about being hunted by every city, county, state, and federal law enforcement agency in the country. You can't say that doesn't matter. You just hate to admit there's a positive side to anything."

"Treadwell is not trying to get us arrested," Klaus said. "He simply wants Riviera to know we are alive and in Los Angeles."

"He already knows that," Agent Parker said. "I told him. Well, the part about being alive, anyway."

Mary tried to calm them down. "I think Klaus' point here is that Treadwell knew that making the information public forces Riviera to acknowledge he was conned six years ago, and now he's got to pull out all the stops and open the contract to anybody who wants to try to collect."

"I understand," Agent Parker said. "All of which just helps underline the urgency of my point that we need to get our act together and work out how we're going to gull him the second time."

"I say we disappear first," Klaus said.

Parker shook his head. "Think about it," he said. "Anybody looking for you—professional law enforcement or professional killer—is going to put himself in your shoes and assume you'd get out of L.A. as soon as possible. So not only is this one of the last places they might look, even if they do, it's a big town. Hard to find two people among fifteen million."

"I vote we stay," Bob said. "We lay low, do the traps. See if we can stop the bugs."

"And all the while we can be trying to figure out how to fleece Riviera."

"Haven't we had this conversation before?"

Chapter Seventy-nine

Sergio Esparza was born near the famous Valenciana Silver Mine in Guanajuato, Mexico. The area later became one of the main pork-producing regions of the country. The local feed lots and processing plants were prime sources of employment and held the fate of many local men.

Sergio's mother wanted him to finish school and go to college, but constant goading by friends—during which the issue of masculinity was raised—took its toll on young Sergio and he eventually took an entry level job with the Mexican Swine Confederation, the only game in town. During his orientation, he was led to believe that with his eight years of schooling, he had a bright future in pork.

But with NAFTA came cheap U.S. and Canadian pork imports, followed by a currency devaluation and increased costs of production that sent the Mexican pork industry into the tank. As the downward spiral continued, Sergio was forced to take jobs lower and lower on the industry chain, eventually ending in the slaughterhouse. His job was a gruesome education in violence, blood, and death. And although he was growing immune to the gore, he never did like it all that much, and one day, as they say, the axe just fell.

The slaughterhouse was shut down without warning, leaving Sergio and a hundred other men suddenly unemployed and angry. Over shots of sugar cane liquor, there was a lot of talk about killing Mr. Garcia, the head of the Mexican Swine Confederation who ran off with the pension money. The betrayal left Sergio angrier than the rest. He sat and listened to all the macho declarations about killing Mr. Garcia but no one followed through. They were all talk. The same blowhards who had talked him into taking the goddamn job in the first place, talked him into believing he would rise in the ranks, they even talked him into buying a round for the boys.

Finally, Sergio decided he would do the talking. He stood and announced that if no one else had the cajones to kill Mr. Garcia, he would do it. He passed his hat and collected thirty-seven dollars. And for that sum, he carved the man into spare ribs and roasts and fed him to the pigs.

Since then Sergio had killed journalists and judges for drug lords. And he had killed drug lords for the Mexican government. He didn't care who he killed as long as he got paid. So when Sergio Esparza heard there was a twenty-million-dollar contract on two gringos in Los Angeles, he packed an overnight bag and headed for the border.

Chapter Eighty

Winston Archer had not achieved his lofty ratings by sitting idly by, hoping for the best. As he liked to say when he spoke to his attorney and business manager: Hope is not a strategy.

Pragmatists that they were, Winston and his producer were enthusiastic proponents of audience research. They employed one of the nation's most respected media research companies to do weekly testing to find out how they might reinforce the loyalty of their current audience and how they might expand to reach new listeners.

The most current research showed that Winston Archer's audience was more interested in the events unfolding in Los Angeles than any other news story they tested. Further analysis of the data showed that taking the end-time angle offered their best chance to expand the audience.

"We already own 90 percent of the crowd that wants to hear these two guys are terrorists and traitors," the producer said. "The data also suggests we can pick up three to five points and a few new markets if we give the bug story more of an end-time spin. What's great is, we don't run any risk of losing the pro-terror audience by focusing on the end of the world. Just remember to bring up 9/11 every now and then."

"In what context?"

"Doesn't matter," his producer said. "Just bring it up." He gave Winston a slap on the back and sent him out to the set. "Now go get 'em, tiger."

Coming out of a stirring introduction that featured golden eagles and F-117 stealth fighters soaring over a hill with three crosses perched on top, Winston Archer shot his cuffs, puffed up, and looked at camera one, saying, "Welcome to the *Winston Archer Report*, my friends." He pointed at the lens. "Your source for the truth, the whole truth, and nothing but!"

"Amen, Archer!"

Turning to camera two, he said, "Well, here we go again." He cupped a hand behind one ear, cuing the sound of a toilet flushing. "What's that, you say? That, my friends, is the sound of your tax dollars twirling down the drain that is a special prosecutor." He rolled his eyes to help convey the absurdity of the situation for those who might otherwise miss the point. "Heaven knows how much this is going to cost us, and for what? Because some kook in the lib-brull press has concocted a crazy story about a patriotic employee of the Department of Defense releasing genetically engineered insects on Hollywood."

To the sound of a cuckoo-clock, Archer crossed his eyes and rotated his index finger by the side of his head for a moment before continuing, "And, sure enough, before you can say 'sagging poll numbers,' some desperate lib-brull Congressman has demanded an investigation. Can you believe it? This story is so nutty, nobody in Hollywood would have bought it from Oliver Stone."

They all laughed and shouted, "Amen, Archer!"

"It's just lib-brull business as usual," he said. "More pseudoscience, like their favorite fairy tale, Evil-lution. I mean, think about it. Tell me where you've heard this before. They take something that's a proven matter of fact, like…Creation, as in Genesis, my friends, and then, after the fact, they make up some 'science' to explain it. 'Oh, it's evolution,' they say. And why? Because they want to take religion out of our lives, just like Stalin did in Russia."

The audience offered up a long boooooooooo and a sea of down-turned thumbs. Off-camera, the producer put his hands together and looked skyward in mock prayer. Archer saw him and nodded agreement before he continued, "So this week's fantasy passed off as a 'scientific' explanation about 'transgenic bugs as weapons' is just more of the same. The atheist lib-brulls simply refuse to accept the fact that it may, indeed, be prophecy coming true."

Here the audience broke into sustained and reverent applause while the producer offered two big thumbs up.

Archer basked in this for a moment before holding hands out to quiet the crowd. He said, "Now think about it. Man can create remarkable bombs and missiles and other fantastic ways to kill and maim and destroy, but they can't make anything that remotely approaches the complexity of, say, a butterfly's wing or the eyes of a mosquito. So the idea that this swarm of deadly bugs was made by 'scientists' is absurd. No. Worse. It's blasphemy. Man can't create anything as sophisticated as these things; only God can."

"Amen, Archer!"

His producer stood by with the broad smile of a proud parent. Nobody understood how to do this better than Winston Archer, he thought. This guy was an artist. He was money in the bank. In Archer we trust.

"Now since I'm no expert on the subject of Biblical prophecy," Archer said, "I asked a religious scholar to explain about the deadly swarms in Revelation and in the Book of Joel. He pointed out—and I found this interesting—that the authors of these texts weren't specialists in modern biological taxonomy. He said the original Aramaic word was probably just a generic reference to insects and the bugs that have descended on Hollywood could be referred to correctly as locusts, in a metaphoric sense. And you don't need me to tell you the connection between the coming of plagues and the end of times."

Winston Archer turned to camera three which pushed in on his sincerity as he said, "There are compelling arguments, my friends, that we have lived through the tribulation and the abomination and that the seventh trumpet is ready to sound. And I've got to tell you folks, seeing so many people of faith in the streets of La-La Land celebrating the End Times just warms my heart."

As the audience shot to their feet with a standing ovation, Winston pointed at the camera and said, "Praise His name, we'll be right back after a word from our sponsors."

Chapter Eighty-one

"Whew!" Katy pinched her nose and said, "Something stinks in here."

"Ahhh," Klaus said. "The sweet scent of pheromone-binding proteins."

They were at Professor Lang's lab at UCLA. Bob was putting one of the transgenic assassins into a glass tube connected to a Kovin box so they could measure sensillum-lymph cavities in the bug's endoplasmic reticulum. After he sealed the box, Mary gave him a kiss and said, "We'll be back in an hour or so."

"Don't get caught in the rapture," Bob said.

These days you couldn't go anywhere in Los Angeles without running into the religious fervor that had gripped the public at large. While the massive crowds and rallies were taking place a few miles down Wilshire Boulevard, even as Mary and Katy walked south across the campus, they saw groups of believers handing out pamphlets and huddled in prayer.

A young man tried to hand a leaflet to Katy. "No, thanks," she said. "I'm good." She waved a sheet of paper at him as she sidestepped him. The document consisted of a list of names and a map that Mary had downloaded from the Internet. It was, in a sense, about the end of the world, though not in an Armageddon sort of way. Katy read the list as they walked. "I've never heard of any of these people," she said.

"You've never heard of Marilyn Monroe?"

"Well, duh. Okay, one."

"Dean Martin? Frank Zappa?"

"Dweezil's dad?"

"The original Mother of Invention," Mary said with a nod. "Let's see, who else?" She pointed at the list. "Truman Capote, Rodney Dangerfield, Walter Matthau."

"Oh, yeah." A flash of recognition on Katy's face. "That guy from the grumpy old men movie."

They were heading for Pierce Brothers Westwood Village Memorial Cemetery. The bone yard of the stars, as some called it, was near the UCLA campus, hidden behind a movie theater and lurking in the shadows of a pair of skyscrapers.

They walked down the broad alley that fed the underground garages of the office towers and led to the cemetery gate. As they got closer, Mary noticed the line of parked cars and the somber crowd dressed in black. She stopped and said, "Sweetie, it looks like there's a funeral going on."

It would turn out to be the service for Ian Grayson, a young star who played one of the gay NASCAR drivers in *Pole Position*. He had been killed by the bugs a few days earlier at his home in Benedict Canyon.

As Mary and Katy stood there, a bus with Ohio plates and the words Great Awakening Baptist Church on the side rolled past them, heading for the entrance to the cemetery. The two cops at the gate stopped the bus. One of them approached the driver's side and pointed, apparently telling him to put it in reverse. That's when the door opened and the congregation piled out, led by a man with a bullhorn in his hand. The Reverend Peter McDowell was a leather-faced minister of the old school. "Here we go," he said. "Let them know you by your deeds and your words!"

The congregants carried American flags and signs with slogans like:

"Thank God for bugs!"

"Pray for more dead actors!"

"God damns the Hollywood agenda!"

Reverend McDowell pressed the bullhorn to his lips and announced, "We are here to celebrate the death of Ian Grayson," he said. "Let us give thanks to God for sending another one of them to Hell!"

This was celebrity funeral number sixty-two for Reverend McDowell and the folks from Great Awakening Baptist Church. They had driven from Ohio as soon as they heard what was going on and had made it in time to crash the service for Lawrence Roberts, who was the first actor laid to rest after the bug attacks.

Katy elbowed Mary. "Who are those guys?"

Mary hesitated a moment. "Uh, they're Christians," she said. "Sort of."

"Sort of? I thought it was an all-or-none proposition."

Behind them, a horn honked. Mary and Katy stepped aside to all another bus to pass. This one had Arizona plates and the words Emerging Church of Jesus on the side. When the bus stopped, the doors opened, and the congregants piled out like a military unit, carrying more signs:

"Love thy Neighbor! Leviticus 19:18"

"He that loveth not, knoweth not God—for God is love. John 4:8"

"Depart from evil and do good; seek peace and pursue it. Psalm 34:14"

The Reverend Lew Hopkins, the pastor of the Emerging Church of Jesus, raised his own bullhorn, aiming it at the Great Awakening Baptists. "Stop the hate!" He said. "These rancid, fraudulent Christians defile the name of the Lord and do not speak the true word of God!"

"Okay," Katy said. "Who are these guys?"

"Uh, they're Christians too," Mary said. "Just a different… brand."

The words of the Reverend Hopkins seemed to get under the skin of the folks from Ohio, especially the Reverend McDowell, who pointed a crooked finger at the Arizona Baptists and shouted, "There is but one true path. We have come to cause this evil nation to know its abomination! The foolish shall not stand in thy sight, thou hatest all workers of iniquity," he said, quoting Psalm 5:5.

Katy nudged Mary and said, "Are they all crazy?"

Mary was tempted to say they were just crazy about Jesus, but instead, she said, "Let's just say they hold their beliefs very strongly."

The two groups of Baptists approached each other like lynch mobs, stabbing their signs toward the heavens with each furious step they took. Soon they were face to face, like soldiers in a Civil War battle line fighting—for the time being—with words instead of weapons.

A young woman from Tucson with a baby on her hip quoted Corinthians 13:13. "These three remain: Faith, hope and love," she said. "But the greatest of these is love."

This sentiment seemed to enrage a man from the Great Awakening congregation. He leaned into the woman's face with rancid fury on his breath and countered with Jeremiah 6:15. He screamed, "Were they ashamed when they had committed abomination? Nay, they were not at all ashamed, neither could they blush!"

Here, the rest of the Great Awakening Baptists joined in, shouting in unison, "Therefore they shall fall among them that fall: at the time that I visit them they shall be cast down, saith the Lord!"

As one, the Baptists from Arizona shouted back: "Love they neighbor as thyself!"

"You will burn in Hell for eternity!"

It was unclear who cast the first stone that day, but cast it was. And there was precious little turning of the other cheek after the fists began to fly. They tore the signs off their axe handles and wielded them like the clubs of avenging angels. It was eye-for-an-eye and tooth-for-a-tooth, and there was a great deal of faith-based skull-bashing. As the situation began to deteriorate, a cop called for backup. "And send some paramedics too," he said. By the time the riot squad arrived, television crews from six news organizations had peeled off from the larger gatherings in Beverly Hills to cover the action at the cemetery.

Mary tugged on Katy's arm, saying, "Honey, I think we should cut and run."

At first, Katy resisted. "Wait," she said. Something about the confrontation and the passion of those engaged in it made her mind race. Amidst all the violence and chaos and prayer, Katy had the feeling that the answer to a great question was right in front of her, staring her in the face. She wanted to stay until she understood what it was. But when she got her first whiff of tear gas, she said, "Yeah, let's get the hell out of here."

Chapter Eighty-two

Professor Lang said, "Well, for the past eleven years I've specialized in the identification and synthesis of pheromones, kairomones and other semiochemicals mediating insect behavior."

They cut to Traci for a moment, her head nodding with the standard television reporter's appearance of concentrated interest, before cutting back to Professor Lang saying, "As soon as I heard about the attacks, I started working on these pheromone-based traps." He held one up for the camera, a cardboard pup tent the size of a shoe box. "As you see, the trap itself is very simple," he said. "You've probably noticed medfly traps just like this all over Los Angeles. Obviously these are much larger because the transgenic assassins are so big. But the principal is the same. The pheromone lures the insect inside where an inorganic contact pesticide kills them."

They cut to a map of central Los Angeles. "These red push pins indicate the location of known bug attacks," Professor Lang said. "We'll use this to determine trap locations."

They cut to a row of long tables inside the lab, covered with several hundred traps. Traci said, "Professor, how long do you think it will take you to get all these traps out there?"

"Well, by myself it would take several weeks to do it," he said with a sly smile. "But that's why they make graduate students."

Cut to Traci standing in the foreground, behind her, a dozen graduate students loaded the traps into trucks from the

Department of Evolutionary Biology. Traci said, "Professor Lang and his students hope to have all the traps in place by Tuesday evening. In the meanwhile, they've established a transgenic assassin hotline. If you see any of these deadly insects, do not attempt to catch them yourself. Call the number on your screen. 1-800-Bug-Kill. Reporting from the campus at UCLA, I'm Traci Taylor for *Eyewitness Action News*."

Chapter Eighty-three

"It's just a little hematoma," Lauren said, touching the firm purple spot peeking from under the bandages on the side of Leon's face. "The doctor said your body should reabsorb the blood pretty soon." What she failed to tell him was that the doctor also said if his body failed to do so, the hematoma would continue to grow, compressing the tissue and preventing oxygen circulation, leading to infection, possible wound separation, and necrosis. "You're going to be fine," Lauren said. And she wanted to believe it too. She had fallen in love.

Leon gave a weak nod and turned his eyes toward the lavish flower arrangement Lauren had brought. "Thanks," he said.

"Lauren Bacall sent those." It wasn't true, but she thought it would cheer him up. "The doctor started you on some new antibiotics, just to be safe." She gave him a tender stroke on the arm, then picked up the hospital bed's control and pushed a button.

As it lifted him into sitting position, the pain caused Leon to make a noise like air being forced from an old vinyl cushion.

"There," she said. "That's better, isn't it?"

He tried to shake his head but he couldn't due to the nerve damage.

Lauren sounded almost naughty when she said, "I've got a surprise for you." As if she might strip right there and give him a lap dance. Instead, she rolled the over-bed table so it was in front of Leon. "I brought your laptop and your notes so you can work on the script." She booted the computer, put the legal pad next to it. "I hope you don't mind, but I looked at your pages, and I've got to say…you are totally brilliant. And you were right: This is a story only you could tell."

Lauren pulled up a chair and took a set of notes from her purse. "Seriously, this is the edgiest, smartest, most original thriller I've read in years. And I love the humor you've injected. It was such a surprise, but the contrast really sets off the dramatic action."

Leon's eyebrows huddled in confusion as he tried to remember any humor he might have put in the script, but nothing came to mind.

"So anyway," she said. "I wanted to go over some notes we had before you take another whack at it." She glanced at her notes. "First," she said. "We absolutely love the killer's brio and total confidence, but we were thinking—and by we, I mean my development people—does he really have to be a loner? It forces you to use voice-over to get to his thoughts, so we were thinking, what if—just go with me on this—what if he was forced, by whoever hired him, to team up with a girl who was expert in some sexy martial art?" Lauren flipped through her notes. "In fact there's one scene that got me thinking—and this goes back to the humor angle—if we went with the thing where he and the girl are in, say, Vegas searching for their target, what if something happened where they were forced to get married so they don't blow their covers? They go to the Elvis wedding chapel, right? And the girl's mother is there, she's a total whack job—we were thinking Cloris Leachman, the way she does crazy—anyway, one thing leads to another and our guy ends up handcuffed to his crazy mother-in-law and he does the second act with her attached to his wrist. In Vegas! Don't you love it?"

Chapter Eighty-four

The six o'clock news was on with the sound muted. In the silence, on the sloping green hills of Forest Lawn Memorial Park, Reverend McDowell and the folks from Great Awakening Baptist Church were inflicting some more faith-based violence on the mourning family of a recently deceased literary agent.

Father Paul was propped up on the sofa, facing the television, though it was hard to tell if he was actually watching. Since beginning his fast, he had lost thirty pounds, and he hadn't shaved since leaving Oregon. With his sunken eyes staring vacantly ahead, his hollow cheeks and his long, scraggly beard, Father Paul looked like a deranged hermit in a priest costume.

Bob, Mary, Klaus, and Agent Parker were sitting around the room, eating pizza off paper plates.

"We placed all five hundred traps," Bob said to Mary. "Probably covered a hundred square miles. Oh, and we saw Gene Hackman's house."

"Really? That's pretty cool." She wiped some tomato sauce from her cheek.

"Yeah," Bob said. "I bought one of those Maps to the Stars homes."

"What we saw," Klaus said in a clarifying tone, "was a tall hedge purporting to be in front of Mr. Hackman's estate."

Bob held out his hands and said, "Why would they lie?"

Klaus just shook his head and looked toward the ceiling.

Mary said, "So what's next?"

"Tomorrow," Klaus said gravely, "we will go back out, risking our lives to check fifty randomly selected traps. If they have worked, and if we do not get killed in the process of checking them, we will remove the old ones and replace them with fresh traps."

Mary smiled and said, "Oh, that reminds me." She jumped up and went to the kitchen, returning with a paper sack which she tossed to Klaus. "I got you something."

Klaus pulled the Groucho Marx glasses from the sack and flashed a narrow, sarcastic smile in Mary's general direction.

"No need to thank me," she said, holding up her hands. "I just hate to see you worry so much about being recognized." She wiggled a finger at him. "Go ahead, see if they fit."

Klaus put them on just as Katy walked into the room, carrying some papers. She skidded to a stop, looked at Klaus, and said, "Yeah, that'll work."

"Hey, Doodlebug," Bob said. "Whatcha got there?" He reached for the papers but she pulled them away.

"Okay," Katy said. "I've got it all figured out."

"What?"

"How to con Riviera." She looked at her dad. "And you'll be glad to know there are no teeth or fingers involved. In fact there's no dismemberment of any kind."

Agent Parker set his pizza down and wiped his hands, saying, "So, talk to me." After a moment of silence, he noticed the other adults looking at him in a damning fashion. He seemed unfazed. "Hey, outta the mouths of babes and all that," he said, turning to Katy. "So, give."

Katy shook her head. "Not until I get a number." She pointed at Agent Parker, then Bob. "From both of you."

"A number of what?"

"And I want it in writing."

"What are you talking about?"

"My cut," Katy said. "I figured if I came up with a workable plan, I should get a cut of the proceeds from both sides.

It seems fair. And I'm not talking about some lame increase in my allowance."

Although no one noticed, Father Paul had turned his head slightly, as if to listen.

Figuring there was little chance that Katy had actually conceived of a viable plan, they cut her in for a million each. After getting it in writing, Katy held up the documents and said, "Okay, so here's what I'm thinking…"

Chapter Eighty-five

"Are you crazy?" Mary sputtered for a moment before she blurted, "That would cost a fortune!"

"Well, duh," Katy said, having anticipated her mother's objection. "There's always costs involved. But you gotta spend money to make money. Somebody said that once."

"And where is all this money coming from?"

"The back end," Katy said.

"The back end of what?"

"Guh! Back end points," Katy said. "Don't you guys ever watch Entertainment Tonight? Profit participation, like they do in the movies. Instead of paying some big star twenty million up front to be in your movie, you promise a percentage of the box office. Points," she said. "You can get people to do anything in this town for points."

Agent Parker shook his head. "I hate to be the one to say this, but it just might work."

Katy did a little two-million-dollar dance.

"Plus I can provide a helicopter," Parker said. "No charge."

"Don't encourage her," Mary said. "She —" Out of the corner of her eye, Mary noticed Father Paul moving. He was standing up very slowly as if being lifted by a power other than his own. She said, "Father? You okay?"

Father Paul's head tilted back as he raised his hands to the heavens and said, "Behold, I will send Elijah before the coming of the great and dreadful day of the Lord: And he shall turn the heart of the fathers to the children, and the heart of the children to their fathers, lest I come and smite the earth with a curse."

God's instructions, it turned out, had finally been revealed to Father Paul. He staggered forward, reaching for a side table for support, knocking it over, shattering a ceramic lamp on the floor. He began to tremble and choke and his hands went to this throat.

Bob and Mary got to him just before his legs gave way. They eased him to his knees, brushing the ceramic shards aside. They laid him down on the floor where he lapsed into a sudden and violent seizure. Mary saw blood where the nylon cord was tearing his skin. She looked up at Katy. "Get something to cut this."

"Be careful," Klaus said. He and Agent Parker watched with misgiving as Katy came from the kitchen with a knife.

"Hold him still," Mary said. "I don't want to cut his wrists." Bob tried to steady him as Mary worked carefully to cut the nylon.

Father Paul's eyelids fluttered like a pair of moths and he began smacking his lips.

"Maybe it's epilepsy," Bob said, trying to pin him down as the seizure grew more intense.

"Got it!" The cord cut, Father Paul's arms flailed wildly, catching Mary on the side of the head, causing her to drop the knife and careen backwards.

Klaus and Agent Parker went for their guns but, by the time they were drawn, Father Paul had the knife at Bob's throat. "Drop the guns," he said. "Everybody calm down. I don't want to hurt him."

Klaus and Agent Parker eyed one another, then slowly laid their guns on the floor.

"Katy, you too," Father Paul said softly.

She seemed embarrassed, looking at her feet, she said, "I left mine in my room."

"All right everybody, hands up," Father Paul said. He pressed the knife slightly to Bob's throat. "Stand." The two of them got to their feet.

Klaus said, "What do you want?"

"Three things," Father Paul said. "First, let me help. Second, I want a cut of the proceeds. Third, I want a slice of that pizza."

"Okay," Agent Parker said. "And exactly how do you propose to help?"

"If you want to do this right," Father Paul said, "you're going to need a prophet."

Chapter Eighty-six

"Be sure to tune in tomorrow," Winston Archer said. "We have a very special guest coming in. An embattled defender of this nation, Mr. Joshua Treadwell will be joining us. We'll be talking about everything that's been going on in Los Angeles, the bugs, his work with the Department of Defense, and his fight with the lib-brull media which has attacked him on the issue of his faith." Winston shook his head, pressed his hands together, and looked to the ceiling.

He then turned to camera two and said, "Now let's talk about this most recent business out in Holly-weird. Last night, a sound stage at one of the film studios burned to the ground." He paused a moment to give an exaggerated frown.

"Awwww," the audience said.

Winston dabbed the corner of his eye with a tissue. "Naturally, the lib-brull press blamed it on—can you guess?—that's right, they blamed it on Christians who have gathered there lately in response to everything that's going on."

"Booooo."

Archer nodded like a bobble-head before continuing. "Now, were there eyewitnesses? No. Did anyone confess? Of course not. It's as if these people want to give us even more evidence of their lib-brull bias," he said.

"Amen, Archer!"

"It's no big loss, if you ask me," he said. "It's just a building. But here's the question: Is the lib-brull media looking into the possibility of insurance fraud?" He shook his head. "I doubt it, not when they have their favorite villains to blame. Seriously, friends, if you ask me, it seems far more likely that the liberals burned it down themselves so they could blame their enemies. It's a common tactic. But is the lamestream press exploring that angle?" He shook his head somberly. "No. And why? Because they've got to stay on message, and the message is, Christians are dangerous."

"Amen, Archer!"

He held his hand up to quiet the audience. "Now, I've said it before, but it bears repeating: what's dangerous is Holly-weird. The whole lib-brull entertainment industry—everybody from the music industry to television to film are all out there pushing the radical homosexual agenda—they've infected this nation for too long."

The audience broke into fevered applause, as if they believed they could resurrect the Pax Network by slapping their hands together hard enough.

"Holly-weird has always been anti-Christian," Archer said. "Well, except for our buddy Mel Gibson." His wink drew more laughter from the audience. "These are the same limousine liberals who have been waging the War on Christmas, forcing all that 'Happy Holiday' crap down our throats like Aunt Lulu's fruitcake! Well, I tell you what, if they want a war, somebody should give it to them. I mean, wouldn't it be something if Holly-weird was simply torn down and remade in His image? Wouldn't that be something?"

"Amen, Archer!"

Chapter Eighty-seven

They stayed up past midnight poking and prodding at Katy's plan, looking for weak spots. But aside from the pure nuttiness of the thing, they couldn't find a good reason not to try it. Klaus got in touch with Audrey, the Hollywood costume designer, and asked her to help. She said she knew exactly who to call. Bob spoke to Traci Taylor who also got on board.

The next morning Mary and Agent Parker were on the phones, telling vendors what they needed and negotiating the terms.

Father Paul nibbled cold pizza and worked on the script.

Klaus was waiting for Bob, standing at the door in his Groucho glasses. Bob kissed Mary on the top of her head and said they'd be back as soon as they finished checking the traps. He slipped a vial of the Rapture into his shirt pocket in case any of the traps needed more bait. He was reaching for a piece of the pizza when his cell phone chirped.

It was Professor Lang.

Bob listened for a minute, his expression growing serious. "You sure? Okay, we'll check it out." He paused. "Yeah, I've got something in my truck. I'll call you when we get there." He flipped it shut and said, "They got a call on the hot line. Some guy walking his dog on a fire road near Stone Canyon says he saw what looked like a nest of the bugs."

"A nest?" Klaus seemed dubious.

"That's how he described it," Bob said. "Like a breeding colony."

"Does that seem possible?"

"First time in the wild, who knows? But I figured we'd bring some ethylene chlorohydrin just to be safe," Bob said on his way out the door.

Twenty minutes later, Klaus was steering the rented cargo van along a winding road in the hills above Los Angeles. Bob was consulting his map, occasionally looking out the window for landmarks. They passed a paver-stone driveway with a double gate. Bob pointed excitedly and said, "I think that's Ben Stiller's house."

"You mean his driveway," Klaus said.

"Okay, fine, the whole thing is one big fraud."

"No," Klaus said. "Just a small one. Katy's is a big fraud." He smiled like a proud uncle, thinking about her crazy plan. "Now, where is this fire road?"

"Keep going," Bob said. "About a quarter mile up, take a right."

They turned on the wide dirt road and stopped at the Park Service gate. Bob hopped out and found it was open. Klaus drove through, and Bob got back into the van. "Looks like somebody cut the lock," he said. "Probably kids on dirt bikes."

Half a mile later they came to a bend in the road. Ahead they saw a man, Hispanic, wearing jeans, a white guayabera, and a two-tone straw cowboy hat. He was leaning against a car parked in the shade. He held up his hand as if expecting them. "I guess that's our guy," Bob said.

And in a sense, it was. Several days ago Sergio Esparza had to make a choice. He could stand for hours in airport security lines while his fellow travelers argued about whether their hand lotion should be X-rayed or confiscated, then face more delays and hassles with U.S. Customs agents at LAX before having to go out and find someone in Los Angeles willing to sell him a gun. Or he could sashay across a virtually unguarded border carrying the weapon of his choice.

After arriving in San Diego, Sergio rented a car and drove to Los Angeles. Once there, however, he didn't have much luck.

It was one hell of a big city, and none of his contacts had a clue where to look for Bob and Klaus now that they'd been declared fugitives.

But two days ago, while standing in line at Pink's Hot Dogs reading *La Opinión,* Sergio caught a break. An article about his targets, the killer insects, and the recall of the Rapture. It said an entomologist from UCLA was working with a couple of local experts to trap the deadly bugs. Having followed the bug story since the attacks at the after-parties, Sergio was willing to bet that Bob and Klaus were the experts. He called the hotline several times to report bug sightings, but they always sent college kids to deal with it. So Sergio decided to up the ante, concocting the story about a colony of the things.

Klaus parked behind the man's car and got out, dust swirling all around. A couple on horseback moseyed by as Bob and Klaus stood there, taking in the view. It was a clear day. From their vantage point, they could see most of the L.A. basin. They could see smoke rising from a sound stage burning in Hollywood and another one down in Culver City. A talent agency was going up in flames on Wilshire Boulevard. The office of a record label in Santa Monica smoldered.

Bob walked to the back of the van and took the stainless steel spray tank. He pumped up the pressure, attached the long spray wand, then strapped the tank to his back. He grabbed a few traps and the small glass tube containing the pheromone. He handed the traps to Klaus and approached the man in the hat. "You called about the bugs?"

"*Sí.*" Sergio nodded and pointed down a path. "Down there," he said. "I will show you."

As they followed him down the slope Klaus got a funny feeling. He looked over his shoulder at Bob and said, "Why would the bugs be this far from a residential area?" The nearest houses were half a mile down the hills.

Bob thought about it and said, "Maybe somebody wearing the fragrance jogs up here or, better, maybe someone came up here to throw theirs away. Just chunked it into the weeds, hit a rock. Two ounces on the ground could draw a bunch of bugs, might look like a nest."

"Maybe," Klaus said, but he didn't believe it. A couple of things still bothered him. First, Klaus had noticed a bar code on the window of the man's car, marking it as a rental. Second, the man who called the hotline said he had been walking a dog. So where was this mutt?

"Over here," Sergio said, leading them further into the scrub where they couldn't be seen by anyone on the fire road. He pointed down the path, behind a fallen tree. Then he stepped aside so Klaus and Bob could pass him.

Klaus stopped and shook his head. He didn't like the idea of a stranger behind his back. This was a trap.

"What's up?" The moment Bob asked the question, he sensed the sudden change in everyone's body language. He tensed, knowing something bad was about to happen. He just wished he knew what.

Sergio didn't like the look in Klaus' eyes. That's what set him off. He could see the man was suspicious, and he knew he was dangerous. Sergio decided it was now or never. He took another step backwards while making the telltale reach, his elbow going up and out while his hand went for his waistband.

Klaus shouted, "Gun!"

The three men drew their weapons at the same time. Two pistols and a spray wand.

Sergio didn't have time to think about it, all he could do was react. He could tell Klaus was reaching for a gun so he decided to shoot him first.

The two guns fired simultaneously as Bob brought the spray wand up and let fly with a full blast of the ethylene chlorohydrin.

Klaus staggered backwards, eyes wide in shock. He pitched awkwardly down the hill, tripping over, and disappearing behind, the fallen tree.

Sergio turned, firing a second shot at Bob. But, blinded by the powerful pesticide dripping into his eyes, his aim was nothing to brag about. Sergio spit and sputtered as he squeezed off a couple of a wild shots before stumbling into the chaparral, stabbed by the sharp leaves of the yucca plants that seemed to grow everywhere. He groped his way past manzanita and grease-wood, hoping to find cover. By the time he squatted behind a large scrub oak and pried one of his red eyes open, neither of his targets was anywhere to be seen.

By now Bob had unstrapped the spray tank from his back and was pressed to the trunk of a mountain-mahogany. In the flash of chaos he hadn't seen whether Klaus had been hit. He yelled for him, but there was no reply. Bob didn't know if that meant the worst or if Klaus just didn't want to give away his position. He could hear some movement in the scrub but he didn't know who it was or where they were going.

It turned out to be Sergio. After a minute he called out to Bob. "I have your friend," he said. "He is not dead…yet."

"Klaus?"

"Yeah," he answered, though he sounded a bit groggy. Sergio's shot had caught the edge of Klaus' Kevlar vest, wounding him under the arm and knocking the breath out of him. The impact, along with the fact he was standing on a steep incline, pushed him backwards until he tripped over the log. He whacked his head pretty hard when he landed. He didn't lose consciousness but was confused and disoriented long enough for Sergio to find him.

"You okay?"

"It's all right, Bob, I'm only bleeding a little," Klaus said. "But he has a gun to my head."

Bob peeked out from his tree, looking back at where the whole thing had started. Klaus' gun was on the ground amidst the scattered bug traps. Bob crept out and grabbed it.

Then he heard something. A retching sound. Severe vomiting, followed by the sound of a man gasping for breath.

"What was that?"

"He threw up on my shoes," Klaus said. "Did you hit him with the chlorohydrin?"

"Yeah." Bob cupped his hands and called out, "Hey, buddy, let me explain what's happening. That stuff I sprayed you with?

It's a neurotoxic agent. On top of your nausea, you're probably getting dizzy, and if you don't already have a headache, you're about to get one."

"It will take more than that to kill me," Sergio boasted.

"Yeah, well, there's plenty more to come," Bob said. "Any minute now, your blood pressure's going to bottom out like Enron stock. Then delirium will set in and you'll start to hallucinate just before you have complete cardiac and respiratory collapse. We'll just wait."

To show what a man he was, Sergio fired a couple of shots in the general direction of Bob's diagnosis. But his machismo was undermined when he threw up again. Still, he managed to keep the gun to Klaus' head. Sergio spit the acid from his mouth before he said, "Come out and I won't kill your friend."

"Can't do it," Bob said. "I'd say we have a bit of a trust issue, me and you. But I tell you what, maybe we can make a deal."

"What kind of deal?"

"The kind where we all walk away," Bob said. "But you better hurry." He really had no idea if Sergio had been exposed to enough of the poison to kill him, but he figured it was best to act as if his death was inevitable.

Sergio tried to vomit some more but he was on empty. His abdominal muscles were sore. The membranes around his eyes and mouth burned like crazy. His head throbbed and his vision blurred. He tried to lick his lips, but his tongue was like a stick of chalk. He said, "Go ahead."

"I've got the antidote."

"Bullshit." Again with the machismo.

"Are you kidding?" Bob couldn't believe this guy. "You think I'm going to strap a tank of this shit on my back without having an antidote? Let Klaus go and throw out your gun. I'll toss you the cure," Bob said. "What do you say? Your time's running out."

After a moment, Sergio said, "I will let your friend go. But I keep my gun."

"All right," Bob said. "But then you go your way, and we'll go ours. Deal?"

"Deal."

A moment later, Klaus came walking through the brush. "All right," Bob said. "Here it comes." He pulled a small glass vial marked Rapture from his pocket and tossed it toward Sergio. "Now, don't drink that," he said. "It's a topical. Rub it on your skin where the poison absorbed."

"How fast does this work?"

"Trust me," Bob said. "You'll forget about the poison in no time."

Chapter Eighty-eight

"So the witch hunt is officially underway," Winston Archer said into camera one. "Activist judges have appointed an unaccountable special prosecutor to look into who may have leaked the names of a couple of guys whose work was, debatably, classified but hardly a matter of serious national security." He turned to his guest, and said, "Mr. Treadwell, what do you know about the state of that investigation?"

"Winston, I'm sorry to say my attorneys have advised me not to comment on any grand jury proceedings with which I may be familiar," Treadwell said. "It's ongoing, and frankly I'm not worried about it, because I answer to a court of higher rank." Treadwell pointed not-too-subtly toward the ceiling.

Archer nodded his understanding and said, "But don't you think that the mere act of appointing a special prosecutor will be taken as a tremendous victory by the terrorists?"

"I can't imagine how they could see it any other way," Treadwell said.

"Fair enough," Archer said. "Let's move on to less temporal matters." He picked up a sheet of paper. "This morning when I got to the set, my producer handed me this interesting little document." Archer put on his reading glasses. "Let's see, in the last twenty-four hours there have been two major volcanic eruptions, one on Montserrat, the other in Ecuador. Another deadly tsunami in Indonesia. Ten thousand more dead from famine in Africa resulting from the ongoing drought. A super-typhoon hit China with winds nearly 140 miles an hour, killing thousands. The list goes on and on and, although the number of deaths from insects seems to be down a bit, the list does include another earthquake in La-La Land this morning." He pulled off his glasses and pointed an earpiece at Treadwell. "What do you make of all this?"

"Well, I think it's both revealing and affirming," Treadwell said. "One of the great gifts we have been given is satellite technology, which allows up to know almost instantaneously what's going on all over the world. We can see if all is calm and idyllic or, when it's upon us, it can give us a clear picture of what may very well be the End of Times. I think it's fascinating."

Archer gave a serious nod and said, "Because it's well documented that these sorts of events will increase both in frequency and intensity as the time draws near for His return."

"If I have the quote right," Treadwell said with a squint, "there will be famine and pestilence and earthquakes in diverse places." He shook his head. "I'm certainly not going to argue with Matthew 24:7."

"Well, no," Archer said. "You'd be up for a week!"

The audience burst into laughter and applause.

Treadwell chuckled and said, "Twenty-four, seven. I'm going to steal that one."

"Feel free," Archer said before turning serious again. "Now yesterday we were talking about the lib-brull press coverage of the fires in Holly-weird. Since then—as if to warm the heart of this old broadcaster—the offices of two more so-called 'talent' agencies, a television production facility, and one of the big rap record labels were also burned down." Archer broke into a giddy smile and clapped his hands like a cartoon clown before returning to his sober newsman face and saying, "Naturally, the lamestream press continues to play the blame game on this, allegedly 'reporting' on who might have set the fires."

"As if it matters," Treadwell said. "You know, it's almost as if they don't understand the effect of all the negative stuff they put out there. Of course they say, 'But it's the truth.'" He shook his head. "What difference does that make? If it's negative, it has a corrosive effect on the public's perceptions. I think we should be looking for the positive in everything."

"Exactly," Archer said. "We need to see this as an opportunity."

"I agree!" He pointed at Archer and said, "People need to see this for what it is: The birth pangs of a new Hollywood. Now we don't know if Jesus is coming tomorrow or a year from tomorrow, but we do know He's coming. And in the meanwhile, people of faith must do whatever they can to help make this a truly Christian nation."

"The choice is simple," Archer said. "Do you want to live in a Christian nation or have to get out there and choose a wedding dress for your son's gay marriage?"

"Amen, Archer!"

Chapter Eighty-nine

A young nurse approached the doctor standing outside Leon's room. She peeked inside and said, "That's him? That's the guy who saved Lauren Bacall from those bugs?"

"That's the man," the doctor said as he wrote something on the chart. "A genuine hero."

"Wow." The nurse shook her head sadly. "How ironic."

"Yeah, ironic." Given the news he was about to share with them.

The nurse looked back into the room. Lauren was fluffing his pillows. "Do they know?"

The doctor shook his head. "On my way to tell them now."

Inside, after some small talk, the doctor said, "I'm sorry to have to tell you, but the infection is resistant to antibiotics."

Lauren took a sharp breath and covered her mouth with her hand. Then she said, "You mean, it's…"

"It's what's known as a super-bug." The doctor nodded gravely. "Vancomycin-resistant staph aureus," he said. "It's a gram-positive coccus, a non-spore-forming facultative anaerobe."

"There's nothing you can do?"

The doctor could only shake his head.

"How long does he have?"

The doctor looked at the chart for a moment. "Hard to say. Too many variables at work. Could be hours, could be days." He took a syringe from the small case he carried. "What he needs now is rest." He injected a sedative into a port in the I.V. line. "He should relax now."

When the doctor left, Lauren dried her eyes and pulled the chair close to the bed. She stroked Leon's arm and said, "You're going to be fine."

Leon turned his head toward her. "The infection doesn't cause deafness," he said. "I heard the prognosis. It's over."

"Oh, stop. He doesn't know what he's talking about," Lauren said. "I've got a call into a specialist I know at Cedars. You'll be good as new in no time."

"You're sweet." Leon gave a little laugh. "All the things I've done in my life? Close calls, car chases, shoot-outs? It's not how I expected to go."

"You're not going anywhere," Lauren said. "You've got a script to finish."

He sighed. "You may have to finish that yourself."

"No way. It's a story only you can tell right, remember?"

"Yeah, well…that was before we added the part about the hero being handcuffed to his mother-in-law in Las Vegas."

Lauren smiled. "That was just a 'what-if,' silly. You don't have to use it if you don't want."

"Thanks." His eyelids were getting heavy. He took a long, deep breath.

She sat there for a moment, just looking at him. Then she leaned close and said, "Hey, I just had an idea for another script, you want to hear it?"

"Sure." He closed his eyes and said, "Pitch me."

"Okay. It's a medical-spy thriller," she said. "Sort of, I don't know, *Outbreak* meets *The Bourne Identity,* but about something, you know? Not just action for action's sake."

"I like it so far."

"Yeah? I'm thinking a handsome French intelligence agent on the trail of terrorists."

Leon gave a sleepy nod then said, "Maybe he falls in love with a beautiful woman he meets at a bar."

She smiled as a tear came to her eye. "Boy meets girl, exactly. That's good."

"How's it end?" Leon asked. "At the Elvis chapel in Vegas?"

"I don't know exactly," she said. "But happy." She wiped the tear from her eye. "I'd like a happy ending."

Chapter Ninety

After the first day, someone brought an orange crate for him to stand on so that he might be seen and heard by more of the gathered crowd. He wore the traditional himation over a sleeveless, ankle-length tunic of rough, dirty wool spun by means not employed in a thousand years. His wide belt and sandals were hand-crafted from ancient scarred leather. His scraggly gray beard and sunken eyes gave him the look of a man who had spent time wandering the desert without food.

"I'm standing near the corner of Wilshire and Santa Monica Boulevards," Traci Taylor said. "Where, for the past two days, this mysterious man has been preaching to ever-growing crowds."

Ronnie zoomed in on Father Paul's ascetic face as he said, "I am the one about whom it was written: I will send my messenger ahead of you, who will prepare your way before you."

A young man in the crowd turned to his friend and said, "Luke, chapter seven, verse twenty-seven."

"He is Elijah," the friend said.

"A witness to the Book of Revelation," said another. "But where is Enoch?"

Ronnie panned the camera back to Traci. "In our life and times," she said, "there has been no shortage of people claiming to be prophets. But few have convinced as many as this man in so short a time."

Ronnie panned back to Father Paul. Some in the crowd were reaching out to touch the hem of his garment. Others pleaded for answers to questions that have haunted for generations. As the camera showed the scene, Traci continued by saying, "Although he has never actually claimed to be the prophet Elijah, those who have heard him preach believe that's exactly who he is. From his authentic attire and his grasp of scripture to his facility with Latin, Greek, and what I believe is Aramaic, he has captivated this crowd."

Ronnie panned back to Traci as she said, "But who exactly is, or rather, was this Elijah? I asked Dr. Karen Watson, professor of comparative theology at USC."

Cut to a prerecorded segment with Dr. Watson in her office. "Elijah," she said, "was a ninth-century B.C. prophet from the northern kingdom during the reigns of Ahab, Ahaziah, and Jehoram. Many Christians believe Elijah, like Enoch, never died, and is alive today. He was said to have been taken into heaven where he lived in the presence of God Himself. According to popular interpretations, Elijah's return to earth is a precursor to the Second Coming."

Cut back to Traci who said, "All of which raises an age-old question, namely, when a man shows up claiming to be a prophet, how do you know if he's telling the truth? The Bible warns repeatedly of false prophets, though it doesn't give specific instructions on how to tell a charlatan from a lunatic from the real thing. Can such a claim be proved or disproved? Are such things beyond the reach of reason? Is it only by faith that we can know the answer?" Traci shook her head. "Not if you're on the *Eyewitness Action News* team, where seeing is believing. If this man is a prophet, it's news, and we'll be there to cover the story, no matter how long it takes."

Ronnie panned across the sea of faces. Someone in the crowd shouted, "Prophet Elijah! When is He coming?"

Father Paul held up an open hand, gazing at it as if it contained a crystal ball. "We know not the day or the hour," he said. Then after a moment he continued, "But I do know the place."

The crowd gasped.

Father Paul lowered his hand. Someone helped him down from the orange crate. The crowd, estimated at over fifty thousand, parted like the Red Sea. "It is this way," he said. "Follow me."

Like sheep trailing a shepherd, the throngs followed Father Paul down the wide road, toward Fairfax and the stretch of Wilshire Boulevard known as the Miracle Mile.

Chapter Ninety-one

Father Paul's supplement to Katy's plan was inspired. It created a ticking bomb that every news organization on earth had to cover.

And that was the whole point.

Feeding into the media-induced End Time frenzy, the story of Elijah's return took over the talking-heads circuit, generating more heated debate than a presidential stain on a WMD. From *The Winston Archer Report* to *HardHeads*—rabbis, ministers, and imams were going head-to-head with preachers, cardinals, and grand lamas. Some of the debates were pitched battles of chapter and verse, others were nuanced and erudite explorations of history and etymology, most were fraught with self-serving error in interpretation and translation.

Still, it was generally agreed that if this man was, indeed, Elijah, then the Second Advent had to be near. "However, if he is a fraud," one of them pointed out, "we will know soon, because scripture tells us Elijah will return three days before the coming of the Messiah."

The result was the most televised news event in history. Broadcast crews from 153 of the 192 countries on earth had set up all around the sprawling five-point intersection where Father Paul had led the flock.

It was also the place where, for the past two days, certain men and women had been preparing the way for His return in accordance with Katy's plan.

Fanned by the unbridled media coverage, the crowd expanded by the hour. By sundown, police estimated there were nearly three-quarters of a million people. It was like Times Square on New Year's Eve, except that instead waiting for a ball to drop, the crowd—in the grip of a virulent, reason-resistant, Apocalyptic fever—was hoping for bodies to come exploding out of their graves.

As the multitude spread, denominations began forming camps, displaying signs to declare their brand of Christianity, like delegates at a political convention. Anabaptists held ground near a Starbucks on the south side of Wilshire. Calvinists had staked out an area in the median on San Vicente. New Adventists had the sidewalk at the corner of Sweetzer. Orthodox reconstructionists were up front, near the small stage someone had built for the Prophet Elijah.

The whole thing started out peacefully enough. Starting at dawn people were testifying, enjoying fellowship, and singing hymns.

But late that afternoon, a group of charismatic Pentecostals took umbrage when they heard a Lutheran confessionalist saying, "How many snake handlers does it take to change a light bulb?"

And before he got to the punch line, all Hell broke loose.

Divided by their common belief, skirmishes broke out along the borders of the camps. The fight for possession of absolute truth was joined as moderate Episcopalians took offense at the First Church of Divine Prosperity, whose members were passing the plate among the crowd, promising big returns in this life instead of the next. Punches were thrown, coins spilled.

Further up San Vicente, some eco-vegan-Christians were taking a beating from a group of dispensationalists who, while roundly rejecting Darwin's theory of evolution, warmly embraced the whole notion of survival of the fittest.

The troubles continued into the night as a contingent from First Church of Christ Holiness raged against members of the New Testament Church Apostolic over the issue of day care, the former promoting the notion that it was a way to help single, working mothers, the latter citing scripture to support their argument that single, working mothers deserved what they got.

Around midnight, as a gang of orthodox Lutherans got into a good old fashioned brawl with some Roman Catholics over the terms of the Joint Declaration on the Doctrine of Justification, there came a sound so awful and ungodly, that even Elijah looked surprised.

Chapter Ninety-two

It started as a strange and ominous rumbling resonating in the streets. It grew into a divine and resounding noise, rending the air, and giving the combatants pause. Fists stopped in mid-flight as the frightful sound began to vibrate the earth itself, a thunderous low frequency that could be felt for a mile in all directions.

A hellish fear swept through the crowd and all eyes turned to the Prophet Elijah.

Father Paul, standing on his stage, held both hands up to the heavens and said, "For you know that the day of the Lord will come like a thief in the night."

As if on cue, fire began to rain down from the skies. Vast, roiling fireballs of orange, gold, and black exploded from the tops of the skyscrapers lining Wilshire Boulevard drawing fearful eyes upward in time to witness bolts of silver-blue lightning arcing between the buildings and the night sky. The air filled with a blaring chorus of trumpets and what was assumed to be Gabriel's horn, followed by what sounded like the screams of all those who had died in His name. The unearthly sounds were terrifying and shook windows to breaking.

As glass rained down on the sidewalks, there was much wailing and gnashing of teeth. Rending of clothes. Fainting. Screaming. Testifying. Weeping and praising. Skeptical eyes were covered to hide the fear of exposure. Tears flowed as if to wash away any remaining doubt. Some ran for cover, begging forgiveness, while others were so deeply stunned they simply stared slack jawed at the awesome and fiery display of His coming.

Here and there in the windows of the office towers all around them appeared the ghostly iridescent figures of seraphim and cherubim in fine twined linen of blue, purple, and scarlet.

Perched like three vulturous judges on the ledge of one of the buildings were the Archangels Gabriel, Raphael, and Michael.

Then, between the two tallest buildings, there rose a mushrooming cloud, thick and white as a billowing field of bleached cotton. The cloud soon filled with a blinding golden light out of which Jesus appeared, fifty feet tall, His eyes burning with His magnificence.

Suddenly, all sound ceased. All motion stopped. Not an eye blinked.

After a moment hovering in the cloud, he spoke. "Look, I've got to make this quick," he said. "I'm really not even supposed to be here. There are a lot of rules about coming back and I had to bend a few to make this trip. So real fast, this isn't 'The Second Coming,'" he said, using his fingers for quotation marks. "Okay? Think of this as version one-point-five. Like an update." He paused to let that sink in.

He pointed at the crowd and added a disapproving tone when he said, "Now, would you take a look at yourselves? You're at each other's throats." He shook his head and switched to light sarcasm, saying, "Are the rules too complicated? Is that the problem?" He counted them on his fingers as he said, "Don't kill, don't steal, don't covet, love your neighbor. Pretty simple, right? Nothing to interpret. No hidden meanings. Yet you've managed to argue your way into thirty thousand different denominations—and that's just the Protestants. And each one superior to the other. And don't try to sell me the 'invisible unity' nonsense either. I'm not buying. I know how you think."

Jesus shook his head, folded his arms and said, "But you'll be glad to know that's not why I'm here. I came about the bugs that started this mess. The thing is, they're not a plague. They're not a Biblical thing at all. They're a government thing. Actually they're an example of what can happen when you don't separate church and state. A few knuckleheads using your tax dollars and their interpretation of scripture to justify killing people they disapprove of."

He shook his head. "Anyway, I saw how the media was hyping things the way they do with all their 'terrifying updates' and 'shocking developments'," again using his fingers for quotations. "And of course I couldn't help but notice you guys getting all worked up about the whole 'Judgment Day' thing and, well, I figured the best idea was to drop by and tell you to get back to your lives. The bugs are under control. The End, 'capital E,' isn't here just yet. And, by the way, it's not up to you to choose the time of my return. I'll be back when I'm good and ready. M-kay?" He gazed upon the crowd for anyone who might want to argue. "Well, all right then, 'nuff said." He flashed the peace sign and said, "*Pax vobiscum.*"

What followed looked and sounded like a tear in the space-time continuum. Vast fluid sheets of sea-green plasma appeared from nowhere, floating and rolling mysteriously over the crowd before soaring to the heavens and disappearing. Hellish explosions billowed again from the rooftops as jagged fingers of electricity bolted across the sky accompanied by a deafening soundtrack of unearthly origins, scale, and fortissimo.

The crowd covered their ears and their eyes until one final thundering roar was sucked into a black hole and the sensory spectacle was replaced by void and He was gone.

Chapter Ninety-three

The silence that followed didn't linger. First came the growing hum of mumbled prayers punctuated now and again with increasingly obstreperous ejaculations for the Holy Name of Jesus. After a few moments, as the prayer continued, one could hear the narrow voices as they resumed their rancorous debate.

But even that didn't last long, being quickly trumped by a frightening and unmistakable sound coming from the east.

And spiritual it wasn't.

It was steel-belted squealing and the growl of V-8 engines. Automatic weapon fire and police sirens wailing straight for the crowd like an action picture that had jumped its tracks. The faithful, already aroused, scattered like crickets to the sidewalks as the flashing lights and gunplay careened toward them.

First they saw a three-segmented beast riding the roof of a truck. Four feet long, eyes glowing red. Six legs clutching an Uzi that sparked and smoked and hooked the eye. Bob was at the wheel, a tightly wound bundle of wild-eyed determination. Klaus was leaning out the passenger side like Machine Gun Kelly firing at the LAPD cruisers that were giving chase.

Cameras from around the world trained their polished lenses on the high-speed drama as it unfolded in front of them. From the inky skies, a black Bell 206 III helicopter swooped down and hovered like a huge violet-tail dragonfly (*Argia violacea*) with an SX16 Nite-sun floodlight mounted on its abdomen. Its beam shone down like God's light pouring into the dark soul of a dirty city.

It was too late when the crowd's parting revealed the concrete barriers police had set up for crowd control. Bob jumped on the brakes, skidding grill-first into the roadblock. The impact ripped the fiberglass bug from its mooring, launching it through a department store window where it came to rest among a family of mannequins having a picnic. None of them looked particularly surprised at this turn of events.

Bob and Klaus felt like they'd been punched in the face. When the air bags deflated, Bob and Klaus saw that the black-and-whites had pulled up short in a semicircle, trapping them in the perfect position for Ronnie to capture everything that happened. Traci was there too, posturing like a war correspondent in the midst of a firefight. She peeked over one of the concrete barriers then looked back over her shoulder at the camera, shouting to be heard over the helicopter. "This is the most remarkable thing I've seen in all my years of broadcasting." She paused, thinking about how that comment would play after recent events. Then she said, "With the obvious exception of the Second Coming."

Just then a black SUV came skidding to a stop behind the LAPD cars. Windows as dark as the paint.

Ronnie panned over just in time to catch Agent Parker getting out of the driver's side. He had the radio mike in one hand and a Brugger & Thomet MP 9 tactical machine pistol with the thirty-round magazine in the other. Standing in plain view, Agent Parker keyed the mic and said, "This is Agent Nick Parker, C.I.A.," his voice boomed from a bullhorn mounted behind the SUV's grill. "Repeat, this is the C.I.A. Everyone hold your fire." A few military hand signals had the cops lowering their weapons. Parker keyed the mike again and said, "Bob, Klaus, this is the end of the road. Nowhere to go, and we have you outgunned. What do you say we make this easy on everybody? Drop your weapons and come out with your hands up."

The crowd was too large to control. Their morbid curiosity trumped any semblance of common sense, and they crept slowly closer for a better view. After so many years of seeing the news packaged as entertainment, they'd come to believe it was true. This wasn't some potentially deadly situation, this was nothing more than a literal version of eyewitness action news shown on the biggest screen they'd ever seen. The crowd reacted to the sequence of events like it was a mere change of the channel. One minute Jesus was entertaining them, the next a high-speed chase commanded their attention. Now it was a hostage drama. And with no commercials.

Agent Parker said, "Bob? Klaus? Let's go. Nobody's been hurt yet, let's keep it that way."

Bob looked at Klaus. "What do you think? Should we just get out now?"

Klaus seemed mildly disappointed in his friend. "You have no sense of drama," he said, shaking his head slightly. "We have to string this out. Increase the tension as much as possible. Give the press time to do background stories on who we are, what we have done, that sort of thing."

"We haven't done anything," Bob said.

"We have to leave that conclusion to the press."

Bob nodded, thinking on it. "Maybe we should negotiate for something."

Klaus seemed to like the idea. "All right. Like what?"

"I don't know. You hungry?"

"Not really." Klaus looked across the street and gestured at the Starbucks. "But coffee would be nice."

Bob pointed at Klaus. "Okay, good." He turned to yelled to Agent Parker. "We want coffee."

"What?" Somewhat surprised.

"Coffee!"

"What kind?" A little exasperated.

"Uh, hang on." Bob looked at Klaus and they both nearly giggled at the absurdity of the moment. After a moment, Bob composed himself and said, "Okay, I want a tall affogato-style java chip Frappuccino wet double shot."

"That it?" Something else was creeping into Parker's voice now.

"No, Klaus wants a double split shot iced soy milk caramel latte."

"He want whipped cream with that?" It was sarcasm.

Bob, stifling a laugh, turned to Klaus. "You want whipped cream?"

Klaus had to bite his lip to say, with a straight face, "No, thanks."

"No whipped cream," Bob yelled. "Also, see if they have the crumbly coffee cake. No, wait, the walnut sticky buns."

A few minutes later, Ronnie framed his shot with the barista delivering coffee to the truck in the background, while Traci was in the foreground saying, "In a stunning development, sources at the State Department tell me the men in that truck are Bob Dillon and Klaus Müller, the former Defense Department employees wanted for questioning in connection with the release of the transgenic assassin bugs. A highly place FBI official confirms that Dillon was once employed by the CIA as an assassin known as the Exterminator. He is alleged to have killed Bolivian drug lord Ronaldo DeJesus Riviera, brother of Miguel DeJesus Riviera, who currently runs the cartel bearing the family name. Müller is also said to have been an assassin. He is credited with the killing of African dictator Ooganda Namidii, among many others."

Back at the center of attention, Agent Parker sipped his Grande Banana Coconut Frappacino, then checked his watch. He set the drink on the hood of the SUV and keyed the mike again. "Time's running out, you two. What's it going to be?"

Inside the cab of the truck, Bob wiggled his cup to see how much Frappuccino was left. "What do you think," he said, looking at Klaus. "You ready to do this?"

Klaus brushed some crumbs from his lap. He looked out at the sea of people and said, "I have my doubts that anyone could be ready to do this."

Bob laughed. "You may be right, but we've sort of limited our options at this point."

Klaus smiled, thinking about what was about to happen. He said, "You know, there are times when I am sorry I ever met you."

"That's a fine thing to say to somebody who saved your life."

"Hey, I saved yours several times," Klaus said.

"Oh, right," Bob said, "throw that in my face."

Klaus smiled again. "But you know, most of the time, I am glad we met." He held out his hand to Bob. They shook on it. Klaus gave a nod and said, "Let's do it."

"All right," Bob turned and yelled out the window. "Hold your fire. We're getting out."

"Guns first," Parker said.

When she saw the activity, Traci's voice pitched up a notch. "Wait a second, something's happening," she said. "Bob and Klaus have dropped their guns onto the street and appear to be getting out of the truck. Their hands are raised. For those of you watching, Klaus Müller is the man on the left, wearing the white cotton dress shirt and khakis. The man on the right, wearing the light tan crew and jeans is Bob Dillon, also known as Javier Martinez.

"Nice and easy," Agent Parker said. "Just walk toward me and keep the hands up."

Traci narrated as Ronnie kept his camera trained on Bob and Klaus. "It looks like they've negotiated a peaceful ending to this potentially bloody stand-off, with the two alleged assassins—wait a—ohmigod!"

Bob and Klaus suddenly reached to the small of their backs, drawing guns.

Agent Parker yelled, "No!" He raised the MP 9 and squeezed off two rapid bursts. He used all thirty rounds in half a second. His aim was perfect.

Bob and Klaus felt the sting of each hit. They jerked and twitched like electrocuted puppets. Blood immediately sponged into the fabric of their shirts, forming irregular circles at the entry wounds. From the back, television cameras picked up the bloody, tissue-filled spray as the bullets made their exit. Lenses zoomed in on Bob clutching his chest, staggering backwards into the truck where he slid down to his knees, leaving a red trail on the door before he collapsed sideways. Klaus stood where he was shot, stunned and unblinking. He wobbled for a moment before crumbling to the ground.

They both ended face-up on the street.

There was a moment of calm before the chaos broke out. Where some had screamed and scrambled for cover, others pressed in for a closer look at the carnage. The police linked arms to block the advancing gawkers.

Ronnie and Traci were allowed to sneak past them. Ronnie rushed in for a close-up of the wounds and the death masks before Traci pulled him toward Agent Parker for a reaction shot. "Agent Parker, I'm Traci Taylor, *Eyewitness Action News.* What can you tell us about—"

He pushed her aside. "Get back," he barked. "Get her away from me. Somebody get some tape around this scene, now!" He made his face available to Ronnie's camera as he shouted, "Keep the press back! This ain't family entertainment."

Two ambulances were on the scene immediately, forcing their way through the crowd with urgent squawks from their sirens. The EMTs rushed in to attend to the wounded. Ronnie captured the whole frantic opera for all the world to see.

Agent Parker signaled something to the black helicopter. The pilot killed the Nite-sun, banked to the right and disappeared into the darkness. Ronnie kept the camera on Agent Parker as he conferred with the EMTs, nodding, grim faced, at what they said.

From off camera you could hear Traci yell, "Agent Parker, what is it? For the record, what did they say?"

Ronnie zoomed in on Parker's face as he said, "They're dead. You happy? They're both dead!"

Chapter Ninety-four

Lauren had fallen asleep in the chair, the script resting in her lap.

Leon's gnawing infection kept him awake, his face washed in the blue-gray glow of the television. He couldn't tell if he was hallucinating as he watched the televised Second Coming of Jesus Christ. It seemed real enough and, for a moment, he wondered what Hell was like and if that was his fate.

Before he could wade too deeply into existential dread, Leon found himself watching the CIA capture and kill two men. And not just any two men, but the targets he had come to Los Angeles looking for. What happened, he wondered. What happened?

He slipped away quietly an hour later without ever finding an answer to the question.

The nurse woke Lauren and told her he was gone.

A few days later she accompanied his body back to France for burial.

Chapter Ninety-five

Bob's funeral was held on a sound stage in Burbank, the crowd of mourners courtesy of the green screen process.

The brushed silver casket shimmered under the bright lights, in stark contrast to the gaping black hole next to it.

Mary and Katy sat bravely at grave side, red-eyed, sobbing, ruined. Trying to be brave. Mary dabbed her eyes with a linen handkerchief. Katy, her lips turned down at the edges, clutched something in her lap as she cried.

Father Paul officiated.

They only needed enough to edit together a two minute segment.

Traci Taylor was there to cover the funeral, an exclusive for *Eyewitness Action News*. She stood a respectful distance from the grave. Ronnie was a little closer, to capture the images.

Traci narrated quietly, "Earlier this morning, they laid to rest the ashes of their friend, Klaus Müller, in accordance with his wishes." She paused. "Now, I believe they're about to lower the casket into the— no, wait a minute, little Katy is getting up and approaching the casket."

Ronnie zoomed in to follow the action as Traci narrated, "It looks like she's going to lay something on top of it, possibly a flower or…no…it's a plastic model of an insect. Oh, doesn't that just break your heart? I'm not mistaken, that's an antlion, which, in its larval stage, is known as a doodlebug.

I'm told that was the nickname her father gave her when she was just a baby."

Sitting in the darkness off-camera in a director's chair, Klaus nudged Bob and said, "That's a nice touch."

Bob nodded. "It's my favorite part."

◇◇◇

Bob had shaved his head and grown a goatee. Klaus sported a Vandyke and tortoise-shell glasses that took some getting used to after so many years wearing contacts.

They were sitting with Mary in the offices of Sight and Soundscapes Unlimited, a special effects firm in Los Angeles. They were going over the invoices. "Wait a minute," Mary said, pointing at a line item. "How many cherubim did we get?"

The man on the other side of the desk looked at his copy. "I think we had twenty, plus ten seraphim, and the three guardian angels."

"Right," she said. "But this can't be the per-cherub price, can it?"

"No, that's for all of them."

"All right, fine," Mary said, flipping to the next page. "Now about the lightning and fire."

The man chewed a bit at the inside of his lip. "I know, we went over budget but—"

"Yeah, well, about that…" Mary pulled off her glasses and said, "It was spectacular."

"Oh, thanks." His anxiety turned to immodesty. "We thought it was pretty damn—"

"Unfortunately," Klaus interrupted. "The contract gives you only 10 percent wiggle room." He tapped the invoice and said, "Not thirty."

"Are you kidding?" The guy couldn't believe they were chiseling him on this. "It looked like the Second Coming, for Christ's sake. How about twenty-five?"

Bob glanced at Mary who nodded. "Fifteen," Bob said.

"Twenty."

"Fair enough."

◇◇◇

After settling the bill for special effects, Bob, Mary, and Katy drove Klaus and Audrey down to a restaurant near the harbor in Long Beach. They had decided to split up on the docks that night, agreeing it was best not to be seen in one another's company for a while.

Agent Parker and Father Paul met them for dinner at The Crusty Crab. Agent Parker handed manila envelopes to Bob, Mary, Katy, and Klaus. "New ID's," he said. "Passports, driver's license, Social Security numbers, everything you need."

They were sitting in the bar, waiting for their table when Katy pointed up at the television.

Traci Taylor was standing on a dirt road in the Santa Monica Mountains. "We lost so much more than just talented people in those terrible days. We will never know what films, what beloved characters, what thrill-ride special effects were lost forever. The loss to our culture, indeed, to the entire world, can never be truly quantified." She paused for a moment, turned her head slightly and said, "For *Eyewitness Action News*, reporting from the hills above Los Angles, I'm Traci Taylor."

"I'll bet a thousand bucks she wins a Pulitzer," Agent Parker said.

"I think I'll just send her the thousand bucks," Bob replied. "We couldn't have done this without her." He raised his glass.

Later, over dinner, Mary turned to Agent Parker and asked if he'd made any plans now that he was a rich man. "I mean other than placing thousand-dollar bets on a whim," she said.

Parker seemed troubled by the question. He looked at his scotch as if the answer might be hiding under the ice cubes. Finally he said, "You know, if you'd asked me a few days ago I would have had a different answer. But after the other night, the religious spectacle, and seeing all those people with so much absolute, unshakable, faith, I'm not so sure anymore. I'm thinking about going to a monastery."

Father Paul spewed wine from his nose and mouth. "What?"

Agent Parker handed him a napkin. "Kidding," he said. "I've got an appointment with a Realtor. Says she has just what I'm looking for in River Oaks."

Katy said, "Are you still going to work at the CIA?"

He cracked a crab leg and said, "Haven't decided."

"Because I think that's what I want to do after college."

"You've got what it takes," he said. "You want my advice? Learn Arabic."

"Guh," she said with a pained face. "As if."

After dinner, they drove over to the docks. Klaus was taking Audrey on a cruise through the Panama canal to St. Thomas, where they would catch a flight to destinations unknown.

As they were about to leave, Agent Parker looked at Katy and said, "Call me if you're serious about the CIA thing. I can arrange for an internship, if you want. Just keep your salary expectations low."

"Thanks," she said. "It'll just be a few years. I need to learn to drive first."

◇◇◇

As the ship sailed, Katy walked alongside to the end of the dock, waving to Klaus and Audrey on the top deck. "Bon voyage!" she yelled.

Mary noticed that Bob seemed a little sad. She said, "You know, this isn't the end of it."

It caught him off guard. "The end of what?"

"Your dream," she said. "I know you can't just give it up. I don't want you to. Someday you're going to perfect the assassin bug and have the world's first all natural pest control business."

Bob looked at her and smiled. "You think?"

"I know."

"But we should put it on the back burner for a while," he said. "Just to keep the profile low."

◇◇◇

Father Paul returned to Seattle, where he retired from Saint Martin's.

He bought a building on the south edge of downtown and christened it St. Elijah the Prophet Old Catholic Church, thus joining a loose community of Christian churches that had split from the Roman Catholics in the 1870s after a dispute about Papal infallibility.

He wanted to serve those rejected by the official church. He baptized the children of the unwed. He performed weddings for the divorced. He brought in a couple of priests who had left the church so they could marry and start families. He opened a day care and a health care center, and had professionals there to discuss family planning.

They passed the plate at every service. The congregants gave generously, since they knew St. Elijah wasn't recognized by the Vatican and so wasn't required to kick money upstairs to pay off the lawsuits. They knew the money would actually get to the poor. And this, they found comforting and more in keeping with what they believed Jesus had in mind.

◇◇◇

Agent Parker's real estate agent found the perfect house for him. It was a two-story, three-bedroom, two-and-a-half-bath colonial on a nicely wooded acre. The new interior featured Brazilian cherry hardwood floors, granite counters, skylight, exposed brick, a new deck, gourmet kitchen, a new roof, and central air. Best of all it was a fifteen-minute drive to CIA headquarters.

He received a raise, a promotion, and a commendation for his brave actions in killing the two fugitives without any collateral damage. No one said it, but it helped that it was all done in front of a worldwide television audience, burnishing the reputation of the long beleaguered agency.

The promotion didn't last long, however. Parker found that with financial independence came an inability or unwillingness to grovel, suck up, kiss ass, or generally take shit of any sort.

He retired a month later, opting to take a year off to work on a screenplay.

Chapter Ninety-six

A special prosecutor was appointed to investigate the leak of Bob's and Klaus' names and the details of their work with DARPA, in violation of national security laws.

Judy Rendon and William Cooper were the first to be subpoenaed. Judy held out, refusing to testify, saying she was duty-bound to protect her sources and was willing to accept the consequences. In truth, she feared reprisal from certain radical ideologues and figured taking one for the team by spending a few months in jail would be amply rewarded in due course, not to mention the value of the subsequent book and film rights.

William Cooper, on the other hand, folded like wet cardboard. Threatened with a prison term for contempt of court and obstruction of justice, the tender, fleshy reporter started singing like a church choir, explaining how Charles Browning had not only given him the information on Bob and Klaus but had paid him two thousand dollars to write the story. His biggest regret, he said, was how cheaply he had sold himself.

Based on William Cooper's testimony, Charles Browning was brought before the grand jury. He worked out a deal for immunity and played Judas to Joshua Treadwell's Jesus—not the original Judas, the one thought to have betrayed the Lord, but the later Judas, the one discovered in the Gnostic gospels to have been in cahoots with Jesus all along.

The press played it up as a kiss-on-the-cheek betrayal, the immunity from prosecution his forty pieces of silver. But it had been in the works all along. Charles Browning would testify that he had leaked the information only after getting authorization from Treadwell to do so. This full disclosure got him off the hook.

When Joshua Treadwell was called to explain himself, he and his attorney trotted out an elegant end-run on the Classified Information Procedures Act, managing an effective gray-mail defense. They insisted that Treadwell would have to request and reveal copious amounts of classified information in order to fully defend himself.

The Special Prosecutor knew that denying access to such material would provide a jury with doubt about the fairness of the trial and leave them considering the possibility that the unreleased material might clear the defendant. A few months later, the government dropped the case.

After the ceremony where Treadwell received the Presidential Medal of Freedom for his work at the Department of Defense, he put his arm around his friend and said, "You did a heckuva job, Browning."

Joshua Treadwell left DARPA to take a position as a political commentator for television and radio, quickly becoming a darling of the conservative media. He was a frequent guest on the *Winston Archer Report* and even sat in to host the show on occasion.

There was even talk of his own cable news show. *The Truth According to Treadwell.*

He became a highly sought-after speaker on the conservative lecture circuit, where he talked modestly about his martyrdom and being hounded out of his job because of his faith.

Treadwell got a million-dollar advance for his autobiography. When it was published, he set out on a book tour. Big crowds, too. First New York. Then D.C. Then, moving down the East Coast, Richmond. The fourth stop was Charlotte, North Carolina, where the marketing had been aimed at church groups.

Treadwell did his presentation followed by a short question-and-answer period, then the crowd lined up to get their signed copies.

An attractive young woman approached and shyly handed him the book. She was too intimidated to speak. Treadwell opened the book to the slip of paper with the woman's name on it. He looked up and said, "Hi, Theresa, where're you from?"

"First Baptist in Charlotte," she said, blushing. "I think you're the best."

"Thanks," he said as he scrawled his name. He handed her the book and she walked away touching his signature as if it were a holy relic.

Next in line was an older man with unruly eyebrows and a yellow WWJD bracelet. Treadwell asked where he was from. "Blood of the Lamb Presbyterian in Brevard," he said. "Little town south of Asheville. I just wanted to thank you for all you've done."

"You're welcome," Treadwell said, signing the book "God bless."

Next in line was a younger man, maybe late twenties, clean cut and disciplined-looking. Treadwell smiled and waited for the man to hand him a book. But he just stood there, empty-handed.

Finally, Treadwell said, "Hi, where're you from?"

The young man said, "Great Awakening Baptist Church in Ohio."

"Ohio? Wow, that's a long drive," Treadwell said. "You know I think I'm scheduled to do an event in Columbus next week."

"I know," the man said. "This couldn't wait."

Treadwell smiled, assuming it was a compliment. "You have a book you want me to sign?"

"No, I came to tell you that I disapprove of your philosophy and your methods."

Treadwell tried to be cordial, even if he didn't feel he needed to be. He said, "Let me guess: you think I'm too conservative?"

The guy shook his head as he pulled his gun. "Too liberal."